LANDFILL MOUNTAINS

PRAISE FOR LANDFILL MOUNTAINS

'A compulsively readable look at the future we'll face if climate change isn't addressed.'

Lauren James author of 'The Loneliest Girl in the Universe'

'Powerful prose and a plot that thrums with energy.'

Dewi Hargreaves, author of 'Shield Road'

'I was gripped from the start, a profound lesson on the eternal importance of storytelling.'

Emily Inkpen, author of The Dex Legacy series

'A speculative fiction debut about the power of community and storytelling.'

The Bookseller

'An ode to the fragile beauty of our planet and the timeless art of oral storytelling.'

Library Laura Podcast

'The kind of story that makes you yearn to spend the day curled up on the sofa and getting lost in the splendor of each page.'

Big Kids Book Club

LANDFILL MOUNTAINS

BY RAB FERGUSON

ONWE

First published in Great Britain in 2021 by Onwe Press Ltd. This paperback edition was first published in 2021

1 3 5 7 9 10 8 6 4 2

 A CIP catalogue record for this book is available from the British Library.

eBook ISBN 978-1-913872-05-2
Paperback ISBN 978-1-913872-04-5

Printed and bounded by Clays Ltd, Elcograf S.p.A.

www.onwe.co | @weareonwe

For Ashton and Hazel,

with all my love.

THE TOWN
DRY STREAM
THE WELL
THE FALLEN FOREST
THE MOUNTAINS
THE WITCH'S SHACK
BURNT GROUND

WHERE THE SUN RISES
WHERE THE HUNTERS ROAM
RECYCLING CENTER
THE MECHANIC'S GARAGE
AUTOMATED RECYCLING TRUCK ROUTE
MOUNTAINS
THE FLATLANDS
THE BROKEN ROAD
THE TOWN
ROLLING HILLS
MADERA
THE FISHER PEOPLE'S VILLAGE
THE GARDENS
WHERE THE SUN SETS
THE SEA

PROLOGUE

Somewhere, a field of crops turns yellow and dies. A wheat mill is lost to flooding. Bovine corpses lie slack across dry earth patched with receding grass.

The systems that depend on this food fail. Prices rise, economies crash. Entire cities starve.

The people hear of potential aid, potential war, potential further disaster. Then the broadcasts stop, and the signals fall away, and they hear nothing more.

The Earth is thrown away, hitting the inside of the bin and dragging the black bag down with it.

Or tell it differently.

Despite his lover's protests, the prince begins to chop away at the first of many trees. He will clear this forest, and build a city upon the land: the greatest city the world has ever seen.

CHAPTER ONE

'It's your fault we live here!'

Joe regretted the words as soon as they came out. His father, David, did not reply. He just stood there, looking hurt. The guilt that swelled up in Joe was heightened by how close together they were. He could see every line of David's weary face, from the greasy hair on his forehead to the slight sag on his cheeks.

In their cramped home, there was no way for Joe to step back. The shack's wood-panelled walls warped inwards like a closing hand, pressing father and his sixteen-year-old son together. The ceiling was low and made of sheet metal, which grew so hot in the daytime that if Joe stood up straight, it burned a welt across his scalp.

A lightbulb hung down between Joe and David, dangling on a long wire, but there was no electricity. The only illumination came from the moon shining through a square hole where there once was a window. The warm night rolled in through the hole as well, carrying with it the thick smell of rot.

On the far wall, there was a stove that didn't heat and a faucet without water. Three lumpy mattresses were laid over the splintered floor, with threads stretched and broken across them. Joe's grandfather, also called Joseph, had been asleep on one of the mattresses. He was stirring now, disturbed by Joe's raised voice. Grandad was skeletally thin apart from a bloated little stomach, like all the people of the town.

Between Grandad and the wall, a line of cloth sacks were filled to bursting and tied at the top. A string-less acoustic guitar was slumped next to the sacks in the corner. A snapped plastic guard across the guitar's surface displayed an illustration of a species of bird that Joe had never seen, and probably never would.

Joe had been pushing his father for an explanation of how they had ended up living in a ramshackle town, scavenging waste to survive. David told him the same he always did. Everyone had known the world was getting warmer. There were news reports on the risk of shortages and economic collapse, but life in the city of Madera had gone on the same.

David was one of the many who ignored the signs, carrying on as if things would somehow return to normal in the future. Despite concerns from Grandad and Joe's mother, still living then, he convinced both they should stay. Even as fuel reserves ran low, and options for travel became scarce, still he stalled.

Soon, food supplies dwindled in Madera and costs surged. Eventually, there was nothing left in the shops. It was only then that David finally took action, when it was too late to properly search for a new place to live. He lifted Joe in his arms, and their family walked out of the city with thousands of others who'd let everything slip away. From there, they'd walked for miles till they'd found this place that once used to dispose of the city's waste. It was a fitting place for them to end up.

'It's just difficult knowing how life was in the city, before everything,' Joe said, reluctantly trying to take the sting out of his previous words.

David nodded. He looked as sad and broken as the guitar in the corner.

'I could tell you a story about the city.' Grandad murmured, sitting up on his mattress and scratching sleepily at his beard. Everyone called Madera *the city* now, as if it was the only one that had ever existed. 'About what it is and how it came to be.'

Joe crouched down, looking into his grandfather's rheumy eyes. 'Another time, Grandad. Sorry I woke you.'

Grandad relaxed down again, then spoke muffled on his side. 'You raised your voice before. Don't forget the tale of the man who shouted often, and the man who whispered only once.'

'I won't,' Joe said. 'I remember all your stories. And I

remember which man the people listened to.'

Grandad murmured assent, closing his eyes. Joe and David waited as the old man drifted back to sleep, the only sound his wheezing breath.

Once his grandfather was asleep, Joe went to the shack's window-hole. Part of him still wanted to rage and yell, and get his anger out. He knew it wouldn't really help, especially since his father never argued back. Joe sighed as he looked out over the town.

Shacks similar to their own were packed in tight rows down the slope. There was a gap through the rows where a trench ran down the hill, splitting the town in half. The townspeople called it the stream, though the ground within it was as dry and hard as the rest. Beyond there rose the mountains, gigantic summits of waste once known as landfill. All the rubbish there had been thrown away by Madera, back when the city still functioned. The mountains were black in the night, dwarfing the hill they lived on.

Above the mountains, tiny shapes swirled over the stars. It was impossible to tell which were plastic bags lifted on the wind and which were crows. When Joe looked at the mountains, their moulding stench grew stronger. It was as if the sight of them pushed their poison into his lungs.

David joined Joe by the window-hole and looked out.

'How could one city throw all this away?' Joe asked. 'You

couldn't have saved anything for us?'

David scratched dirt out from under his nails. 'When I look out at those mountains, I always wonder how much I threw away. I'm sorry this is the life we live, Joe. I wanted better for you.'

David's apology only irritated Joe. Sorry didn't change anything. He turned away from his father and left through the front door, out into the night where the full moon shone overhead. Joe envied the moon, separate and away from it all. He knew if he stayed he would end up saying more that he'd regret, and he didn't want that. He strode quickly away, aware of his father's moonlit face watching him go.

CHAPTER TWO

Joe squeezed through the spaces between shacks, heading towards the dry stream. He avoided the shacks' window-holes, where he might be caught by someone wanting to talk, and held his nose as he passed one of the shared outhouse toilets that stank as badly as the mountains. The toilet was nothing more than a wooden box over a pit in the ground.

At one point he stopped abruptly, having almost stepped on the leaves of Ms Winnipeg's carrots. Some of the shacks, such as hers, had vegetables growing around the walls. They never amounted to much, twisted morsels that were barely even a mouthful of food. There wasn't enough nutrition in the earth, and the sun was too cruel.

What a place to live, Joe thought. *Even plants can't grow properly here.*

All the real food came from the other three communities: the gardeners, the fisherpeople, and the hunters. It was brought to the town by the drifters, who drove electric cars and vans, charged at an old building called the recycling centre that had a solar powered charging point. Electric vehicles were the only ones that worked anymore, as all the petrol stations had run dry before everyone started leaving the city.

The automatic sorting machines at the recycling centre let you charge a vehicle in exchange for depositing recycling, so drifters would trade food for recyclable waste collected from the mountains. Occasionally, if a townsperson had collected enough, they'd purchase some seeds or a plant from the drifters as well, more as something to tend than something to eat.

Those carrots don't look like they have much life left in them, Joe thought, looking at their flaky brown leaves sticking out from the ground, but he still watched where he stepped. He walked by more shacks he knew well. He passed Alice's with a smooth stone dug into the earth before the door as a ramp, the Artist Sisters' surrounded by animal shapes crafted from reused tin, and the Singing Family's where he imagined he heard all four of them – father, mother, son and daughter – snoring in harmony.

Joe reached the edge of the dry stream and jumped down where the dirt banks were taller than his head on either side. He went uphill until the trench flattened out, then turned to see the whole town below him. A few hundred sheet metal roofs glittered like water in the moonlight, parted by the dry stream cutting through their middle.

Even there at the top of the hill, the mountains towered dark and high above him. The town was surrounded by desert, which wasn't made from sand but hard earth with dust across its surface. To Joe's left, the desert was rolling hills, cracked brown slopes like the one the town sat upon. None of them were nearly as tall as the mountains. To his right, it was flat, stretching out to the horizon where the city twinkled as a single light, like a star that had fallen from the sky.

'The lights are still on in Madera,' Joe muttered to himself.

But Joe's father had told him that a lot of the street lights and office buildings were powered by similar automated renewable systems as the recycling centre. It was part of the too small and too late efforts that had been made to combat climate change. It didn't tell them anything about what it was like in the city now. All of humanity could die out, and Madera's light would carry on twinkling.

Joe walked down the other side of the hill, so the town was out of sight behind him. Here was the fallen forest, where dead trees lay in scattered patterns across the earth. There were thick oaks with roots that clawed upwards out of the dirt, birch trees snapped and white, and hollow willows with long branches draped across the ground like hair. There was wood to be found on the mountains, so this quiet and still place was left untouched by the townspeople.

Grandad had told Joe a story once, of a desperate man who'd come to the fallen forest in the night for wood to sell to the drifters. He'd been met with crows perched along every one of the logs, watching him sullenly. It was said in the town that the crows listened to the whispers of an old woman they called the Witch.

Rumour had it that it was the Witch who'd talked the termites out of the dead trees, and killed the rot inside their wood with a well-placed word. No desperation was worth crossing her and risking a curse placed inside your heart with her bony fingers.

The man turned from the forest and instead walked out into the desert, even though walking there meant death. When the daylight came, the sun burned the water from his body and the pink from his skin, until he was only a black mark on the earth. Grandad told him no one knew if it was the Witch's power that had caused the man to walk out into death, or if it was the man's fear of her power. Grandad said one was not too different from the other.

As Joe walked through the fallen forest, there appeared to be so many of the collapsed trees that they became indistinguishable, so that it would be impossible to find a comfortable log one night then return to sit on it the next.

To do so required the same trick as finding your way on the mountains, where the waste had to be looked at not as a whole but as its constituent parts. On the mountains, Joe saw the shapes made by the rise and fall of countless rubbish-filled bags. Here, he saw the shapes made by the particular trees that lay together.

With the knowledge of a thousand nights walking through the forest, Joe found his way to a fallen oak that was long enough to lie down on and speckled with white dust. The contours of this log were like his own fingerprints, an integral grain within Joe's life. He sat down on the oak and looked out at Madera's light sparkling beneath the moon.

'Joe,' said a gentle voice from the top of the hill. She was a distance away, but she cared for quietness, and knew how far her voice could travel. At seventeen years old, she was slightly older than Joe, both of them on the cusp of adulthood together. Her name was Sonya.

She had braided hair, with loose tufts and curls sticking out. Her brown skin was flecked with scratches from their work. Her clothes were tattered and losing their colour, like all fabric collected from the mountains. She carried the thinness and bloated belly that life in the town gave with a simple acceptance. Her footsteps were soft but audible as she walked through the fallen trees toward him. She sat down by his side and linked her arm through his.

'I heard you shouting before,' she said.

Sonya was the reason this oak log was special to Joe, why out of all the trees in the fallen forest, this one was significant. This was where she sat with him. This was where once, when they were much younger, she found him after a similar argument with his father. She'd given him a rock to hit against another rock in the ground, and told him to keep on doing it until his anger was gone. It worked, because she'd laughed at how silly he looked smacking rocks together, and he'd ended up laughing as well.

This log in the fallen forest was where they told each other stories, built from the stars in the sky or the rubbish on the mountains. This was where they made each other laugh, at the strangeness of their town and its people, at how they lived off waste and smelled of it too. This was where they argued, but not how Joe argued with his father. They were good arguments that made it feel as though talking about things mattered.

This log was where they took off their clothes and lay together, and she made him feel the closest he could imagine to the exhilaration of swimming in a river. Afterwards, when they were done, was the only time when his body felt soft and clean. It changed the inside of him as well, as if barbed emotions like bitterness and anger could no longer snag in his chest. Instead, they floated away with his easy breathing.

'I was arguing with my father,' Joe said, smiling simply

because she was there.

'I know,' Sonya replied. 'As does the rest of the town, the crows in the sky, and anyone who happens to be on the moon.'

He laughed and pulled her close into his side. 'I wasn't that loud.'

'You're still banging rocks together, Joe,' she said, 'after all these years.'

'Except I wasn't hitting against rocks tonight.' Joe rested his cheek on Sonya's head. 'I was hitting against my father. We were talking about how the world used to be, and I got so angry. I said what I knew would hurt, and I wish I hadn't. It's like Grandad's story, where each time the man cuts someone with his knife, he cuts into his own soul as well. I don't want to be someone who hurts people. Not Dad, or anyone else.'

'Of course you don't.' She rubbed her thumb along his arm, keeping his stress from building. 'You're made up of kindness, Joe. Anger's just something that gets tangled up inside you.'

Sonya always described Joe as the sort of person he wanted to be. Sometimes he could almost believe her. They both watched a dim, almost imperceptible light move across the horizon, heading towards the brighter light of the city. It was one of the automated trucks that travelled back and forth from the recycling centre, the place the drifters visited to use sorting machines and charge their electric vehicles. The trucks were never manned, driving in an endless loop between the city and the centre.

'I think,' Joe said, speaking aloud something he'd been considering for a while, 'I think I need to see it. The city that threw away the mountains, that my father took me away from. The light that we see every night, but we don't really know what's there. It feels like a missing piece of my life, like if I saw it I could make some sense of myself.'

Sonya's thumb stopped moving on his arm. 'I still remember it there, more than you do. I remember starving for days, even worse than it gets here. My mother and I lived with hundreds of people under a bridge because we couldn't afford to stay in the empty houses. Mum said that even then, there were places they didn't want people who looked like we did to live.'

She took her hand away, and ran her fingertips idly across the texture of their log as she went on. 'We huddled around fires in oil cans. Everyone just kept leaving, standing up and walking away from the city. Some people hotwired abandoned cars, looking for any that still had petrol left in them, and drove as far they could on what was in the tank. When we did the same, we had to drive so slowly because the roads were full of people. They were as far forward and behind as you could see, carrying what they could and getting out. We were lucky to find this place. You were too. There's nothing in the city for us.'

'That was a long time ago. Maybe things are better there now,' Joe said. He felt Sonya shake her head, nuzzling against his neck. He knew what she was thinking. 'It might not be like your mother's dream.'

'It wasn't a dream, it was a vision. She saw the city still going on without a single person in it. Traffic lights changed on deserted roads. The man turned green and beeped away, but no one crossed. The street lights came on at night, but only for the wolves. In the offices, the computers' fans whirred and symbols bounced around on their screens. The video adverts still played in the underground stations, even while the trains sat unmoving on their tracks.'

'But when you were in the city, people still lived there. No one's actually seen it empty.'

Sonya pushed herself up on the oak, sitting straight and leaving a space between them. 'All the adults say that life in the cities fell apart. Everyone left. It was on the news, on the tablets and phones, before the signal fell out of the sky. If it all started working again, they'd need the mountains. There used to be a road here, where the trucks came down to dump their waste. If they'd made a better life there again, wouldn't they have fixed the roads? Wouldn't the trucks be coming here?'

'Maybe it's different,' Joe said. 'Maybe they're not throwing everything away anymore. Or maybe it's the same, and they're dumping the waste somewhere else, and couldn't care less about having a road to us.'

'There's no way to leave the town. Walking out is death, and the drifters won't take anyone with them. Even if they did, none of them would ever go to the city. They're too frightened of the journey. If you start dreaming of it as a better place, it's only going to torture you. There are good things about our life here. We have food, water and shelter, and the people in this town look after each other. We've got me and you.'

'It's not about if it's better or worse than here.' Joe put his arm around Sonya's shoulder and drew her to his side, pointing up at the full moon. 'Look at the moon. We don't know what it'd be like up there, if it'd be good or bad. But wouldn't you go if you got the chance? Wouldn't you risk everything to see what you could find there, walking in its dunes and caves, to see the night sky from standing on its strange grey earth? Even just to look back, and see here from another place? It'd give you new sights and new thoughts. Wouldn't you want that?'

'No,' she said, snuggling down under his arm. 'I'd be afraid that for all that new, I'd lose the old things I care about. But I know you'd go, if you could.'

She wrapped her arms around him, then laughed. Her laugh was silk on the air, and it tickled in Joe's ear.

'What's funny, Sonya?'

'The city's already too far to reach. But the moon? You're going to have to practise jumping.'

'I will,' he said, breaking free of her arms and springing up from their oak. He leapt over a fallen tree. 'I'll practise every day.' He jumped over another. 'You'll see me in the mornings, getting higher and higher. One day you'll be collecting and you'll see me jump right over the mountains.'

Sonya laughed again, shifting her weight on the log. Joe took her hands and pulled her up, so she stood close to him. He could smell the sweet scent of yarrow oil in her hair. Her and her mother kept yarrow flowers from the gardens in plastic pots around their shack, and boiled the petals over a fire to extract the softening oil for their braids.

'I'll jump to the moon, grab you a moon rock, and jump back here to give it to you.'

'I hope you're as good at landing as you are at jumping,' Sonya said, then kissed him. She smiled, leaning back with her arms around his waist. 'If there's something missing inside you, then you'll find it inside you. You could walk the whole world, looking outwards, and still feel wrong.'

'How do I find something inside me?' Joe asked, the feeling of her lips still tingling on his.

'Maybe you need to bring everything else together first.' Sonya swayed herself from side to side on Joe's hips. 'Your mind's looking for the city, trying to remake it from the waste on the mountains. Your heart's on the moon, leaping over craters and cheering at stars. If you pulled yourself back together, if all of you was here in one place, maybe you'd feel more whole.'

He caught her mid-sway and held her close. They turned

as they talked, half-dancing between the fallen trees. 'I know I can't go to the city. But sometimes I wish I could get out of the town, just for a little while.'

'You should go to see the Witch. She helped my mother.'

Sonya's mother Demeta sometimes went to the Witch's shack for visions. It was there that she'd seen the empty city. Sonya had described her mother's experience to Joe. She'd told him how the Witch had bled a dead crow into a pot with a fire below it, then stirred herbs in as well, and waited until black steam rose up from the bubbling crow's blood.

After that, the Witch pinched a mushroom and dipped her hand into the boiling mixture, showing no signs of pain. She lifted the mushroom out, now a congealed red blot between her fingers, like the heart of one of the rats watching from the shack's corners. Demeta opened her mouth and the Witch pushed the rat's heart to the back of her throat, then flicked it down her gullet.

As the Witch pulled her fingers out of Demeta's mouth, the shadows fell from the walls and Demeta felt her body dissolve away, rising with the smoke. Her mind was left floating in the Witch's shack, open and unprotected, filling with images of an empty city that she took for signs.

'I don't want to see the Witch,' Joe said. 'It'd do as much good to get drunk with the Moonshine Brothers, and see what dreams swim in my head then.'

'My mother said the Witch's visions show you what you need to know, even if it's something you didn't realise you needed.'

Joe let go of Sonya and crossed his arms over his chest.

'You only don't want to go because you're afraid of her!' Sonya said.

'Yes.' Joe nodded. 'Yes, I am. She's a scary old lady who talks to rats and crows, and everyone says can put a curse on your soul. She's without a doubt the most frightening person I've ever met. I'd say more, but I'm scared she'll hear me somehow and crows will peck out my eyes.'

Sonya laughed again, then raised her chin so he could kiss her. They stayed like that for a long time, kissing slowly because there was enough night to last. Eventually she stepped back from him and drew a square of foil out of her pocket.

Condoms could sometimes be found amongst the rubbish on the mountains, their packets airless and limp. They were just another item that had been easy for people living in the city to throw away, emptied out from pub machines and pharmacists' stockrooms. Even using the condoms, the risk of pregnancy was still there, which would be hell while living in the town. The last children to survive birth were twins named Tiger and Lily, six years ago. Every pregnancy since, and several before, had ended in either miscarriage or stillbirth.

With the condoms, they did the best they could to prevent

that. They only slept together when they had them, and they'd been lucky so far. Joe took Sonya's hands, squeezing them in his own before pulling her to him. The gasp Sonya let out was the long breath of a flowing stream.

Joe felt warm light flickering on top of his eyelids, as if he lay under water with the sun breaking across its surface. He sat up and opened his eyes. Sonya was lying on their oak next to him. The stars were gone, the sky blue. The sun was rising behind the mountains, highlighting their edges with an orange glow so it appeared they were aflame. Joe nudged Sonya and she smiled as she sat up next to him. Neither spoke, both enjoying the peace.

They knew a day of collecting on the mountains approached, working where the ground shifted underneath them. Where if one glass bottle was knocked out of place, it might be followed by rolling bin bags, then a yellowed fridge-freezer or a cracked ceramic bathtub. Once something that size was dislodged, the whole side of a mountain could start to slide towards them. When there was an avalanche, all they could do was run. If they were caught up in the bags and the waste, they'd be crushed beneath their weight.

It was important to take pleasure in the quiet moments. They lived a dangerous life, scavenging from the landfill mountains.

CHAPTER THREE

By the time Joe returned to his shack, the sun had risen above the mountains. He went quickly inside, his head already beginning to ache from the heat. Grandad sat inside, in front of their counter built across a stove that didn't heat and a faucet without water. He was on one of three mismatched stools they had taken from the mountains, eating porridge.

David had already gone. He'd be up on the mountains, finding new places to dig into and fill a sack with anything he could sell. The size of the mountains, and the relatively small population of the town, meant that the vast majority of the landfill was undisturbed. Madera had thrown enough away that in fourteen or so years the scavengers had barely scratched the surface of what lay within the waste.

Of the whole town, it was often Joe's father who'd collected the most when a drifter arrived with food to trade. He'd start collecting even before the mountains were lit by the sunrise, picking out items in the first embers of the orange glow. He'd still be there when the sun set behind the fallen forest, continuing on as everything turned to deep blue.

'You should eat.' Grandad indicated a bowl of porridge for Joe on top of the dead stove. Through the open back door an empty pan and a jar of oats were on the ground next to the remains of a fire, a thin wisp of smoke still rising up.

Joe lifted a brown bottle from a bunch in the shack's corner – all glass, as the drifters paid more for plastic – and went to a bucket of water between two of the mattresses. He dunked the bottle under the surface to fill it. David took the bucket to the stone well and back before sunrise each morning. It was the one miracle of the town, the deep well that tapped into spring water that flowed far beneath the earth. If David waited for the daylight to fetch their drinking water, the metal handle would become scorching hot and burn a blister across his palm.

Joe filled another bottle and handed it to Grandad, who wetted his beard slightly as he drank. Joe sat down with him and ate the porridge. It was made by boiling oats in water, and Joe had to drink between each spoonful to push the grey slime down his throat. When he'd finished eating, it left a sticky sensation on his tongue.

'You're often angry at your father,' Grandad commented.

'I don't mean to be. I get frustrated when we talk about how things used to be.' Joe got down from his stool. He picked up two more glass bottles, the size that used to hold wine, and went to the bucket.

'You blame him for our lives here.'

Joe pushed a bottle under the water, air bubbles rising from it. 'I don't... I know he couldn't change what happened to the world. But I wish he'd tried to do something, rather than convincing you and Mum to stay in the city.'

Grandad had turned around on his stool to look at Joe. 'He did try to do something. He tried staying. That was the choice he made. Be careful how you tell his story. It will affect how you tell your own as well.'

It was for good reason that Grandad was known in the town as the Storyteller. He told tales to the townspeople, and his mind worked to the patterns of stories. However, if anyone said that to him, he'd reply that all minds did.

Joe put the second bottle in, but it clunked against the bucket's base. He lifted the bucket instead, pouring the water carefully into the neck of the bottle. Afterwards, he put the full bottles into his and Grandad's cloth collecting sacks. Both already contained poles and tarp for casting shade, as well as a few filled water bottles that David placed in them earlier that morning.

'Let's go,' Joe said, lifting both sacks and carrying them

towards the front door.

Grandad followed him, walking stiffly but well for a man of his age. 'Maybe you can learn something about a person from how they raise their children. Your father taught you to be kind. You carry my collecting sack without me even having to ask.'

'Will you tell a story in the dry stream?' Joe said, changing the subject. The heat prickled his skin as they walked out into the sunlight. The morning was warming up, though was nowhere close to the intense temperatures that would be reached around midday.

Grandad's walnut face cracked into a huge smile. 'I will, Little Joe,' he said, using Joe's childhood nickname. 'I'll tell The Boy Who Learned What Fear Was.'

'Good choice. I like that one.'

They squeezed through the shacks until they got to the bank of the dry stream. Joe took Grandad's hand and helped him down, joining the flow of people heading towards the mountains. During the daytime, the mountains weren't black but vivid and multicoloured. Every aspect of human waste spilled from bin bags of various colours and sizes. A crowd formed around Grandad, knowing a story might be coming.

The townspeople had various skin tones, a diversity of races and cultures having found their way to the mountains as the old society crumbled around them. Those who had rarely mixed in the city were neighbours in the town. They had different structures to their faces, and different lilts and expressions to their voices, relics of the times when people used to move around the world.

What brought them together was their thinness and their bloated little bellies. Their round joints bulged from their limbs, the shape of their skeletons clear. In that way at least, they were all the same.

'*Back in the old days, when the air was not so hot,*' Grandad began, '*when people lived in the city and talked on phones, watched television and worked in buildings that scraped the sky, there was a man who had a son. His son was not like other children. He'd never once felt his breath tremble or his heart pound, he'd never been afraid, and he asked his father to teach him what fear was…*'

The crowd around Grandad grew as they walked down the dry stream, more townspeople descending the dirt banks and joining the listeners. Tiger and Lily, the young twins, scrambled down, carrying a duffel bag between them. Their tired-eyed older sister, Rose, He didn't want her be hurt followed behind. Ms Winnipeg, the grey-haired woman who lived near Joe, sat on the bank and lowered herself into the trench, shushing those who offered to help so she could hear Grandad's telling.

Further down the stream, two men that the townspeople called the Husbands saw the story coming and stopped to wait for it, empty bin bags in their hands. They were a couple. The taller of them was called Marco. He was dark haired and serious, and would engage Joe in discussion around ideas of how less wasteful societies might be created in the future. The shorter man, Harvey, preferred casual conversation and laughter.

The titles some people in the town were given, like everyone calling Marco and Harvey the Husbands, or Grandad the Storyteller, were used more often than their actual names. There was no official giving of these titles. They developed through talk on the mountains, and then ended up sticking.

Joe had once overheard Marco telling Harvey that he disliked the title they shared, saying that he didn't like being described in a different way from other couples in the town. Neither of them had gone on to ask the others to stop calling them the Husbands, but since hearing that Joe didn't use the term, and used their names instead.

Joe realised he wasn't listening properly, and returned his attention to Grandad's voice. Several of Grandad's stories were set in the city, and how he described it changed from telling to telling. In this tale, the city was a place where people were afraid to venture out from beneath the street lights at night because there were things that crept in the dark, shadows that moved through the derelict buildings, empty playgrounds, and abandoned churches.

'The boy saw how his father stayed under the bright lights, and he knew this was because his father was afraid, but he couldn't understand what

afraid meant or how it felt. Since everyone else seemed to understand, the boy thought he must be missing out on something important.

'He told his father he wanted to learn what fear was. The father was too scared to go into the night himself to teach his son, so he used his computer to post an advert, offering good money to the person who taught his boy what fear was.

'A poor man saw it as a chance to make easy profit. He hid in a gutter where he knew the boy would pass, dressed in black clothes, and held a knife in each hand. When he saw the boy, he leapt out, brandishing the blades above his head. Without speaking a word the boy grabbed the poor man's hands and jammed the knives into each of his thighs, then walked on without even quickening his breath.

'The father was horrified when he found out what had happened. Now he was scared not only of the night but of the boy, and so cast him out of his house. The boy walked out onto the dark streets, muttering that it was no use, that he'd never learn what fear was. But a voice behind his ear said: "Are you sure of that? Would you bet your life and soul on it?"

'The boy turned and there was a rich man behind him, smelling of money as rich men do. The rich man held out a key between his manicured fingers, a plastic tag tied to it by a string.

'He said, "If you stay one night in this flat, your life will be blessed with a woman who loves you, and you'll always have enough money to eat what you choose and live where you want. However, if you fail and leave the flat in fear before the night is over, your soul will be mine."

'The boy thought this over. He did not trust this man. He had heard

stories of a devil that lived in the alleyways and gambled for unsuspecting souls to add to his collection. Yet, knowing no fear, he did not think he could possibly be scared out of the flat and lose the bet. He said "I accept" and took the keys.'

By this point, the crowd was quiet and focused on the story, even Tiger and Lily listening intently. Joe kept his eyes out for Sonya walking ahead, knowing that she hated to miss Grandad's storytelling, but he didn't see her.

'The boy found the building by the address on the plastic tag, and saw that the flat was on the top floor. He climbed the stairs, up and up and up. When he reached the door, he didn't hesitate to let himself in.

'Inside the flat, a dead woman hung by a rope from the ceiling fan, her face blue and her tongue bulging out of her mouth. The boy almost laughed. The rich man's lost his bet, he thought, if he expected me to run away just because of a dead woman. So he sat down on a chair and waited for morning, imagining what he'd eat when he could eat whatever he chose.

'Three hours passed, and then the dead woman's eyes snapped open. Despite her bulging tongue blocking her lips from moving, she spoke to him with a demon's voice. She taunted him to come over and kiss her, and told him how she'd scratch away his flesh and claw the marrow from his bones.

'He only snorted in reply. She still hung from the fan and posed no threat. He turned his chair away from her, ignored her words and imagined where he'd live, when he could live wherever he chose.

'Three more hours passed, then there was a crash behind him. The fan had dropped from the ceiling and the woman's body was on the floor. She

clambered to her feet, reaching forward to claw at his eyes. The boy knew his living limbs were more nimble than hers, which were stiff with death.

'He walked calmly around her, unknotted the rope from the fan, and tied it instead to the radiator. He walked around her again and sat back down in his chair, turning it to face her. She stretched her arms out towards him, but the rope held firm no matter how much she pulled. He watched her, looking at her blue face, bloated tongue, and the red mark the rope made around her neck, and imagined what the woman who loved him would look like.

'Three more hours passed, and then the sun rose. When the light hit the woman's face her tongue shrank, the blue faded from her cheeks, and she became the most beautiful girl the boy had ever seen. He untied her and she thanked him, saying that he'd broken her curse, set on her by the devil of the alleyways.

'They immediately fell in love, and a few days later the boy was employed by a successful company. For the rest of their lives, they were able to choose what they ate and where they lived. They never saw their devil again.

'The boy learned what fear was, because when the girl he loved walked with him at night, he knew the dangers that lay waiting in the dark. He didn't want her to be hurt, or for him to be lost, leaving her alone. Maybe he would never know the sensation of fear, but through his love for her, he knew what it meant.'

Grandad finished the story at the bottom of the dry stream. There was a brief silence, then applause from the crowd, including enthusiastic clapping from Joe. Several people approached Grandad to tell him they were looking forward to hearing him at the next celebration. Eventually the crowd dispersed across the empty ground leading from the end of the town to the start of the mountains.

The earth near the mountains was stained dark shades of purple and green, in a tideline that seeped out of the waste and stopped before the town. Nothing would grow in the purple-green ground, despite multiple efforts that had been made. It revealed what the mountains really were, the congealed scabbing of a wound that bled out into the dirt. The waste even stank like an infected injury.

Some of the townspeople no longer noticed the smell, but not Joe. It forced its way through his nose, and he even tasted it in his mouth. He and Grandad stood where the earth was still brown, next to the stone well. The well only reached as high as Joe's knees, but it plunged deep into the ground.

'You changed the story's end,' Joe commented.

'The story changes every time I tell it. But it's important, when you change the ending. It makes a difference to everything that came before. I've told you how this well is older than the town and the mountains, haven't I?'

Joe nodded.

'Stories are like the well. Very old and used by many different people, in many different times. Even when you think you're telling a new story, you shape it out of all the stories you've heard before. You build your well out of those same old stones.'

Grandad hmm-ed, working out his words. 'The original ending of that story doesn't sit right with me. The girl throws fish in the boy's bed, there's a creeping sensation on his skin and he knows what fear is – what's that? It's a cheap trick. If I tell it that way, it feels like lying. A storyteller can move the stones around, but they can't just place them wherever they want. There has to be truth under the surface. The well has to draw water.'

Joe often had the impression that when Grandad spoke about stories, he was talking about more than just stories. Mr Rajarshi, Grandad's friend, joined them by the stone well with a heavy-duty bin bag in his hand. Joe gave Grandad the cloth sack he'd been carrying for him, then watched as the two old men walked together towards the mountains.

There was no exact point where the mountains began, only a gradual increase in waste over the purple-green ground. First there was a scattering of lighter rubbish, such as empty shopping bags, crumbling polystyrene and foil wrappers. Then dotted amongst it there were bin bags, these early ones already torn open with nothing of worth left inside. In many, thick green mould clumped over what remained of the contents.

The bin bags increased in number until they piled on top of each other. The gaps between them were crammed with materials that couldn't be sold and so had been left, unrecyclable packaging, ruined cardboard, broken metal and infested fabrics all shoved together. The waste built higher, and larger objects could be seen, including glimpses of rusted appliances, crumbling furniture, even skeleton shells of cars and other vehicles that David said were never supposed to come to the landfill.

High up around the peak of the first mountain there were townspeople collecting. *They look like insects from here*, Joe thought. From the top, they'd be able to see four more peaks with dipping valleys between them, all infested with more people setting up shade and picking through the rubbish.

So much waste had been left behind from the city that even though they'd been collecting for years, there was still much more to find than had already been scavenged. Most of what they sold to the drifters were recyclables – tin cans, plastic bottles and clean cardboard. Some electronics were also recyclable and had good value for trade, such as the battery-dead smartphones and tablets.

The drifters took it all to the recycling centre, where they deposited the collections into sorting machines in return for credit to charge their cars and vans. The centre had been part of an environmental scheme prior to society falling apart. The items that had been valued in that scheme were ones that drifters would trade more for.

Recycling at the centre was poured into automated trucks that took it away to the city, like the one Joe and Sonya had seen the night before. When the trucks came back to the recycling centre, they were empty and ready to be refilled.

Where does it all go? Joe wondered to himself, as he waited for more of his collecting group to arrive, so they could head up the mountains together.

The townspeople were unsure of how much of the automatic system still survived, and it seemed likely the recycling was all ending up piled somewhere in the city. The only reason the drifters kept coming back for the recycling was for the credit to charge their vans. A few of the drifters had owned electric vehicles when living in the city, though most had acquired them as a means of survival before leaving. Driving the electric vehicles, and having control over trade, meant the drifters were the people who had to worry least about having enough to eat.

Non-recyclables were sold to the drifters as well, including tools such as shovels, nets or axes. Joe had recently found a set of fishhooks, which he'd exchanged for wolf meat when they'd last had a drifter visit. These sorts of items were sold onto the other three communities, the gardeners who grew grain and other food on fertile land called the gardens, the fisherpeople who lived by the sea and fished from boats, and the hunters who roamed wild, stalking the few animals that were left in the parched desert.

There was the Mechanic as well, a woman who lived by herself away from the communities, in a dilapidated garage.

She worked with a store of parts, as well as salvage brought to her from the desert, to keep the drifters travelling. It was a situation that couldn't last forever.

When the electric cars and vans started to fail, they'd need to work out a new way of surviving. Everyone said that with the Mechanic's skills and the long-lasting batteries, it would be ten or twenty tears, maybe more, before that problem arose. What they'd do then was a question Joe had often asked, but had never had properly answered.

The townspeople heard news from the other communities through the drifters, but hadn't seen the places where the others lived. The drifters refused to carry passengers. None of them were willing to take the risk of someone trying to steal their vehicle. Everyone stayed apart, even as they relied on each other to survive.

All the adults in the town and the other communities, anyone who was more than a few years older than Joe, had some part in building either these mountains or similar ones elsewhere.

How many of them feel the shame my Dad does, Joe contemplated, *and carry the weight of the mountains on their back? And how many of them don't think about it at all?*

Now, running across the purple-green ground towards Joe, dodging through the scattered waste, were Tiger and Lily. Two children who'd done nothing to make the mountains, but had to live off them all the same. Their older sister, Rose, who'd looked after the twins since their parents were lost in an avalanche, couldn't collect enough to feed the three of them by herself, so they had to collect as well. It was the only way they'd have enough recyclables and sellable objects to trade by the time the next drifter arrived.

Rose followed after the twins, looking bemused by her younger siblings' antics. Tiger and Lily skidded to a stop in front of him and held their hands outs, with string entwined around their fingers. Lily separated her palms, stretching out a spiderweb pattern between them. Tiger had a single length of string leading from one index finger to the other. Both twins' hands were rough from collecting on the mountains, their skin marked with lines and scratches.

'We learned a new trick!' Tiger exclaimed.

'Can we show you?' Lily asked.

'Go on then,' Joe replied.

Tiger and Lily jumped apart, and Lily thrust the spiderweb pattern towards Tiger. He pulled his line of string taut between his two fingers and Lily swept her hands back and forth, so the spiderweb drifted like a wave. Tiger brought the string down between Lily's hands, somehow passing it through the rippling pattern, then lifted it up and out again. Once Tiger's string was free at the top, they both turned proudly back to Joe. It was a good trick.

'That was brilliant,' Joe said, crouching down and helping

them remove the string from their fingers. 'Where'd you learn that?'

The twins pointed towards the Witch's shack, closer to the mountains than the rest. It had no window-holes, though there were little hollows at the base of the walls for the rats to come and go. The roof was wooden, not sheet metal, and was covered in crows. The birds stared towards Joe and the twins, as if they'd been watching the trick.

Joe knew that Tiger and Lily were lying. The Witch didn't play games with string. It was more likely to have been Grandad who'd shown them how to do it. He'd have taught them as well that the story of a trick affects its magic, and that saying the mysterious Witch told them how to do it would help wow their audience.

'Come on, let's get up the mountains. We can meet the others up there,' Joe said, anxious to move away from the crows' glittering black eyes. He'd joked with Sonya the night before, but the Witch really did send a tremble running down his spine. The rats and crows nesting in her shack, the mixes of blood and herbs to send people into trances, her ability to predict how someone's illness would progress – all of it unnerved him.

What bothered Joe most about the Witch was that no one knew her real name. She was only her title. It was as if she only had featureless skin where her face should be. Joe led the twins towards the mountains, Rose following close behind. All the way, Joe felt the crows' eyes fixed on the back of his neck.

CHAPTER FOUR

Later that day, Joe was on the mountains. His knees were crunched into one bin bag as he tore another in front of him open with his hands. A tarp was stretched over his back, pressing him down. It was fastened to poles stabbed into the waste, pulling it out into a rectangle that gave shade from the sun.

Sonya was under the tarp as well, rooting through loose rubbish next to a black-haired girl called Maya. Behind Joe, the twins were searching through smaller carrier bags. Rose was with them, never slowing her work despite the deep shadows under her eyes.

A boy with a snout nose called Buddy collected next to Joe. Buddy was the son of one of the Moonshine Brothers, three men who made alcohol by fermenting oats in old bathtubs they'd taken from the mountains. They either sold the whisky to the drifters or shared it with the rest of the town during rain celebrations.

Buddy was in a relationship with Maya. She lived in a shack by herself as she didn't have any family left, but often stayed with Buddy and his father Kane. Buddy was currently slicing bags open with his knife, one that he'd kept from the mountains rather than selling. The blade flipped out from a wooden handle, originally designed as a weapon.

This was the group Joe worked with every day on the mountains, setting up shade and digging into the waste to find items to trade to the drifters. They were some of the youngest townspeople, all teenagers apart from the six-year-old twins.

While they knew their ages, they were not able to pin down their exact birthday each year, as there were no calendars anymore. They didn't talk about dates, or even name days of the week. The only sign of time passing was the moon's cycle at night, and the permanently hot days growing short then long again.

There were just three other young townspeople who didn't work with their group. The son and daughter of the Singing Family were young teenagers, and a nine-year-old girl called Hope collected with her father, Bill. Due to the rarity of successful pregnancy, the rest of the townspeople were older than Joe and his friends.

The bin bag stuck to Joe's hands with sweat, and his limbs were aching. The items in the bag were blurred and difficult to focus on. It hurt to swallow, his throat as cracked and dry as the desert earth. He crawled across to the edge of the tarp and picked up a bottle from the hole the group had dug in the waste to keep their water together. They dug these holes so they could find the bottles again. Anything dropped on the mountains was easily lost.

After taking a long draft, the lukewarm water soothing his raw throat, Joe's eyes refocused. He looked out over the side of the mountains where the desert was flat. He could see the sparse remains of the road that had once led to the city, an occasional shred of tarmac suggesting the path it had taken. In the daytime, Madera couldn't be seen, but Joe knew from many nights spent gazing at the twinkling light its exact point on the horizon.

He took another drink and then sat down so that he faced towards his home. From there he could see how small it really was. The shacks huddled together on their little hill as if hiding under the mountains, terrified of the vast expanse of empty desert all around.

Movement far below him caught Joe's eye. A woman named Alice pushed herself along the stained purple-green ground in an office chair, using a washing-line pole to navigate through the loose waste. Her curly blonde hair caught the light as she moved in and out of the shade she'd set up at the bottom of the mountains.

Alice was in her mid-twenties. She had cerebral palsy, and used the office chair to get around. She moved forward by pushing her pole into the dirt, switching sides as if rowing. Her pole acted as a harpoon as well. Alice speared it through the tops of bags, before lifting them up and dropping them onto her lap to search through. Plastic carrier bags dangled from either side of her office chair, ready to deposit her collections into.

The townspeople called her Office Chair Alice. Her title was different from the rest, in that it prefixed her name rather than replacing it. They saw Alice and her collecting as a symbol of triumph over the adversity they lived in, impressed by the rigorous physiotherapy routine she went through to continue to be able to work. It was one she'd learned as a child in the city, and adapted as she'd grown older in the town.

Joe thought they'd got it wrong with Alice's title. Her office chair shouldn't have been used to define her. She was a funny and empathetic woman in her mid-twenties, who knew how to lift others' spirits. In Joe's case, when she saw him looking serious or moping, she'd whack his shins with her pole and shout 'remember to smile!'

There was a tug on Joe's arm. Lily had crawled up beside him.

'Joe, will we get good trade for this?'

Tiger was behind her, holding a teddy bear. Its fur was matted and sticky, a dark splotch on its head shutting one of its eyes. When Joe was the twins' age, already living in the town, he had a bear that his mother had given to him before she died.

He remembered the bear, with a buttoned waistcoat and a stitched-on hat, but he couldn't remember her. David said she'd got sick in their first few days in the town and never recovered. Joe had sold the bear to a drifter, at a time when they were low on food.

'It won't recycle, but they might buy it to sell on,' Joe said. 'Do you know what it is?'

Lily shook her head. Tiger was already putting the bear away into the duffel bag the twins shared for collecting.

'It's a friend,' said Joe. 'Children give them names, and they go with them on their adventures. So they've got someone to talk to wherever they go.'

The twins stared at him wide-eyed, but neither opened the duffel bag to look at the teddy bear again. They went back to their work, pushing their little hands into the waste.

'Thank you for telling them that,' Rose said, moving nearer to Joe under the tarp. 'I want them to learn about where everything came from.'

'Hey, what do you think this is?' Maya called over from next to Sonya. She held up a small hand-held device with two screens. It flipped open and shut, with buttons around the bottom screen. Joe found it difficult to imagine a screen actually working. He'd seen so many of them on the mountains, televisions, laptops, tablets and phones. They'd only ever been black.

When Joe and his family first came to the town, most people still had phones and other technology, turning them on occasionally to see if signal had returned. Eventually every battery ran out. The technology on the mountains was all dead, and was collected only to be sold on to the drifters. The machines at the recycling centre gave high charging credit for electronic equipment, so it was seen as *good trade*, which the drifters would exchange a lot of food for.

'Maybe it's a mobile phone?' Rose suggested.

'But then why's it got two screens?' Maya replied, fiddling with the buttons as if she was using the device.

'It could have been a businessman's,' Sonya said. 'Someone who worked for a big company, in one of the skyscraper buildings. Who always had hundreds of meetings to go to, and messages to send, and calls to take. He was so busy that when he was talking to someone on the top screen, he was doing his work on the bottom one.'

Joe caught Sonya's eye and grinned. They often played this game on the mountains, imagining who'd owned the objects they'd found. Sonya was good at it, able to invent whole characters from tiny details and even develop a deeper story for them. By the evening, she'd have come up with family history, hobbies and a love interest for the businessman.

'It's not a phone, or anything else,' Buddy grunted without looking up from the rubbish he was rifling through. 'It's just trade. That's all anything is here.' He rose up so he was half-standing under the tarp, and held his hand out towards Maya. 'If you don't want it, I'll have it.'

'No.' Maya put it into her collecting bag, a black bin bag that fastened with red tape at the top. 'It's electronics.'

'See,' Buddy crouched back down. 'It's something that sells, or it isn't. That's it.'

Maya opened her mouth and Joe thought she was going to argue. Instead she sighed, and Joe was surprised to see a small smile on her face as she turned back to her collecting. He had never understood what she saw in Buddy, but their relationship seemed to work. Joe took a last drink from his water, then placed it with the other bottles and returned to his spot next to Buddy.

There was a hole in the waste where Joe had already removed and emptied several bin bags. He reached down and found the rubbish at the bottom was only loosely packed, so he could dig through it with little risk of it shifting beneath him. He lifted out a full bin bag, putting it with a few others he'd piled to the side. A greasy take-away box, foil crisp packets and a plastic bottle were all flattened beneath where the bag had been.

Joe put the plastic bottle into his collecting sack, then ripped the clean parts from the take-away box and put them in as well. He spotted the edge of something metal, and moved another bin bag, hoping for electronics. It was only a CD, utterly worthless.

'Hey, this guy was a dirty-Bertie,' Buddy said, on the other side of the pile of bin bags Joe had made. Joe leaned round and saw Buddy had opened a bag filled with blocks of magazines. Each block was in plastic packaging, protecting them from the powdery green mould in the bag.

Buddy wiped the mould from the top of one of the blocks, revealing a woman with her legs spread open on the cover of a porn magazine. Joe had seen it all before. There was no censorship on the mountains. Everyone, including Tiger and Lily, had seen the porn scattered amongst the waste, alongside disturbing violent imagery and everything else that had existed in dark corners of the city. They'd even found weapons, and the skeletons of people who'd been thrown away.

Joe couldn't read, but he could see that the women in the magazines were being sold like any other product from the city. Buddy wiped mould away from the other blocks, revealing covers showing sports and cars.

'That's a good find,' Joe commented.

'Yeah, and I'll have all the trade from it,' Buddy said, shoving the magazines into the hiking rucksack he took with him on the mountains.

Joe rolled his eyes. Buddy would never share a find, and Joe would never ask. Joe thought Buddy would have fitted in well in the city. He only bothered about what something was worth to him and beyond that didn't care at all. He'd have thrown away a whole mountain by himself, if he'd lived there when times were good.

Joe went back to his own hole in the mountainside, lifting up a new bag. Its bottom gave out, pouring waste over his legs. It was mostly gloopy mould and unrecyclable types of plastic, but he collected a couple of tin cans and a juice carton with oranges on the side.

He remembered the last time he'd eaten oranges. Charlotte and Lacey, the Artist Sisters, had given them out at a rain celebration. Joe had three segments and they'd tasted glorious, bursting with juice as if they'd been filled by the sun. Since then, they'd heard that the gardeners' orange tree had died. The closest any of them would come to holding an orange again was the dried peel that they sometimes found on the mountains, curled and brittle like ancient flower petals.

Something else in the waste caught Joe's eye, a white and blue picture obscured underneath the dirty remains of paper towels. He pinched the edge of the picture and lifted it, revealing a book that he held by the front cover. He quickly supported the book's spine with his other hand to prevent it from ripping.

The cover showed an iceberg, a white tip above the water that plunged into an ethereal blue spike beneath the surface. Joe wished he could step inside the image and feel what it was like to be cold. Even when the rain fell and the stream ran with water, the town was still warm.

The Librarian, an old man who was friends with Grandad, saved books collected from the mountains in his shack. Some townspeople helped him, giving him any they found, though others sold books to the drifters. The Librarian let others read his books, but wouldn't allow them to be taken from his shack. He was too afraid of a book being sold to a drifter and lost.

The words written inside the books conveyed nothing to Joe, as if all their meaning had been used up when they were in the city. It was the same anywhere he found text, even the faint and broken words on the T-shirt he was currently wearing. The words felt purposeless now.

In the past, the Librarian had offered to teach him and the other young people to read. After working on the mountains until sunset it was too exhausting to spend the evening squinting at pages they could barely see. Before long, none of them returned for the Librarian's lessons.

'What've you got, Joe?' Sonya asked, and Joe held up the book. Buddy's head appeared around Joe's bin bag pile.

'That a book, mate?' Buddy said. 'That's good trade.'

Joe nodded.

'Here, you didn't get that from my magazine bag, did you?'

'No, Buddy. I found it down here.'

'What are you going to do with it?' Rose asked, from behind them.

'That's a stupid question,' Buddy replied before Joe could answer. 'He's going to sell it, isn't he?'

'He could give it to the Librarian,' Rose said.

'Might as well piss on food,' Buddy snorted. 'It'd just sit in the old guy's shack.'

'The Librarian thinks it's important.' Rose crossed her arms.

'Yeah, most people think having what they want is important. Half the time he can't even afford to pay for them.'

'He doesn't just want the books for him,' Rose said. 'He wants to save them for the future. So when the time comes, kids like Tiger and Lily can learn to read.'

'Little tip for you.' Buddy wagged his finger at Rose. 'There's no point in saving for the future, if you're starving in the present.'

There was a tense silence.

'Which will you do, Joe?' Maya asked.

'I'm not sure,' Joe said, looking at the book in his hand. He heard Sonya laughing.

'What?' he asked her.

'You don't know yourself that well,' she said. 'You'll worry about it for a while, not wanting to waste its worth in trade, but also not wanting to sell it if it might help children here in the future. In the end, you won't be able to stand profiting from it, not when it could help others. It'll be in the Librarian's house before the next drifter arrives.'

Joe put the book into his collecting sack, knowing then that he'd give it to the Librarian. He heard the sound of someone gagging. He turned in time to see Lily, at the very edge of the tarp, bend over and spill watery vomit onto Tiger's shoes. He scrambled over the waste towards them, Rose hurrying across too. Lily staggered forward, and Rose caught her before she fell.

Joe clasped Tiger's shoulders. 'I need you to tell me what happened. Did she eat anything? Was there a bad smell, or an animal?'

Tiger nodded at the second question. 'There was a snake, under the bags.'

'What colours was it?'

'A black and grey one…'

The young boy trailed off, gaping over Joe's shoulder. Joe felt the mountain rumbling beneath him before he heard the shouting.

'Avalanche!'

Joe turned and saw full bin bags rolling down towards them like boulders. Sonya and the others higher up the slope scattered out from the shade. The waste under Rose and Lily slid away, sweeping them from sight. Joe hoisted Tiger up as the waste gave way beneath them as well. The tarp twisted violently around them both, fastening Joe and Tiger together and dragging them down the mountainside.

Bags bounced all around them as Joe used his free arm to shove against the rushing waste, trying to stop himself and Tiger from being pulled into the faster undercurrent below. A bag slammed against Joe's back, then Tiger's head butted into his chest and winded him.

Joe glimpsed what was pushing the avalanche towards them – a section of brick wall with a brass fireplace as if ripped straight from a house – then his legs jammed together and he and Tiger were sucked down into the waste. Something ceramic smashed against Joe's head. As he tried to stay conscious, he was aware of the mountain closing above him, blocking out the light.

CHAPTER FIVE

The roar of movement above them stopped. Joe opened his eyes, but everything was still dark. He could feel Tiger crushed against his chest, one of his arms pinned behind the boy's back. Tiger was still breathing, but Joe couldn't do the same. Panic gripped his imprisoned body. He tried to move his arms and his legs, but nothing budged the black wall of bin bags pressing in all around them. He kicked and wriggled as hard as he could, but to no avail.

Joe's limbs were failing against the pressure, getting weaker as he struggled. He still couldn't draw in breath. He realised with a sudden certainty, there was nothing he could do. The mountain had him. He had minutes left to live. Sonya and the others would find his body in the waste, but they would be too late.

Too late for him, but perhaps not too late for Tiger. With the arm stuck behind Tiger, Joe did his best to shove against the weight pressing down on the boy's back. If Tiger could breathe for a little longer, the others might get to him in time. Joe's head grew light, the pressure in his lungs unbelievable. Little white lights sparkled in his vision, like stars against the darkness they were trapped in.

A third presence joined them, emerging as if it had travelled directly through the waste. It was the shape of a boy, younger and smaller than himself. Joe couldn't make sense of what he was perceiving, this silhouette of a boy somehow standing out in the darkness. How could he pass through full bin bags like they were nothing?

It must be a hallucination, Joe thought, *brought on by the lack of air.* He could still feel his lungs demanding breath, but it was less urgent now, as if behind a veil. His mind was slipping away from his body, losing its grip on reality.

The figure reached towards him. A wave of incredible calm emanated out from where the boy's fingertips touched Joe's side. In that moment, Joe knew with absolute certainty that this was the Boy Who Learned What Fear Was from Grandad's story. Joe didn't understand how it could be the character from the story, but he knew it as surely as he knew the waste was crushing down on top of him.

The Boy adjusted the bin bags, moving them here and there to give room for Joe to breathe. Joe felt the waste above him shift, the restriction on his chest loosening. He sucked in one breath, then another. His breathing grew more powerful, deep and shuddering, lifting Tiger up and down on his chest. Tiger let out a grumbling sound, thankfully still breathing. The figure of the Boy faded away, darkness into dark, and was gone.

There were voices above them! Someone was yelling out their names.

'We're down here,' Joe tried to call out, the strength lost from his voice. Above, they just kept on yelling. He wasn't sure if anyone had heard him.

A crack of light opened on Tiger's hair.

'Down here,' Joe tried again. This time there was a response. Someone above yelled others over. The crack of light opened wider, so Joe could see Tiger's ear. The weight on top of him rapidly lessened, until the bags covering them were lifted away. He stared into the blazing sun, blinded with white light as his arms were pulled open and Tiger was taken from his chest.

Joe was helped to his feet by someone. His arms and legs were aching, and felt as stiff as if they were made from wood. The mountainside was too bright and his vision filled with swirling black spots. As if from far away, he heard Buddy complaining about losing the collecting bags and water bottles.

Ahead, Joe saw the blurred shape of Rose standing with one of the twins, the other twin lying amongst the rubbish. He stumbled backwards but the person holding him pressed their body against his shoulder blades, wrapping their arms around his waist to support him. It was Sonya. Her hold tightened as he felt himself sag. She was asking if he was okay.

Joe tried to respond, to tell her about the presence inside the mountain. Instead, he choked on the first word and coughed harshly, convulsing in her arms. Rose and the twins came into focus. Miraculously, Tiger was standing, covered in mould and slime but apparently unharmed. Lily was laid out on the waste, her breathing slow and her chest damp with sick. There were wisps of red blood in her vomit. Rose was bent over her, crying.

'Joe,' Sonya was saying. 'You need to go back to the town. Go with Maya and Rose, and the twins.'

'Someone in the mountains,' he mumbled.

'Buddy and I are going to look for the collecting bags.'

'I'll help,' Joe tried to turn to her, but slumped in her grip.

'You can't. You need to go back.'

He put his hand on her forearm, attempting to stand, but slipped into her again. 'It's dangerous. Loose ground. You come back too.'

'We can't. None of us can afford to lose a day's work.'

'Not safe.'

Sonya shifted so her mouth was next to his ear. 'What food have your family got at the moment, Joe?'

He tried to think, looking up at the intensely blue sky. He could feel his skin burning. 'Just oats. Potato and oats. Ran out since last drifter.'

'See, I've got to stay to find the bags.'

'I don't wanna leave you.'

'The twins need you to go down the mountains,' Sonya said in his ear. 'Go with them, so you can look after them.'

With that, she propelled him forward. Maya moved next to him and guided him with an arm across his back. Tiger held Maya's other hand and Rose carried Lily in her arms. Dazed and unable to lift his weight from Maya's side, Joe managed to put one foot in front of the other on the waste. They went down the mountains together.

By the time they stepped down onto the purple-green ground at the base of the mountains, Joe's vision had cleared and he walked independently of Maya. He felt deep pain across his body. As well as the aching, his skin was burning and his head seared with dehydration, the impact of walking unsheltered from the sun.

He'd thought of the presence in the mountains as they'd walked. Logic said it must have been a hallucination, brought on by being unable to breathe. Yet, he was sure he had felt hands brush against him as the bags were moved.

Lily's mouth hung open as her older sister carried her down off the bottom of the mountains. Rose's eyes were red, her expression fearful. A pair of puncture marks above Lily's ankle had risen into red mounds. Joe had seen snake bites before, as well as rodent bites and insect stings. Vermin were not uncommon in the waste. He'd never seen it have this effect before, especially not from one of the black and grey snakes. Their bites didn't even sting.

There were a few people between the base of the mountains and the town. The three Moonshine Brothers took collecting bags towards the dry stream. Despite not being actually related, the Brothers all had wide set shoulders and bushy beards. The tallest of the three, who was bald, was Buddy's father Kane, the other two Matthias and Scott.

Sonya's mother Demeta was there too, helping a group of older women including Ms Winnipeg lower a bucket down the stone well. Like Sonya, Demeta wore her hair in braids, though hers were longer than her daughter's. Sonya said the late nights spent rebraiding their hair together were a special time.

Demeta was also taller than her daughter, with more wrinkles around her eyes and prouder cheekbones. She let out a gasp when she saw Lily hanging in Rose's arms, and everyone looked up towards them.

Joe and the others were quickly surrounded, the Moonshine Brothers urging them towards the town for shade. Ms Winnipeg and the other old women followed behind asking questions: were they sure it was a snake, had they seen its colours, had there been any strange smells, had Lily eaten anything from the mountainside?

Only Demeta didn't come to them, running instead to the closest shack to the mountains, with crows perched across its roof. The Witch would be waiting inside. She was the only person in the town who didn't collect on the mountains, as she didn't do trade with the drifters. Other townspeople gave her food in return for her dream-giving potions and her knowledge of healing, or gifted it to her in the hope of good luck.

Demeta raised her hand to knock as she reached the door, but it was already inching inwards. The Moonshine Brothers stopped rushing everyone towards the town, and Ms Winnipeg and the other old women fell silent. The crowd separated, leaving Rose holding Lily in the middle. Joe, Maya and Tiger stood behind her.

The Witch's hands appeared, clawed around a knotted stick. The stick, rumoured to be from the fallen forest, struck down onto the earth and lifted dust. The wood bent as she dragged herself out into the sun. For all the townspeople's awe and fear of her, she was a tiny woman, the hunch of her back higher than her head. She was dressed in rags, the same dirty brown as the ground. Her hair was mostly gone, a few grey strands still dangling down from her temples.

Three crows flapped up from her shack's roof, then swooped down and landed on her hunched back. She showed no surprise or pain as they dug their talons into her spine, wobbling on their perch. Her tongue pushed out past her thin lips, tasting the air. The Witch raised her stick, stretched out her arms, and jammed the wood into the ground once more. She pulled herself forward another step.

'Bring her to me, and lay her down,' commanded the Witch. She shared Sonya's ability to speak quietly and be heard. But unlike Sonya's soft voice, the Witch's was abrasive, scratching inside the ear. Rose carried Lily forward, then placed her down in front of the Witch.

'She was bitten by a snake,' Rose said. It was hard for Joe to shake the feeling that the Witch already knew that just by looking at Lily's figure laid across the ground.

The Witch lowered herself using her stick, until her legs buckled and she dropped to her knees over Lily, the crows still clinging to her back. The three crows all faced in different directions. One looked towards Demeta, standing by the Witch's open door, another looked up towards the mountains, and the last stared directly at Joe.

The crows descended with the Witch's back as she placed her stick onto the ground and brought her ear to Lily's mouth to listen to her breathing. Then she inspected the puncture marks above Lily's ankle.

'Can you help her?' Rose asked.

'I can try.' The Witch rarely used more words than were needed. She pushed a hand into her rags, drawing out several strands of long yellow grass pinched between her fingers.

The Witch bit off the ends of the yellow grass, chewing it while leaning over Lily, as if about to kiss her. She closed Lily's nose with one hand and pulled the child's mouth open with the other. A strand of yellow spit trailed down from her mouth into Lily's, followed by a splodge of mushed grass spat with force. The Witch clamped Lily's mouth shut, then grasped her chin and jerked her head up. Joe saw Lily's throat move as she swallowed.

'Will she live?' Rose asked the Witch. It was a dangerous question. The townspeople knew that the Witch's predictions for sickness and health were unerringly accurate. Whatever she forecast always came to pass.

'She'll wake up soon, but not fully. She'll fall asleep again before nightfall. That sleep will be long and deep. She must awake from that slumber by the setting of the next full moon, or she will die.'

Rose sobbed. Lily stirred on the ground, writhing in the dirt.

'Joe, you're hurt. Come to the shade.' David stood next to him, holding a cloth collecting sack. His father's words reminded Joe of his pain, his body aching as if it were still being crushed inside the mountain. David held out an arm to support him, and Joe staggered into the shade provided by the first line of shacks.

Lily sat suddenly bolt upright. Her eyes were blank, as if

replaced by beads of glass. Tiger spoke to her, but she showed no sign of hearing him. He tried again, Rose watching on aghast. Maya tried to turn Tiger away from his twin, but Tiger yanked free, refusing to leave Lily's side. Throughout, one of the three crows on the Witch's back still peered at Joe.

'I heard the avalanche,' David said, offering a bottle of water to him. 'Are you okay?'

There was a feeling inside Joe like great weight crashing down, as if something inside himself had shifted and caused an avalanche like on the mountains. Nothing was okay. Not while Tiger shook Lily's arm, desperately trying to make her respond to him.

'Of course I'm not okay,' Joe said through gritted teeth. The roar of his internal avalanche was getting louder as he tried to restrain it.

'Joe...' David cautioned.

His father's mild tone only heightened Joe's overwhelming sense of everything being wrong.

'None of this is okay!' Joe jabbed his finger towards Lily. 'She's only a child, and so is Tiger. They shouldn't have to risk their lives every day. It's not right!'

Demeta watched him openly from next to the Witch's shack, while the other townspeople were trying not to make it obvious they were looking over. Joe felt his face burning red. Only Tiger, Rose and the Witch were focused on Lily. She was who everyone should have been paying attention to.

'You know what we see, every day on those mountains?' Joe raised his voice, making sure that all of them heard. 'The wrappers from your food, when you lived in the city. We see how much you all had. Now, a six-year-old girl has to risk her life digging through that rubbish to earn enough to avoid starvation. At her age, you'd have had a hospital to go to, and what's she got? An old woman spitting in her mouth. She deserves better!'

The only sound was Lily heaving. The townspeople looked at Joe with horrified expressions, not because of what he'd said about the mountains – they'd heard that all before – but because he'd spoken badly of the Witch.

She picked up her stick and rose creakingly to her feet, then advanced towards him. Her stick tapped a methodical beat against the earth as she approached. All three crows stared at Joe now, fanning out on her spine and tilting their heads. The Witch stared as well, her eyes almost as black as theirs. Her large pupils and dark irises were surrounded by the thinnest line of white.

David stepped between Joe and the Witch, his arms raised slightly to the sides as if to block her from reaching him. Her stick touched the ground between David's feet and she leaned her weight down onto it, standing uncomfortably close to them both. Joe smelled the tang of the yellow grass on her breath.

The mush was still caught between her teeth, like patches of mould. The crows retreated down to the base of her back and cawed at the sky.

'They're afraid of you,' the Witch whispered, her chin almost touching David's shoulder as she brought her face close to Joe's. 'Their eyes see things that human eyes do not. In their simple language they all call out the same word when you come close. Destiny. Destiny. Destiny.'

Each time she said the word, she rapped her stick against the ground and the crows called out. After the third call they flew from her back. She turned, manoeuvring her body around the stick in several steps, and started walking back towards her shack. The three crows landed with the others on its roof. David, who'd often said he didn't believe in the Witch's magic, let out a sigh of relief.

She stopped, speaking while facing away from them. 'The time will come, Joe, when you'll be unable to find the thread that connects your past to your present to your future. Then you will visit me, and you will learn from me.'

The gathered townspeople were silent as the Witch continued her gradual progress towards her shack, passing Lily, who was no longer vomiting. A carrier bag blew against the Witch's leg with the gentle wind, catching for a moment, then drifting away. She made it to the darkness inside her shack, and then the door swung closed behind her.

David looked at Joe for a moment as if about to say something, then decided against it and walked towards the mountains, leaving the bottle of water. Rose carefully picked up Lily, so their chests were touching and Lily's head hung over her shoulder. She carried her towards the town with Tiger following behind. As they passed Joe, Lily's eyelids were fluttering, as if she was already drifting into sleep.

CHAPTER SIX

That night, David came through the front door long after the sun had set. Joe was sitting on one of the stools by the counter across the defunct sink and stove. Grandad lay on his mattress but wasn't quite asleep, having recently returned from telling stories in other shacks. Surprise registered on David's face at the sight of Joe. Normally, by the time he came home, Joe was in the fallen forest with Sonya, especially if he and Joe had argued that day.

David leaned his collecting sack against the wall. 'I saw Demeta on my way back. She told me Lily's in a deep sleep. They can't wake her.'

Joe nodded slowly. He already knew. Sonya had visited earlier, bringing him his collections that she'd recovered from the mountains. She'd told him she was going to stay with Rose and the twins that night, to help in any way she could.

David shifted on the spot, gathering himself before speaking. 'Don't trust the Witch. Even back in the city, there were people who claimed to know your fate and future. They told you lies, for a price. It's an old scam.'

Joe let out an acknowledging grunt. He didn't know what he thought of the Witch's magic, especially after what he had experienced inside the mountains. The events of the day had left him feeling too bitter and exhausted to discuss the topic with his father.

David continued on regardless. 'You've got a good eye, for seeing through the crap that people speak. If she talks to you again, pay attention to what she wants from you.'

Grandad lifted his head from his mattress. 'When somebody makes symbols of everyday things, giving meaning to the flight of birds or the changing of the weather, it suggests there's a way they want the plot to go. She might be trying to see the ending she desires up ahead, or casting foreshadows for it to happen her way.'

Joe had the feeling he'd just been told the same thing twice, in his father's and grandfather's different languages. David took a jar of oats, a bottle of water and a metal pan out through the back door. He then returned for the handmade bow-drill they used to start fires. By the time the porridge was made, Grandad was snoring. David halved the food between himself and Joe, sitting with him at the counter. They ate in silence.

The next day Joe collected with his usual group, minus Rose and Lily. They'd moved to a different area, aware that some waste might still be loose after the avalanche, but there was nowhere on the mountains where it was really safe to work. Buddy and Maya collected up ahead, while Sonya was by Joe's side with Tiger. Tiger wore a backpack with a peeling image of a red and blue superhero on it, the duffel bag he usually shared with Lily too large for him alone.

Joe couldn't help but look out for a snake as he collected, though he saw none. While they could sometimes hear the sounds of creatures moving within the waste, it was only rarely they actually saw them. Even then, it was a fleeting sight as they lifted a bin bag, the rat or snake quickly disappearing back into the mountain.

With snakes, it was usually one of the black and grey ones, like the one that had bitten Lily. Everyone had assumed those snakes weren't very poisonous, as normally their bites ached for a day or two at worst. Even the green and yellow ones, that could make you feel really ill, had never caused what had happened to Lily.

Joe had told Sonya what the Witch had said, but he hadn't yet spoken to her about sensing the Boy Who Learned What Fear Was under the waste. He couldn't find a way to bring it up without sounding ridiculous. This was Sonya, though. She'd listen, if he could just get the words out.

'When I was inside the mountain...' Joe began, and Sonya looked up from her collecting. They were interrupted by shouting in the distance.

A wave of yelling swept over the mountains towards them as closer voices joined in. It wasn't an avalanche this time. The shouting was jubilant and happy. Joe's group clambered out from under their shade, then ran higher up the waste, quickly sweating in the heat.

They looked across the desert, searching the rolling hills and the flatlands. Buddy spotted it first and pointed out towards the hills. The tiny shape of a black van rose to the top of one of them, a dust cloud rising behind. It was heading towards the town.

'Drifter's coming!' Buddy yelled. The rest of the group joined in, then heard townspeople further on shouting the same. Joe watched the van's progress, repeatedly sinking out of sight before re-emerging on the next hill. Something clicked inside of him. He knew what he had to do.

'Buddy,' Joe said, once the yelling died down. 'Can I talk to you?'

Buddy eyed him suspiciously and Joe indicated with a motion of his head for them to walk away from the others.

'What do you want, mate?' Buddy asked, following Joe

further down the mountainside.

'Can I borrow your knife?'

Buddy crossed his arms. 'I heard about yesterday. That you were ranting and raging after Lily got bitten. I don't want someone stabbed with my knife.'

'I'm not going to stab anyone.'

'No, you're not. You're just going to sell it straight to that drifter. How stupid do you think I am?'

Joe clenched his teeth. 'I only want to borrow it. I'll give it back.'

'If you want the knife, give me something that will sell for more than it would. And I still want it back when you're done.'

Joe crouched down and rooted through his collecting sack, producing three flimsy digital cameras, identical apart from their colours – one red, one green, one blue – which together would definitely sell to the drifter for more than the knife.

The cameras were the sort of object that the drifters could trade on to the other communities based on nostalgia, swapping items from the waste for the food supplied by the gardeners, the fisherpeople, and the hunters. Even if no one from another community bought them, the cameras would still be usable as electronics for the recycling centre, letting the drifter charge their vehicle's battery that little bit more.

Joe had found a box containing twelve of the cameras earlier in the day, sealed up with sellotape. Sonya's story for them was that they'd been owned by someone teaching a photography course, or had been stock in a shop that went out of business. He wasn't going to let on to Buddy that he had more.

Joe handed the three cameras across and Buddy inspected them, turning each one over in his hands. Buddy took his time, and Joe felt himself getting light headed from standing out of the shade. He knew this was an act. He'd seen Buddy's eyes gleam when he'd first taken the cameras out of his collecting sack.

'It's not enough,' Buddy said. 'It's my knife, you know. I've had it for years. It's special to me.'

'Fine,' Joe grabbed four plastic bottles from his bag and chucked them one by one at Buddy's feet. 'I'm only borrowing it. That's all you're getting.'

'Pleasure doing business with you.' Buddy grinned, before swinging his backpack off and putting the cameras inside, then gathering up the bottles as well. He drew the switchblade knife from his shorts pocket and passed it to Joe.

'I want that returned. I won't forget.' Buddy trudged up the mountain and called back to Joe. 'And in good nick. Take care of it.'

Joe put the knife into his collecting sack, pushing it below plastic yogurt pots he'd collected earlier in the day.

'Why do you need a knife?' Sonya walked down the mountainside towards him. Higher up and out of earshot,

Buddy rejoined Maya and Tiger, the three of them heading back towards the shade.

'For Lily,' Joe said.

'How will a knife help Lily?'

Joe gazed out towards the drifter's van. Already it seemed larger and closer, though it'd be most of the day before it arrived. 'The drifter will take me to the city. I don't intend on asking.'

Sonya glanced at the van, then looked at Joe with her eyes wide. 'The city? I thought that was play talk the other night. I didn't think you were actually going to try to go.'

'I wasn't. At least, not yet. But after what's happened to Lily, I've realised it can't wait. What if there's a better life there, where Tiger and Lily wouldn't have to put themselves at risk every day? What if there's a hospital, with doctors that could come and help Lily, or give me medicine to bring back to her?'

Sonya placed her hand on his cheek. 'Lily can't collect now, and neither can Rose while she's looking after her. They need you here, to collect, and share what food you can.'

'The rest of the townspeople will do that,' Joe said, his jaw moving against her palm. 'Even without me, there'll still be enough food or there won't. But no one else will go to the city. The Witch said Lily will either recover before the next full moon, or she'll die. What if she dies, and we learn later there was something in the city that could've saved her?'

Sonya took her hand lightly away from his cheek. Joe felt he had to convince her, that he couldn't go if she didn't accept it.

'Something strange happened, when Tiger and I were under the waste,' Joe said. 'I felt like there was someone else there, who moved the bags so I could breathe. It sounds mad, but at the time it felt like it was the Boy Who Learned What Fear Was, from my Grandad's story.'

Sonya's brow wrinkled with confusion. 'I was there when we dug you up, Joe. It was just you and Tiger. I spoke to Tiger about getting trapped as well. He didn't see anything like that.'

'I don't know if it really happened. It's just what it felt like at the time. But at first I wasn't able to breathe, and then the bags shifted, and I was. What if there was a reason I survived? The Witch told me I had a destiny just after Lily was bitten. What if that destiny is having this idea, and finding something in the city that saves her?'

Sonya looked at him sadly, the sun glittering in her eyes. 'Yes. You have to go. Because if you don't, and Lily doesn't get better, you'll always wonder whether you should have. I get it. But try asking the drifter first. I know they say they won't take passengers, or go to the city, but it's still worth trying. See if you're able to persuade them. If not, then consider forcing them.'

Sonya turned away, and set back off towards their shade. Joe followed after her, and saw how she watched the far-off van as they made their way across the waste. She moved as if carrying a new tension across her back and shoulders. It wasn't easy for her to agree to him trying to get to the city, but she understood about Lily.

'That van's less than half a day away, I think,' Joe said. 'It won't be long till we need to go back into the town.'

'Be careful, Joe. The drifters are dangerous people,' Sonya replied.

They reached the shade and ducked under, joining Buddy, Maya and Tiger in collecting their last few objects to sell when the drifter arrived.

CHAPTER SEVEN

As Joe walked up the dry stream, he could hear the rattle of the approaching van's wheels. Despite the fact their electric engines made no sound, it was always possible to hear the drifter's vehicle as they got closer. Their wheels clattered and clanked against the hard earth, the noise travelling easily across the empty desert.

Joe had time to grab the collecting sacks he'd filled, then after that he'd head back down the stream for the drifter's arrival. When Joe stepped through the shack's door, Grandad was already inside, separating out his own collections from the pile against the wall. He had two full sacks and one half-full. Joe had three sacks, plus the partially-filled one in his hand. The remaining five sacks were David's, along with whatever he brought back from collecting that day.

'Penny for your thoughts?' Grandad asked.

'I don't understand my father at all,' Joe said. 'Most of the time he has no fight in him, not that I can see. But when everyone else is exhausted and aching from collecting all day, he's still up on the mountains, working in the dark. He starts before everyone else as well.'

Grandad picked his words carefully, each one considered. 'I don't believe your father worsened our fortunes by delaying leaving Madera. Even if we'd left earlier, we don't know anywhere else better than here we could have gone. You understand our lives based on how he tells the story. You only blame him because he blames himself.'

Joe pictured David on the mountains, late into the evening, ruminating over the choices he'd made and trying to pick up as much as he'd ever thrown away. He'd thought that his father refused to take responsibility for their lives. Grandad was suggesting that the alternative was true, and that David placed too much onto his own shoulders.

'Can I ask you a question?' Joe said to Grandad. Thinking about the waste on the mountains had reminded him of his experience underneath it.

'Always, Little Joe. Though I might not have the answer you want.'

Joe hesitated, unsure how to ask without sounding like he was losing his mind. 'Have you ever had something, or someone, from one of your stories turn up in real life?'

'Most days since I started telling stories,' Grandad replied. 'Stories echo the world, and the world echoes stories.'

Joe had heard Grandad use that phrase before. It was something he said when someone asked him if a story was true. It was a way of saying stories could be true, without necessarily being something that really happened.

'I mean, more than an echo. A story actually becoming real,' Joe probed further.

Grandad gave him a shrewd look. 'I suppose if you wanted to ask me your question directly, you already would have.'

Joe nodded. He wasn't sure how Grandad would react if he started talking about a fictional character appearing inside the mountains. He didn't want to make his grandfather worry.

'Since we all came out here from the city,' Grandad said. 'The boundary between stories and life has felt less clear. This all seems like it could be a tale to me, compared to working in an office when I was young. So who's to say other stories couldn't mix with this one?'

Joe knew that was as much as he'd get out of Grandad without explaining exactly what happened in the mountain. Grandad never gave too specific an answer when the topic was the facts or reality behind his stories. David had described Grandad to Joe as like a magician, who did not want to reveal the technique behind his tricks.

Joe realised he could no longer hear the rattle of the van's wheels. It had stopped somewhere in the town, most likely down near the well.

'Time to go,' Joe said. He lifted two collecting sacks in each hand. Grandad picked up his own collections and followed Joe out. They reached the dry stream and joined the other townspeople walking down with bags of collection for the drifter. There was a large crowd at the base of the stream, so Joe climbed up the dirt bank.

The sun was hot on the back of his neck as he lifted himself out of the trench. He turned his body and sat with his feet dangling into the dry stream, more townspeople passing by his legs as they headed down to see the drifter. From there, he could see all the way to the black van parked by the stone well.

Joe spotted Sonya and Demeta near the front of the crowd. They were speaking to Alice, who said something that made Sonya smile. Kane and the other Moonshine Brothers were behind them, getting tarps and poles out ready to set up shade. Grandad joined Buddy and Maya near the back. David wasn't present. He usually delayed seeing the drifter so he could collect that bit more to sell.

Dust was still rising from the stationary van. The windows were tinted, the drifter hidden inside. The Mechanic had tinted all the electric vehicles' windows, to protect the drifters from being cooked inside their cars and vans by the glaring sun.

Between the van and the stone well, the Mayor stood facing the crowd. While everyone else wore only light clothing, he was in a long corduroy jacket. The Mayor considered his jacket a symbol of his status in the town, though all Joe could think of were the pools of sweat stewing in his armpits.

Before life in the city fell apart, the Mayor had owned the landfill. Because of this, he saw himself as a leader within the town, and wore the jacket to display his authority. It irritated Joe that everyone else let the Mayor take up that role. People still thanked him for 'letting' them live there. They were separate from the old world and the city now. The Mayor had no more claim of ownership over the town or the mountains than any of the rest of them.

The van's door swung open. A leather boot stepped out onto the dry earth below it, shortly followed by a second. The drifter moved into view, towering over the Mayor. He was dressed in faded jeans and a white shirt that stretched around the muscle on his chest. His clothes were old and well-worn, though not as dirty as the townspeople's. A Stetson hat shaded his eyes, the stubble on his chin catching the sunlight.

He was one of the less sociable drifters. Joe had met him before, but all he knew about him was that his name was Leigh. The Mayor stuck out his hand officiously and Leigh shook it, then the Mayor angled himself so that he was half speaking to Leigh, half to the townspeople.

'Welcome, drifter, to our humble town,' the Mayor announced. 'We comb these mountains to ensure that what has been left here does not go to waste. It is hard work, and it is rough work, but it is proud work. There's much to be found on these mountains of ours. You can trust that if there's anything you desire, it will be provided for you.

'There's great difficulty in collecting, with the oppressive heat and danger on the mountains. We hope that you'll bear these hardships in mind when offering trade for our collections. Having met you in the past, we know you're a kind and generous man. We're delighted to invite you into our town, and our homes.'

Leigh gave a slight nod to the Mayor, then another to the crowd.

'How's this old town doing?' The drifter's voice was rough and low, gritty with years of travelling through dust. 'Been a while since I've been around these parts.'

'You visit us at a dark time, I'm afraid.' The Mayor clutched his hands over his heart, and Joe cringed. 'A young girl, Lily, has been bitten by a snake and fallen into a deep sickly sleep. It is only with the utmost struggle that her older sister has been able to make her swallow food. We're all banding together in order to collect and sell enough to feed her, and to keep her well. Her twin brother has worked especially hard for her today.'

'You'll be Tiger, then,' Leigh said, crouching down towards

where the Mayor was looking. Tiger stepped forward, miniature in comparison to the drifter. 'I remember the first time I saw you and your sister. Came by here not long after you were born, saw you in your mama's arms. Been travelling these communities for years, only pair of twins I ever saw. Something special you got there, kid. You going to look after her?'

Tiger nodded and Leigh shook his hand, taking longer over it than he had the Mayor's. Leigh rose to his feet, and the Mayor assumed a prim position next to him, speaking out towards the crowd again. 'You are welcome to stay in one of our homes, all of which are open to you, or to sleep in your vehicle, which others choose and would cause no offence.'

Leigh's jaw tightened. The Mayor's pomp and ceremony clearly annoyed him.

'If it's all the same to you, for the few days I'm here I'll stay with her' – the drifter pointed to elderly Ms Winnipeg in the crowd – 'just like I always do.'

The Mayor puffed out his chest, oblivious. 'Certainly. Now, all there is left to do is announce that trading's open. Is there anything you'd like before we begin?'

'A table and chair, if it ain't trouble. And shade.'

There was a brief conversation at the front of the crowd, then three of them hurried away to provide a table and chair. Others worked together to set up shade where Leigh would sit and where the townspeople would queue. This shade was tall enough to stand under, and more securely fastened than what they cobbled together on the mountains.

Leigh busied himself emptying out the rear of his van, arranging various foods for sale. The back of the van was packed with cardboard boxes from the gardeners that contained oats or potatoes, as well as a few holding peppers and mushrooms. After those, he unloaded a set of pepper plants growing out of plastic pots, which some townspeople would attempt to cultivate in the hard earth around their shacks.

Leigh brought out herring in tubs filled with salt, from the fisherpeople. He followed that with meat similarly preserved in salt, most likely rabbit and wolf from the red shapes Joe could see poking out. They'd have been caught by the hunters, or possibly by Leigh himself. Once everything was ready, the drifter sat down behind the table and took a drink from the bottle of water that had been placed there for him.

The Mayor moved next to Leigh again and addressed himself to the townspeople, some of whom had already started to queue under the shade. 'I declare that trading is now open. I remind you to keep the line orderly and not to overcrowd our guest. There'll be enough time for everyone to perform their desired transactions. I suggest some of you at the rear leave and return later, to avoid unnecessarily wasting time.'

There seemed to be a huge amount of food in the boxes surrounding the back of the van, but Joe knew each customer would only buy a stock of oats and potatoes, then maybe one or two luxuries like a plant, a piece of meat or half a fish. Joe joined the queue forming under the shade, which folded in on itself several times.

He was behind Grandad's friend Mr Rajarshi, who had lost his hearing as he aged, and got by through lipreading. Grandad was further ahead now, with other townspeople waiting behind him. A few people, including Sonya and Demeta, were heading up the mountains to do some more collecting before coming back later.

Leigh was leaning back on his chair with his hat pulled low. The townspeople approached him one by one and emptied their collecting bags onto the table. He looked across each set of collections and made an offer for all of it by saying a number that they could spend. He had written 'prices' on his boxes, a scoop of oats costing '1', a piece of rabbit meat '4'. The seller always accepted the drifters offer without debate, and then picked what they wanted from the boxes. It was rare that he turned an item away. The townspeople had a good idea of what the drifters were able to sell on, or recycle to charge their vehicles.

The line progressed slowly. Each time they took a forward step they all hefted their bags up, before dropping them again with a crunch on the hard ground. The heat seemed to be getting to Mr Rajarshi. Even under the shade he was sweating profusely, and he drank repeatedly from his water bottle. When the line moved forward, he struggled to carry his three heavy-duty bin bags forward.

Mr Rajarshi rejected Joe's first two offers to move the bags for him, but relented on the third. When it was his turn to go to Leigh, Mr Rajarshi carried them himself again, his arms locked downwards with their weight. He dropped the bags on the ground before lifting them, one at a time, and emptying them onto the table. Joe watched from a respectful distance, next in line with the queue still long behind him.

Leigh must have remembered Mr Rajarshi from previous visits, as he lifted the brim of his hat then raised his face before speaking. Mr Rajarshi accepted Leigh's offer for his collections, then went to the boxes and picked out oats, potatoes and a single portion of herring. Leigh wrapped the fish in paper and salt, then helped Mr Rajarshi pour the oats into metal tins the old man had brought with him. Mr Rajarshi put all of his food into one of his bin bags, carrying it away in one hand, the two empty bags in the other.

After Leigh had sorted out Mr Rajarshi's collections, Joe approached the table. The Mayor hovered nearby, ready to shout out and tell someone else to get anything Leigh asked for. A strong fish scent emanated from the boxes by the van, almost covering the stink of the mountains. Up close, Joe could see that despite his large muscles, Leigh had the same gaunt cheeks that were common amongst the townspeople. The drifters were better fed than them, but not by much.

'What you got for me?' Leigh asked. He didn't look at Joe, focusing instead on an old silver coin he was rolling deftly through the gaps between his fingers. Joe emptied out his collecting sacks, mostly recycling to be taken to the centre, but also a few things that could be sold on, like clothes, ceramic plates and a trowel. He placed a tied carrier bag down separately. It contained the rest of the digital cameras that he'd concealed from Buddy.

'Twenty five all of it,' Leigh said, glancing across the table, the coin still dancing through his fingers. 'Three of those are for the trowel alone. One of the gardeners will be wanting that.'

Leigh looked at the unopened carrier bag and waited. He was relaxed, slumped back in the chair. Even so the coin moved constantly in his hand. Joe opened the bag of cameras, so they spilled over the table.

'Good electronics recycling,' Leigh said. 'Could maybe even sell a couple, to folk that want to think about how things used to be. You oughta be proud of that find. An extra eight for those. You'll be rich for this town.'

'I don't want trade for them,' Joe said, speaking low so the Mayor wouldn't hear.

Leigh stopped the silver coin's movement, pinching it between his finger and thumb, then looked up and met Joe's eyes. 'What do you want? Ain't nothing free around these parts.'

Joe hesitated, aware he was breaking an unwritten rule. Then he said it anyway. 'I want you to take me in your van to the city.'

Leigh pushed his shoulders back and clicked his neck. 'You ever heard of a drifter giving someone transport?'

'No.'

'That's because we don't.'

'I'll pay. Not just the cameras. Everything.'

Leigh shifted in his chair, and Joe got the impression he was checking whether the Mayor was listening. 'I don't go to the city, kid. No one does.'

'But for all of this?' Joe indicated his collections on the table.

'It's dangerous. You don't know what's between here and there.'

'Do you?' Joe asked.

Leigh's laugh was as dry as the desert. 'I see what you're doing. Drifters are the wild sort, right? So you're playing on my sense of adventure.'

'Maybe you're too scared,' Joe replied. He didn't know if he was going too far, but he wanted to keep the drifter talking.

'I'll let you in on a secret.' Leigh leaned forward over the table, close enough that Joe could see the thin lines scoured across his face by years of dust and heat. 'I am scared. There ain't just death that way. There's something wrong with the desert round the city. The shadows that you thought only lived in your head – in your nightmares – walk in the open there. I ain't crossing through that for what you've picked up off the mountains.'

'How much does it cost for you to stop telling stories?' Joe said. Leigh relaxed back, rolling the silver coin in his hand again.

'I know that sort of tale,' Joe continued. 'You're raising your price. Name it, and I'll pay.'

'You can't afford it. No one here could. Except maybe that Librarian, but he ain't in the habit of selling his books.'

'How much more would you need? I'll get more for you.'

'You got gall. I like you, but I can't help you. What do you want with that city anyway?'

'You heard about the little girl who's sick. Lily. It's the only place where there might be medicine or help for her. It could save her life.'

'It's a noble cause. It really is. That poor girl, and her brother.' Leigh fell quiet for a moment, moving his mouth as if mulling it over.

He's genuinely considering it, Joe thought. For the first time he felt hopeful that the drifter might actually accept his offer.

Then Leigh shook his head. 'Sorry. I ain't your guy. Maybe one of the other drifters will take you.'

Joe opened his mouth to respond, but was interrupted by a shout from the Mayor. 'Joseph! There's a queue waiting behind you. I beg you to think of them.'

A sardonic grin appeared on the drifter's face. 'You'd better make your choices. Don't forget to add your trade from the cameras as well.'

Joe went to the boxes at the back of the van. He filled up five jars of oats, then bought rabbit meat, herring and potatoes as well. He didn't plan on staying in the town long enough to eat it all, but he could at least leave something behind for his father and grandfather.

'You've still got one left,' Leigh said, across to him. Joe was certain he'd spent exactly what he'd earned, but he took an extra scoop of oats anyway.

'Good luck finding someone to take you to the city, kid. It ain't going to be easy.'

'I'll ask the next drifter,' Joe lied. 'Thank you.'

'Joseph!' The Mayor shouted again. Joe picked up the collecting sack he'd filled with the food, stuffed the other empty sacks in as well, and walked away. Leigh slid Joe's collections from the table into his own bin bags, the silver coin still held between his fingers.

CHAPTER EIGHT

After speaking to Leigh, Joe walked up towards his shack. Sonya was standing outside his front door. The sun setting at the top of the hill cast her long shadow down towards him.

'What did the drifter say?' she asked.

Joe put his cloth sack of food down. 'He said no. I offered him everything I'd collected, but he wasn't interested.'

'Maybe it's worth waiting.' She pulled at the fabric of her shorts. 'You can make an offer to the next drifter.'

'I don't think the answer would be any different. And Lily's sick now. By the time they come, it might already be too late.'

Sonya struggled to keep the worry out of her voice. 'He looks strong, and drifters usually carry weapons. He might have a gun.'

Joe raised his hand and stroked his fingers through her braids, feeling their texture speckled with grit from the mountains. 'I have to try. I'm going to sneak into Ms Winnipeg's shack at night and catch him when he's sleeping. Then it won't matter what weapons he's got.'

Sonya stepped back, a braid pulling through his fingers then falling free. She drew a glittering knife from her waistband. It was ornamental, with a curved blade, and a red ribbon wrapped around the hilt. The weapon was shaped for cutting throats. It looked wrong in Sonya's hand, as if both she and the blade couldn't be held in focus at once.

'I'm coming with you.'

Joe blinked. 'I didn't think, even if he'd agreed to take me… I wouldn't ask you to.'

'If you manage to threaten him into driving you to the city, you won't be safe alone in his van. You'll need someone else with you to keep an eye on him.' Sonya's tone left no room for argument.

'Where'd you get the knife?' Joe asked.

Sonya looked it over in her hand, smiling at some memory as she did. 'It's Maya's. Buddy gave it to her.' Her smile fell away. 'So we'll go into Ms Winnipeg's shack while they're asleep?'

'Yeah. We'll have to make sure she doesn't shout for help.'

Sonya's expression took on an unusual blankness. Joe normally found her easy to read, and was able to recognise a complexity of feeling in her subtle shifts and mannerisms. Now her face was dull, her body neutral, showing him nothing.

'I'll make sure Ms Winnipeg keeps quiet,' she said, 'if you stay focused on the drifter.'

'Are you sure?' Joe asked. 'You don't have to come. I can do this alone.'

'I've made my decision,' Sonya replied, resolute. 'I'm coming with you.'

Joe knew there was no point in arguing – she wouldn't change her mind. They were both stubborn, just in different ways. When Joe was set on doing something, he charged towards it, crashing through everything in his path. When Sonya was similarly determined, she became immutable, steadily moving yet impossible to stop.

'He'll leave soon, to take his first load to the recycling centre,' Sonya said. 'Were you planning on going there later tonight, when he's back?'

Joe hadn't considered timing. Leigh would be in and out of the town for a couple of days, taking trips to the recycling centre, where he'd deposit their recycling for credit to recharge his van. Joe wanted to leave as soon as possible. However, because people knew Leigh would still be around for a day or two, some of them wouldn't have traded with him yet.

'Let's make it tomorrow night,' Joe said. 'He'll definitely still be here then, but it lets people trade with him tomorrow. I don't want anyone to starve because of this.'

Sonya's bottom lip trembled, breaking her blank expression. 'Make sure you leave things well with your father and grandfather. And you should take that book to the Librarian before we go.'

'I don't think we should tell anyone what we're doing,' Joe said, aware of how Sonya talked everything through with her mother. 'They'll try to stop us, and we might not get another chance.'

'I know.' Sonya's lip stiffened and her face was blank again. 'I'm not coming to the fallen forest tonight. We should both spend some time with our families. I'll see you tomorrow, on the mountains.'

Joe knocked on the Librarian's door. Overhead, a thin sliver was missing from the right-hand side of the moon and the first stars were emerging in the deep blue sky. Joe's own shack had been empty, David still on the mountains and Grandad somewhere telling stories.

The Librarian's shack was the only one in the town with a lock, a contraption the Librarian had created using parts from a suitcase's combination dial. Every time the Librarian left for the mountains, he set a new number on the combination, which needed to be entered to open the door.

His window-holes were blocked with the same sheet metal that was used for the shacks' roofs. Anyone could force the sheet metal out of place with one firm push, or kick through the door and its flimsy lock. The townspeople tactfully avoided mentioning that to the Librarian.

There was the sound of movement behind the door, then the numbered dials clicked round as the Librarian manipulated them from inside. The mechanism popped open, and the door drew back to reveal two magnified eyes looking at Joe through circular glasses. The Librarian's eyebrows protruded over the top of the frames.

'Ah m'boy!' The Librarian's reedy voice spun upwards with excitement. 'Have you brought me another book?'

'Yes.' Joe held up the book with the iceberg on the cover.

'Excellent!' The Librarian exclaimed, pulling the door fully open. As soon as Joe stepped inside, the Librarian shut the door, then turned the dials to relock it. Joe's eyes took a few moments to adjust to the musty darkness, the only light a candle on a low table by the opposite wall.

The entire interior was crammed with bookshelves lined up in tight rows, like the shacks on the hill. Each bookshelf was a different shape and size, some handmade and others recovered from the mountains. Most were overloaded, with books wedged into gaps that had already been filled twice over.

In the candlelight, the shack became a labyrinth of right angles, made from the corners of books, shelves and shadows. The air smelled as if it hadn't been disturbed in years, left to become dense and heavy.

The Librarian had disappeared from his locking mechanism and was now somewhere inside the bookshelf maze. The creak of his old bones sounded further away than was possible in the enclosed shack.

From outside, the Librarian's home appeared too small to contain all these bookshelves. Joe wondered if he'd left room for a mattress anywhere. The Librarian reappeared at the opposite end of the shack and sat down on a chair behind the candle, its flame reflected in his glasses.

'Sit down,' the Librarian called to him. Joe edged between bookshelves, knowing that if he knocked against one he'd send multiple books clattering to the floor. He headed towards the light of the candle. The Librarian made his own candles. He traded items he'd collected to other townspeople for oil or wax they found on the mountains, and also bought meat from the drifters to drain off fat to use as tallow. This left him with shrunken meat and little trade to spend on oats or other food, starving himself to keep the candles burning.

'You asked if I'd brought you another book.' Joe passed the last of the bookshelves and stopped in front of the Librarian. 'I don't think I've brought you one before.'

'Nonsense, nonsense!' the Librarian replied. 'I remember every book I'm given. It was a set of Ray Bradbury's short stories. Come to think of it, you were much smaller then. Your father came with you, after you found it on the mountains.'

Joe placed the iceberg book on the low table. The Librarian was in the only chair, so Joe sat on the floor.

Behind the candlelight reflected in his lenses, the Librarian's eyes didn't register Joe or the book. He looked beyond Joe's shoulder into somewhere else. 'Ah yes, Bradbury. He was good. He was really very good. He understood, you see. He knew that the worlds he created lived in the poetry of his language. That's why his stories swirled and sparkled and fizzled and roared. He chose his words in such a way that a single sentence contained as much as another author's novel.'

The Librarian refocused on Joe. 'That's what I'm doing here. That's my task. These books all contain worlds within them. I'm their protector. You brought me Bradbury, who would have approved of this duty I'm undertaking. In one of his stories he described lost people walking in a dying country, carrying whole books in their heads. They were saving them, for when everything could be rebuilt. That's what I'm doing, and I don't even need to hold them in my head.'

The old man suddenly grasped Joe's wrists. 'This book you've brought me tonight, or the Bradbury you gave me before, they could be the last copies in existence. What do we know that's left? The city, which we hear nothing from. It might be completely bare. Every bookshop empty, every building hollow, every library burned. Then there's the communities and settlements formed by those who left the city. Our town, the gardeners, the fisherpeople by the sea, the hunters in their ever-moving tents, and the Mechanic alone in her garage. All too far away from each other to meet, but connected by the drifters. Beyond that, beyond our little circumference, for all we know, is oblivion. Where else then, other than here, other than the mountains, do we know for certain that there are books?'

'Nowhere,' Joe said. The Librarian released his wrists, though Joe could still feel the grip on his skin.

'Exactly. That's why I cannot stand to see books go to the drifters.' The Librarian sniffed, and Joe thought there might be tears forming behind his glasses. 'The idea that they could end up in the recycling centre, the worlds inside them shredded and turned to pulp, is too much to bear.'

The Librarian fell quiet, sniffling.

'So what's this one?' Joe indicated the iceberg book on the table.

'It's an entirely different type of world, m'boy.' The Librarian lifted the book close to his face. 'It's a textbook, containing knowledge from its time, or at least what people thought they knew. This one's a world of weather, detailing how and why some places were getting warmer, and others colder.' The Librarian placed the book down next to the candle. 'We'll need it, when the time comes. We'll need all of the books. We'll need to learn as much as we can, from all the different worlds, to build one here worth living in.'

'Do you think that'll happen?' Joe asked. 'A time when children in a place like this will learn to read again?'

'I believe so, yes,' the Librarian said. 'Because of youths like you, who are full of fire. The ones who want to understand everything, who want to hear every story and know every truth. Who want to learn so they can be clever, so they can contribute, so they can make things better. I've met young people the same before, who are burning up inside. You'll change the way things are, and you'll get your chance to learn.'

The reflected flames swayed in the Librarian's glasses. For a moment Joe felt it wasn't candlelight he saw in the lenses, but the fire that the Librarian perceived inside of him. He heard the rumble of wheels on hard earth from outside, the drifter driving away towards the recycling centre.

'I should go,' Joe said, standing.

The Librarian nodded and stood up as well. Joe moved through the darkness between bookshelves, the Librarian close behind. The door surprised Joe, his hands brushing against it before he realised that he was at the end of the shack. He stopped and waited as the Librarian wound the dials to unlock the mechanism.

Joe stepped out into the night, then turned back to the Librarian in the doorway. 'Do you read them all?'

'As many as I can, for as long as I can keep a candle burning.

It costs me, in lost sleep and the food I can afford from the drifters, but I make a willing sacrifice. The worlds only live when they're being read, when they're thought of or dreamed of. I keep them spinning. Thank you for the book, truly.'

The Librarian shut the door, then the combination dial clicked round again as he relocked the shack, protecting the books and worlds inside them. Joe walked away, heading to the dry stream. When he reached its bank, a quiet but carrying voice called his name. He turned, expecting Sonya.

Instead it was her mother, Demeta. The silver cross on her necklace glinted in the moonlight. She was similar to Sonya in many ways. She had the soft walk, the braided hair, the air of calm. While Sonya's calmness seemed inherent to her personality, something about the lines on either side of Demeta's mouth made Joe suspect that for her, it was an acquired trait, one that she'd worked on and learned. He guessed that when Demeta was younger, she'd been a woman who snapped and snarled.

'Try not to get my daughter into too much trouble, won't you?'

When Joe didn't reply, Demeta laughed. Her laughter had a cynical edge that Sonya's lacked. 'You two are the same as when you were children. If you were hiding something, neither of you'd tell a lie. You'd just both stop speaking altogether. Be safe, whatever you're up to.'

Joe was careful not to nod.

'I was there yesterday, when the Witch approached you. If she wants to speak to you, it's worth listening. She's closer to nature than we are. She sees connections we don't, how everything holds together. She could help you.'

'But how do I know there's any truth to what she says?' Joe asked. 'How do I know she's not just an old woman who's learned a few tricks with animals and herbs, so she won't have to work on the mountains?'

'Sometimes, Joe, you remind me extraordinarily of your father.'

Joe hadn't expected that. Perhaps it showed on his face, because Demeta smiled, then told him once more to be safe before walking away towards her shack.

When Joe returned home, both his father and grandfather were asleep on their mattresses. He spent a long time watching their chests rise and fall. He wondered when he'd see them again if he and Sonya succeeded the following night, and what would happen if they failed.

Collecting the next day was slow work. With Rose and Lily missing, and Tiger subdued by their absence, it was quiet on the mountains. Sonya told Joe that at the Witch's advice, Rose was making Lily swallow water with small amounts of food mixed in. It was working, but the child didn't even stir when Rose gave her the bitty drink.

Joe knew by the way Sonya watched for Leigh's van on the desert that she was constantly thinking about the night ahead, just like he was. When the van was in view, heading away from the town or returning from the recycling centre, it became almost impossible for either of them to focus on their work. Neither Buddy nor Maya asked why they wanted the knives, though Buddy made no attempt to conceal his curious glances at Joe.

When they finally descended the mountains at the end of the long day, Leigh was no longer taking trips to the recycling centre and had left his van parked by the stone well. Joe and Sonya walked up the dry stream and agreed that they'd meet in the fallen forest when the sun set that night, then separated towards their shacks.

Grandad was there when Joe returned home, David still on the mountains. Grandad lit a fire out the back, and cooked a portion of rabbit and potato for them to share. Joe could barely eat his meal. He kept moving from place to place in the shack, unable to settle. His grandfather didn't ask him what was wrong, but did ask if he wanted to listen to a story. Joe assented, needing something to occupy his mind. Grandad asked which story he wanted to hear. Joe thought about where he'd be going, if the plan worked.

'The city,' Joe said. 'Tell me a story about the city.'

Grandad told him the tale of a rich prince and a forest woman, of a suit made from night sky and a dress made from earth, and of the doomed love upon which the city was built. It was a long story. By the time Grandad finished, the sun had set and the night had grown dark. Sonya was probably already in the fallen forest, but David hadn't come back from the mountains. Joe wanted to see his father before leaving.

Eventually, he knew he shouldn't keep Sonya waiting any longer, and told Grandad he was going to the fallen forest. He started towards the door, but right at that moment, David opened it from the other side, carrying a collecting sack. He stood aside to let Joe pass, but Joe stopped where he was.

'Are you okay?' David placed his cloth sack down.

'Yeah,' Joe said. He didn't know what to say, so he asked the same question the townspeople always asked. 'Any good finds on the mountains?'

David looked at him for a moment, then replied as if this small talk was usual between them. 'Mainly plastic and card recycling today. I thought I might have found strings for the guitar, but it was only an empty packet. Yourself?'

'I found a book yesterday,' Joe said, overeager in having identified a topic to talk about. 'I gave it to the Librarian.'

'For free?' David asked.

'Yes.' It hadn't even occurred to Joe to ask for trade for the book when he was in the Librarian's shack.

'That's good.' David hesitated, then added, 'I'm proud of you. That's a good thing to do, giving it to the Librarian.'

'I hope you find the guitar strings someday.'

'Me too.' David smiled, but his lips curled inwards as if he tasted something bitter. 'If I ever do, I'll teach you how to play. If you want me to. I think you'd like it.'

'I could play at the rain celebrations,' Joe said, then went to the door. 'I'm going to go see Sonya in the forest. Goodnight.'

'Take care, Joe.'

Joe stepped out and shut the door behind him. From inside, he heard David sigh, then a rustling sound as his father sorted through collections from the day. Their last conversation before he left had been free from arguments or anger. He'd wanted to give his father that, at least.

CHAPTER NINE

Sonya was sitting on their log in the fallen forest, facing out towards the flatlands and the stars. A black plastic bin bag and a cloth sack were next to her on the ground, both tied at the top. As Joe approached her, a branch cracked under his foot and she jolted. When she turned towards him, the fear was still there in her eyes.

'What's in the bags?' he asked.

'There's oats, potatoes and herring in the black bag, as well as a pan and a flint-light. The cloth sack's one of yours, with as many bottles of water as I could fit in. I didn't know when we'd get the chance to refill them.'

'I hadn't thought of that,' Joe said. The fear that was apparent in Sonya's expression rose up inside him as well. He wasn't prepared.

'We can get water wherever the drifter does. And when we've watched the trucks' – Sonya pointed out over the flat desert, where a faint light travelled towards the bright dot of the city – 'they don't seem to take too long. I doubt it'll be more than a three-day drive, but I don't know how long we'll be in the city. I think I've packed enough food to last us about twelve days.'

Sonya had considered so much that Joe hadn't. He felt as if he was standing on a cliff, about to pull her off the edge with him in an attempt to fly.

'Maybe you were right about waiting for the next drifter,' he said. 'Maybe we shouldn't do this tonight.'

Sonya dropped her head into her hands. With her sitting on the log and Joe standing, she only came up to his waist. After a pause, she asked, 'Why?'

'Because it's so dangerous. Even having the knives, all it takes is a struggle, the drifter to get hold of one–'

Sonya let out a pained sound. Joe knew she was imagining a blade sinking into flesh.

'And if it works,' Joe said, 'we'll be going out into the desert. No one from the town's ever come back from the desert.'

'That's why we need the drifter though.' Sonya let her hands fall and shook her head. There was a note of disbelief in her voice, at her own words. 'People who walk out don't survive. But the drifters do, in their cars and vans.'

She looked up at Joe and smiled sadly. 'You don't really think we shouldn't go, you're just afraid. Nothing's actually changed. Lily's still ill. If we don't do this tonight, and the drifter leaves tomorrow, you'll be ashamed. You're not someone who lets fear turn you from the path you think is right.'

Joe knelt down and put his arms around her. 'Sonya, you always describe me like a hero in a story.'

Their mouths were close. The last time they'd kissed had been here, in the fallen forest, before the avalanche and Lily's snake bite.

'I wish we could stay in the forest for a while, just being us,' Joe said. 'But if we stay here even a second longer, I'm not sure I'll be able to do this.' He stood and offered his hand to her. 'Shall we go?'

She took his hand, and for a moment her smile was a little less sad. 'We shall.'

'Are you sure you want to come with me?'

Sonya gripped his hand and pulled herself up. 'Of course. To the moon and back.'

Sonya and Joe didn't need to conceal themselves as they walked through the town. There was nothing suspicious about them walking together at night. Yet they still took wide paths around every window-hole and avoided where the grey moonlight broke between the shacks.

Joe felt they'd become two ghosts. They were unreal

compared to the solid town, flickering apparitions passing through. Or they were real and the town wasn't, the ground only a notion beneath their feet. The whole night felt like make-believe. They wouldn't *really* sneak into Ms Winnipeg's shack and threaten Leigh. They weren't *really* bound for the city. It was like they were young children again, playing at being characters from one of Grandad's stories.

When they arrived at Ms Winnipeg's shack, reality faded back into place. They were going to do this. They'd made a hurried plan as they left the fallen forest. If Leigh or Ms Winnipeg was awake, they'd immediately threaten them with the knives and demand the drifter drive them to the city. If both were asleep, Joe and Sonya would get into position with the blades at their throats before waking them up.

A curtain sewn together from torn clothing and patches of fabric was draped over the window-hole, blocking them from seeing inside. They crept round the side of the shack, stepping over Ms Winnipeg's vegetables. Once they reached the back door, they laid their bags onto the ground.

Sonya slipped her knife out from under her T-shirt, the red ribbon dangling from its handle. Joe pulled his from his pocket, pressing the catch so that the blade sprung out with a click. He nodded at Sonya, and then slowly pulled the door open, letting in as little moonlight as possible. They entered through the gap, stepping inside into the darkness.

At first Joe saw nothing but the glint of their knives. Then his eyes adjusted and he made out the outline of Leigh lying on a bed nailed together from wooden planks. A thin line of moonlight stretched across from the back door towards the drifter, broken by their shadows. The grey light crossed the corner of the mattress where Ms Winnipeg lay on the floor. They took another cautious step forwards, and Ms Winnipeg jerked forward, coughing loudly.

Joe and Sonya both froze. She coughed twice more, deep and rough, before settling again. Sonya crept across the floor to Ms Winnipeg. She held the knife at her neck and hovered her other hand over Ms Winnipeg's mouth, close enough she'd be able to feel the elderly woman's breath.

Joe edged around Ms Winnipeg's mattress, stepping over her feet poking out at the end. As Joe neared Leigh's bed, he didn't know where to stand. He needed to be near Leigh's neck, but that put him within reach of his muscular arms. Joe moved slowly up the bed, aware of Sonya's hand close enough to Ms Winnipeg's face to wake her at any moment. He edged towards Leigh's upper body, raising the knife.

Ms Winnipeg's breath scratched in the air, every catch in her throat possibly the beginning of a coughing fit. Joe was sure Leigh and Ms Winnipeg couldn't remain asleep for long. His and Sonya's presence echoed in the shack, sending ripples of disturbance across both sleepers. The drifter's face twitched.

Joe's arm shot out instinctively, holding the knife above Leigh's throat. He'd thought his hand would shake, but it was utterly still. The knife was too close though, a hair's breadth between the blade and his neck. Leigh shifted. Joe knew he should pull the knife back, but his arm had stiffened. The blade touched against the skin of Leigh's neck.

Ms Winnipeg let out the start of a scream, and Sonya muffled the sound with her hand over the old woman's mouth. Leigh's fist crashed into Joe's ribs, throwing him into the wooden wall. Joe scrabbled for the knife that he'd dropped in the dark, and accidentally pulled down on Ms Winnipeg's sewn-together curtain. The curtain broke to the side and let a ray of moonlight into the shack, highlighting Leigh reaching for a handgun over the side of his bed.

Joe lunged forward, tripping over Ms Winnipeg's foot and landing flat on top of the gun. Leigh's arm was beneath Joe's stomach, pushing for the weapon. Joe clutched his arm with both hands, but Leigh had already gripped the gun's handle. Joe yanked it out of the drifter's grasp and staggered backwards, only just managing to avoid falling over Ms Winnipeg a second time.

'Get back!' Joe shouted, aiming the gun. Leigh was halfway out of the bed. He tightened as if to pounce forward at Joe, but stopped when he saw Sonya with her hand over Ms Winnipeg's mouth. He climbed back onto the bed and held his palms up.

'Alright, you win,' Leigh said. 'There ain't no good in anyone getting shot.'

Ms Winnipeg squirmed on her mattress, making terrified sounds against Sonya's hand. Sonya bent over her and muttered something aggressive into her ear, and Ms Winnipeg fell silent. Joe was shocked by Sonya's viciousness, then realised she was behaving how they both needed to, if this was going to work.

'Nobody has to get shot if you do what we want,' Joe said, with his most convincing snarl. He hoped his trembling chest wasn't visible in the dark.

'Ain't you ever heard it's bad luck to rob a drifter? Especially this one.' The growl in Leigh's voice matched Joe's with ease.

'We're not robbing you,' Joe said. 'We're going to your van, and you're going to drive us where we tell you to.'

Leigh's shoulders dropped, some of the tension falling away from his body. 'It's you, kid. I'm guessing we're driving straight to the city, right?'

'Hurry up,' Joe replied, ignoring him. 'We're going now. Out the door.'

Leigh clambered over the side of the bed and moved towards Joe.

'Stay back!' Joe snapped, keeping the gun pointed at him.

'Easy,' Leigh said, raising his palms again. 'I'm going to the door. You stay calm with that gun in your hand.'

Leigh walked out into the moonlight. He wore loose shorts,

and a sleeveless vest that revealed his arms. His hair was ruffled from sleep, his head appearing strangely large without his hat. His face was caught between emotions, his brow tight but his mouth a bemused half-smile. He let his hands fall to his sides as Joe followed him out.

'Why don't we leave the lady in her shack,' Leigh said. 'She's got nothing to do with this.'

Joe was about to agree, but Sonya interjected from inside. 'No. She might go for help. She's coming with us.'

Ms Winnipeg emerged from the shack, walking very upright and shaking with nerves. Sonya followed directly behind her, still holding the knife. Leigh's expression hardened into anger.

'Here's what we're going to do,' Sonya said, then indicated their bags to Leigh. 'You're going to carry those. Joe's going to walk near you with the gun out of sight but always aimed at you. I'm going to walk behind Ms Winnipeg with my knife. Anyone sees us, it'll look like we're having a normal walk. As long as neither of you tries to draw attention, no one gets hurt.'

'Please,' Ms Winnipeg let out a sob. 'Sonya. Joe. Just leave him alone.'

Tears ran down Ms Winnipeg's cheeks and she began to sniffle. Behind her, Sonya's face was pained, but she spoke firmly. 'We're all going to be silent as we go down the hill. You're going to have to stop crying.'

Ms Winnipeg shuddered, appearing for a moment as if she

was going to lose control of herself. Then she pursed her lips, reining her emotion in.

Leigh looked sideways at Joe. 'Reckon you should give your girl the gun. Seems to me she's in charge.'

'Be quiet,' Joe said. 'And start moving.'

They walked as Sonya had described, Joe and Leigh, followed by her and Ms Winnipeg. Even with the weapons hidden, it'd be immediately obvious to any onlooker that there was something wrong with the tense group moving through the night. Joe kept expecting a voice to yell out, telling them to stop, but none did.

When they reached the dry stream, where they'd be out of sight of the window-holes, Joe let out a shaky breath. He signalled with the gun for everybody to get into the stream. Immediately, Leigh jumped down and vanished into the trench. Joe swore and leapt after him, landing close and raising the gun. Leigh looked at Joe, then started walking down the stream, still carrying their bags. Joe wasn't sure if he'd been attempting an escape or not. Either way, Leigh cooperated as they went to the bottom of the stream, then out into the gap between the town and the mountains. Ahead of them, his van was parked next to the stone well.

As they left the bottom of the dry stream, Joe knew with a sudden certainty that they were being watched. He looked around and saw that on top of the Witch's shack there was an owl with a white face, brown markings, and round, staring eyes.

Joe had only ever seen owls two or three times before in his life, flying over the mountains at night.

'Get in, now!' Joe snapped at Leigh, once they were next to the van. None of the others had noticed the owl.

'Hold your horses, kid.' Leigh unlocked the rear of the van and threw the bags inside, where they landed on top of townspeople's collections with a crunch. He reached into the van, then took out his hat and put it on his head. 'That's better. Feel naked without it.'

Leigh turned towards Sonya and Ms Winnipeg. Joe lifted the gun, but all Leigh did was take Ms Winnipeg's hand delicately in his own. 'Don't worry. I'll be coming back, you know that. Let the others know as well. Don't let them be thinking these two cost the town a drifter's trade.'

Ms Winnipeg nodded, tears running down her cheeks again. With her and Leigh opposite each other in the moonlight, Joe noticed the similar structure to their faces. They were family. Further back, a white shape swooped down from the Witch's roof.

'Now!' Joe hissed.

'Alright.' Leigh let go of Ms Winnipeg's hand and got into the driver's seat. 'Didn't your pa ever teach you manners?'

Joe ignored him and climbed into the passenger seat, not once directing the gun away from Leigh. He looked out for the owl in the corner of his eye, but had lost track of the bird.

Sonya squeezed past Joe and into the rear of the van, sitting down on a pile of bin bags filled with collections.

'Drive!' Joe shouted and pulled the door shut. Leigh clicked his tongue, leaned forward and turned on the van. The headlights illuminated the discoloured purple-green ground ahead. Leigh drove forwards, the van's wheels scraping loudly across the earth. The sound must have woken up half the town. Joe imagined his father and grandfather sitting up on their mattresses and seeing that his own was empty. Would they assume that he was in the fallen forest with Sonya, or would they guess that he was part of the drifter's unexpected late-night departure?

They accelerated, plastic carrier bags catching on the bonnet and loose waste bumping under the wheels. They swung away from the mountains and out onto the flat desert that stretched all the way to the city's twinkling light. Joe glanced out of the back window. Though he couldn't see it, he felt like he could almost sense the owl, following them from above.

CHAPTER TEN

The sky grew paler as they drove, the stars disappearing and the city's light becoming difficult to distinguish from the rest of the horizon. The dark shape of the mountains had shrunk behind them, the town long out of view. Leigh was following the old route to the city, the dusty earth more compressed where the road had once been. Sometimes the van bumped up onto the tarmac remains, and for a while the ride was smoother. Then they'd drop back down onto the hard desert earth, where the van would judder and shake.

Joe kept the gun aimed at Leigh, who stared resolutely ahead with both hands on the wheel. As the night wore on, Joe's head filled with heavy exhaustion, so that he had to fight against falling asleep. The story Grandad had told him the night before, the tale of How The City Came To Be, ran through his mind. The imagined sights threatened to become dreams. He repurposed the story as a way of staying awake, telling himself the tale as Grandad had told it to him.

There is a story of how the city of Madera came to be. A story that, were it written with needles on the inner corners of the eyes of men, would serve as a warning to those who take heed. It begins in a time when the world was fuller, when there were many people and many places. There was a prince whose land, like ours, was dry and hot. While our desert is cracked and brown, his was fine golden sand.

The prince's father, the sultan, ruled over many cities. They lived together in a palace in the capital, which was the richest of all of their cities. The capital contained the most radiant jewels and metals, the greatest poets and storytellers, and the cleverest scientists and philosophers.

The prince could have anything he desired with a wave of his royal hand. When he was hungry, the palace cooks brought him whatever food he asked for, from delicious sweetmeats to tender fruit, preparing his meals with rare and exotic spices. There were endless varieties of flavour and enchanting tastes, and he would eat until he was full.

When he was restless, there was sport. The prince led great expeditions into the golden desert, hunting fantastic prey. The prince and his warriors sought out towns plagued by ghouls, shapeshifting creatures that took on the form of hyenas and stole children away from their homes. The ghouls flew from the prince as hawks, or turned to fight him as lions, but whichever form they chose, he bested them. If he tired of ghouls, the prince would explore caves looking for ifrits, beasts of wings and fire that could not be killed by conventional weapons and had to be defeated through wit and words.

When he was lustful, there were women. His father had the largest harem in the land. Within it, there were women from every corner of the globe. Like the cooks' food, there was an endless variety of flavours for the prince to sample.

Yet he was not happy. He found that even when he had eaten well, there was a hunger within him that he did not understand. For all of his adventures, he craved an excitement he did not know. When he should have felt satisfied, there was a lust within him for a pleasure he could not describe. What he desired was like a colour never before seen, impossible to comprehend or to put into language. He did not even know if what he desired was real. All he knew for certain was that the desire itself existed.

The prince went to his father and told him of his troubles. The sultan had heard him make these complaints many times before, and knew they would not easily be solved. He advised his son to travel to a forest many miles from the borders of their country.

'In that forest,' the sultan said, 'a man finds what he searches for.'

The prince set out, taking with him his money and his maps, his strongest warriors and his most steadfast horses. He journeyed across lands and oceans, meeting with heroes and villains, angels and demons, and spirits both light and dark.

Eventually the prince arrived at the edge of the forest, years older and alone. He no longer had his money, or his maps, or even a horse to ride upon. The only thing that he still carried with him was his inexplicable desire.

As he walked deep into the forest, he found it was very different from his home. The air, while warm, was sticky and wet. There was the sound of a thousand insects buzzing, yet he could not see a single one. The undergrowth was verdant and crunched beneath his boots. Overhead, the trees reached out to each other and hid the sun, the light in the forest filtered emerald by their leaves. There was a taste on his tongue, akin to herbs or vegetables. It was the taste of life, of the forest's ancient soul in the air around him. He feared this place, so unlike anywhere that he had known, but he had not travelled this far by giving into fear.

After a long time walking, he came across a woman. She wore brown rags and carried a simple spear, but seemed to mean him no harm.

'Do you know where in this forest I can find what I am searching for?' the prince asked.

He was ready to ask again in a hundred different languages, not expecting an answer in his own. To his surprise the woman understood him, nodding once and pointing deeper into the forest. He tried to ask her more, but she stepped out of sight, disappearing amongst the trees. The prince followed where the woman had pointed and walked further into the forest. Soon he met a man, who was dressed similarly to the woman, and carried a simple net for catching fish.

'Do you know where in this forest I can find what I am searching for?' the prince asked.

The man nodded, and pointed deeper into the forest. Again, the prince tried to ask him more, but he stepped out of sight, disappearing amongst the trees. The prince followed where the man had pointed and walked further into the forest. Soon, he saw a figure ahead of him. He approached, meaning to ask his question again, but when he saw the woman more clearly, he realised he did not need to. She walked naked, as free as an animal, plucking berries from the trees and dropping them into a woven basket. Occasionally she tasted one, puckering her lips as she drew out its bitter juice in her mouth.

The prince saw her in greater focus and more detail than he had the other forest people, or anyone else before in his life. He saw her curly black hair, reaching down over her shoulders. He saw the way she moved with nature, how she was as much a part of the forest as the trees, as the buzzing of insects, as the taste in the air. He saw the attention she paid to the texture of each berry between her fingers, the careful way she picked them without damaging the rest of the plant, and how she altered the position of her bare feet in response to the shift of the undergrowth beneath her. He knew that she was aware of him watching her. He also knew that he had fallen instantly in love with her. He spoke to her as a poet does:

'I have come to find you
for I have been well fed but I have been hungry,
I have had adventure but I have been restless,
I have been embraced but I have been lustful.

When one hungers but not for food,
one hungers for love.
When one is restless but not for action,
one is restless for love.
When one lusts but not for sex,
one lusts for love.

A loveless man has hollow thoughts,
empty sentences waiting to be filled by love.
Let yourself be the person who fills my thoughts.
Let yourself be the person who gives my words meaning.'

As he had fallen in love with the poetry of her movements, she fell in love with the poetry of his language. They spoke together for a long time. She explained to him how she understood his words because of the visitors they had from all over the world, and how those who visited the forest left with more peace inside them than when they had arrived. She described to him how her people lived from the forest itself, with no towns or cities, and only the simplest of tools. He told her in turn of his land, of all his people's wonders and of the exquisite way in which they lived. She listened with wide eyes, and he told her that it would all be hers if she returned with him.

Her wide eyes then filled with tears. She told him no, that she could not leave her people and family. She said that sometimes those who visited decided to stay and live with the humble forest people, and invited him to stay with her. At that the prince's heart swelled, because now he had found her, he could not imagine being separated from her, even for a day. He agreed, and kissed her, and promised to give her the best of all lives.

By the time they had finished speaking, it was night. She took him to a hill where the trees' branches parted and revealed the sky. There they made love on the mossy slope. Afterwards, they looked up at the night sky and told each other the stories they knew about the stars.

From then on, the prince did everything he could to keep his promise to give her the best of all lives. First he cut down trees, to make log cabins for her people to live in. She protested, screaming at the wound in the forest as if it was a wound in her. When he told her how their homes would protect them as they slept, and prevent predators from taking away the forest people's children, she accepted his choice. It was not only his logic that convinced her, but the poetry in his words that she had fallen in love with.

*The prince's work continued, breaking rocks and uprooting trees so that he could make more buildings for the forest people. Madera was born (*the city that you see on the horizon, Little Joe*), growing taller than the trees ever had. Everything had to be the best for his love, greater even than his father's capital. For the forest people, the prince invented cars so that they could travel faster than horses and camels, televisions so that they could see storytellers and actors in their own homes, and phones so that they would not have to wait for messengers to arrive.*

For each new invention more of the forest was lost, and each time the prince's lover protested. However, his words were like music to her, and each time he won her over. He convinced her that this was what was best, for her and her people. When he took the sweetness and the colour from the air, and filled it with waves and static, they argued for days. She cried fiercely for the lost soul of the forest, for the life that had been extinguished. But eventually, when he had persuaded her of the education and connection it would bring to her people, she dried her eyes. There was death inside her, sadness for every tree that had fallen and every rock that had been smashed. She held it inside, telling herself that the prince was doing what was best for her people.

In the end, the forest was gone, leaving only the city. Only one small patch of trees remained, far away from the high-reaching buildings. This was the hill where they had first made love. They went there often, to look up at the stars through the parting in the branches. On those nights, he would walk naked like she did, to sense the world around them. During those times, she did not feel the death that she carried inside her, only her love for him.

'Truly, we have built the world's greatest city,' the prince said to her one night, lying between those trees. 'The forest people now live the best lives of any in the world. Much of what we have created has been shared, but all people know that it comes from here.'

She was uneasy. This was the sort of talk that led to him making something new. But what else could be added? And what would be destroyed, so that it could be made?

'We are lord and lady of the city,' the prince continued. 'We should wear finer robes than any other royalty. For you, there must always be the best.'

With that the prince stood, and ripped two strips of cloth out of the night sky. From one, he made himself a suit. From the other, he made her *a dress. Both were deep blue-black and sparkling with stars. She looked in horror at the damage he had done to the night, at the two empty black gashes where no stars shone (*that even now, Joe, I can point out for you in the sky*). He pulled on his suit, but she threw down the dress.*

'The cost is too great!' she shouted, then spoke as a poet, as she'd learned from him:

'You say you love me,
but how can you?
I was the forest,
and you cut down the trees.
I was the sweetness in the air,
and you stole away the taste.
I was naked and free,
under the stars in the sky,
and you ripped them away
to wrap me in clothes.
I say I love you,
but how can I?
When you killed everything that was me,
who is I that loves you?
Love causes one to remain still
while another claws wounds in their chest.
So I curse love and I curse you,
and I curse what love has caused.'

She lifted earth from the ground, shaping it into a dress around her body. 'This hill, where we first made love, is all that's left of my forest,' she said. 'I will wear its earth and be part of the forest still, even though all the rest is gone.'

With that she left him, stepping out of sight between the trees, as the other forest people had done before. The prince searched the tiny patch of forest, but somehow she had disappeared. Enraged, he stamped the ground, causing all of the trees to fall. Even then she could not be seen. He lifted the night-sky dress, and with the stars on his suit twinkling, set out across the bare lands to look for her. He was determined to find her, and through his lyrical words, convince her to wear his dress and be his queen.

With the two of them gone, a wrongness emerged in Madera. The city began to fall apart, and many of the once-forest people who'd lived there left it behind. Some say that the wrongness was due to the prince no longer continuing to build, suggesting that, like a forest, a city must always be growing. Others claim that it was his lover's curse 'on what love had caused.' Myself, I sometimes wonder if that place was always wrong, and it was only the prince's words that blinded the people to it. As for the prince himself, even now he is travelling still, searching for his lost love.

After Joe had told himself the story three times over, he felt a change in the movement of the van. It was as if the wheels had lifted an inch from the ground, so they floated above the earth, rather than rumbling over it. By this point, it was drawing closer to morning, the sky greyish through the van's tinted windows.

Squinting through the darkened glass, Joe saw faint lines appearing over the dry desert. It was the outline of a forest, like the one from the story. The trees and their leaves were almost invisible, like scratches that had been carved out of the air. Joe glanced around confused at Sonya and Leigh, but she was asleep and the drifter was focused on the road ahead, as if nothing at all had changed.

The shadow of a large black cat appeared next to the van's window, impossibly keeping up with the drifter's driving. Like in a dream, Joe felt as if he should be shocked, but the emotion never actually arrived. He found himself strangely immobilised, unable to do anything but watch as the dark shape of the cat sauntered alongside them, matching the vehicle's pace while not even breaking into a run.

The feline shadow lifted and formed into the shape of a woman. A dress made of earth covered her body, the encrusted brown dirt flecked with pebbles and stones. The Forest Woman kept stride with the van, and locked eyes with Joe. Her irises were brilliant amber. Curly black hair rolled down either side of her face.

'Continue your quest. Seek out a way to the city, and the girl will be healed,' the Forest Woman said.

Then she and her hazy forest vanished and the desert was bare once more.

CHAPTER ELEVEN

Joe shook his head, and wiped grit from his eyes. He looked in the rear of the van, where Sonya was sitting up and yawning. The mountains were little more than a bump in the distance behind her.

The van felt like it was travelling on solid earth again. Joe would have dismissed the woman and her words as a waking dream, brought on by staying awake for too long, had it not been for the hands that shifted the waste away from him inside the mountain. There was more to it. Stories were influencing his real life, but how could that possibly be true? He wished he could speak to Sonya, but there was no way to bring it up in front of the drifter.

The sky grew brighter as they drove on. The van still smelled of herring, though Leigh had sold all of his fish to the townspeople. Joe found the scent oddly refreshing, clearing his mind after the long night. It took him a moment to realise why he liked the smell. It was the absence of the landfill's rotting stink mingled in with it.

'You'll want to lower your window,' Leigh said.

'Why?' Joe lifted the gun from his lap, its barrel pointed towards the drifter.

Leigh noted the weapon and rolled his eyes. 'The sun's about to come up. I wager you and your lady ain't ever seen it rise over the horizon, instead of over those mountains.'

Keeping his eyes and the gun on Leigh, Joe found the switch and brought the darkened window down.

'For God's sake, point that somewhere else,' Leigh exclaimed. 'I ain't going to try anything while I'm driving, am I? I'd prefer not to have my head blown off if we go over a rock.'

Joe relented, aiming the gun down but keeping it in his hand.

'Are those clouds?' Sonya exclaimed, grabbing the back of Joe's seat and pulling herself forward. Orange light rose up from the horizon, and above it a line of clouds rippled with soft colours.

'Maybe there'll be a celebration soon,' Sonya said, close to laughter with excitement. 'Those clouds look big enough for rain. And we might have seen them before anyone in the town!'

Joe realised he'd dropped his guard, but when he glanced back Leigh was watching the sky as well. The orange light was gentle on Leigh's face, and his smile was genuine, lacking its sarcastic edge.

When Joe looked out again, the sunrise had begun. He felt the same warm light on his own face, and the air rushing across his cheeks through the open window. The horizon itself seemed to burn, the seam between land and sky blazing, then the brightest flame lifted separately. In the shape of a ball, it broke away from the rest and became the sun.

'Beautiful,' Sonya said, in breathless awe.

'Amazing,' Joe agreed.

'It's something to see,' Leigh said. 'That's what it is. Now roll the window up, sunlight melts the seats.'

Joe did as he was asked. The tinted glass closed out the sunlight, replacing it with shades of blue and grey. Even the windshield was darkened, so inside the van the atmosphere was more similar to evening time than early morning.

'Tell me, then, what is it that takes us to the city?' Leigh asked.

'It's like I said in the town,' Joe replied. 'We're going to see if there's anything that can help Lily. Medicine, or a doctor.'

'The young girl who's sick.' Leigh tapped his hands on the wheel. 'Sure is a good reason. Thing I've found about good reasons is they're often why someone says they're doing something, but ain't always why they're actually doing it.'

Joe heard Sonya let out a delicate sigh in the back of the van.

'It's about finding out if there's a better life there as well,' he said. 'For children like Tiger and Lily. And for me, and Sonya, and everyone.'

'Mhmm.' Leigh raised his eyebrows.

'My father told me about the city,' Joe went on. 'The hospitals, and schools, and cinemas, and fairgrounds, and bookshops, and restaurants. He had all of that. Everyone your age did. I've always wanted to see what's left. But we wouldn't be going now, if it wasn't for Lily.'

Leigh's arm was suddenly across Joe, and Joe raised the gun in fright. Leigh's hand froze on the glove compartment.

'I'm just getting water,' he snarled. 'You've already hijacked my van, can't I even have a drink?'

'I'll get it.' Joe's voice was cold, but his heart was hammering. Leigh put his hand back on the wheel, and Joe lowered the gun again. Joe reached forward and opened the glove compartment. It was jammed full.

There was a radio with wires sticking out, a bronze tin with something inside that clinked, and a stopped wristwatch with a frayed leather strap. Sure enough, there was a glass bottle sloshing with water. There was also a large hunting knife beneath it.

Leigh might have been attempting to get the knife, or to pull the gun out of Joe's grasp. Or he might have been reaching for his water. Joe handed the bottle over and closed the glove compartment. Leigh opened the screw cap, took a long draft, replaced the cap and pushed the bottle down into the side pocket of his door – all without slowing down the van.

'The past wasn't some perfect world, kid. There were plenty of people who had nothing. But people like me, and your father from what you're saying, yeah, we had a little. More than you've ever had. Trying to figure out where it all went, that sounds reasonable enough.' Leigh shifted his jaw. 'Sounds like you're looking for someone to blame as well. Ought to be careful with that. You can spend your whole life pointing fingers without fixing a thing.'

Leigh dropped one hand from the wheel and onto the dashboard. The plastic there was mottled, hundreds of little circles burned into it. He ran his finger around one of them. 'I used to smoke, back when there were still cigarettes. That's what these are, from stubbing them out. Back then, I got real sick. Now which of these burns, which one of those little cigarettes, was responsible for clogging up my lungs? Way I reckon it, the world's something like that. You know it ain't always been this hot?'

Joe nodded. Sonya bent forward in the back of the van and listened intently.

'From what I understand, that's because of the fossil fuels we used to burn. Filled the world up with too much smoke, so the heat couldn't get out. The world was a sick lung, just like mine. Lots of stuff filled up that lung. If you used electricity in your house, caught a train, bought a phone, whatever, you were burning that fuel and contributing.'

Leigh laughed, and Joe imagined a cloud of smoke coming out of his mouth as he did. 'You two are getting a glimpse of what runs through my head, when I'm driving from place to place. What I'm saying, is it was hard to live in the world without hurting it. People tried, but like me with my cigarettes, mankind was addicted to the way we were already living. We were just too damn slow to change.'

Leigh braked hard, surprising Joe and sending him smacking into the glove compartment. The gun slipped in Joe's fingers. He grasped it before it fell, panicking, and managed to keep a hold of it. He twisted quickly and dropped back against the van's door to aim at the drifter.

'You can put that down,' Leigh said, without even looking across. 'I only stopped because I wanted to show you something. Let's get out of the van.'

'We didn't tell you to stop before the city.'

'That's what I'm showing you. You can see the city from here.'

'You first,' Joe said, motioning with the gun towards the door.

'Fair enough.' Leigh got out onto the desert, then raised his hands in a bored and mocking surrender. 'You've got the gun, remember. I ain't trying nothing.'

Joe climbed out of the van, Sonya close behind him. Being out on the open flatlands was like standing on a giant frying pan, the heat sizzling in the air around them. Immediately Joe's head began to ache, and he could feel his skin burning. It was easy to imagine how people died out here in the sun.

As his eyes adjusted to the bright light, he saw it, tiny in the distance. Several roads led out from its black centre and then broke away into nothing in the desert, like a crushed spider with its legs sticking out around it. The city. Madera.

'What are you doing?' Sonya cried out. Leigh was out of sight, the van's back door open. Sonya walked towards the van with her knife in hand, and Leigh stepped out and smashed the butt of a rifle into her stomach. Sonya collapsed onto the ground, dropping the knife. Joe raised the handgun, panicking.

Leigh brought the rifle up and took careful aim at Joe. 'I don't reckon you've ever fired a gun before. Why don't you go ahead and put that down.'

Joe could barely breathe. Everything had gone wrong so quickly. The gun shook in his hands.

'Leave it, Joe,' Sonya begged from the ground. 'There's nothing you can do.'

'You should listen to the lady.' Leigh inclined his head to look down the rifle's sight, the butt against his shoulder.

'How do I know you won't shoot us anyway?' Joe shouted.

'For God's sake, put the gun down so I don't have to!'

Sonya's eyes implored Joe, brimming with tears. He placed the gun down onto the earth.

'I should leave you both to burn in the sun,' Leigh growled. 'It would serve you right.'

The drifter lowered his rifle.

'Get into the back of the van,' Leigh said. 'I'm taking you idiots home. No one in your damn town would forgive me if I didn't bring you back.'

Leigh stepped back as Joe went to Sonya. Joe gripped her hand and helped her to her feet. As they walked to the van, Joe took a last look over his shoulder at the crushed spider in the distance. He wondered if that was as close as they'd ever get to the city.

Joe sat with Sonya on the bin bags in the back of the van. Her arms were around his waist, and her head was laid on his shoulder. For a while she'd cried quietly, and had now settled into slow breathing. As for Joe, he stared forwards as his body moved with the rhythm of the van, replaying everything that had happened in his head.

Joe cursed himself for letting his guard down when he saw the city, and for not properly understanding how a gun worked. He didn't want to have actually shot Leigh, but if he'd been paying attention, he might have been able to stop the drifter before he'd got to the rifle. He tried to come up with a plan to force the drifter to turn back, but couldn't think of anything. He was drained. With the handgun and Sonya's knife in the glove compartment, and the rifle across Leigh's lap, there was nothing they could do.

'Sorry, kids,' Leigh said eventually, tapping the wheel. 'No joyride to the city today. It's a good thing you put that gun down. I'd have shot you if I needed to.'

Joe didn't reply. Sonya made a noise in her mouth that almost sounded grateful.

'We wouldn't have made it across the flatlands anyway,' Leigh added. 'There's worse than me out there.'

'You showed us,' Joe said. 'The desert's empty all the way to the city.'

'Looks that way, doesn't it,' Leigh said. 'Closer to the city, the desert changes. There are voices without bodies, and the shadows of unseen people. If you travel that way, you'll only end up joining the ghosts.'

'I've heard the stories,' Joe said. 'Everyone has. But no one's seen it for themselves, have they? There's nothing there, just empty desert, so people fill it with stories.'

'You think I've never tried to drive to the city? Or that none of the other drifters have? I'm one of the lucky ones, kid. I came back. It wasn't always like this, but it ain't natural that direction, not anymore.'

Joe snorted.

'Sounds like the sort of notion that people get, when they travel alone too long, right?' Leigh said. 'Except last time I tried to go that way, I wasn't as alone as I thought. I was miles into the flatlands, parked and getting ready to sleep for the night. Then there was a knock on my van's door, out where nobody on God's earth has any right to be.

'There wasn't a vehicle in sight, but the shadow at my window was in the shape of a man. I lowered the window and the man was in a fine suit, one I've not seen the likes of before or since. It was the colour of the night sky, dotted with glittering stars.

'The man offered me the world back as it used to be, rebuilt and shining, if I could help him find the woman he was looking for.'

Joe felt a tremble run through him. Leigh had not reacted at all when the forest had appeared outside the van, nor when the woman had walked alongside them. There was no way he could have known what Joe had seen, or the story that Joe had been telling himself to stay awake in the van. And yet, it was the Prince the drifter was describing, in his night-sky suit, looking for his lost love.

'Did you help him?' Sonya asked from Joe's shoulder.

'He asked me where the gardeners lived, and the fisherpeople. I told him that much and he started to walk away. I drove after him, trying to convince him to get into the van.

I couldn't see him too well, because his suit blended into the night. I kept losing track of him and finding him again, then he just folded away into the shadows and the stars.

'I drove around looking for him, but it was as if he'd vanished. Even when he was gone, I still felt something watching me, out there in the dark. I ain't gone that way since. I don't know what his kind is, but I don't fancy meeting it again.'

'His kind is stories,' Joe snapped. 'The Prince in his suit made of night is a story. He's not real.'

'Well,' Leigh said evenly, as if he'd expected that reaction. 'If that's true, then stories live in the desert by the city.'

Joe had no response. How could both he and the drifter have seen stories walking in the real world? Sonya was falling asleep again, her arms slack around him and her breath brushing on his neck. Only a week ago, Joe would have been certain Leigh was lying, or at least telling stories of his own. Now, he didn't know what to believe.

'Kid, I know what you're going to do,' Leigh said, when the mountains were large in front of them and the town was in sight. Sonya was snoring on Joe's shoulder.

'You're going to try to go to the city again,' Leigh said, when Joe didn't reply. 'I'd advise you not to attempt it at all, despite how satisfying it would be to see you get what you deserve for pulling my own gun on me. But I know you're too bullheaded to listen to me.

'So I'll tell you this, there's no drifter that will drive through those flatlands for you. Too many have headed out that way and not come back. Not every drifter's got people they care about in your town like I do, and they won't be as forgiving if you try to force them to drive you. Maybe you could make a deal for a lift, but not straight to the city.'

Joe could tell Leigh was hinting at something. 'Where would I go instead then, that would help me get to Madera?'

'I ain't saying nothing more. I don't want responsibility for what you do.'

'I need to go there,' Joe insisted. 'For Lily.'

But Leigh only shook his head, his mouth a stubborn line. They passed into the shadow of the mountains, travelling along the purple-green ground. The stone well came into view ahead, a few people milling around between it and the town.

'She seems a fine lady you've got with you,' Leigh said, speaking again after a few moments of quiet. 'Consider what all this does to her. Because if you try this again, she'll either go with you or she won't. I don't know what would be worse for her.'

Leigh brought the van to a halt. Sonya stirred, her hand moving across Joe's T-shirt. Joe looked out through the windshield, and saw the Mayor stopping Alice and Marco at the stone well. He told them something that made Marco look up despairingly to the sky, and Alice slump low in her office chair. None of the three were hurrying to get out of the sun, nor paying the van as much attention as they should.

Sonya lifted her head from Joe's shoulder. She smiled when she saw the mountains. Her smile fell away when she looked at his face, and knew as he did that something was wrong.

CHAPTER TWELVE

Joe and Sonya stood outside the van. At the stone well, the Mayor, Marco and Alice still conferred in hushed voices. Marco caught Joe's gaze for a moment before quickly averting his eyes.

Leigh opened the back of the van, taking great satisfaction in throwing Joe and Sonya's bags out as far as he could. At least they hadn't lost all the food that was inside. After retrieving the bags, Joe and Sonya headed over to the stone well. The group there fell silent, opening out to face them.

'Joe, Sonya,' the Mayor said. 'Ms Winnipeg told us what happened. We can discuss that another time. I trust you're both unhurt?'

'Yeah, we're fine,' Joe said, and Sonya nodded.

'There's something I'm afraid we must tell you.' The Mayor spoke as if each word took effort to pronounce. Alice had tears in her eyes. Marco held his hands clasped in front of his hips.

'It might be best if we find you somewhere in the shade to sit down,' the Mayor said after a brief pause. Joe had lived in the town long enough to know death well. He heard its echoes in the Mayor's voice, and saw its shadow cast across the others' faces. Joe thought of his father, so often alone on the mountains as the sky grew dark, then realised who it must be.

'Lily,' Joe said.

The Mayor shook his head. Marco stepped forward and put his hand on Joe's shoulder, then looked across at Sonya as well. 'It's Buddy. He was caught in an avalanche. They dug him out, but he was already gone.'

A wave of relief washed through Joe. It wasn't his father or grandfather, or little Lily. The space the relief left was quickly filled with shame. He hadn't been close with Buddy, but that didn't matter now. His collecting mate would never grow up, never get the chance to become a man. He and Maya would never get to have a future together. It could have just as easily been Joe, when he and Tiger were caught in the avalanche.

Sonya was no longer at his side. She'd returned to Leigh's van, and was explaining something to the drifter. Leigh let out an exasperated sigh, but stood aside and allowed Sonya into the van. She came out with the red-ribbon knife that Buddy had given to Maya. Joe realised that he wasn't paying attention to Marco, who'd just asked if he needed anything.

'No, I don't,' Joe replied. 'I'm okay.'

Sonya returned and Marco asked her the same. Once they'd both assured him that they'd be alright, Marco left them and set off towards the mountains. The Mayor headed in the same direction, but stopped on the stained purple-green ground, waiting to share the news with anyone who passed by. Alice was the last to leave, giving Joe and Sonya a distressed look before turning away.

'Where's Buddy's knife?' Sonya asked.

Joe was suddenly aware of how long it had been since he'd last slept. He struggled to get his words in order. 'I dropped it in Ms Winnipeg's house. When Leigh hit me.'

'We'll need to get it back,' Sonya said. 'We should give it to Maya.'

'Yeah,' Joe hollowly repeated, 'we should.'

Sonya shot him an annoyed look. 'We need to go to Ms Winnipeg's shack to apologise anyway. We can ask for it back then.'

Joe could only nod. The news about Buddy had taken him by surprise. Nothing seemed to make sense anymore. All he could feel was shame at his initial relieved reaction.

'We should have been here,' Sonya sounded angry at both Joe and herself.

'I'm going to find Maya. She would have been with him when it happened.'

Joe must have looked lost, because Sonya added, 'You should get some sleep. You're too tired to be on the mountains. I'll meet you at sunset to go apologise to Ms Winnipeg. Hopefully word will get to our parents that we're here and we're safe.'

They headed up the dry stream, both of them so exhausted they were almost sleepwalking. When Sonya turned off towards Maya's shack, she didn't have the energy to speak. Instead she just gestured towards the stream's bank and then climbed out.

Joe passed her up the bags she'd packed for their journey. Sonya carried them away without saying goodbye, and Joe continued on towards his home.

As Joe approached his shack, he heard David's raised voice from inside. 'I'm proud of him, yes. Of both of them!'

A low and insistent female voice replied, too quiet for Joe to make out the words.

'Because they're right,' David retorted. 'To not accept this life, and to look for something better. To try to make change happen, rather than just wishing things were different.'

Joe had shouted similar words at his father, and received little or no response. But here David was, echoing him as he defended him. The woman spoke again. This time Joe recognised the similarities to Sonya's voice. It was Demeta. David replied more gently than before, and Joe moved closer to the shack's window-hole to hear.

'I know,' David was saying, 'I'd give away every collection on the mountains for working phones. But that's not how the world is anymore. Just because we're trapped here, doesn't mean they have to be.'

'This town isn't a trap. It's our home,' Demeta replied.

'It's a trap for me. And it was for you once. We were like them, remember? When we had enough youth left in us. We ran away from the town too.'

That was something Joe had never heard. No one left the town. There was nowhere to go, except to burn in the desert. Joe opened the door and stepped inside. David and Demeta both looked round in surprise. Demeta rushed over and hugged Joe, then shoved him back.

'Sonya,' she said, bending forward so her cross necklace dangled in the air. 'Is she here? Is she okay?'

'Yes. She's gone to see Maya.'

'Good. This is where she belongs.' Demeta straightened up, her eyes flaring at Joe. 'We've got a hard life here, but that doesn't mean it isn't sacred and special. And we only get one. Remember that next time you decide to risk yours, or Sonya's. Now if you'll excuse me, I'm going to find my daughter.'

She walked outside and then stopped, taking a deep breath. 'I gave you some advice last time we spoke. Try talking to the Witch before you do anything else stupid.'

She strode away. Through the window-hole, Joe saw her

heading towards the dry stream. David came to his side, offering him a bottle of water. Joe drank greedily, the water soothing a burning thirst that he hadn't acknowledged until that moment.

'So you're okay, and Sonya too?' Worry creased David's forehead.

'Yeah, we're both alright.'

Joe expected further questions about their journey in the van, but David only waited for him to finish drinking and then took the bottle away.

'And you've heard about Buddy?'

'Yes,' Joe replied. 'They told us when we got back.'

David sat down on a stool. 'He collected with you on the mountains.'

'He was there every day.' Joe stood awkwardly over his father, but to sit down next to him felt wrong as well.

'How are you feeling?' David asked.

'I...' Joe began, but couldn't continue. He wanted to tell David about the awful relief he'd felt, that it had been Buddy and not someone he was closer to. But saying it seemed like crossing a forbidden line, like speaking badly of the Witch. As if, like her, Buddy would somehow hear. That it would insult Buddy's memory, and somehow hurt further a young man who had already lost his life.

'You don't have to talk about it, if you don't want to,' David said. 'But I'm here if you do.'

When Joe overheard David and Demeta arguing, he'd been surprised by the anger in his father's voice. Joe had tried so many times to draw him into a fight, and he'd never risen to it. Now that he'd finally heard him angry, Joe knew that David either couldn't or wouldn't react to him in that way. If Joe could tell anyone how he'd felt without fear of being judged, it was him.

'I don't know what to say yet.'

'That's okay,' David replied. 'It's okay not to know.'

After that, David encouraged him to get some rest. Joe lay down and for a while drifted in and out of sleep, aware that David stayed with him in the shack. In the times when he was awake, he thought of his vision in the desert.

The Forest Woman had said that if he travelled to the city, Lily would be healed. It had seemed like a dream, but alongside the Boy Who Learned What Fear Was saving him in the mountains, and what the Witch had said to him about destiny, it all felt like too much to be ignored.

But how could he travel there now? Leigh had said that no drifter would take him directly to the city. Yet, he had hinted that one might take Joe somewhere else, and from there he'd be able to get to Madera. Where had he meant? Joe needed to work it out before the next drifter came, if he were to have any chance of helping Lily.

Joe's thoughts kept him awake, full of questions that he did not have answers to. The brightness and warmth of the day began to irritate him, to the point where he could no longer lie still and was constantly shifting position on his mattress. He sat up and told David that they should be collecting on the mountains.

David convinced him to eat before they went, and took a pan outside to cook two small pieces of herring. The smell of it reminded Joe of inside Leigh's van. When they climbed the mountains, Joe and David stayed together rather than splitting off to find their usual groups. For the first time since Joe was a small child, father and son collected together on the mountains.

They returned home as the sun was setting. Sonya was standing by the door, waiting for Joe to go with her to Ms Winnipeg's shack. David nodded respectfully to Sonya, then took Joe's collecting sack and went inside. Sonya's eyes were bloodshot, her expression dull. Joe asked after Maya. Sonya told him that she'd been broken down on a mattress, unable to do anything but cry.

They didn't talk on the way to Ms Winnipeg's. Sonya was someone who was comfortable not speaking – she easily dropped into silence and listened to the world – but this was different. Normally, her quietness was attentive and expressive, and Joe could speak to her even while she was silent.

Now she was withdrawn, and it seemed that if he spoke he'd be interrupting her. He'd decided against bringing up the vision he'd seen in the desert for the moment. He wanted to give her time to think about Buddy.

As they came close to Ms Winnipeg's shack, they saw Leigh stepping out of it. He looked back inside, and spoke through the open door.

'One last trip to the centre, to drop off what's left of the recycling. Maybe I can manage that without any of your town's damn kids pulling a gun on me. I'm paying a visit to the fisherpeople next. Last time I saw the Mechanic, she told me she'd heard they have machines now to do their fishing for them. Reckon that's something to see.'

Leigh moved back inside for a moment, and they heard him say goodbye. Joe and Sonya hung back, and he left without seeing them. He headed away in the other direction, past the end of the shacks and down towards his van.

When they arrived at the shack, the door was shut. Joe saw Ms Winnipeg's patchwork curtains were still hanging loose from where he'd fallen into them. Sonya knocked and Ms Winnipeg's voice called them in. Joe braced himself as Sonya opened the door, uncertain what response to expect from Ms Winnipeg.

The old woman was sitting in a chair. She'd been crying, little tears caught in the wrinkles below her eyes. Despite her age, Ms Winnipeg jumped to her feet as they came in, both of her knees clicking, an involuntary flash of fear across her face. Then she smiled weakly.

'It's good to see the two of you,' she said, but stayed on the other side of the shack, keeping her distance. 'I was so afraid you wouldn't come back from the desert. After what's happened to poor Buddy, I thought we might have lost you as well.'

Ms Winnipeg sat back down, one leg shaking. She'd known Joe and Sonya as long as they'd lived in the town. Now, even though she tried to conceal it, Joe could tell she was frightened of them. It wasn't a good feeling.

'Ms Winnipeg,' Sonya said. 'We came to say sorry.'

'There's no need, no need at all.' She flapped her hand at Sonya and Joe. 'No one was hurt, were they? Though you did give me quite a scare.'

'We're truly sorry,' Sonya said, and Joe repeated the sentiment. He meant it. He hadn't anticipated the impact their plans would have on her.

'Oh don't worry about me, I'm just silly, I get myself into a fuss too easily. I'm just glad everyone came back in one piece. You were lucky it was Leigh you picked. With some drifters, you wouldn't have made it home. We don't want to lose anyone else.'

Joe felt Sonya glancing across at him. When he looked at her, she was focused on Ms Winnipeg, her face unreadable.

'You two collected with Buddy, didn't you?' Ms Winnipeg

asked. They talked about Buddy for a while, Joe and Sonya sitting on the floor, in front of Ms Winnipeg's chair. There was tension in her elderly body, as if she were ready to spring up at any moment. Joe hated that they had done this to her, who cared so much about the young people of the town that she'd fight against herself to sit with them anyway.

Joe tried his best to contribute to the conversation as Sonya and Ms Winnipeg discussed their memories of Buddy. He wanted to support the two of them as best he could, but he found it hard to know what to say. The shame he felt for his initial reaction to Buddy's death kept coming back to him, making him feel sure he would say the wrong thing, even as all he focused on was trying his best to be kind.

'We actually wanted to ask you something to do with Buddy,' Sonya said eventually. 'When we came here, the other night, we left a knife. It was his. We were hoping to give it to Maya.'

Ms Winnipeg shuddered at the mention of the knife. She'd been gradually relaxing as they spoke about Buddy, but now her whole body tensed again. Joe's stomach turned, guilt piling on top of guilt.

Ms Winnipeg stood, slowly and carefully this time, and went across to the wooden bed at the side of her shack. She bent down and picked up the knife from the floor between the bed and the window-hole, unmoved from where it had fallen during their break-in. She hesitated before lifting it, as if it might be burning hot. Her hand trembled as she gave it to Sonya.

There was the sound of the van's wheels rumbling across the earth from outside, as Leigh left the town. Joe saw Ms Winnipeg's eyes well up with tears again. He remembered the familial resemblance between her and the drifter.

'You both look so tired,' Ms Winnipeg said. 'You should go home. Get as much rest as you can. Do visit again, please. I mean that. Regardless of what happened, I do like to see you. There's so few of us, especially you younger ones, and I like to know how you're doing. And be careful when you're collecting. We're all so easily lost.'

They told Ms Winnipeg they were sorry again, and she told them how sorry she was about Buddy. Then they said their goodbyes, and left her in her shack alone.

CHAPTER THIRTEEN

Over the next couple of days, Joe, Sonya and Tiger climbed the mountains together. They were the only three left of their usual collecting group. Maya was too devastated to work or even leave her mattress, and Rose was keeping watch over Lily. As well as their collecting work, the three of them looked for ruined wood – either badly warped or weakened by termites – that couldn't be sold or put to any purpose other than burning.

All the townspeople were doing the same, for Buddy's pyre. His funeral was set for three nights after Joe and Sonya had returned home. When Joe was younger he'd never understood why everyone was tasked with finding wood for the funeral pyres. There was always too much, and most of it ended up being saved for use while cooking. He saw now that it gave all of them something to do, a way to feel as though they were helping.

Every time Joe saw Tiger collecting next to him, he was reminded of the countdown hanging over Lily. He'd worked out they had just over twenty days till the next full moon. They'd almost certainly see another drifter in that time.

Before the next drifter came, Joe had to work out the way to the city Leigh had been alluding to. He wished he could talk to Sonya about it as they collected, but he knew the thought of travelling out again would distress her. It wouldn't be right to do that to her while they prepared for Buddy's funeral.

In the evenings, Joe's shack was busy with people visiting Grandad, David waiting by the door to let them in. As the Storyteller, Grandad would speak at the funeral, so people came to share their memories of Buddy. Many visited, including those who hadn't known Buddy well and only wanted to share a brief memory.

This included the Artist Sisters, who said that he'd complimented their creations and advised them to ask for more in trade from the drifters for what they made, and Mr Rajarshi, who praised how he'd always been hardworking and polite. People didn't expect everything they said to be retold at the funeral, but they each contributed to Grandad's construction of Buddy's story. Like the wood for the pyre, they all gave something.

Buddy's father, Kane, the bald Moonshine Brother, visited

the most. He came to the shack's door again and again, his face strained and his cheeks the colour of beetroot, each time bearing another story he was desperate to be told at the funeral.

Kane's stories ranged from Buddy's first words during the journey out from the city, to the way he pointed out at the waste from his cobbled-together carrier, to how quickly he picked up the method to make moonshine in a repurposed bathtub. He spoke about Buddy's relationship with Maya as well. He described when she first visited their shack and he was sure Buddy had taken a liking to her, and when he'd embarrassed them by catching them together amongst collecting bags.

Sonya visited the evening before Buddy's funeral. Joe found it strange hearing her discuss Buddy. She described him in such a positive way. He knew Sonya had often found Buddy difficult and annoying, like he had.

She spoke about his hard-working attitude, and how he'd focused on getting value for his collecting in order to make things as comfortable as he could for Maya, who didn't have a family to collect with. Joe loved Sonya for how she was able to find the good in people and put it into words.

Sonya also delivered a message from Maya, asking if Grandad could visit her shack to talk about Buddy, as she didn't feel up to walking through the town. When Sonya left, Grandad followed her out of the door, leaving Joe alone with David.

'You haven't spoken to Grandad about Buddy,' David said,

almost a question.

'No,' Joe replied, sitting with his back against the shack's wall. 'I don't know what to say.'

David rested his chin on his hand, open and listening.

'I'm so sad that he's dead,' Joe said, then spoke his difficult truth aloud. 'But Buddy and I didn't like each other. We never got along. It makes it hard to know what to say.'

Joe was surprised to see David smile a little.

'It's okay to feel that way,' his father said.

'When I found out what happened, I felt relieved. That it wasn't you, or Grandad, or Lily, or anyone I was closer to,' said Joe. 'I hated that I felt that way. It's like I'm wrong inside.'

There was sympathetic pain in David's eyes. His expression told Joe that he'd felt similarly wrong before, that maybe everyone who'd lived long enough had, and that he understood.

'You can't control your emotions. That relief didn't come from a bad place. You didn't want Buddy hurt. It was relief that other people were alright. And you don't have to pretend you got along with Buddy to feel sad about his death.'

'Yeah, you're right.'

David smiled again. 'I'm about to sound like Grandad. We all tell ourselves stories, Joe. It's how we understand the world, how we fit together our memories. You could lie to yourself and say that you and Buddy were always the best of friends. But when you tell yourself dishonest stories, life becomes murky very quickly. It becomes difficult to know which of your own stories to believe in. That's no way to live.'

Joe could hear the ghosts of old pain in his father's voice. They would have talked further, but there was a knock at the shack's door. David gave him a last smile before standing and answering the door. It was Kane, anxious to see Grandad again.

David welcomed him inside, sitting him down on one of the stools and offering him a bottle of water. Kane's leg bounced incessantly. When he drank the water, he spilled some onto his lap. As soon as Grandad walked in through the door, Kane started talking about Buddy's ideas to increase the amount of food drifters would trade for the moonshine.

Joe thought the real reason Kane visited so often was Grandad's voice. Kane was high-pitched and frantic as he described his memories of Buddy, which Grandad then told back to him in the tone he used for storytelling.

There was a rhythm to Grandad's words, along with a subtle emphasis on images or moments of detail, that was calming. It drew Kane's voice level. By the time he left the shack he seemed more in control of himself, until the next time he came knocking, overwrought again.

Joe woke up to Kane's shrill voice the next morning. He was standing over Grandad's mattress, talking fast as the old man slowly sat up. Joe rose on his own mattress, and saw David was awake too.

'The clouds are out?' Grandad asked.

'Yes!' Kane wrung his hands, pulling at them as if he was trying to break his own fingers. 'I don't know what to do. What if it rains tonight? We can't have a celebration if Buddy's waiting to be cremated, and we can't have a funeral in the rain!'

Grandad attempted to stand, but his legs locked halfway up. Joe moved swiftly across, ducking under his arm and helping him upright. Once he was standing, Grandad lifted his arm from Joe's shoulders and went to the window-hole. The sun hadn't yet risen. The sky was covered with cloud, in deep red with flickers of yellow. Grandad's face was lit by the colour. His beard, his wrinkles and his rheumy eyes were all red.

'The celebrations are a time when everything is washed, when the past is cleaned so it may become the future,' Grandad said. 'It would be wrong to leave Buddy waiting while the rain falls. The funeral will be this morning. We'll go to the base of the mountains, and gather the townspeople from there as they arrive to start their collecting. It's fitting, for one as young as him, that he'll leave us with the rising sun. The funeral will be for his death, and the celebration when the rain falls for his life.'

Kane nodded. 'I'll go to the mountains now. I'll make sure no one goes up.'

'We'll get dressed and then join you,' David said, and Kane headed out of the door. Joe was amazed by his grandfather.

It was a small story that he'd told, of Buddy leaving with the rising sun, and of the link between the funeral and the rain celebration, but it had changed things for Kane. Grandad had let it be okay for the funeral to be in the morning, rather than at sunset as was traditional, and for there to be a celebration soon after.

After having dressed and eaten, Joe, David and Grandad headed down the dry stream. David carried a bowl of porridge for Kane. There was already a crowd around the stone well when they arrived. The early risers, who'd met Kane on their way to the mountains, had gone back into the town and gathered townspeople.

Maya was standing near Kane, her eyes puffy. She wasn't quite crying, but occasionally let out small hiccups that were accompanied by a streak of tears down her cheeks. Rose stood next to Maya, with an arm around her shoulders.

Rose's other arm was outstretched to hold hands with Tiger, who looked confused and upset. Joe had been told that Charlotte, the Artist Sister, was keeping an eye on Lily so that Rose could be there. If Joe did not work out a way to the city soon, the next funeral Rose and Tiger attended might be their sister's.

'It's a pity we don't have suits,' David said to Grandad, 'and black dresses. It was a good sign of respect, the smart clothes.

Even now it's strange, having nothing different to wear.'

The townspeople's clothes were the usual selection of faded colours and torn fabrics. Joe couldn't imagine them in suits and dresses, in the immaculate way those clothes appeared in the magazines and photographs found on the mountains. That perfection didn't exist anymore. Everything they owned was marked by its history.

'It's a different time,' Grandad said, 'which needs its own traditions. There's practicality, even in respect.'

A hand squeezed Joe's. Sonya was there. She gave him a brief, sad smile and then looked across at the Witch's shack. The door was open and the Witch moved towards them, supporting herself with her stick. No crows rode on her back, nor had she induced rodents or snakes to follow her footsteps. She approached the crowd and joined them. For this, she was just an old woman.

In the face of death, there were no titles. No Librarian, no Witch, no Mayor. The only one who'd take up his role was Grandad. Only the Storyteller. But not yet. For now, he was just an old man. They were all just people, because a teenage boy who'd been one of them had died.

Missing only Lily and Charlotte, the townspeople walked together up the dry stream, moving in a long line of twos and threes. There was quiet conversation, a murmur as if the stream flowed again. Sonya told Joe that she didn't know how Maya could cope, how she'd get back to collecting on the mountains and live on. She wasn't sure how to help, or even if she could. Joe had no answers to give, but he was glad to be there to listen to her.

As they walked out from the top of the dry stream and passed into the fallen forest, the talking ceased. The procession was slowed as they milled through the fallen trees. No one stepped over the logs or overtook one another. They moved patiently, following the same path as those ahead of them. Once they reached the far end of the fallen forest, they walked down the side of the hill that led towards the flatlands. Below them, there was a wooden pyre topped by a body. A white lace material had been laid over him, what looked like a woman's shawl from the city now repurposed as a funeral veil.

Kane's Moonshine Brothers, Matthias and Scott, stood solemnly next to the pyre. The two men had built it the night before, using the ruined wood that the townspeople had collected. They'd brought the body to it this morning, after Kane had told them that the funeral would be early.

There was no shade set up. For once, with the cloudy sky, it wasn't needed. There was black ground under the stacked wood, and the earth all around the pyre was dusted with grey. This was where they burned all those who died in the town. Joe's mother had been the first.

As they came close to the pyre, they saw through the veil

that Buddy's body was the wrong colour. Sonya let out an involuntary cry and gripped Joe's hand tightly. Buddy's skin was purple-green, the same as the land by the mountains. The entirety of his flesh was bruised, deformed by lumps and scratches. His face was barely visible, his eyes squished almost shut by the bruising. His lips were blue.

Joe wished that Buddy's lips could move once again, even if it was just to argue with him. He hadn't been there to help Buddy when the avalanche had happened. He could only hope he still had the chance to help Lily.

Matthias, the Moonshine Brother with shoulder-length hair and early grey in his beard, walked to the front and stood at the base of the pyre. The rest of the townspeople sat down on the dusty ground, waiting for him to speak. Even Alice climbed down from her chair and onto the earth.

'Now, we all know why we're here.' Matthias's voice was gruff. He shifted uncomfortably in front of the large crowd. 'Buddy was like family to me. He couldn't have been a better young man.'

Matthias coughed, staring awkwardly out at them all. The silence stretched, but he'd be given all the time he needed. No one broke the quiet.

'He loved his work,' Matthias said. 'Both collecting on the mountains, and making drink with us. He wasn't afraid to put effort in. He wanted to be good at things. I liked that about him.'

Matthias fell silent again. He appeared more settled this time. He pressed his hands together, gathering his thoughts.

'Everything he did, he worked at. Whether it was the moonshine, or growing plants, or cooking food' – Matthias looked across to where Maya sat – 'or being with Maya.'

Maya was sitting next to Kane. She had no family of her own to be with. Her chest heaved, but she made no sound.

'Buddy gave it his all. He wasn't the sort to put in less than a hundred percent, to save himself excuses for if it went wrong. Now I, well–' Matthias coughed again, swallowed then continued. 'I don't have a way with words. But that's why I liked him.'

Joe wondered why they did it this way. Why did they wait to tell these stories of what was liked about a person, of why they were loved, until after their death?

'Kane,' Matthias said. 'If you want to say a few words. If you feel able.'

'Yes.' Kane sounded like a rat squeaking. He stood slowly, as if his body ached. He swallowed, and forced his words out in a high rasp. 'I'll speak.'

Kane walked to the front in a stiff stride, and Matthias sat down with the rest of the townspeople.

'I haven't been sleeping.' There was very little breath behind Kane's voice. 'Not since he died. I've been turning it over and over in my head. What to say, and what to ask the Storyteller to say. I wanted to capture Buddy, who he was. I wanted it to be perfect for him. I–'

His voice rattled, and died away. Scott passed a bottle of water to Matthias, who handed it up to Kane. He drank, then continued.

'I worked it out last night. There are no words good enough. It doesn't matter how many stories you tell. Buddy was too much to describe. Buddy was everything he ever did, or thought, or felt. No one else can do or think or feel those things. Not ever. So how can we describe him using the same words we use for everyone else? How can we do that, when there's too much of him that's gone? He was my son–'

Kane's voice squeaked upwards. He drank again, then tried to speak. His mouth made the shape of words, but there was only a weak hiss, like something deflating. Kane finished the bottle of water, then took several deep breaths.

'Buddy was–' came out, but nothing more. The bottle fell from his hand, a glittering explosion as the glass shattered. Kane motioned for another drink.

'Kane,' Matthias said.

Kane shook his head and stuck his arm out for a bottle. Marco, sitting near the front, stretched forward and offered him one. Kane drank half of the bottle. When he attempted to speak again, his voice was no longer even a rat's squeak, only the scratching of its claws. David helped Grandad to his feet, and Maya went forward, taking Kane's hand. He looked at her like he didn't know who she was, tears streaking down his face. Maya's chest shook, but she stayed strong as she led him away and they sat down together.

Grandad went to the front. 'I'm going to tell you, as much as I can, the story of Buddy's life. Kane speaks truthfully when he says that no story could give us all of Buddy. This tale is woven from the memories of him that you shared with me. These memories were gifts from Buddy, given by living and being who he was. By sharing these gifts, we'll all have a little more of him to hold on to.

'Today we mourn, as we can talk with Buddy no more. Yet we'll find in the coming times that Buddy does speak to us, and move us, through our memories of him, which are gifts he left behind. The body is made of earth and sky, so it returns to earth and sky. The soul is made of mind and feeling, so it returns to mind and feeling. Buddy's soul does not leave us today, but is split between all of us who knew him. It's an honour to carry him with us.'

After that introduction, Grandad told Buddy's story. Like Joe, Buddy was born in the city but took his first tottering steps in the town. Buddy grew, made alcohol with his father, lost his mother, and loved Maya. Joe couldn't concentrate on Grandad's voice. The story faded away, and instead Joe became aware of the hard ground beneath him.

The people around him had their heads bowed, or their eyes shut, or stared towards Grandad. All of them were inside the story, watching Buddy climb the mountains. Sonya's hand was sweating, and Joe could feel the cool space between their palms. His clothes itched against his skin, and there was an ache in one of his legs. All of the sensations anchored him to the dry earth and prevented him from focusing on Buddy's tale. He heard Grandad's words and knew their meaning, but didn't feel their effects.

A memory of Buddy came to him. Not as a sight or a feeling, only as a fact in his mind. Joe remembered that he'd traded Buddy three cameras along with some plastic recycling to borrow his knife. He hadn't told Buddy that he'd found a whole box of the cameras on the mountains. If Buddy had gone to Leigh first, he'd have had good trade for the three that Joe had given him. If it was after Joe had sold Leigh the rest of the cameras, their value would have gone down. No rareness or novelty, only an addition to the drifter's electronics recycling.

Buddy might have died angry at Joe. Maybe if he was alive, their group would currently be collecting together on the mountains, and Buddy would be refusing to work with Joe, calling him a cheat and a liar. He'd still have got his knife back, and gained some of Joe's collections in the process, but there was no chance that Buddy would have let it lie there. Then again, if things had been different, Joe might have been in the city with the knife, its return to Buddy uncertain.

So many ifs, Joe thought. *But it's all happened now and none of it can be changed.*

Joe only realised that Grandad had finished speaking when Sonya raised her head. Others shifted and adjusted their sitting positions, groggily as if waking from a dream. Maya sobbed aloud.

'Soon we'll let his body return to where it came from,' Grandad said. 'What the fire doesn't take to the sky, will be given back to the earth. Now is the time for goodbyes, and to say what shouldn't be left unsaid.'

Maya's sobbing was joined by Kane's. Like a wave, others in the crowd fell to crying as well. No tears came to Joe, though his eyes stung when Sonya clenched his hand and began to weep. Kane was the first to stand and go to the pyre. His head was level with his dead son's stomach. He stroked Buddy's battered face through the veil, whispering to him. Joe didn't know if Kane actually managed to make any sound or if he was only mouthing the words. From Kane's desperate expression and the imploring look in his eyes, Joe thought that he might have been apologising for something. Kane's hands dropped from Buddy's cheeks and he walked stiffly away from the pyre.

Maya was next. As she approached Buddy, she brushed her hair back from her face and wiped her hand across her eyes.

Her expression became tight and determined. She improved her posture, moving her chest forward and straightening her back. Everyone else stayed at a respectful distance while one of them was at the pyre. Even so, Joe could hear that Maya spoke more clearly than Kane, with an almost formal edge to her voice. She maintained her control as she walked away, though silent tears slipped down her puffy cheeks.

One by one, every townsperson went to Buddy. Once they'd finished, they returned to the others and stayed standing to show that they'd gone to him. Even the Witch went to the pyre. She didn't speak, but spent a few minutes there, staring quietly at Buddy. There was a grave sadness on her face. Her deep wrinkles were set as if she'd worn this expression many times before, as if she didn't mourn only Buddy, but every death she'd ever seen. She mourned death itself, and the way of things, that all must happen as it did.

Eventually, Joe went to the pyre. There was no planning to the order. Simply when one person left, another approached. Joe reached out his hand and touched it to Buddy's, the fabric of the veil between them. His old collecting mate's hand wasn't cold, but it lacked life's heat.

'I'm sorry,' Joe whispered, 'about the cameras. I hope you got to the drifter before me.'

Buddy's bruised eyes squinted up towards the clouded sky.

'I'm sorry this happened. I know we didn't get along, but I'd have wanted you to live. You deserved more time.'

There didn't seem to be anything left to say.

'Goodbye, Buddy.'

Joe returned to the crowd. Sonya went next, speaking to Buddy for a long while. Joe knew she'd have thought over what to say during the last few days. When she returned she stood by Joe and watched with bloodshot eyes as the remaining townspeople went to Buddy. The time came when everyone was standing, and Alice was back in her chair. Maya and Kane went to the front once more, Maya's upper body trembling and Kane looking like a lost little boy at her side. They approached Buddy and said goodbye, Maya repeating it several times, Kane in a single squeak.

Kane took a matchbox from his pocket, and he and Maya each drew out a match. Matches were rarely found on the mountains. They were saved only for this, for the funerals. Kane's didn't light on first striking, but Maya's did. She held it beneath his until they were both flickering. They bent down and lit the cardboard inserted under the wood, then retreated and joined the others. The wood caught the flames, and the townspeople stood together, watching Buddy burn.

CHAPTER FOURTEEN

After the funeral, Joe, Sonya and Tiger collected on the mountains. They'd had to hurry onto the waste. The clouds were heavy overhead, and when the rain fell it would be torrential. The only collecting they'd get done that day was what they managed before the downpour. They all kept glancing up as they worked, waiting for it to begin.

Joe had decided that evening, at the rain celebration, he would speak to Sonya about his vision of the Forest Woman and Leigh's hints around a way to the city. He didn't want to explain what the Forest Woman had said about Lily, not while Tiger was within earshot. Things were already confusing enough for the young boy.

The rain came late into the evening, when the sun was low beneath the western clouds. It was sudden and powerful, the mountains echoing with the sound of water smacking against plastic bin bags. The deluge flattened their hair and clothes in seconds, utterly drenching them.

Joe carried Tiger in a piggyback, and Sonya took their collecting bags, heading back towards the town. The mountainside shone beneath them, the damp waste catching the light of the evening sun, even through the thudding rain. Despite the beauty, they had to be careful. The steep slopes were even more dangerous when wet. A misstep could send you crashing down the slippery mountainside. Cascading torrents of water gushed through the waste, which could wash away the bags beneath their feet. The last thing the town needed was another death. Yet Joe couldn't keep from smiling.

The mountains were never safe, but this was worth it. To see Sonya with her braids soaked and shining, the water rushing down her skin. To hear Tiger, who'd been so sombre throughout Lily's illness, ooh-ing and aah-ing with amazement at the rain as it bounced upwards from the bin bags. To know that when they got to the town, the stream would be flowing and that this night would be different from all the rest. Maybe, for a short time, they could forget their problems.

Joe stopped for a moment and opened his mouth towards the sky, closing his eyes as the downpour smacked into his face. To his side, he saw Sonya encouraging Tiger to do the same. The raindrops hammering into his mouth tasted fresher than anything taken from the well, unaffected by the grime and history of the mountains. It tasted as rain would have at the beginning of everything, when the world hadn't yet been shaped and the soil sparkled with potential. As it crashed over Joe, he felt clean and new as well.

When they reached the bottom of the final slope, Sonya began to leap. With nowhere left to fall, she jumped from bag to bag, sending up splashes. Joe's heart swelled, and he chased after her, Tiger cheering on his back. Joe loved her, and he knew it truly in that moment. There were a thousand sides to her, a thousand stories that could be told of who she was. He loved them all, because all of them were Sonya.

As the rain spurred them down onto the purple-green ground, they were joined by others. Joe saw Marco and Harvey sit down together and slide down the last few bags on the mountainside. David and Demeta did the same, along with the other adults from their collecting group. The Artist Sisters raced down the end of the waste, scrambling competitively down the final part of the slope. At the mountain's base, Grandad stood with Mr Rajarshi and the Librarian, laughing at it all.

When they reached the end of the waste, Joe and Sonya ran to the stone well, where Joe let Tiger climb down from his back. Tiger's eyes widened with joy as the watery mud squelched beneath his feet. He began to stamp around, giggling as the mud became more and more liquid with the unrelenting rain.

Infected by Tiger's enthusiasm, Joe copied his big right-angle steps. His knees reached as high as Tiger's head. Soon Sonya joined in too, then more of the townspeople. It became a strange dance. Marco and Harvey linked arms and circled each other as they did the high steps, David and Demeta doing the same. Those four swapped partners, David switching across to dance with Harvey and Demeta with Marco. Joe grinned and offered his arm to Sonya, who hooked hers through and stamped in a circle with him.

'I think it's about time,' Grandad shouted, 'that we take Tiger to the stream!'

David slipped free from dancing with Harvey, swept Tiger up and hefted him onto his shoulders. Joe's father's hair was slicked down against his head.

'Stick your arms out, Tiger!' David exclaimed over the thunderous rain. 'Did you know you can fly?'

To Joe's disbelief, David dashed off with Tiger's legs dangling on either side of his neck. The young boy spread his arms out, water crashing off them in the shape of wings.

Grandad walked over next to Joe and Sonya, and shouted. 'He used to do that with you, you know! Do you think I'm too old for the stream?'

'You're never too old!' Joe replied.

Grandad smiled, water running down through his beard. 'Little Joe, you tell stories almost as well as I do!'

They followed David's path to the stream. Water tumbled down the trench, pooling out at its end. It appeared natural and alive, like blood rushing through a vein. There were people all along the stream, dipping their hands under or dunking their heads. Alice's office chair was empty, its wheels stuck in the mud. She was in the stream, and splashed water at Joe as they passed.

David had his hands under Tiger's armpits, the young boy laughing ecstatically as Joe's father bounced him in and out of the water. Grandad went to join them, leaving Joe and Sonya standing together at the edge of the stream.

'Shall we?' Joe said to Sonya, indicating the water.

'We shall,' Sonya replied.

They jumped down, soaking their feet, then both dunked their heads under. A storm cloud of bubbles swept across Joe's face, the stream wondrously cool. He lifted his head out at the same time as Sonya, who whipped her head back so an arc of water flew up from her hair. She grabbed him and pulled him down, so that the stream ran over them both, cleansing the heat and the waste from their skin. For a moment, all the youth the mountains had stolen from them returned, and they were joyous and free.

The initial downpour had eased, but it still rained steadily as the townspeople worked together to set up the bonfire. They built it from ruined wood, collected that day on the mountains. There'd been surplus from Buddy's pyre, but they never used wood intended for a funeral on a celebration fire, or vice versa. They stacked the wood in a great square near the stone well, Joe and Sonya helping place some larger pieces of plywood, alongside broken bits of pine furniture. Once completed, it stood roughly at Joe's height and ten paces wide, sinking down under its own weight into the sodden ground.

This was where they always held the celebrations. Unlike where they built the funeral pyres, there was no ashen land nor black marks on the earth. It was a strange fire that the Witch called up in the pouring rain, and it left no damage to the ground. The townspeople waited for the Witch now, standing round the unlit bonfire and watching the door of her shack.

The door opened inwards, and the Witch emerged without her stick. She squelched her feet through the mud, her hunched back pushing her nose towards the soaking ground. Each step forward seemed to cause her bony ankles to sink deeper. The circle of townspeople around the bonfire parted as the Witch approached. Her damp brown rags stuck to her skin.

It's impossible to tell where the mud ends, Joe thought, *and the rags begin.*

The Witch snapped her head towards Joe like a bird, staring at him as if she'd heard his thoughts. Rainwater streamed down her face, following the lines of her wrinkles. She jerked her head away and walked on, still birdlike, her hands clasped behind her. She transformed when she reached the bonfire, climbing up the side with her spindly limbs sticking out like a spider's legs.

When she stood on top of the wood, she changed again and moved as a snake. She coiled her body as she flicked her tongue in and out of her shrivelled lips, tasting the rain and the air. She determined something from that taste and reared up, pushed her hands inside her rags and flung out a handful of powder to each side. Two purple clouds floated momentarily, before being brought down by the rain into the wood.

The Witch reached into her rags again and drew out a thin glass bottle. Squinting through the rainfall, Joe could make out the rainbows twisted and knotted within the liquid inside. The Witch poured the liquid across the bonfire, laying the rainbows flat along the wood. She produced more of the bottles, emptying them until the entire top layer of wood was covered in the glimmering substance.

She took out a lump of a rock and a simple metal blade, then struck them together so that sparks sprinkled down onto the bonfire. As soon as the sparks landed on the wood they erupted into giant purple flames. The Witch moved like a spider again, fast but calm even as the fire spread behind her. She leapt down onto the mud as the last of the wood cracked into flames, showering her back with purple sparks. She walked on unconcerned, violet embers dropping from her rags.

The townspeople closed in around the fire, their faces lit purple. They peeled off their damp clothes and threw them to the side, so they only wore their underwear. The cool of the rain and the warmth of the fire felt good together on their skin. There was no need for modesty, not when they were celebrating the feeling of water running down their skin.

'Let's sit down there,' Sonya said, indicating a space by the fire.

Joe sat with her, muddy water pooling around them. Most people positioned themselves similarly, sitting either cross-legged or with their feet out towards the fire. Grandad, Mr Rajarshi, and the Librarian were together on chairs. Partway around the fire, Joe could see Ms Winnipeg was in the centre of another group of older people also using chairs. She was chatting with a bald wrinkle-headed woman named Mrs Polward and a rosy-cheeked man who refused to be called his last name and went by Benjamin.

Despite her age, the Witch sat on the ground, closer to the fire than the rest of them. She hadn't taken off her mud-coloured rags, so it looked like she was caked in the wet dirt. She was bent towards the fire, her head following loops and twitches in the flames that Joe couldn't perceive.

It was hard to tell through the blur of the rain and the purple-tinged smoke, but Joe thought very few of the townspeople were missing from around the bonfire. Rose had stayed in her shack with Lily, whose long sleep continued. The rest of the townspeople were taking collective responsibility for looking after Tiger at the celebration.

Maya wasn't present, and neither were the Moonshine Brothers, though Matthias had said they would bring down their latest brew at some point. Joe hadn't expected Kane to come with them, but when he saw the glint of the metal barrel in the rain – a flash of purple as it reflected the fire – all three Moonshine Brothers carried it.

They brought it to every townsperson, who each held up a glass for the Brothers to heft up the barrel and pour them a measure from the hole in the top. Even the Witch had some, poured into her carved wooden bowl. It was a testament to how many times the Moonshine Brothers had shared out whisky that not a single drop was spilled. The golden brown alcohol's smell was sharp, burning in Joe's nose as his glass was filled. He placed his palm over the top of his glass, to keep the smell in and the rain out. Several more townspeople did the same.

'Name the drink,' Grandad announced to the Moonshine Brothers when they'd finished sharing it out, his words travelling over the crackling of rain meeting fire. Each whisky the Brothers made tasted subtly different, so each was given its own name.

'Buddy's Sky.' Kane's voice wavered, but it was loud enough to be heard and no longer high-pitched.

'Buddy's Sky,' Grandad shouted, raising his glass. The townspeople raised their glasses and echoed him, then tilted their heads up and drank. The whisky burned down Joe's throat like a sliver cut from the sun, before settling at a comfortable heat in his stomach. The Moonshine Brothers placed the still mostly-full barrel down into the mud. The trio laid out a sheet to sit on, but remained clothed and separate from the others.

Next, the townspeople shared fish, meat and vegetables with each other, everyone producing bowls and food they'd brought with them from their shacks. This would be a good feast, as the drifter's visit had been recent, so there would be a greater variety of food.

Joe cut himself a small section from his herring and then gave the rest to Sonya, who cut herself a piece before handing the fish on to the people to their right. Sonya passed Joe a bunch of kale leaves, and he put one in his bowl before handing them on to the left. All around, people shared food, taking small portions and passing the rest on, until their bowls were filled with eclectic mixtures. Joe's ended up holding rabbit and wolf meat, kale, peppers, herring, and an oat biscuit that someone had made a batch of for the celebration.

'It's like having a proper meal again,' Joe overheard David say to Demeta, the two of them sitting near Sonya and Joe.

The townspeople protected their bowls as best they could, with their hands or with clothing that wasn't covered in mud.

The bowls inevitably filled with rainwater, which had to be poured away while carefully keeping the food inside. They used long forks with wooden or plastic handles, so that they could hold their food up to the purple flames to heat it.

The sizzle of rain falling into the fire was joined by the satisfied sounds of people eating, enjoying the variety of flavours. Conversation was sparse. The few words that were spoken focused on the smell and taste of the food, the fire's lapping purple light, and the feeling of the rain washing their skin. They thought only of the wonder of sensations, not of what came before or after.

The Mayor and Harvey lugged the barrel around the fire, enlisting the townspeople's help in refilling glasses. The Moonshine Brothers had left after the food was shared out, taking some for themselves and Maya, as well as a glass bottle filled with Buddy's Sky. Once the barrel had travelled around everyone, they all raised their glasses once more, this time all cheering.

'Cheers,' Sonya said, holding her drink out with a sly smile. Rainwater splashed in the amber liquid.

'Cheers,' Joe replied. He hooked his arm through hers, and they both drank at the same time.

There was a flash of light from the bonfire. It was no longer purple, instead blazing white with strokes of gold slipping down from the tips of the flames. The Witch's arm was stretched out, her hand open towards the fire, the remains of some mysterious powder being washed from her fingers by the rain.

Joe heard them before he saw them. Four voices, singing wordless harmonies. He could just make them out, standing on the other side of the white-gold fire. The Singing Family, mother and father in the middle, with their son and daughter on either side. The father's voice, the lowest, set a rhythm while the others swung above it. They built up a melody, low and sombre, then the mother began to sing the lyrics.

It was an old sad song from the city, one that Joe didn't entirely understand. When Grandad's stories included the city, everything was explained and described for the younger townspeople. This song had been written for people who already knew what it was like to live there. Joe didn't know how it felt to drive under street lights at night, or to look at the moon through a high-rise window. Rain was mentioned, but it didn't hold the same joy in the city as it did for the town.

The chorus was easy to remember though, and Joe knew what it meant to feel blue. He was no good at singing in pitch, but he could throw emotion into his voice when they all sang the chorus together. He sang with his arm around Sonya, swaying in time.

It's strange how good it can feel, Joe thought, *to sing a sad song.*

Sonya was giggling at him.

'What?' he asked.

'You were thinking deep thoughts as you sung,' she said. 'I could tell.'

The Singing Family followed it with a happier tune, the son and daughter trading lyrics back and forth, as their parents sang a jaunty melody behind them. As with all of the Family's songs, everyone joined in for the chorus. Once the Family finished singing and sat down to great applause, Buddy's Sky was passed around again. As the whisky washed down his throat, Joe felt a fuzziness in his chest and behind his eyes. The drink gave everything a gentle haze, softening the light of the white and gold fire.

The Artist Sisters stood up next. There was no pre-planned order; people simply stood if they wanted to share something. The Witch blew a cloud of powder from her hand again, and the flames leapt up in pink. The Artist Sisters went to her and asked something. It was a rare thing, to see a smile creep up on the Witch's ancient lips. She reached into her rags and threw out a different powder, the flames turning the deep blue of oceans.

'That's a beautiful colour,' Sonya gasped.

The Artist Sisters moved around the blue fire, placing down objects made of miscellaneous metals. Sliced-open drinks cans, copper wire and bent cutlery were fastened together to form abstract shapes. When the shapes were put in front of the fire, their shadows made people, gaps in the shapes letting the blue firelight through. A woman holding a blue umbrella, a man on a bike with blue between the spokes, a child with a blue balloon.

The townspeople walked around the bonfire in a circle, inspecting the objects and the shadows that they made. Joe's favourites were the ones that cast shadows resembling people from the town. There was Alice, pushing her office chair with her pole. The Librarian reading, with blue light glinting where his glasses would be. Grandad, orating a story.

'This one's amazing,' Sonya said, tugging on Joe's arm. 'Look at her hair.'

It was the shadow of a woman, her hair blowing out behind her as if in the wind. The foil triangle that cast the shadow of her hair was perforated, causing the firelight to flicker through, as though she had glittering blue hair.

'Who do you think she is?' Joe asked, because he knew Sonya would like the question.

'The Lady with Blue Hair,' Sonya said. 'Maybe she's the reason it rains. She lives on the clouds. When the time comes for rain, she dances on top of them to let it fall.'

Joe saw the Lady in the shadow, and the way she'd tap and twirl her feet on the tops of clouds.

'Who do you see?' Sonya asked him.

'I like the Lady with the Blue Hair,' Joe replied. 'That's who she is.'

Once people had seen all of the objects and the shadows,

they went back to their own clothes and sat down. The Artist Sisters gathered their creations, which they'd sell to coming drifters. They'd make something else, new and enticing, before the next rainfall. Grandad rose to his feet, and everyone fell silent. It was time for the story.

CHAPTER FIFTEEN

Behind Grandad, the Witch produced a jar filled with grey paste from her rags. She opened the lid and scooped out a ball of paste, rolling it between her fingers until it crumbled into her skin. She flung her hand out and nothing visible passed between her and the fire, but the flames swung back, turning to green. Black smoke rose from them, uncurling as it climbed towards the clouds.

Grandad stood taller when he told stories. It was like the Artist Sisters' creations, when an object was closer to the fire and cast a longer shadow.

'I'll tell you the tale of the man who dodged death.'

Joe knew the story well. It was one Grandad often told after deaths in the town.

'Before we left the city, there was a time when people knew the whole

world. Before then, there was a time like now, when people did not. In that time, the oceans were wide and blue, and travelling across them held all the adventure of sailing a ship up into the stars.

'During those days, there was a young man by the name of Daniel Yorvick, who'd run so far from home he couldn't tell you where he'd begun. All he knew was that if he stayed in one place too long, he grew tired of having the same earth beneath his feet. He was much more comfortable at sea, where the water below him was ever-changing. Daniel found his way to the water time and time again, as a sailor, as a stowaway, as a pirate.

'There are many stories of Daniel's adventures, several of which I've told you before. This tale begins when he was fifteen, at sea with a rowdy pirate crew, who he intended to slip away from at the next port. He'd already had to defend himself from some of the other crew members, who'd thought that picking off the youngest and smallest of them would be an easy way to increase their share of the bounty. They were stronger than him, but Daniel was faster and his blade was sharp. After taking one man's hand, another man's eye, and a third man's life, the pirates realised Daniel Yorvick was not such an easy target.

'The ship they travelled on was called Redbeard's Revenge. Its black flag, bearing the insignia of a lizard's skull, was one of the most feared on the ocean. The ship was named for its captain, a giant man with a bushy ginger beard, wild copper hair and madness in his eyes. No one knew what injustice had birthed Oruc Redbeard's desire for vengeance, only that he'd once worked for the British East India Company. Now he took whatever goods the company's merchant ships carried, along with the lives of their

crew.

'Oruc hired the low and the cruel to work on his ship, searching the dirtiest drinking holes for men with anger in their spit and hatred in their belly. Daniel was a fine liar. Just as he could disguise himself as a noble aristocrat to gain passage on a royal galleon, so could he convincingly pretend to have a black enough heart to travel on Redbeard's Revenge. In reality, he'd sooner steal away on a lifeboat than draw the blood of an innocent man.

'This wasn't the only way Daniel Yorvick was different from the rest of the pirate crew. Of all of them, all those rogues and scoundrels, it was Daniel who loved life the most. He loved life at its wildest, when he was dancing, and singing, and drinking, and fighting. He loved life too at its quietest, when he tasted the salt on the air in the morning, when he listened to waves at night while everyone else lay sleeping, when he looked out across the sea and remembered all the things he'd done. He loved people, making friends and making enemies, and he loved women – often.'

That drew a laugh from the townspeople. Through the rain, Joe could almost see the twinkle in Grandad's eye.

'Of all things, what Daniel loved most was the horizon. That endless line across the edge of the world was full of promise for him. It promised more of everything he loved. More adventures, more people, more life.'

Some of the townspeople closed their eyes as they listened, the same as at Buddy's funeral that morning. Joe gazed into the smoke rising from the emerald fire and saw within it shapes from Grandad's tale. There was a curl here that could be the sail of a pirate ship, a wisp there that could be the edge of a sword. He watched them form and break as Grandad continued on.

'Being so fond of living, Daniel was concerned when he saw Oruc Redbeard hoist the first mate into the air and then launch him over the side of the ship.

"Any dog that throws a rope," Oruc shouted, "joins him in the locker!"

'The cause of their argument was clear. The course that Oruc had plotted took them towards black clouds and stormy weather. Oruc yelled to increase their speed. The crew did so, without question. The storm might spare them; Redbeard would not. The pirates, the rough men with rage in their blood, looked ahead towards the clouds with pale faces and fearful eyes.

'No one questioned Redbeard when the sea grew choppy, nor when the rain splattered on the deck, nor when the lightning cracked around them. The waves grew wild and still he shouted them onwards, his voice as loud as the thunder and the storm. The wind pulled the black sails back and forth, sending the galley close to tipping each way. Barrels and cannons flew overboard. The brute whose eye Daniel had liberated flipped over the side and vanished into the sea.

'Daniel hurriedly fastened a rope from the rigging around his own arm, willing to try anything to stay alive. Still Oruc shouted them on and still the crew complied. It was only when a huge wave lifted them, moments before the ship was hurled onto its side, that one pirate screamed at the captain: "Curse you, you bastard! You've killed us all!"

'As he said it, lightning struck through the black sails and exploded onto

the deck. The wave crashed, the ship tipping over as the wood burst into flames. Daniel fell towards the sea and the rope around his arm pulled tight, leaving him dangling between death by water below, or fire above. Spinning and disorientated, Daniel saw burning pirates fall past him, extinguishing in the dark sea. The ship swung back and he crashed onto the deck. All he could hear was dripping and burning. The water was calm. They were in the eye of the storm.

'Daniel rose to his feet and saw that there was only one other man left aboard. Oruc Redbeard stood at the helm, his back to Daniel and his mighty hands on the wheel. The captain paid no attention to the fires burning around him. Daniel thought quickly, then drew his sword and cut the rope from his arm. He kept his blade drawn as he climbed the stairs to the helm. He'd kill Redbeard, if he must, to prevent them from going back into dangerous waters.

'Daniel stopped halfway up the steps, when he saw a cloud of blue smoke swirling next to the captain. A man strode from the blue cloud towards Oruc, the sounds of his boots death knolls. There was a sword in the man's hand, not forged from steel but instead a giant crab's claw. The inside of the crustacean blade was a curve of mottled teeth, the outside honed into a fine line so sharp that it could cut through sky and sunlight. The weapon dragged on the deck, carving a groove through the wood.

'The man stood in front of Redbeard. Oruc, the dreaded pirate, the scourge of the seven seas, the captain who'd driven his crew to death rather than surrender to the storm, drew his sword. Then he let it go, and dropped to his knees.

'"Please, no," Oruc said. The man lifted the crab-claw blade, then split Redbeard in two. The force of the blow sent both halves of the captain's remains crashing through the decks, and Daniel heard two splashes down below. The man turned towards Daniel, his crustacean weapon splattered with blood. He had a shark's eyes, black and narrow. When he spoke, Daniel saw three rows of pointed-triangle teeth leading down his throat.

'"Daniel Yorvick," he said, his voice as ancient and immutable as the ocean. "This ship is damned."

'He was the death of the oceans, that came to sailors in sinking ships. He was Davy Jones, here to take Daniel Yorvick down to his locker at the bottom of the sea. Daniel turned and ran, heavy footsteps following behind him. There was only so much ship, before water that would steal the breath and warmth from a man in an instant. The footsteps following him were slow, but whenever Daniel glanced back, Jones was close behind. While Daniel dodged around the fires, Davy Jones strode through them, their heat nothing compared to the fathomless depths of darkness and cold from which he came.

'Daniel had an idea, and jumped over a fallen mast, before sliding down the wet sail onto the other side of the deck. He sprinted up the forecastle stairs, breathing hard. He heard Davy Jones ascending the steps behind him, but he saw what he was looking for at the end of the ship. The front cannon. Redbeard kept it loaded, but had never fired it. The cannonball inside had been meant for some specific aspect of his vengeance that would now never be fulfilled.

'Daniel snatched up a burning plank and lit the fuse, then spun the

cannon one hundred and eighty degrees, aiming at Davy Jones's chest. By some miracle, the weapon sounded, not waterlogged by the storm. But even the cannonball, loaded with all of Oruc Redbeard's hatred and lust for revenge, simply flew straight through Davy Jones.

'The crab-claw blade swung and Daniel parried it, losing half of his own sword. Daniel danced around Jones, ducking and weaving away from his deadly blows, not daring to turn his back and run. When the opportunities he'd learned to look for in fights against larger men were presented, Daniel took them without hesitation, nipping forward and stabbing his half-sword into Jones. A gush of saltwater rushed over Daniel's hand each time, but Jones showed no sign of hurt nor injury. After every successful stab, Daniel pulled out his weapon and dodged back before the crustacean blade took off his head.

'The boat was burning and sinking in the centre of a storm, and the man he fought was immortal. Despite this, Daniel continued his dance with Davy Jones all across the ship. He didn't resign himself to his end. It was too important that he see the horizon at least one more time. Daniel was thinking throughout their fight, pushing his mind harder, deeper and faster than ever before. He calculated every inch of the ship, searching the boat in his head for anything that could help him survive. Again and again, he came up with nothing. Eventually, like a ray of light from an approaching sunrise, one final gambit came to him.

'Daniel threw his sword down at Davy Jones's feet and jumped back. He turned and ran up the forecastle stairs once again, death's heavy footsteps following behind. Daniel jumped up onto the cannon, balancing precariously

as he looked out over the wreckage on the water. He sighted his target and jumped down towards the sea, the crab-claw blade slicing hair from the top of his head as he fell.

Daniel landed on a small section of the ship's hull that had broken away, barely the length of his body. It crashed under the water, his hands and knees smacking into the freezing cold, then floated with him on top of it. Daniel grabbed a broken plank to keep his makeshift raft in the storm's calm eye, then looked back at Redbeard's Revenge.

'Davy Jones stared down at him, then faded into blue smoke. Daniel waited, expecting the smoke to reform at his side. It did not. Davy Jones came for drowning men, and while Redbeard's Revenge was doomed to sink, Daniel's piece of hull was not.'

Sonya nudged Joe in the ribs, lifting him out of the story.

'You're a bit of a Daniel,' she whispered.

'What do you mean?' Joe whispered back, close to her ear, so that she could hear him over the rain.

'The city's the horizon, isn't it?' Sonya said. 'An adventure. I bet even when you find it, you'll keep chasing after where the land meets the sky. You'll always be looking for something new.'

The water running down Sonya's face followed the paths of tears. It revealed sadness behind her smile. He put his hand on her waist and kissed her. It was the first time they'd kissed since that night in the fallen forest when he'd told her he wanted to see the city, the night before he and Tiger were caught in the avalanche and Lily was bitten.

The urgency between their lips was as if they were kissing for the first time again. The comfort that had developed between them over the years was gone, replaced with something more desperate. Sonya's bare skin was warm, rainwater trickling under Joe's hand. She took a last soft bite of his lower lip, then placed two fingers on his chin, and turned him back towards the bonfire and Grandad's story.

'After waiting out the storm and surviving his journey back across the sea, Daniel adventured for many more years. What finally caused him to settle down was the love of a woman. Together they bought a farm several acres wide, and worked it until they made enough money to hire farmhands to assist them in tending their wheat, their cows and their sheep.

'By this time, Daniel was a grown man, and his wife had borne him three children. He still loved the horizon, but he loved it remaining in one place. He'd sit on his porch and look out across his land to where the sky began, and not once did he lose his appreciation for the beauty of his home.

'When death came to the farm, it was not made from drowning and dark seas. It was illness, plague and starvation. A skeletal figure in a black cloak, carrying a scythe. Daniel watched the apparition from the porch as it approached across the fields. The animals ran from it, the farmhands shivered unknowing as it passed, even the wheat tilted away from the hooded skeleton. Daniel fingered the trigger of his flintlock pistol, but kept it on his lap. When the reaper stood in front of him, it reached a single bony finger out towards his heart.

'"I met a man like you once before, out at sea," Daniel remarked. "Now

you, reaper, I've heard that you allow a soul to play a game for his life."

'A nod from the skull.

'"I've also heard that whether it's poker, blackjack or chess, you always win. Even on the flip of the coin, or the roll of the dice."

'Another nod.

'"I propose a simple game," Daniel said. "A duel. I get one shot at you with my pistol. If that doesn't kill you, then you can take a swing at me with that scythe of yours. Deal?"

'A third, final nod. Daniel stood, pointing the pistol straight into one of the reaper's empty eye sockets. Then he lowered the gun and slotted it into its holster.

'"Now remember," Daniel said. "You can't take your swing until I take my shot. I don't intend on firing this gun anytime soon. I'd advise you there's little point in staying on my land."

'Then Daniel went inside. When he next returned to the porch, to watch the sunset on the horizon, the reaper was gone.'

Grandad paused as another round of Buddy's Sky was handed out. 'There's very few things worth stopping a story for,' he said, then drank his shot. 'But whisky is one of them.'

'Let's hope he makes it to the end of the story,' David muttered to Demeta, who laughed. Grandad must have heard them over the rain, because he chuckled before telling the final part of the tale.

'There came a time when Daniel was an impossibly old man, living in a flat in the city. The loaded pistol, now a relic, was kept in a drawer by

his bed. He'd seen his wife, his children, his grandchildren and his great-grandchildren die. He still loved the horizon, but it was a sad love now. He loved the memories it gave him, of his family and his youthful adventures. There was nothing else left for him on the edge of the world.

'She visited him as a young woman, with pale skin and black hair. Everything about her was gentle.

'"It's time now, Daniel," she told him.

'"I could work my way out of it, you know," he said. "I'm Daniel Yorvick. I can talk myself onto the finest royal galleon, or the dirtiest pirate ship."

'She smiled and shook her head. "Not this time."

'"No, not this time." Daniel walked to his window and looked out across the roofs of the city. "There's still so much life in the horizon, you know. Just not for me."

'She joined him by the window and took his hand in hers.

'"I suppose that's why we need you," Daniel said. "To give the next lot a chance."

'She squeezed his hand in reply.

'"You were always mine then," Daniel said. "You can dodge them, but never your own. You can't dodge your own."

'Her dark eyes looked upon Daniel fondly.

'"So, how do you do it? You don't have a crab sword or a scythe."

'In response, she led him by his hand to his bed. She laid him down, then joined him on the bed and wrapped her arms around him. Her smell, sweet like freshly-picked flowers, enveloped him. She reminded Daniel of

those nights with his wife, or the women before her, when he woke late and realised that one day he'd no longer exist. That he, like all men, would die.

He remembered how terrified he'd felt at those times, but also how alive, like a white-hot flame pressed between two eternities of darkness. He remembered how he'd pull the woman in bed with him closer and hold her tight, grateful just to be living. He put his arms around the black-haired woman and held her in that same way. Eventually, as had happened with all the women in all the beds before, his thoughts of death gradually gave way to sleep. He never rose to see the horizon again.'

The story ended and everyone was silent, Daniel Yorvick and his death hanging in the air together. Someone started clapping, then a cascade of others joined in. The applause brought them back into the real world, sitting around the green fire in the rain.

Grandad called that silence after the end of a story 'the breath out'. He said that by measuring the length of the breath, rather than the volume of the applause, one could gauge how much a story had moved its audience. By either measure, the story had been successful.

CHAPTER SIXTEEN

'I enjoyed the story,' Joe said, finding Grandad by the green fire light. 'Daniel Yorvick is one of my favourites.'

Grandad grinned. There was water dripping from his beard, and the effect of the whisky was clear in his eyes. 'I'm glad you enjoyed it. You always liked the pirate part best when you were little.'

'Can I ask you something about stories?' Joe said, emboldened by the warmth of the whisky in his chest.

'Something around stories appearing in real life?' Grandad asked, astute despite the slight slur in his voice. 'Like you asked before?'

'There's been two times when I thought maybe I met someone from a story. When I was caught in the avalanche, it felt like the Boy Who Learned What Fear Was helped me stay alive. When I went out in Leigh's van, I swear I saw the Forest Woman from the story of How The City Came To Be.' Joe hadn't meant for everything to come out at once, and so quickly qualified what he was saying. 'I couldn't breathe in the mountains, and I was half asleep in the van, so I know it could just be in my head.'

'Our whole lives happen in our head,' Grandad said. 'All we can do is try to make sense of it all. In answer to your question, it's like I said before. The boundary between the world and stories has felt weaker since we moved out here. There's the tales the drifters tell, of the desert around the city. And there's someone in the town who always felt like a character from a story to me...'

Joe followed his Grandad's gaze, to where the Witch was half-sunk in the mud, closest to the fire.

'I'm not sure, Joe,' Grandad went on, 'I've always believed stories to be powerful things. But I've felt that power out here more than anywhere before.'

The Mayor strode past them, stopping next to the fire to make an announcement.

'It's time for the giving of gifts!' the Mayor bellowed out.

'Now, that's a good idea,' said Grandad. Between celebrations, the townspeople collected gifts for each other on the mountains. Usually they were items that would be essentially worthless to the drifters: tokens they knew their friends or family would appreciate, but had little practical use.

Joe opened the sack he had with him, and gave Grandad a spiky purple crystal he'd found amongst the bin bags on the mountains. Grandad identified the stone as amethyst. He gave Joe a pair of tough leather shoes he'd found in his size, telling him that there was nothing worth as much in the world as shoes that could last a long distance.

Next, Joe went to Sonya. He gave her a sun made from stained glass, dangling red triangles with a golden circle in their centre. When the light from the real sun caught it, it would shine. Sonya clutched it to her chest and smiled, then told Joe she wanted to give him her gift last.

As Sonya went to Demeta, Joe watched his father and grandfather exchange gifts. David gave a small figurine of a faerie woman with wings like a butterfly. In return Grandad gave a strange metal fork with two blunt prongs. David raised the fork, then struck it against a rock. A musical note chimed out, and David's face lit up. He turned and saw Joe, and they both hesitated awkwardly.

Joe reached into his bag, and pulled out a little silver coffee pot. He'd searched that day for something good to give his father. He knew what it meant to David to see objects that were mostly lost from the old world. David thanked Joe, speaking carefully as if one wrong word could break the moment. He opened his own cloth sack and handed Joe a small bum bag. Joe tried it on. He liked the way it clipped around his waist.

The bonfire flared and caught Joe's eye. At first, he thought it was back to the usual colours of flame, then he realised the difference. The fire was reversed. The centre was dull orange, while the spikes blazed yellow-white. Something tiny and burning shot out from the fire, then swooped towards Joe. He caught it before it hit his chest. A crow's feather.

The ends of its barbs glowed yellow, then faded, leaving the feather jagged. Next to the fire, the Witch stared at him, unblinking. Then she snapped her head back to the flames, so close it seemed they'd burn her nose. Joe had never heard of the Witch giving a gift before, though she always received many. No one else appeared to have seen him receiving this one, everyone else still exchanging gifts and talking in loud whisky voices. It was like Grandad said. She felt almost like a character from a story.

Joe looked across at Sonya. She'd just given Tiger a yo-yo. He was showing it off to Hope and her father Bill. Hope was the only one at the celebration other than Tiger who was too young to drink the whisky. Sonya noticed Joe watching her, and beckoned him over to her bin bag.

'Look inside,' she said. 'But be careful not to let the rain in.'

Inside there was a plastic carrier bag. With one hand Joe held the bin bag open, water dripping over the entrance like the mouth of a cave. With his other hand he lifted open the carrier bag. Inside, lit by the backwards firelight, there was a pile of postcards. On the top card, there was an image of a black and white woman with bobbed hair and a pearl necklace. There were towering buildings and old-fashioned cars behind her.

Joe flicked through the postcards, only touching their edges to avoid getting them wet. They were all black and white pictures of the city. They showed polished shoes on display in a shop window, a blimp passing over the tall buildings' spires, a cinema with electric lights and a glowing sign. Many of the cards showed people: an old man feeding pigeons from a bench, children kicking a ball across a road, lovers dancing down concrete stairs. Joe tucked the carrier bag under itself, so that the postcards were protected from the rain, then closed the bin bag over it as well.

Sonya sat watching Joe with the beginnings of a smile on her face, waiting for his reaction. She knew she'd picked well, but he wasn't sure she realised just how well. Joe knew that his desire to see the city ran counter to her way of thinking. She'd always believed in making their lives in the town as good as they could be, rather than taking on the risks of travelling out to look for answers.

It was hard for her, with Lily's illness hanging over them. She must've known that Joe was desperate to take any chance to head out towards the city. Despite it all, she accepted who he was, and showed him that with the gift. He took her wrist and pulled her towards him. She grinned, but moved her hand in front of her mouth to stop him from kissing her. She pointed to Joe's left.

He followed her direction, and saw Demeta holding a necklace of wooden beads that David had given her. She put them around her neck, then passed David a flat cardboard box. There was an image on the top of the box that David stared at, before suddenly laughing, a barking and loud sound, as if it had built up in pressure during all the time he'd spent sunken and unsmiling. Joe couldn't remember the last time he'd heard his father laugh.

David ripped open the top of the box, then lifted out circular rolls of copper and steel wire. Joe didn't know what they were, but David clearly did. He jumped in the air, gripped Demeta in a tight hug, then ran towards the town. Joe had never seen him with so much energy.

'What did she give him?' Joe asked Sonya.

The rain ran over Sonya's lips as she smiled. 'Guitar strings.'

Demeta moved around the bonfire and spoke to the Singing Family. The Family stood again, all four humming together. There were no words, only a simple and repeated rhythm that resonated in Joe's chest. Their humming grew louder, the pace slow but steady. Around the fire, Joe saw people getting to their feet and moving in time. It was the beginning of a dancing song.

Joe and Sonya stood, and she put her arms around his waist, swaying back and forth. Her hands slipped across the sides of his stomach, damp with the rain. They rocked gently together, waiting for the Singing Family's languishing rhythm to launch into the cacophony of sounds they bent their voices into, the drop where the real dancing began. The Family maintained their rhythm, keeping everyone trapped on the edge.

A metallic ringing matched the Singing Family's pitch. David stood by the fire, the newly-strung guitar strapped across his shoulders by a length of rope. He stood tall, like Grandad telling stories, taller than Joe had ever seen him. The Witch threw her hands forwards, tossing sparkling glitter into the bonfire. The flames caved inwards, becoming a layer of white-hot pressure over the wood.

All four members of the Singing Family altered their voices into a sound like drums. Each vocal beat sent a different-coloured flame shooting up from the pressurised white. As the flames leapt, the townspeople danced. Sonya clung onto Joe's waist and they spun through the crowd. Alice and Demeta bounced to the rhythm together, Sonya's mother grinning at the young couple as they passed. Mr Rajarshi shifted his body to the vibrations of the music, moving stiffly in time with the Librarian and Ms Winnipeg. Marco held Harvey's waist, then twirled him under one hand. Grandad demonstrated a shuffling dance to Tiger, the young boy guffawing at the criss-crossing steps.

The only person not dancing was David, who stood stationary with his guitar, having played nothing after that initial strike to start the Singing Family's vocal drumbeat. Even as they danced, the townspeople's eyes were continually drawn to him, waiting for him to play.

As the Singing Family's voices faded away, he began. He played with the fingers on his right hand curled like hooks, twanging notes from the thinner strings, while his thumb flicked against the heavier strings above them. His left hand danced like the townspeople, making different shapes across the fretboard. The sound was clearer and sharper than when the Singing Family sang, but similar in tone. It was as if the sound of singing had been trapped inside the metal wires, released only when David plucked them.

The white fire matched his music with upward bursts of colour. He drew a rapid series of sounds from the instrument, and as he did, the shooting flames clambered over one and other in a blazing multicoloured fountain.

The Singing Family joined in again, creating a beat behind David's music. The townspeople, who'd stopped in awe to listen to David play, began to dance once more. Joe remained motionless, watching his father as the others danced, until Sonya pulled him back into the movement.

The world, aided by Buddy's Sky, became a blur of coloured

flames, dancing figures, and falling rain. Only Sonya was in focus, no longer spinning but sliding back and forth with Joe. His eyes dropped down to her lips, then to the rainwater running down her neck. Joe thought of how her mouth would open and her breath would escape if he kissed where that water ran. Their eyes met, and they kissed on the lips, still dancing. David played a last chord and the Singing Family sang a harmony, then the tune fell to its end. The flames tumbled down from colourful fountains back into the subdued white.

'Shall we go to the forest?' Joe said in Sonya's ear.

'Let's dance a while first,' Sonya replied. 'There's no need to leave everyone yet. We're having so much fun.'

'Yeah,' Joe said, as David struck his fingers across the strings and the Singing Family began again. 'I guess we are.'

And they danced in the rain.

CHAPTER SEVENTEEN

Later, after the fire had died down to a bed of multicoloured embers, Joe and Sonya left the celebration together and went to the fallen forest. They kissed on their log, alcohol blurring the world around them. The rain was almost finished, only flickers of moisture left in the air.

Most people had already gone home to their shacks, though in the distance the Singing Family could still be heard along with the sound of David playing the guitar. Joe and Sonya's log was soft after the rainfall. Dampened, the wood smelled sweet. Joe imagined the forest must have smelled like this when the trees still stood, their green leaves blocking out the sun.

Their bodies were pressed comfortably together. Their chests pushed back and forth with their breathing, and drops of moisture trickled down their skin. Abruptly, Sonya pulled back, separating away from Joe.

'You still want to go to the city, don't you?' Sonya asked.

'Yeah, I do,' said Joe, taken aback by the suddenness of the question. 'I was going to talk to you about it tonight.'

'What were you going to say?'

'That night, in the van, there was another character from a story. Like the Boy Who Learned What Fear Was in the mountains, but this time I actually saw them. It was the Forest Woman, who the Prince wants to marry in the tale of How The City Came To Be. She told me that if I go to the city, Lily will get better. It felt like a dream, but I'm sure I was awake.'

There was something resigned about Sonya's expression. 'It's just like we said last time. You have to go. Otherwise, you'll always wonder if it would have helped Lily. I don't think you're going to be able to get a drifter to take you, though. How are you planning on getting there?'

'I'm not sure. Leigh said the same, that a drifter would never take me, but he suggested there was another way. I didn't know what he meant.'

Joe looked out towards Madera as it twinkled on the horizon. Was that light only from automated renewable systems, the same as allowed the drifters to charge their vans at the recycling centre, or was there more to it? He thought he spotted the dim headlights of an automated recycling truck heading out from the city towards the centre, but couldn't find them again. Then shock jolted through him as he realised what Leigh had been hinting at.

'There's a chance I could make a deal with a drifter to take me to the recycling centre, because they go there anyway,' Joe said, explaining it to himself as well as to Sonya. 'If I can get to the centre, I could ride a recycling truck into the city.'

Sonya moved away from him on their log. She wrapped her arms around her ribs, where Joe's fingertips had been moments before.

'I wouldn't expect you to come with me,' Joe added.

Sonya pushed her toes into the mud and stared up to where the moon broke through the clouds. Nearly half of it was in shadow. The next full moon was drawing closer, the time the Witch had given Lily growing shorter.

'I wouldn't,' Sonya said. 'Not after what happened last time, coming back and finding Buddy dead. I want to be here, helping the people who need me here. But if you didn't come back when you were supposed to, I'd never know if you were coming back at all. Years could pass. I could spend my whole life waiting for you.' There was no crack in Sonya's voice, though Joe knew there were waves of emotion held behind her words.

She looked down from the moon and met his eyes. 'How can you have a night like tonight, and want to leave? That's what I don't understand. I know your *reason* for going, that you think it might help Lily, but you've always *wanted* to leave, since long before all this happened. This morning – the funeral – showed how everyone here can come together and support each other. Then tonight there was food, and drinking, and gifts, and songs, and art, and stories, and dancing. What is it that you're looking for, that you can't find here?'

Joe couldn't think of any answer that he'd not already given. Sonya was satisfied with what they had, but there had been so much more in the world once.

'Is it me?' Sonya said, and Joe heard how she forced her voice to remain level. 'Am I not enough for you?'

'Sonya, I love you. More than the moon, the rain, the city. More than the stories, and the songs, and the dancing, all put together.'

'How can you say that?' Sonya asked, still forcibly calm. Joe wished she'd allow her control to break, and express the feelings to match her words. 'This place is everything I am. My work is the mountains, my family are the townspeople, my home is the town. I'm made from dancing around the fire in celebrations, from collecting on the mountains, from loving you here in the forest. These are the things I am, and they're not enough for you. So how can I be enough for you?'

Joe wanted to reach out and take her hand, but her arms were still tight across her chest. 'Those things are part of me, too. Going to the city wouldn't change that. If I do manage to get a lift to the recycling centre, and you stay here, I swear I'll come back to you.'

'You can't promise that. Even if you survived the journey, I wonder if the city would be enough for you. Sometimes I think you'd see it then just keep on walking.'

'Would I?' Joe snapped. 'Would I forget Lily, and why I'd gone?'

Sonya didn't rise to Joe's tone. 'If you didn't find anything for her, Lily would be your reason for continuing on. If you did, then travelling away would have helped, and you'd do it again.'

'You're right. If I had the chance, and it'd help people here, I'd leave the town again. I'd want to go. Is it so bad that I'd like to see more than just this one place?'

'There it is,' Sonya said. 'You want more. More than what's here. I understand. I'm not saying this to make you feel guilty or wrong. I just needed to be sure I understood.'

'No.' Joe stood up from the log, facing Sonya. 'You don't understand. It's not that I don't care enough or that you're not enough. There's a risk of me not coming back, but not because I'd decide to leave you behind. It would only be if something happened to me, the same risk we face every time we go on the mountains.'

Joe's stomach lurched as he spoke. The alcohol's taste had turned sour. 'Part of the reason we spend so many nights together in this forest is because each one might be our last. If you don't want to spend those nights with me anymore because I'm going to try to get to the city, then maybe it's me who's not enough for you.'

Sonya shook her head. 'We're getting this all mixed up. After the whisky and everything that's happened today. We shouldn't have talked about this now.'

Joe felt limp and heavy. 'When you gave me those postcards, I thought we were going to be okay. I thought we'd be good again.'

Sonya bent forward on the log, as if a great weight pressed down on her as well. 'It's because I can't sleep with you tonight.'

'What? You know it's fine if you don't want to–'

'I want to,' Sonya said. 'With everything that's happened, I just want to be as connected to you as possible. But I can't.'

'Why not?'

Sonya's eyebrows pushed down. She was working out the best way to tell him something. In the end, she just said it. 'Maya is pregnant.'

Joe's mind stopped, suddenly blank. He sat back down next to Sonya.

'She's known for a little while,' Sonya went on. 'But she hadn't told Buddy yet.'

'Why didn't she tell him?'

'Why would she? Most of the time, they're gone soon after you realise.'

Joe pressed his hands onto the soft texture of their log, feeling it imprint on his palms. 'Didn't they use condoms?'

'The condoms are too old. They've been up there in the heat on the mountains.'

'Yeah, I know. But they've always worked for us.'

Sonya said nothing, letting his words linger in the air between them.

'I'm not sure they do anything at all,' Sonya said, finally breaking the silence. Still, she wouldn't look at him. Joe felt a chill, as if rainwater ran along the underside of his skin.

'Why didn't you tell me?' he asked.

Sonya turned towards him and spoke matter-of-factly. 'The same reason that Maya didn't tell Buddy. The same reason the women never say when they're pregnant. Pregnancies don't last.'

'Were you, you know, certain that you were?'

There was no proper way of testing pregnancy in the town, although some went to the Witch to ask. Due to malnutrition, women's blood didn't flow as regularly as it was supposed to, so menstruation was useless as a measure.

'There were two times when I was certain. The beginnings of the baby came out with my blood.'

'Sonya,' he whispered, and opened his arms towards her, his immediate instinct to hold her. She showed no sign of wanting to be held, and his arms were left dangling awkwardly. 'I wish you'd told me.'

Sonya took Joe's hands and lowered them onto the damp bark, laying her fingers over his. 'It would have only hurt you. I never wanted that.'

'I could've helped. You didn't have to go through that alone.'

'I had my mother, and the other women in the town. We always deal with it among the women. It's hard sometimes, but it's just life.'

It was as though she'd pulled away the ground and revealed a system of mines under the town. There was a whole world in his home that Joe knew nothing of.

'Do the other men know?' Joe asked.

'They have a way of knowing, without knowing.' Sonya rubbed her thumb along his finger. 'The same as you. You knew the last pregnancy that made it to birth was Tiger and Lily, and that the condoms were too old to be reliable. You knew that on the rare times you could see a woman was pregnant, she didn't speak openly about it. Eventually she wasn't pregnant anymore, and there was no child.'

Joe shook his head, which ached with whisky.

'Look at it like this,' Sonya said. 'You must've known there were pregnancies you were never told about. But you didn't think about it, so you never considered who might have been pregnant, or when. You never thought about the fact that a woman you were speaking to could've been pregnant in the past, or currently carrying a child.'

'You're right.' Joe tried to collect his jumbled thoughts. 'I knew there were pregnancies I didn't hear about. I never thought, never even suspected, that it might have been you.'

'Don't feel guilty. My mother said it's always been like this, in a way.' Sonya laughed a little, then saw how far from laughing Joe was. Her look changed to one of concern. 'I didn't tell you this to give you pain. I wanted you to know why I can't sleep with you. If Maya's baby survives, and they both make it through the birth, she'll be looking after it alone.'

Sonya took her hands from Joe's and placed them together on her lap. 'I look at her and I can't help but think what if that was me? What if we sleep together, and you leave, and I have a child without you here? I can be strong. I can keep going through birthing almost-children, through knowing every day that someone I love could be lost on the mountains, through Lily being ill and Buddy being dead, but I couldn't go through that. Not by myself.'

'Sonya.' Joe felt as if he was calling out to her. The space between them felt as wide and dark as the gap between the earth and the moon.

'It's okay. It's just how things are. You have to go, for Lily and for yourself. And while you wait for a drifter to arrive and take you away, I need to not spend my nights here in the forest with you. Even if we said we wouldn't, we'd end up sleeping together.' Sonya stood up. 'I'll see you tomorrow, on the mountains,' she said and walked away towards the town.

The distant music had long since stopped. Joe sat alone in the fallen forest for a long time, until the moisture was gone from the air and from his skin, and the night was dry once more.

CHAPTER EIGHTEEN

The next day on the mountains, things were almost normal between Joe and Sonya. When they saw Tiger nodding off as he searched through a bin bag, exhausted from the celebration night, they laughed together. They discovered strange objects and called each other over to see them.

Joe found old speakers with their mesh torn away, revealing cracked tubing, and Sonya found a notebook filled with a child's drawings of giraffes and houses. Joe noticed that Sonya hadn't drunk for a while and handed her a bottle of water. Before Joe even realised his muscles were aching, Sonya encouraged him to take a rest break.

However, throughout the day they never touched. Not even once. The comfort of her fingertips on his arm, of their hands briefly clasped, of stopping for a moment to kiss and think of the forest, was gone. At the end of the day, they climbed down the mountains, and neither of them suggested meeting in the fallen forest that night.

While Joe would desperately miss the time they spent together amongst the trees, he understood Sonya's decision. He wouldn't try to tempt her back there. He had watched the desert throughout the day for an incoming drifter, and still planned to barter for a lift to the recycling centre, then ride a recycling truck all the way to the city. He didn't want to make his leaving any harder for her than it had to be.

When David stepped into their shack, late after the sun had set behind the mountains, he seemed surprised to see Joe sitting inside. Grandad was absent, having been asked to visit Rose's shack. Lily was worsening. Before, her constant sleep had at least been peaceful. Now, she was tossed around by nightmares like a boat in a storm.

Rose had previously been able to make Lily swallow water with small amounts of food mixed in, but because of the tossing and turning she was struggling to give her anything. The hope was that if Grandad's stories could reach her, perhaps they could make her dreams less cruel. Until Grandad returned, it was just Joe and his father.

'I thought you might go to the forest tonight.' There was a question within David's statement. By not asking directly, he'd given Joe the option of ignoring it.

'Sonya doesn't want to see me there at the moment.'

David sat down on the stool next to him and waited for him to continue.

'It doesn't make sense,' Joe said. 'Why do I love someone who wants to stay, when I want to go? Why does Sonya love me, when all I talk about is leaving, and she loves this place? It's like nothing's put together right.'

David sighed. Not his usual world-weary sigh, but one that was bittersweet and followed by an almost nostalgic half-smile. 'I can't tell you why. I also don't know why we sometimes love people who don't love us. I don't know why we have a feeling deep in our chests, like an ancient instinct, that if two people are in love, it'll be enough to overcome any differences, when so often it isn't. I don't know why love hurts so much when it's going wrong, when it goes wrong so easily.'

There was a new sort of sadness in David's eyes. It wasn't tired or dull. His eyes were bright and filled with memory. 'The pain of a broken heart – that's normal, that's human. It's part of the way the world's supposed to be. But the pain that's caused by everything in this town that makes you so angry, like the shacks we live in and the landfill we call mountains, that pain shouldn't exist. It's the product of something broken in the world that needs to be fixed.

'But working out how to love people and be loved, with all the hurt that comes with it, that's a big part of what living is. I worried this place might take that away from you, but it hasn't. You're still living, Joe, even here. It hurts, but at least it's the right sort of pain.'

David spoke with a confidence that Joe had seldom heard in him. It reminded Joe of how he was when he held the guitar the night before.

'It was amazing hearing you play guitar last night,' Joe said. 'I'm so glad Demeta found the strings. I can't believe I might never have heard how a guitar actually sounds.'

David scratched his thumb across the fingertips of his left hand, which he'd used to press the metal strings against the fretboard. 'When I lived in the city and first started playing guitar, it hardened the ends of my fingers. They calloused, so it was easier to hold down the strings. But here, even after so long without playing, my fingertips were already hard from collecting on the mountains. If you'd like me to teach you how to play, your hands will already be ready.'

When Grandad came through the shack's door, Joe was standing with the guitar secured across his shoulders by the rope-strap, shifting his fingers into the chord shapes David was describing. Before he strummed a chord, David would step forward and adjust one or two of his fingers, sliding them onto the correct frets. Then Joe would strike across the strings as his father had shown him, the sound reverberating in the shack.

Grandad sat on a stool and watched as Joe attempted to

go through the chords he'd been taught. David let him try to puzzle out his misplaced fingers by himself, before offering corrections. When Joe played a chord properly, the sound was clear as glass.

It was difficult to believe that the sound of guitars was once common. The instrument seemed imbued with power as the wood vibrated against Joe's chest, possessed with a magic that was now mostly lost from the world.

'Emotion and music are one and the same,' Grandad said, while Joe ran through the chords. 'It's like they're made of the same material. They ring together.'

Grandad looked with proud eyes at David. 'Anyone can trap emotion in words, but there's always a gap between what we say and what other people hear. The feeling gets muddled and diluted and changed along the way. For musicians there is no vessel. They play the emotion itself to us, so it resonates in our hearts and through our blood.'

The next few evenings followed the same pattern. After a day spent collecting and watching out for an approaching drifter, Joe would say goodbye to Sonya at the bottom of the mountains, then go home to wait for his father. David would return after sunset, and they'd play guitar together. They'd start by going through what Joe had already learned, before moving on to something new.

David was endlessly patient. Joe often misplaced his fingers on the fretboard or hit more strings than he should, and the sound jarred in the air. His father, whose hands knew the music well and would never so much as bend it out of place, only smiled.

He'd make Joe take a deep breath before playing again, and said that each broken chord or missed note was a step forwards. When Joe grew frustrated, David asked him to play something that he'd previously struggled with but now was able to manage.

Knowing that Joe was waiting for him each evening, David started coming home earlier, beating the setting sun so that they would have longer to play together. Grandad – who was finding collecting on the mountains more tiring than he once did – stayed in the shack, too, rather than taxing his stiff legs to go out visiting people. When someone wanted a story, they came to him.

The only visit Grandad made was to Lily, once a day, who was still being rocked by nightmares. When people came to hear a story, they'd often stay afterwards to listen to Joe and David practising.

The Librarian told Joe he was looking forward to hearing him play at the next celebration. Marco said he'd been keeping an eye out for guitars on the mountains, so that Joe and his father could have one each. Some people started calling the two of them the Musicians. Joe wasn't sure he'd earned the title, but at least he was learning and improving.

The moon turned each night through the shack's window-hole. It became a white fingernail, then not visible at all, the time the Witch had given Lily to recover half spent. It continued to turn, coming back into view. Still Lily stayed in her deep sleep, and still no drifter arrived.

One night, Sonya and Demeta came to hear one of Grandad's stories, and to listen to Joe and David play. That night, Joe's shack felt like the forest, a similar comfort between the five of them as he and Sonya had shared amongst the fallen trees. Each time Joe finished a tune, Sonya demanded another, making David and Demeta laugh.

After Joe had played everything he knew twice round and they'd all applauded, David took the guitar. Sonya sat with Joe on his mattress, while Demeta and Grandad sat on the stools, and they watched David play. Sonya laid her head on Joe's shoulder.

Listening to his father's music, Joe felt he'd found something worth doing. Being the Musician, with Sonya by his side, and he and his father's relationship better than it had ever been, was close to perfect. When Sonya and Demeta reluctantly departed, arranging to visit again in three nights' time, Joe almost told Sonya that he'd stay, that even if a drifter came, he'd stay.

The next morning, Joe was woken by the noise of wheels on the dry earth outside. It was before sunrise, the shack still dark. The noise slowed then stopped, replaced by the sound of Grandad's wheezing snore.

'A drifter's arrived,' David whispered from the next mattress.

'Yeah,' Joe replied. He stood up and went to the window-hole. He couldn't see the drifter's vehicle from there, but the shacks further down the hill were framed by bright headlights. The light struck upwards from the sheet metal roofs, shooting beams into the sky.

'You have another plan to get to the city, don't you?' his father asked.

'I want to bargain for a lift to the recycling centre. From there I can ride one of the trucks to the city.'

'You should speak to the drifter now. You can avoid the crowds,' David said. 'Take the guitar with you. Keep practising, and working out what sounds good.'

'It's better off here, so people can listen to you play. I can't even tune it properly yet.' Joe wished the drifter had waited just a few more days, so that he could have played guitar for Sonya again. He leaned out of the window-hole, and felt anxiety rising in his throat. 'I don't have a choice. I have to go. For Lily.'

'Don't tell yourself you don't have a choice.' David joined him at the window-hole. 'That only ends in regret. When it finally came to us leaving the city, your mother changed her mind. She said she wasn't sure that we should go. I told her, and myself, that we had no choice anymore. I said that so if we walked out and found nothing, if baby Joe starved, then it wouldn't be my fault. The truth is, it was a choice to stay in the first place, and a choice to go when we did.'

Joe studied David's face. His father was staring up at the black shapes of the mountains behind the vehicle's lights, as if he could see the past within them. He had never told Joe any of this before.

David looked down from the mountains. 'If things work out badly from a decision which we consider and acknowledge that we're making, then at least we know we had our reasons. We can reflect on the past, understand that we decided based on what we knew at the time, and make peace with ourselves. Whatever you choose, know that you're choosing it.'

For a moment they were both silent, standing side by side at the window-hole, as Grandad snored behind them. The headlights felt like a beacon, calling Joe down. He thought of the Forest Woman, telling him that travelling to the city would save Lily. He hadn't told his father about the Forest Woman and the Boy Who Learned What Fear Was. He wished he had, because it was all too much to explain now.

'I'm going to go,' Joe said. 'I'll see which drifter it is, and if they'll take me.'

'That makes sense,' David replied. 'I hope it's good news.'

As Joe walked out through the door, he didn't know what good news would be. He went to the dry stream and climbed in, heading down towards the stone well and the mountains. As he neared his destination, the inside of the trench seemed to grow darker. The headlights shone above the dirt banks and hid the dawn sky from view.

When Joe stepped out from the bottom of the stream, the headlights were pointed towards him, two miniature suns that burned colours into his eyes. He squinted as he approached, and saw the vehicle was a car, with two silhouettes standing next to it. He walked beyond the glare of the headlights, and the figures shifted into focus. There was the Mayor, in his corduroy jacket, and a drifter. She was a wide-shouldered woman, taller than Joe, with asymmetrical hair shaved short above her right ear.

'The name's Niv, stop it with that *drifter* nonsense,' she was saying to the Mayor, then she spotted Joe approaching. 'Hi there! I'm not trading, just passing through. Will be back in two or three weeks, stocked-up. Thought I'd let you lot know on my way past.'

Joe had spoken to Niv when she'd come through the town before. They'd always got along well. He knew that if he just asked her for what he wanted, he'd get a straight answer. There was no need to hide it from the Mayor anymore either. Everyone knew that he and Sonya had tried to force Leigh to take them to the city.

'It's not trade I'm looking for,' Joe said. 'It's travel.'

Niv's laugh was a bellow, bouncing off the mountains. 'Ha! Hello, Joe. I didn't recognise you in the dark. You've grown taller, though I'd hoped you'd turn out handsome. I was warned about you on the way here. Heard you stole a cowboy's gun.'

The Mayor glowered at Joe.

'No need to give him that look, Mr Mayor. Leigh's living a fantasy, imagining he's the quickest draw in the Wild West. Good job giving him a scare, Joey! You know I'm not taking you to the city, right?'

'I want to go to the recycling centre. I can make my own way to the city from there.'

The Mayor shook his head and let out an exasperated sound, but Niv ignored him and said, 'I'm on my way to the centre now.'

'I'll pay to travel with you. I've got a sack and a half of collections that you can have.'

'You'll be planning to ride a recycling truck to Madera?' Niv asked.

Joe nodded.

'And you've heard the stories about what it's like on the way to the city?'

'I have. I still want to go.' Joe had more reason than ever to believe there might be some truth in those tales, but it didn't change his plans.

'First time in years someone's asked to travel with me. People used to ask all the time, and I used to say no all the time.' Niv paused, considering it. 'You don't look so tough. No offence. But you were willing to go up against Leigh to get yourself to the city.'

Another silence, as Niv looked over him. The moment stretched out, and Joe felt a tension inside his chest, like his fate hung in the balance.

'You're trouble,' she said. 'So I'd probably be doing everyone a favour by just taking you to the recycling centre, and seeing you off. And I'll tell you the truth, Joey. I'm bored as hell. I've been driving the same routes for too long, with nothing ever changing. You're at least interesting. Can you bring down those collections for me, and be ready to go for sunrise?'

Joe looked up and saw the sky's blue was losing its depth. He didn't have long to pack or to tell Sonya what he was doing. If he didn't leave now, there might not be another drifter before the next full moon.

'Yeah, I can do that.'

'Don't be late. I won't wait around.'

Joe thanked her, shaking on the deal. He turned to walk away, but felt a hand on his shoulder. It was the Mayor.

'No tricks, Joseph. The drifters supply the town with food. It's important we behave accordingly around them.'

Joe was aware of the space within him where anger would have usually flared up, but there was nothing there. The Mayor was right.

'No tricks,' Joe said. 'Not this time.'

David was waiting for him in the shack, Grandad still asleep. Joe explained that he planned to leave with Niv. David nodded, though his face was lined with worry. He didn't question Joe, or attempt to talk him out of it. Instead, he offered to help pack.

He gave Joe a thin blanket large enough to cover him, a metal pan, a bowl and spoon, and a magnifying glass for starting fires. Joe decided against taking paper and wood with him. If he couldn't find anything to burn, he'd soak the oats and eat them raw. David dug out several plastic bottles from his own collections and filled them with water, suggesting they'd be lighter to carry than glass.

They put everything into one of the cloth sacks, which David then loaded with more oats and potatoes than he kept behind for himself and Grandad. When Joe protested, David pointed out that they'd be able to buy more when the next drifter arrived, whereas Joe might not get the chance to replenish his supplies.

'Let me help in this way,' David added. 'It's the only way I can.'

David put a last small water bottle into the bum bag he'd given Joe at the celebration, then clipped the bag around Joe's waist. He said that he'd wake Grandad and take care of carrying everything down to the car if Joe wanted to go and see Sonya before he left. Joe thanked his father and headed out.

The sky was pale, a touch of yellow light behind the mountains. The few stars that remained were faint and almost gone. Joe had a sudden feeling that if he left the town, he'd never see the stars again. He'd be some other place and the sun would set and night would fall. The sky would be entirely black, empty all the way into infinity.

Joe stopped at the edge of the dry stream, which he needed to cross to get to Sonya's. Rose and the twins' shack was on the other side. Tiger sat against the door, fiddling with a piece of string in his hand.

Lily's frightened moans carried out from the window-hole, some nightmare distressing her. Tiger didn't react, focused on the string between his fingers. There were bags beneath his eyes, similar to those that Rose always had. They made him look older than he was.

Joe's doubts left him. He took his father's advice, and acknowledged that he was making the decision to go. Even if he came to regret it, he could look back on this moment – Tiger sitting outside the shack while Lily moaned within – and know why he'd made this choice.

I still want to see the city and find out what's happened there, Joe acknowledged to himself. *I always have. But that's not why I'm going. I'm going for Lily, and Tiger too. I just hope the Forest Woman was right, and I really do find a way of waking Lily up.*

He knew that he couldn't go to Sonya. It wasn't long until sunrise, and he didn't think he could say goodbye to her quickly. He wasn't sure he could say goodbye to her at all, not without losing his resolve and letting Niv leave without him. If Sonya found it hard to see him go and offered to come, he might be weak enough to accept. He knew that wouldn't be right either. He climbed into the dry stream and headed down towards Niv's car.

When Joe reached the bottom of the stream, the sun was rising over the top of the mountains. Niv had turned off her headlights, and stood talking to the Mayor and Ms Winnipeg. David and Grandad were already there with Joe's supplies and the collections he'd promised Niv. As Joe walked over, he heard Ms Winnipeg asking for news of the last drifter.

'Leigh's fine, though not so cocky since meeting our boy here.' Niv nodded towards Joe, her hair flicking over the shaved part of her head. Ms Winnipeg startled at seeing him behind her. Joe hoped his father and grandfather didn't notice her fear.

'Did you speak to Sonya?' David asked.

'No. I couldn't.'

David winced, feeling Joe's pain. 'Is there anything you'd like me to tell her?'

'Tell her…' Joe said, and the words caught in his throat. It seemed like adding insult to injury, to leave without speaking to her and then say that he loved her. 'Tell her I'll try my hardest to come back.'

Grandad stepped forward. Joe was surprised to see his eyes were moist with tears.

'Be safe, Little Joe,' Grandad said, his voice cracking. 'And make it home. There's more stories to tell, and music to play.'

Joe told Grandad that he would, and then said his goodbyes to them both. As he did, he couldn't help but look over his father and grandfather's shoulders towards the town. The mountains' shadows stretched over the shacks, the sun only touching the highest of the townspeople's homes. He was watching for Sonya, appearing from the bottom of the stream or out from between the shacks. As he hugged David and Grandad, as Niv put his supplies and collections into the boot, as he climbed into the passenger seat, he still watched for her.

Niv started to drive, and Joe lifted his hand in farewell. David's expression was stoic, while tears ran down Grandad's face. They both raised their hands in return, even Ms Winnipeg and the Mayor waving Joe goodbye. The four of them grew small as Niv drove on. Then the town grew small, and eventually the mountains did as well. Joe still looked back, watching somehow for Sonya.

CHAPTER NINETEEN

'I nearly didn't wait for you,' Niv said. The car rushed through the flatlands, the mountains already far behind them. 'But I thought I'd need a big man as a bodyguard.'

Joe snorted. He wasn't in the mood for jokes. He'd been mostly silent for the journey so far, resisting Niv's attempts to start conversation.

'You're very serious,' she observed. 'You're not a poet, are you? I lived with a poet once. It was terrible.'

Joe didn't reply. He sat in a cramped position, pushed forward by bin bags on the seats behind him. The bags themselves were taken from the mountains, but their content was from the gardens. Joe could tell by the thick green scent wafting out from them.

'Hold tight, serious boy,' Niv said. She twisted the steering wheel, swerving the car and crashing Joe into the door.

'What are you doing?' Joe exclaimed, pulling himself back onto his seat.

'I said hold tight,' she retorted, and swerved again. This time Joe grabbed the headrest quickly enough to stay on his seat. He yanked his safety belt across his chest.

'Safety first,' Niv said cheerfully, and swung the car just in time to prevent Joe from fastening the clasp. His shoulder hit the door and the belt twanged out of his hands.

'Stop it!' Joe pulled the safety belt on and clicked it into place.

'We've got a freeloader,' Niv replied, raising her eyebrows at the rear-view mirror. Joe glimpsed the black shape of a bird as they swerved again. He turned in his seat. Through a gap in the bin bags, he could see a crow perched on the boot of the car. Each time Niv swung the car, the crow beat its wings but somehow managed to cling on. Its glittering eyes and long beak were fixed on Joe.

Niv put her foot down, driving in S shapes as she they accelerated. The crow flapped wildly, then finally lost its grip. It hit the ground, spinning along in the dirt, and collapsed in a crumpled heap. A trail of black feathers spun after the car, the crow left behind with its wings broken at abrupt angles. Its head stared after them, its neck snapped. There was nothing in the town that was said to give worse luck than killing a crow. Joe could only hope that the Witch's power didn't extend this far.

'Persistent bugger,' Niv said. 'Must've been after something in the car.'

'It was,' Joe said. 'Me.'

Niv glanced sideways at Joe. He'd almost forgotten how the crows watched him, and the owl he'd seen when he and Sonya left with Leigh.

'The Witch in our town has a connection with animals. The crows flock around her shack, and perch on her spine. She told me they were afraid of me, because I have a destiny. Since then, I've seen her crows watching me, and when I first left the town, an owl followed the van.'

Niv looked at him for a moment, then burst out into her explosive laugh. She slapped the wheel for emphasis, her laugh getting progressively louder.

'You don't believe me,' Joe said, when her laughter had subsided.

'Oh, I believe you.' Niv squinted through tears, a big smile on her face. 'I just find you funny. Oh, birds are frightened of me! I was chased through the town by a caterpillar! A dog barked to me about destiny, then licked its bum!'

'Very funny. It's the truth.'

'I'm sure it is. That's why it's funny!' Niv wiped her eyes with the back of her hand. 'You've got to laugh, Joey. What about the town, what did you laugh about there?'

'I don't want to talk about the town.'

Niv poked Joe's arm hard. 'I let you come with me so I'd have someone to talk to, not for you to sulk. You want to be mopey, you can walk.'

'There was this girl, Sonya,' Joe said reluctantly. 'We laughed at everything. We laughed at the moon.'

'You sound like a poet again. None of that in my car.'

Joe let out an exasperated sigh.

'You'll learn not to take me so personally,' she said. 'What's funny about the moon?'

'I was jumping over logs in the fallen forest. I said I was practising jumping, so I could reach the moon one day. You had to be us, and be there, for it to be funny.'

'That's often the way,' Niv said. 'The moon's not a bad thing to laugh at. Now this girl, she can always make you laugh, as long as you can see the moon.'

'Who's the poet now?'

'Ha! I like you, Joe. You can be fun when you're not moping.'

Joe couldn't keep the sadness out of his voice. 'I know I can. It's dangerous living in the town. A young girl got sick recently, and she's not been able to wake up since. A boy my age was killed in an avalanche.'

The smile that had been flickering at the side of Niv's mouth tightened.

'But despite the danger, we often have fun. We really do. When it rains, we have celebrations, and it's like all the fear washes away. We listen to stories, and music, and drink and eat and dance together. It's like the celebration is all there is in the world, and all there needs to be.' Joe looked over at Niv, waiting for a poet comment. She only nodded for him to continue.

'So yeah, I guess I know I can be happy. And have fun.' Joe was usually the first to see everything that was wrong with the town. Now, without Sonya by his side to remind him, it felt important that he remembered the good things for himself.

'Being a drifter, there's one thing I've learned.' Niv smiled again, a more natural expression for her. 'Maybe I should have learned two or three, but I'm no good at learning. Too stubborn. What I've learned is that everything changes. Everything gets left behind in the end, whether we stay or go. So hold on to your celebrations, and your moon jokes, and anything else that makes you smile. As long as you can smile at it, you've still got it.'

With that, she burst into thunderous laughter. Even though Niv hadn't really said anything funny, Joe found himself laughing as well. It went on for a long time, both of them cackling away as the car sped across the desert. As their laughter reached its peak, tears rolled down Joe's cheeks and Niv was slapping the wheel again.

When their laughter finally died down, they settled into

telling each other funny stories. Niv told Joe the dirty sea rhymes she'd learned from the fisherpeople, and about when she'd spilled seeds from the gardens in her back seat and later found the shoots of a tomato plant growing there.

Joe told her Grandad's comedy tale of a man looking for a violin, and described how he and Sonya had once lost the twins on the mountains and ended up chasing after them, only to find that Lily had been following Tiger, who'd been following a frog.

Their laughter often returned, building up so they had to stop telling their stories until they'd composed themselves. Joe decided that this was one of the times that Niv had been talking about, that he'd later look back on and smile.

'There it is,' Niv said, pointing ahead. The recycling centre was a grey concrete cube jutting out from the flat desert. The car bumped up onto the road, a stretch of surviving asphalt that led up to the recycling centre and then disappeared after the building in a jagged end.

'You'd think they'd have made it look good,' Niv muttered. 'Supposed to be environmental and all. But no. Just a big stupid square.'

They passed a small shelter at the side of the road, with paper adverts still on display behind cracked glass. There was a metal bar across the middle of the shelter, screws sticking out where seats had once been.

'That's the old bus stop,' Niv said. 'Used to be able to get to the city from there.'

They drove past street lights, which had their bulbs removed and wires dangling down from their fittings. Between the street lights, there were taller wooden poles with pairs of horizontal planks at their peak.

'They're telegraph poles,' Niv said, as Joe craned his neck to look up at them through the window. 'They used to be joined by black wires. In some places out in the desert they still are. They're beautiful with the wires swooping between them.'

The road, the bus stop, the street lights and the telegraph poles were all relics from the time of the city, when everything used to be connected together. The grey-cube recycling centre grew closer, and Joe saw that there was something built up against its side. It looked like a miniature version of one of the mountains, a mix of colours pushed into the concrete wall. Then he smelled, faintly, that familiar rotten scent leaking into the car.

'Smells like home?' Niv asked, responding to Joe's crinkled nose.

'I'd hoped that nowhere else smelled like home.'

Like its larger counterparts, the small mountain's waste was mostly contained in bin bags. Their plastic rippled to the side, caught in a gentle wind. An orange carrier bag separated and drifted through the air, before floating down and tumbling across the desert. Plastic bottles and food packaging spilled out from the small mountain's base, along with computer monitors, smartphones and other discarded electrical items. A bitter image came to Joe's mind, of this miniature landfill someday bleeding purple-green into the ground, and leaving another stain on the earth.

'It's where we throw stuff the machines won't take,' Niv commented. They passed the small mountain and drove alongside the front of the recycling centre. The concrete cube had glass windows going up several levels, and large double-doors with a green star printed across them.

The only buildings Joe had seen before were the shacks in the town. The difference that immediately struck him was how solid the centre was. He could tear the sheet metal roof from a shack, or kick down the wooden-panelled walls. The recycling centre was concrete, all one piece in the correct shape. A hundred men couldn't bring it down. When the town was long gone, the shacks had all fallen, and all that was useful from the mountains had been collected, even then the centre would remain.

Niv turned around the corner of the building, driving into the charging station, its lime-green roof attached to the recycling centre's wall. As they swung in, Joe could just make out the edge of the solar panels on top of the roof. The six charging points were round metal poles with small screens on their front, and different coloured charging cables looped up on their sides. Niv parked next to one and turned off the car. She took a leather wallet out of her pocket, then drew out a plastic card.

'Do you know what this is, Joey?' she said, showing him the card.

'I have no idea.'

'This is what lets drifters be drifters. A card from an old scheme to encourage people to use electric vehicles and recycle, that gives you credit to recharge in exchange for putting recycling into the machines. The whole automated system was cutting edge. The driverless recycling trucks were seen as quite impressive at the time.'

'Were you part of the scheme?'

Niv chuckled. 'The card was in the car when I stole it to get out of the city. I won't tell you how I got the key. Ancient history now.'

Niv clicked her door open, a slight smile on her face as she got out of the car. Joe got out too, looking at the screen on the nearest charging point. It was strange to see a screen actually working. It displayed an image of an ID card that looked like the one Niv had just shown him.

Joe had forgotten the cooling effect of the car's darkened windows. The heat raised sweat on his shoulders, despite the roof over the charging points. There was a line where the shadow ended, beyond which the ground blazed white in the sun. Niv lifted two bin bags from the back seat, soil dripping from the rips in their plastic. She looked out over the flatlands behind the centre, in the direction of the city, but there was nothing there.

'You can help me with this,' she said, and held the two bags out to Joe. 'We can keep an eye out for a truck approaching. We'll see when your ride's on its way.'

The bags were heavy, but Joe was used to that. Niv picked up two more from the car, then headed towards the blazing line of sunshine, with Joe following after her. When Niv crossed out of the shade, Joe heard her gasp, and he braced himself for the heat. It slammed down on him as he stepped into the sun, his vision filling with white.

Joe shut his eyes and breathed deeply, forcing the dizziness to fade. He opened his eyes again and walked after Niv, the brightness aching in his head. When he rode the truck to the city, he'd be out in this heat with only his blanket to use for shade. He didn't know how long the trucks' automated route to Madera took, but he doubted it was a quick journey. Joe felt his stomach turn. He could be spending days in the sun.

The green star emblazoned on the centre's double doors split as they entered the building. Stepping out of the direct sunlight felt almost like entering the stream during a celebration. The room was open and wide, with concrete pillars holding up the ceiling. Their footsteps echoed on the smooth stone floor. A series of hatches ran the length of the far wall, organised by various coloured lids. Niv led Joe to the left, stopping at one of the green lids.

'Garden waste and compost,' she said. 'This is us.'

Niv lifted the lid, revealing a chute inside that dropped down into darkness. She untied one of the bin bags and poured out its contents. Dead plants, dried and losing their colour, fell into the chute and slid down. At the end of the bag, a smattering of soil stuck on the metal, which Niv brushed down after the rest.

There was a whirring sound inside the machine, then Joe heard a rumbling move upwards in the wall behind it. The rumbling stopped, and the machine beeped. Niv scanned her plastic card under a red light and there was another beep. She ducked down and opened a smaller door below the green lid. The square space behind the door was empty.

'This is where it spits what it won't take,' Niv said. 'Never have much problem with that in garden waste. It takes pretty much everything.'

As they emptied the compost from the rest of the bags into the same chute, Niv explained how the machines gave charging credit based on the weight and type of the recycling going in. They went back and forth to the car, carrying more of the bags inside and sweating in the hot sun. Each time they went out, they checked the desert for an approaching truck, but saw none.

Most of the bin bags contained decaying plants, though one was filled with broken plastic boxes that the gardeners had previously been using for storage. Niv emptied the plastic boxes into the first of the orange-lidded chutes. There was a clattering in the lower compartment, then the wall rumbled and the machine beeped as usual. Niv opened the compartment, over half of the boxes rejected.

'Wrong sort of plastic,' she said. 'We'll try them in the next one.'

They moved on to the next orange lid, dropping the boxes in. Again it took some, and rejected the rest. They carried the surplus across to the next machine and dropped it into the chute. They continued on until the last machine, with three boxes left. It took two, rejecting one.

'Happens sometimes,' Niv said, taking the box out of the lower compartment. 'They don't accept all plastics. It's for the pile outside. Can you take it?'

She handed it to him. The box was falling apart, one side cracked and barely attached.

'Is it worth trying it through the machines again?' Joe asked, looking down at its broken shape.

'Nah. It'll just get rejected again.' She looked at Joe, noticing his discomfort. 'I don't know what's going on in the city, Joey, but I don't think anyone's waiting for our recycling.

It's all just piling up at the other end anyway.'

As they walked out of the centre, Niv handed Joe the box. She asked him to throw it on the pile, while she got the collections he'd traded her from the car. Joe looked down at the broken plastic and could think of no use for it, no sensible purpose to save it. He went to the fledgling mountain against the centre's wall. The stink was there, not as strong as the mountains at home, but still present. Either the waste had carried the smell with it, or something was rotting beneath the surface.

Joe hesitated with the plastic box in his hand. He didn't want to add to the beginnings of a mountain. The heat was sweltering, and his head was starting to ache again. He couldn't stay standing there in the sun, and there was no point bringing the box back to Niv. He flung the plastic box onto the small mountain, and turned away.

He met Niv going through the centre's doors with the sack and a half of collections he'd given her, and she told him that was everything from the car. They emptied the recycling from Joe's collections into the chutes, moving across the different coloured lids for paper, plastic, electronics and the rest. Niv told Joe to leave anything that the machines wouldn't take in the bottom of the sacks, for her to sort through later and see if there was anything she could sell.

When they were finished, they went back to the car.

Joe picked up his cloth sack of supplies, while Niv plugged the charging cable into a port behind the rear door. She scanned her ID card in front of the screen charging point. An intermittent buzzing sound came from within the metal pole, which Niv frowned at, but then she looked again at the screen and then a dial on her car, and seemed satisfied. She led Joe back inside, going past the chutes and through a small side door. They walked through a narrow hallway with a staircase leading up.

'What's up the stairs?' Joe asked.

'There's recycling machinery on the first floor, then nothing. It used to be offices, but everything's been taken. It's empty all the way up.'

Once, on the mountains, Joe had found a round papery structure almost the size of his chest. When he and Sonya cracked it open, it was filled with hundreds of little holes, all folded in on each other. He'd taken it to his father and grandfather, to ask if they knew what it was. It was a beehive, Grandad had told him, a natural one. It was dried out, and the bees were long gone from it. David said he hadn't seen a bee in years, though he'd heard they had them in the gardens. He said they were magnificent creatures with tiny golden hair, but the way he said it was sad. The recycling centre, with its hollowed rooms, was the human equivalent of the beehive. Like the bees, everything they'd made to fill the structure had shrivelled away, and all the workers were gone.

Joe followed Niv into a small room with a door and window that faced out of the rear of the centre. The room had a worn beige carpet, darkened indents revealing where there had once been furniture. Through the window they could see rows of large steel containers, which Niv said were transported by the recycling trucks. Their metal sides bore the same green star as the centre's doors. They were topped by solar panels, that must have been used to charge the self-driving trucks' batteries during the day time. Plastic tubes sloped down from the floor above, slotting into apertures at the back of each container.

'Perfect timing,' Niv said, and pointed towards the desert. There was a black dot in the distance, growing gradually larger. A truck was coming.

CHAPTER TWENTY

Niv leaned against the wall in the small room, and Joe joined her. The truck was still far off yet, and they had some time to wait. She opened a water bottle she'd taken from her car and offered it towards him.

'Thanks, but that's okay. I've got my own.' He reached down towards his cloth sack, and Niv kicked his hand.

'Hey!' Joe cradled his stinging fingers.

'Take the polite offer,' Niv said with a grin. 'Going to be easier for me to refill than it will be for you.'

Niv held out the water. Joe kept his distance while he took it, pretending to be afraid of her boots. She mock-kicked at him, and they both laughed.

'If only it was a cold beer, eh?' Niv said, after he had a swig and passed her back the bottle.

'I've never had beer. I've seen the cans and bottles on the mountains. Is it good?'

'Stuff I used to drink?' Niv smiled wistfully and shook her head. 'Nah. It was crap. Really cheap lager. My mates used to call it piss-water. But I tell you what, back when the weather wasn't always the same and you had to wait for summer for the hot days, a cold piss-water on a summer's day, that was good.'

She laughed, softer than usual, almost like humming. 'What did I say about holding on to things? I hold on to piss-water in the sun. It reminds me of those friends, and drinking with them. They were funny ones, they were. I was the funniest though. Always have been.' Niv's eyes were damp, but she still smiled.

'We drink moonshine in the town,' Joe said. 'It's strong, so you have to drink it in small amounts. We always have it when it rains, at the celebrations. It's funny, because the whole town drinks it together, so even the people who are normally serious get drunk. Like the Mayor, the one with the coat who welcomes you into the town–'

'The one with the stick up his arse, you mean,' Niv interjected.

'Exactly,' Joe said. 'I saw him throw up once. He'd had too much, and we were round the bonfire. He staggered away to be sick, and ended up doing it right in front of the Witch. He only saw her when he looked up. He jumped back, nearly put his bum in the fire, and had to sit down in the mud to cool it off.

He avoided the Witch for ages after that. He wouldn't admit he was avoiding her, but everyone knew.'

Niv snickered, then dried the damp from her eyes with her shirt. 'I've had some of your town's whisky. It's good stuff.'

'Depends on the brew. It's different each time.'

'Always just tastes like alcohol and fire to me.'

'When you've had it enough it tastes different. There's different flavours.'

'The whole world's gone to hell. You can't even get lager, let alone fancy wine or real ale. But somehow we've still got drinking snobs!' She offered him the water again. 'Here, if it's classy enough for you.'

Joe took it, keeping an overdramatic eye on her boots.

'What's that water taste like?' Niv asked, as he drank. 'Hint of crystal, oakwood and bloody elderberry?'

Joe laughed and spluttered water down his front.

'Do something for me, Joey. If you find any alcohol in the city, you find a bar still stocked up or something like that, try their different beers. Find the nastiest piss-tasting one they've got, and bring it back for me.'

'Will do.'

Niv offered him some kale, which Joe had the sense to accept rather than be kicked again. They ate together, watching as the truck grew larger.

'You can go if you want,' Joe said, once they'd finished

eating, though he appreciated her company. 'If you need to head on.'

'I'm on my own time. We all are, with the way the world is now. If I want to wait for something, like you riding away on that truck, I can make the time for it.'

'You know, you're wiser than you look.'

'Not a compliment!' Niv said, and this time Joe was ready to dance away as she kicked at his legs.

'I'm just preparing for when I'm an old crone,' she said, after catching him on his shin. 'Don't reckon I've got quite the mysterious air to be a witch, but I can be jolly and wise. One of those old ladies who shocks you by saying something really rude, and has a dirty laugh. Wears bright colours that don't match, always has a drink hidden somewhere, and swears like a sailor.'

'You're halfway there,' Joe said, ready for a kick again, but Niv just chuckled.

'What about you? What sort of old man are you going to be?'

'If I make it to that age? I'm not sure. I hope I play music. I've only learned a little, but it feels like something I could keep doing.'

'I can see you playing music. We ever have boybands again, you got the look.'

'What's a boyband?'

'Ha! You're better off not knowing.'

They fell into silence again. The heat wasn't too oppressive in the little room. For once, Joe was able to enjoy the warmth on his skin. He relaxed against the wall and felt his back loosen and unclick. Niv was similarly restful. He saw it in the leisurely way she drank from the bottle, and in her slow sigh as they watched the approaching truck.

Joe felt as if he was in a waking dream. There was nothing for him to do, no mountains to climb and no work to be completed. He wasn't in need of sleep for energy, nor food for sustenance, nor celebration to keep his soul alive. For a while he could simply be, letting his mind drift like a gentle wind over the desert.

The sun passed its highest point in the sky, half of the day left. The truck was close enough for Joe to make out details. Its driverless front had no windows, only an enclosed metal cab.

'It can't last, you know,' Niv said eventually, breaking the silence. Her tone was more serious than before.

'What can't last?' Joe asked.

'How we're living. The electric vehicles' batteries will die. It might take ten years, or twenty, but eventually each and every one of them will go. Even the Mechanic can't stop that.'

'People talk about that in the town sometimes,' Joe replied. 'They say we'll need to work out a new way of doing trade, or how to travel to one of the other communities to work there instead.'

Niv nodded. 'Everyone speaks like we'll have time to work it all out. Which is true if the batteries die off one at a time. But the charging points here didn't always buzz like they do now. That started a couple of years back. If they fail, everything stops very quickly.'

Joe pictured a drifter arriving at the recycling centre, and finding that the charging points were no longer functioning. If they had enough charge, they'd head to one of the communities and share the news. If not, they'd need to wait for another drifter, the only person who knew their way of life was coming to an end.

'When the time comes, however it happens, it'll be worst for your town, and for us drifters,' Niv said. 'The other communities have their own ways of getting food. All drifters have to offer is our vehicles, and your town survives on trading us the recycling to keep them charged.'

Joe was silent. He could come back from the city, and find everything that life in the town relied on had fallen through. It was as if the shacks and the people could vanish into the desert while he was away, leaving him with only the mountains to return to.

The humour returned easily to Niv's voice. 'You're brooding. It's very manly.'

'I don't want to see people starve.'

'Want to make it better? Find something new in the city. If

you get something new into the system, then it can change.'

The truck was getting close now. It was almost time.

'I could be going to a ruin.'

'Maybe.' Niv shrugged. 'But you grew up on the mountains. If it's a ruin, who better to search through it?'

Joe nodded. 'What about you? Where will you go next?'

'Back to the gardens. I need to stock up on food for trade, and I'm curious about something else as well. When I left there, they were talking about using new automated machines for digging and ploughing the ground. They didn't say where they'd got them from. I'd like to find out what happened with that.'

The truck, nearly at the recycling centre, began to turn. Joe got to his feet as the steel container it carried came into view. There was a green star across its side, the same as on the charging points' screens and the entrance to the recycling centre. Joe moved towards the door, but Niv waved her hand at him to wait.

'It needs to drop off its empty container first,' she said. 'Then it'll take a full one.'

The truck turned a full one hundred and eighty degrees so that it faced away from them, then reversed towards the centre, into a space between two of the other containers. Joe found it unnerving to watch the intricate movement and know that it was performed by the truck itself, without human thought or intervention.

A panel on the back of the truck's container slid open while the truck reversed, allowing the entrance of a recycling tube that protruded from the centre's wall. Air hissed out of the truck and its rear sloped downwards, then the catches that held the container sprang loose. The truck scraped forward and with a reverberating clang, the container slammed onto the desert. Dust rose up from the ground around it.

'Go time,' Niv said, lifting Joe's cloth sack and heading towards the door. 'When we see which container the truck's going to take, you can climb on.'

Joe and Niv walked out into the heat. The truck began to reverse towards a new container, and they stepped up next to it. Joe patted the container's side, making a drum-like sound. The steel was painfully hot in the sun. As the truck pushed under the new container, Joe remembered his father's words. He always had a choice. He could turn away. He could ask Niv if he could travel with her to the gardens, and eventually back to the town. The option was there. He made his decision and acknowledged making it.

When the rear of the truck scraped out from under the container, he climbed up. He immediately had to lean forward because of the metal burning his back. Niv handed him his cloth sack, drawing out his blanket as she did. She helped him wrap it around himself, providing a thin layer of material between him and the hot metal, then made a hood with the blanket's top to shade his head.

Joe lurched up and away from her as the container lifted fully from the ground. The truck edged forward, the container's panel sliding closed when the recycling tube slid out. Joe sat facing Niv and the centre, his feet dangling over the desert.

'Thanks for everything, Niv. I hope I see you again.'

The truck had already started to accelerate, the gap between them widening.

'Pleasure travelling with you,' Niv said. Concern crossed her face as Joe pulled away. 'Be safe out there, Joey.'

'I will,' Joe shouted back, then lifted the hood to cover his head.

'Oi!'

Joe lowered the blanket. Niv and the centre were far back now.

'Don't forget the piss-water!' Even across the desert, her laugh was loud.

'I won't!' he shouted back.

He made sure his supplies were secure next to where he sat, pushing the cloth sack into the tight gap between the container and the truck. Then he pulled the blanket hood back over his head, which flopped down over his eyes and blocked out the sun.

In the reddish darkness underneath, he felt as if he was

being cooked. He remembered stories of burnt corpses in the desert. He could only hope that the blanket would be enough to protect him in the long hours until nightfall.

CHAPTER TWENTY-ONE

There was only heat. Joe felt as if he was being cooked from the inside out. The worst pain was in his throat. It was scorched dry, so raw he felt it would split around his Adam's apple, bleeding as the hot air escaped. Even with the hood covering his eyes, Joe felt like everything was spinning.

Joe lost his balance, swaying forwards from his perch and catching a glimpse of the desert rushing below him. He grabbed onto the truck, unsure how far he was bent over the edge. He shifted himself back until his spine was pressed against the steel container, then looked down through the gap in his hood and used his bum bag to fasten one arm to the truck. It was too tight, and whenever there was a bump it jolted his arm painfully, but it prevented him from falling.

With his free arm, he fumbled a plastic water bottle from

his cloth sack. He drank deeply, ignoring the part of his mind that told him to ration. The thirst was too much. The ache in his head grew larger, pressing out against his skull, the pressure building until he felt sure that the bone would crack.

Only water tempered the pain's growth. Joe had lost count of how many bottles he'd finished already. He'd peed into one of the empty bottles, not willing to waste a drop of liquid on the desert ground. He didn't know if he'd drunk from that already and hadn't noticed the taste, or if that was still to come. It didn't matter. It wouldn't stop him drinking it.

Joe's muscles were tight, forcing him to hunch and aggravating the pain in the arm that he'd fastened to the truck. He tried to settle back against the steel container, but his limbs were too stiff for him to properly adjust his position. His mouth was cottony and tasteless, yet he was suddenly overwhelmed by the smell of sick. He didn't think he'd vomited, but he wasn't sure. Everything was swimming and he was losing track of time.

Something passed overhead. Without thinking, Joe pulled down his hood. The brightness burned his eyes. He tried to yank the hood back up, but couldn't manage to grip the fabric. The white light dulled and he saw telegraph wires, sweeping in waves across the desert. They were beautiful, just like Niv said they'd be. The colour was fading from everything, Joe's vision infiltrated by a grey mist. He managed to pull the blanket-hood back over his head, and wondered for a moment if the telegraph wires were the last thing he'd ever see, then lost consciousness.

When Joe awoke, he was under the stream in the town, cool water running over him. He bathed there for a moment then lifted his head out, ready for the celebration. But then his hood slipped down from his face, and he was still sitting on the back of the truck, travelling through the desert night. He was fastened in his upright position by the bum bag clipping his arm in place.

If I hadn't done that with the bum bag, Joe thought, *I'd have fallen off when I blacked out. I wouldn't have survived the impact. Not at this speed.*

There was no stream, only the night's milder air washing over him with the breeze created by the truck's movement. The stars were above him. He found himself looking for the gaps where the Prince had torn away the suit and dress in Grandad's story.

Sensation returned gradually to his body, and he became aware all of his muscles were aching. The inside of his throat burned as if layers of its lining had been scoured away. He rooted through his cloth sack for a water bottle. Their plastic rustled together, all empty.

Joe felt a hot shame rise inside him as he remembered that he'd peed into one of those bottles. He checked the bum bag that secured his arm to the truck, and found that the small bottle his father had put inside was still untouched. He took a sip, just enough to dampen his throat, then zipped it back into the bag.

Joe couldn't believe how much he'd drunk. He'd been in some kind of fever. He still shook with it now, his blanket soaked and stinking of sweat. He couldn't do it. He couldn't face the sun again. Not with only one bottle of water.

After half a day of the sun, he was more broken than he'd ever felt. If the sun began to rise again before they reached the city, he'd unclip his arm and drop head first onto the fast-moving ground below. It was a better way to die than being cooked.

Hunched over, Joe began to cry. He was so dehydrated he barely produced tears. Each sob wracked his chest before he coughed it out. He was an idiot. He'd thrown away Sonya in the forest, playing guitar with his father, all the worlds of Grandad's stories, and for what?

To die by breaking himself on the earth, or burning in the sun. The moon, half-full above him, reminded him of his failure to help Lily. His stomach tensed with the discomfort of crying, and his throat closed so that his sobs were reduced to painful hiccups.

Joe heard voices whispering and sat up, wiping the thin trails of moisture from his cheeks. The flat desert around him was empty, but in the corners of his eyes he saw shadows moving.

The shadows vanished whenever he tried to directly look at them. By fixing his gaze in one direction, he could see them at the edge of his vision, silhouetted figures that somehow walked alongside the speeding truck.

'Who are you?' Joe asked hoarsely. The whispering around him grew louder, a crowd of voices all speaking at once.

'There was a dear little girl' – 'her bracelets jangled' – 'the prettiest creature' – 'called her little red cap.'

Joe felt as though he recognised the voices. At the same time, he knew that he'd never heard them before. They came from all around him, making his head reel.

'Her mother gave her a basket' – 'told her not to talk to strangers' – 'do not leave the path' – 'she was going through the wood.'

'Who are you?' Joe shouted, his raw throat aching.

'She looked into the darkness' – 'she didn't know what a wicked animal' – 'he asked her where she was going.'

There was a sound in the distance like snapping jaws. The whispers shot away in different directions, as if fleeing. Paws padded on the earth as something else approached the truck. Joe felt the impression of great size beside him. When he turned towards it, hot breath blew across the back of his neck. He spun round and heard claws scratching in the dirt, but saw nothing. It snorted near his ear and he turned again, but the beast was always out of sight.

'Joe,' it said. Its voice was saliva, and tongue, and the click of teeth.

'What are you?' Joe asked, pressing himself as flat against the steel container as he could.

'You know me,' it replied in a low growl. 'Are you here to pick flowers, Joe? Have you strayed from the path? Do you think you'll make it to grandmother's cottage?'

'My, what big teeth you have,' Joe said. He spoke calmly, but was breathing hard.

'Very good.'

The Wolf followed the truck, stalking from side to side. Joe perceived it only when it entered the peripherals of his vision, as a darkness that loomed over him. Each time he saw the darkness, he glimpsed a wicked grin, or brutal claws, or mocking eyes staring down. The details changed. First, he saw a mouth filled with sharp triangular teeth, then they were broken and jagged. The claws were curved down into the earth, then they were pointed like blades. The eyes were blood red, then the deepest black.

'Tell me something.' The voice sounded both inside and outside of his head. Joe sensed the Wolf within him, listening to his fear. He felt the beast's grin grow wider. 'Who makes the Wolf? Who conjures me from between the trees? Is it Red Riding Hood, when she stares out into the deep, dark wood? Is it her mother, when she tells Little Red not to stray from the path, and to watch out for strangers in the shadows? Is it your grandfather, when he tells my story around that burning fire? Is it you, when you listen to him, and I prowl through the darkness behind your eyes?'

'You're just another story.' Joe struggled to force the words out from his dry throat. 'You can't hurt me. You're not real.'

'Fool.' A huge shadow flashed across Joe's vision then slammed into the truck, lifting the wheels up from the ground on one side. Joe grabbed his cloth sack just in time, but his blanket fell towards the desert. The wheels dropped back onto the earth, wrenching Joe's fastened arm so that he yelled out in pain. That pain was joined by despair as the truck continued on, and he saw his only protection from the sun disappearing out of sight.

'Stories can hurt,' the Wolf said, triumph in its voice. 'As you'll know when I eat you, piece by piece.'

'If you're the Wolf,' Joe shouted out, 'you lose. Red Riding Hood escapes and you get chopped apart by an axe!'

The Wolf barked wildly, a bloodthirsty sound that shook the truck. It was as if the words themselves hurt it. Joe raised his free arm pathetically in front of his body, expecting an attack.

'The tale is told in different ways,' the Wolf snapped, its spit landing on Joe's skin. 'I am the Wolf that ate Red Riding Hood, and I still have bits of her caught between my teeth.'

Joe wiped wolf spit from his face. He found a single string of red fabric between his fingers. It gave him an idea. It felt like madness, but the whole situation was madness. If there was anything he'd ever learned from Grandad, it was that there was power in storytelling.

'It's not her flesh you feel between your teeth,' he shouted into the dark. 'It's only her hood! And it's not her in your stomach, it's something much heavier. There's a wound down your belly that's been sewn back together.'

An agonized howling filled the night.

'They tricked you, Wolf! The huntsman sliced you open, and Red Riding Hood and her grandmother climbed out. They piled stones inside and sewed you back up. Your stomach is filled with rocks, and they'll be the death of you!'

The howling stopped, and a large weight thudded down onto the desert. As the truck drove on, Joe caught a momentary glimpse of a great shadow slumped in the dirt. It whined, then let out a quiet whimper, then nothing at all.

The Wolf was story, so he'd beaten it with story.

Joe unpacked his supplies, balancing oat-filled jars and carrier bags of potatoes along the rear of the truck. He placed his pan down next to the food, with the bowl, spoon and magnifying glass inside. He flattened the air out of the plastic bottles and laid them in a line, losing a couple to the desert. He'd tried to find the string of red fabric that stuck to his hand, but it must have dropped off, lost to the desert rolling along beneath him.

Once his cloth sack was empty he began to tear along its seam, intending to split it to use as a replacement for the blanket. His fear of the next day was still present, but no longer in control. For now, he was able to think practically. He risked his supplies falling from the truck, but he knew he had no chance of surviving the sun without cover.

For the third time, he had met a character from a story. That felt like it should be mind-blowing, but in the logical mindset he'd entered into to plan for survival, the existence of fictional characters in the real world had become an acceptable fact. He was travelling to the city because a Witch had told him it was his destiny, and a Forest Woman had said it would save Lily. If he took magic and fiction out of the equation, there was no reason for him to be where he was.

Joe could still hear the whispering on the uncertain line between thought and sound, but the figures seemed to be staying back since the Wolf. He wondered if the Wolf itself had scared them off, or if it was how he'd used storytelling to defend himself. It seemed what drifters said about the way to the city was true, but it was possible that Joe discovered a manner of protecting himself from the shadows that they never had.

The truck slowed to a halt and Joe looked around for a cause, but the flat desert and the night were the same as ever. The vehicle shuddered as it stopped. Joe unclipped his arm, but didn't dare dismount. If the truck started moving and he wasn't quick enough to climb back on, which could easily happen with his stiffened muscles, then he'd be dead.

There was a click and a ting from the front of the truck, then the sound of metal swinging open. At the recycling centre, Joe hadn't seen any outline of a door on the truck's cab. Footsteps moved towards him. They sounded human this time.

How can there be people? Joe asked himself. *The trucks are automated.*

Two large men, with white gas masks concealing their faces, appeared round the side of the truck. They wore bottle-green jumpsuits, in a darker shade than the star on the container. They closed in on him. Even if Joe hadn't been weakened from his journey, he wouldn't have been able to resist their firm grip as they twisted his arms behind his back with sudden brutality.

'Where did–' Joe started, and they threw him forward.

He hit the earth and crumpled, the impact too much in his already damaged state. One of the men swept Joe's supplies off the truck, while the other took the last water bottle from his bum bag and poured the contents onto the desert ground. Joe felt each drip as if it was his own blood spilling. The man who emptied the bottle strode over to Joe and swung a kick into his side, knocking the air out of him.

'Hitching a ride to the city?' The voice behind the mask was mocking. 'Where the streets are paved with gold, and the street lights are solid silver. Where the clothes are made from the finest silk, buttoned with diamonds, rubies and sapphires. Where you walk in as a poor man, and you walk out rich. You'll love it.'

The man kicked him again, and Joe heard one of his own ribs crack.

'Let's go!' the other man shouted. 'We don't want to wait around out here.'

The man who'd kicked him walked away. Joe wheezed on the ground, pain stabbing into his side with each breath. He raised his head in time to see one of the men entering the truck's cab, through a door that opened from underneath, where Joe wouldn't have expected a handle. The other man looked around nervously, out towards the whispers, then climbed inside as well.

The cab's door pulled down and shut. The ground vibrated under Joe as it began to move, and he attempted to lift himself up. He faltered and collapsed onto his injured rib, winding himself so his screams were soundless. The truck pulled away, and Joe didn't bother trying to rise from the earth again. He knew it was over. Those men, whoever they were, had killed him by leaving him there. He'd die in the desert.

There was the sound of paws on the earth once more. Joe anticipated the Wolf's voice again, or its teeth. He lay on his front, waiting for the end. The animal circled around him, sniffing the air. It sounded too light to be the Wolf. Joe pushed himself up from the dirt, balancing on trembling arms as the pain penetrated his side.

He used the same method as he had to see the other shadows, staring in a single direction and catching glimpses of the creature when it passed through the corners of his eyes. It was dark and sleek, with something liquid to its movements. After prowling around him several times, it stepped into the centre of his vision without disappearing.

It was a panther, with its amber eyes fixed on him. Joe thought he recognised the shape of the creature, and the colour of those eyes. He hoped it was the animal he had once seen following alongside Leigh's van. His arms ached with the effort of supporting his upper body, but he didn't dare move as the feline approached.

The panther skulked closer, its muscular shoulders rolling in a slow cycle beneath its fur. The shoulders raised up, losing their fur and revealing bare skin, and the front paws lifted from the ground and became hands. Her dress made of earth formed across her, the dirt sparkling with grit. Her black hair curled down on either side of a gentle expression. The Forest Woman's amber eyes were kind as she looked down at him.

She walked with the soft step of the cat, her hips rolling in the same smooth cycle as her shoulders had before. She dropped forward, the dirt dress falling away as her fur returned, and was a panther again by the time she reached Joe.

She wanted him to climb onto her back. The thought was in Joe's head, and he wasn't the one who'd thought it. He had nothing to lose. It was that or the desert. Joe struggled to his feet, nearly falling, and the panther lowered herself down to the ground. He climbed onto her.

She rose up, effortlessly lifting his weight on her back. Joe fell forward, too weak to remain upright, and wrapped his arms around her neck. Her shoulders turned in their circular motion against his chest as she stalked across the desert, each movement sending pain through his ribs.

Joe would later struggle to describe what happened next. He lost his sight, and all feeling apart from the panther's movement beneath him. He heard a voice that sounded at once alike and not alike to Grandad's. It told the narrative of his situation, of riding on the panther, of his injuries and pain, even of hearing the voice telling the narrative. As simply as changing a phrase in a story, the voice changed his location from 'the desert' to 'the fallen forest'. It took away his pain, and melded his rib back together.

Then he was in the fallen forest, still riding the panther and just out of sight of the town. The stars above him were the same as they'd been in the desert. He slipped off the panther's back, landing in the dirt. The cat looked into his eyes, then stepped out of sight as easily as she'd stepped in. Joe looked over towards his and Sonya's log, and called her name.

CHAPTER TWENTY-TWO

Sonya turned, tears running down red paths on her cheeks. Her mouth dropped open when she saw Joe in the fallen forest. She stared at him in disbelief, then hurried over to where he lay on the ground. 'Why are you here? What happened?'

Joe didn't reply. He could still feel the strangeness of his journey home, like a fuzz in the air around him. The voice both similar and dissimilar to his Grandad's still echoed in his head.

'Joe,' Sonya said, her eyes still glistening with tears. 'Are you hurt? I'll get help.'

The peculiar feeling faded, and the world settled back into place around Joe.

'I'm not hurt,' he said. It was true. The Forest Woman's magic had worked. Joe's body felt weak, but no longer in pain. There wasn't even a twinge in his ribs.

'Are you sure you're okay?' Sonya asked.

'No, I'm not okay. I'm just not hurt.'

'I don't understand what's happened.' Her eyes were wide, and her voice was insistent now. 'How can you be back?'

He told her about his journey on the truck. He described the whispers in the desert, then his encounter with the Wolf, and how he was inspired by a string of red fabric that seemed to be from Red Riding Hood's cloak to use storytelling to defend himself. He explained how the men, seemingly from the city, came out from inside the truck and attacked him, before the Forest Woman arrived as a panther and somehow brought him home. It all sounded so bizarre told out loud, especially when only moments ago he'd been living it out there in the desert.

'I felt it when you came back,' Sonya said in awe. 'It was like everything in the fallen forest shifted for a moment, and there was some sort of shadow here with me. Then you called my name.'

Joe looked up at the moon, still half-light, half-dark. He thought of Lily, and a numb exhaustion descended over him.

'I failed.' Joe choked on the words. 'I couldn't help Lily. I...'

Joe couldn't get anything else out. He felt as if his soul itself was weary. Sonya took his head in her hands, and rested him on her lap. She let him lie there for a little while, stroking his hair. When he was ready, she gripped his hand and helped him to his feet.

Sonya took him towards his shack, where they went in through the back door. Wheezy snoring let Joe know Grandad was asleep. David was sitting on a stool, lit by the half-moon's light, awake far later than he usually was. He seemed not to register their entrance, staring at the wall.

For a moment, Joe and Sonya both looked at David. Joe knew it was his journey away that had impacted on his father. Then David became aware of their presence and looked across, gasping when he saw them. He rushed over and hugged Joe tightly, before stepping back and handing him a bottle of water from the side.

Joe drank, remembering the sound of his water being poured away onto the desert earth. He couldn't finish the bottle, overwhelmed by the freshness that ran through him. Sonya took it from his hands and led him onto his mattress. Joe tried to thank her and David, but the words mumbled away on his lips as his tiredness weighed down on him and forced him into sleep.

Joe woke up to the sun shining in through the window-hole. His father and grandfather were gone, but Sonya lay next to him on the mattress with her arm around him. She was already awake.

'How long's the sun been up?' Joe asked.

'It's the middle of the day,' Sonya said, rubbing her thumb between his neck and shoulder. 'Do you want water? Or something to eat?'

He brushed her hand away and sat up on the mattress. 'We need to climb the mountains.'

Sonya sat up as well and looked at him with a worried expression.

'I already lost half of my family's food in the desert,' Joe said. 'I'm not going to make them do my collecting for me.'

Sonya's mouth tightened. She knew there was little point in arguing with him, but her opinion was clear.

'I can't stay here and do nothing,' Joe said. 'I need to be of some use.'

'You are useful,' Sonya said. 'You don't know how good it is for me just having you here.'

Sonya's words helped, but it wasn't enough. He was supposed to go to the city to save Lily, and he'd failed. Everything that had led him to this point – the Boy Who Learned What Fear Was protecting him beneath the waste, the Witch saying he had a destiny, the Forest Woman telling him to travel to the city – all of it had been for nothing.

'How's Lily?' Joe asked.

Sonya sighed. 'The same as before. She still hasn't opened her eyes, and she's spitting up most of what Rose tries to feed her. Your grandfather was here last night, telling her peaceful stories. I hope they get through to her.'

'Me too,' Joe said. It hurt his head to think that Lily might never wake up, and that he might never see her collecting on the mountains again. It felt so long ago that the twins had shown him their spiderweb trick, the same day that Lily was bitten. There had to be something more they could do for her, other than telling her stories to calm her sleep.

After that, Joe went with Sonya towards the mountains to fit in a half day of collecting. As they passed the Witch's shack at the bottom of the hill, Joe saw a rat crawl out of one of the holes at the bottom of her shack. It sniffed the air, then turned its head towards him. It paused like that, staring at him, then darted back inside.

Alice was collecting on the purple-green ground at the base of the mountains. As Joe and Sonya approached, she dropped the bag she was searching through and pushed herself swiftly towards them.

'Joe!' Alice jammed her pole into the ground in front of Joe and Sonya's feet, stopping abruptly. Her expression was bright and excited. 'I heard you'd left with a drifter for the city. How far did you get?'

Joe considered avoiding the question or lying, but he knew the town had an appetite for stories. Alice would be too interested to drop this now. She and others would keep asking until Joe told them something worth hearing. He didn't have the energy to make up a lie that sounded truthful, so he told the truth even though it sounded like a lie.

Word of his tale quickly spread, and he spent most of that day being interrupted from his collecting to retell it. Some people came back for a second time, like the Artist Sisters. The Moonshine Brothers came to listen too, and even Kane seemed swept into the tale. Ms Winnipeg brought Tiger along to make sure he didn't miss out.

After hearing the story, Ms Winnipeg leaned over to Sonya and said, 'At least I wasn't in this one!'

Sonya let out a surprised laugh. David and Grandad arrived and listened while Joe told the story to a small gathering of townspeople. David seemed particularly affected by it. He was close to tears as Joe described how the heat affected him, and being kicked in the side in the desert. Grandad listened seriously too, but also absent-mindedly nodded approval at Joe's telling of the tale.

Joe didn't need to worry about being called a liar. Sonya, David and Grandad all believed him. It was his father's belief that surprised him most. Sonya had always believed in magic more than Joe, due to her mother's faith in the Witch's powers. Grandad seemed to have had some experience of his own around the strange magic behind storytelling.

It was David who was the sceptic, who'd never believed in this sort of thing at all. Perhaps he had seen more than he let on, having lived with Grandad's tales since coming to the town.

Or maybe there was simply no other way he could explain how Joe had left with Niv for the recycling centre, then reappeared in the fallen forest.

The rest of the townspeople received Joe's words as storytelling. They saw it as a fiction he'd created after his journey, rather than a factual account. It was as if they thought this was his own unique take on his grandfather's storytelling, where he cast himself as the lead, and described magical happenings in order to add to the intrigue.

The desert before the city was already the setting of many stories told by drifters, so the Storyteller's grandson going there and returning with a tale of his own made sense to them. The townspeople talked about Joe's story as if it had its own inherent truth, separate from the world. They reacted to it in the same way as they reacted to Grandad's stories, where they'd argue for days about what 'really happened' in a tale.

With any other story, it would have been fun for Joe. Like discovering playing music, he would have enjoyed finding out that he could tell stories, twisting and turning a plot for his audience to chase. But the story they wanted him to tell was one of his own failure. It gave him no joy to tell it repeatedly.

Joe felt similarly apathetic when playing guitar with David that evening. He tried to make it matter to himself, but the truth was that he no longer cared how well he played. Without the pressure of his own motivation he made less mistakes, but he'd lost his drive to learn more.

They played together over the following few evenings, and nothing changed. David perceived Joe's lack of effort on the guitar, but he didn't press Joe on it. He seemed to hope that if they kept playing together, then Joe would come back to himself.

Sonya treated Joe similarly on the mountains. The townspeople had gradually stopped seeking him out during collecting to ask for the story, so it was often just the two of them together. She spoke to him as if everything was normal, making jokes and showing him interesting finds, even though he barely responded.

Sometimes Maya collected with Joe and Sonya, her baby bump just beginning to show. Joe felt sorry for Sonya when Maya was with them. Maya spoke in the same manner as he did, her voice lethargic and lacking emotion. She'd cried all her tears for Buddy, and now there seemed to be nothing left of her. Sonya was stuck between the two of them, trying her best to bring some life back into either.

On the fourth evening after Joe's return, David told Joe that the Singing Family had asked to practice singing alongside the guitar. Joe declined the offer to go with him, though they played together for a while before David headed out to the Singing Family's shack. Joe stayed with Grandad instead, who had been watching them play.

'You don't seem all that interested in playing the right notes,' Grandad commented after David had left. 'You don't seem interested in anything at all. It's not like you.'

Joe was on his mattress, facing away from where Grandad sat on one of the stools. He spoke without turning. 'I'm trying to care. It's just hard at the moment.'

'Why is that? You've always been so full of passion. Now, even when I see you speaking with Sonya, it's as though you're barely listening to her. At this point I'd be glad to hear you argue with your father, if it brought the feeling back to your voice.'

Joe sighed, then rolled over and faced Grandad. 'I thought I was supposed to go to the city to help Lily. But now her time's almost up, and I can't see another way to try to get there. I've failed, and I think she might die. Now people here want me to be one of the Storytellers with you, or one of the Musicians with my father. But how can I stay here and be one of those things, when deep inside I'll know I'm just the person who failed Lily?'

Grandad grumbled phlegm in the back of his throat, then shook his head. 'I don't like the titles we give people in this town. We get it all wrong. It reduces us. The Librarian's only his books, Office Chair Alice only her disability, the Husbands only their love for each other. All of them are more than that. I'm more than just my stories.'

Grandad rose from the stool, standing over Joe as he spoke. 'Listen to me. Names are better than titles. With your name you can play a thousand different roles. You can be a musician, a storyteller, whatever you need to be at the time. You can even be someone who fails sometimes, because we all have to be that.

'Don't trap yourself by saying that you're one thing or another. You're too big and complicated to restrict yourself like that. Just be Joe, because then you can be all that you are. I should know. It's my name as well.'

Grandad smiled down at him. 'I'm proud of what you've done with the name. You did everything you could to try to help Lily, despite the danger to yourself. You have nothing to be ashamed of.'

Joe forced a fake smile, which Grandad undoubtedly saw through but returned nonetheless. Grandad went back to his stool and sat quietly, letting Joe settle on the mattress. Joe lay with his eyes closed, exhausted yet unable to sleep.

Maya didn't collect with Joe and Sonya the next day. She felt sick, Sonya said, and couldn't face the sun. It was the first showing pregnancy there'd been for a long time, and it was now public knowledge in the town.

Maya feeling unwell sent a ripple of worry through the townspeople, despite it being typical in expectant mothers. The child could easily be lost, and so too could Maya. Even if she made it through pregnancy, the chances of them both surviving the birth were low.

Joe and Sonya were looking after Tiger, who over the last few days had been collecting with Ms Winnipeg and a group of the older women. He seemed to have developed a greater comprehension of Lily's situation.

At one point, Joe noticed him sitting at the edge of the shade and staring up at the faint shape of the moon in the blue sky overhead. Did Tiger understand the Witch's prediction for Lily, and know the significance of the moon being almost full? *He's only six years old,* Joe thought, *but he seems so much older now.*

That evening, Sonya came over to Joe's shack and listened to him practice the guitar. She sat on a mattress with David, while Grandad was out telling Lily a story. Joe stood over them and listlessly cycled through tunes. Sonya was complimentary, praising everything he did, trying to get him excited about playing music, but eventually she fell silent when it became clear she was having no effect.

It was an odd scene, Joe repeating the same half-hearted riffs over and over, while Sonya and David stared resignedly up at him. There was an air of ritual to it, as if it had once been done for a purpose, but now was only for tradition's sake. Joe was relieved when he removed the guitar's rope-strap from his shoulders and placed the instrument against the wall.

'Shall we go to the forest?' Sonya asked, when he'd finished playing.

'We shall,' Joe replied, managing a weak smile at their old refrain.

As Joe and Sonya walked away from the shack, Joe heard David playing the guitar and looked back at him through the window-hole. David played a low finger-picked melody, shifting his left hand through chord shapes while he focused on his right hand on the strings.

When he'd found his rhythm he looked up, accidentally meeting eyes with Joe. He had never seen his father's eyes hold such pain as in that moment. There was a slight stumble in the music, then he nodded to Joe and continued playing. Joe knew what he'd seen. It was the pain of a father whose son had returned, but not fully.

When he and Sonya arrived in the forest, Joe sat down on their log, looking up at the moon with only a curve from its left side remaining in shadow. He expected Sonya to sit next to him. Instead, she straddled his legs and kissed him.

Her kiss was more aggressive than usual. It didn't feel like her. She pressed her chest against his and for the first time since he'd returned from the desert he felt a heat rising inside himself. Yet there was a queasiness in his stomach as well.

When Sonya drew a packaged condom from her pocket, his lust disappeared. She leaned in to kiss him again, and he held her back by her shoulder.

'Joe?' There was the tiniest choke in her voice. He was perhaps the only person who'd recognise that sound from her and know the sadness it indicated.

'I might still go, Sonya. If a drifter came tomorrow, and told me they'd drive me to the city, then I'd go.'

'I know that.' Sonya moved to kiss him again, shoving her shoulder against his hand, but he held her firmly.

'What if you get pregnant?'

'That doesn't matter.'

'Sonya!' Joe was shocked by the brazenness of her lie, and how she'd been able to say it as though it were true. 'Yes, it does.'

'Yes,' she conceded. 'It does.'

She climbed off his legs and turned away, standing with her back to him as she looked out towards the stars.

'You shouldn't do that,' Joe said, remaining on the log and speaking to her back. 'You should care about yourself more than that.'

'I do care about myself.' Sonya's speech was measured, brimming with restrained anger.

Behind her, Joe felt too tired to argue, but he couldn't let it lie. 'Not enough. Look at the position you put yourself in.'

'I'm fully aware of that.'

'Why do it, then?'

Sonya's hand clenched, then she uncurled her fingers and

held them straight. 'You know why. I shouldn't have to say. You know it's for you.'

'I've never asked you to hurt yourself for me.'

'No. You haven't.'

Joe struggled for words. The weariness he'd felt since returning from the desert weighed on him. 'You'd never even think about hurting me in the way this could've hurt you.'

Sonya twisted around to face him. Her voice didn't rise, but the way she spat out her words was as if she wanted to yell. 'Don't you dare tell me how to look after myself. I know how. Don't you make me love you, make me care about you more than I care about myself, then tell me not to.'

'I'm not telling you not to love me–'

'No, you're not. You're telling me to put myself first.' Her implication hung at the end of her sentence: *like you do*, the words she meant but didn't say.

'Sometimes you should put yourself first,' Joe replied, after a pause.

'I can't.' Her shoulders went limp. That one barb, that one sentence said to wound, had spent her anger. They were silent for a while, then Sonya sat down next to Joe again, putting her hands on her knees. He clasped his own in his lap.

'You still want to go to the city,' she said.

'It might be too late for Lily already. The moon's so close to full. I think she has a couple of nights left, at most.'

'I have an idea,' she replied. 'I think you should talk to the Witch.'

Joe looked up at her. Her voice was quiet as she went on.

'My mother told me that when you go to the Witch's shack, she shows you what you need to see. If you're supposed to go to the city, maybe she'll show you how. Think about it. It's her sort of magic you saw out there. The strangeness with animals. Maybe whatever power the Wolf has, and the Forest Woman has where she can turn into a panther, maybe she has it too.'

'There was a crow,' Joe said, realising he hadn't told her. 'When Niv drove me to the recycling centre. It clung to the back of the car, and Niv swerved until it fell off. It died when it hit the ground.'

Sonya grimaced. The town's traditions ran deep.

'There was an owl as well,' Joe continued. 'The first time. When you came with me. I saw it, on top of the Witch's shack, when we were getting into Leigh's van. It was watching us.'

'It was watching you, Joe. The Witch said you had a destiny, and you said you thought that destiny was why the Boy Who Learned What Fear Was saved you in the mountains. Maybe it's why the Forest Woman saved you too. Because you've still got things left to do.'

'Do you really believe that? In fate and destiny?' Joe asked. He wasn't sure if he did or not anymore.

'Destiny's the sort of story that makes itself true,' Sonya

replied. 'I think you get to choose. Whether you survived to do something, or just survived.'

'But if it's like the Witch said and I've got a destiny waiting for me, I don't get a choice, do I? My fate's always been whatever it is that I'll do in the future. I'll feel like I'm choosing, but it was always going to happen.' This was more like their old conversations in the forest, where they talked about the world and how it was.

'I think people would always make the choices that they end up making,' Sonya said. 'With who they are at the time of choosing, what they know, and the experiences they've had. But just because you were always going to make a certain choice, that doesn't mean it isn't yours.'

'So I was always going to decide to go with Niv. I was always going to get on the back of that truck, say the right words to beat the Wolf, and end up lying injured in the desert.'

'You'd always have made the choices that you did. But they were still yours.'

'Then it's all been leading to this. Everything that's happened, from the first time you told me I should see the Witch, that night we talked about jumping to the moon and back.' Joe looked around the fallen forest. All the trees lay in the same places, but it felt different now than it had then. 'That time I chose not to, and everything since has led me here, to deciding that I will. Destiny.'

'So you're going to see the Witch?'

'Yeah, I am. She told me that I'd come to her, when I couldn't find the connection between my past, my present and my future. I think that's now. Maybe she can help me figure out what I should do, or how I can get to the city. You're right as well that it's my choice. I learned from my father not to pretend that I'm not making choices.' He smiled at Sonya. 'I think I'll have to go to her now, though, while I'm feeling brave enough. She still scares me.'

Sonya laughed. 'You were never one to let being scared stop you from doing something.'

'That's because of you. You always helped me to be better than that.'

Sonya stood, and reached her hand out to him. 'If we're going to do it before you lose your nerve, shall we go?'

He reached up and took her hand. 'We shall.'

'To destiny,' Sonya said, a ghost of her smile on her lips, and she pulled him up.

CHAPTER TWENTY-THREE

The roof of the Witch's shack was blacker than the night sky behind it. It was only by the glint of beady eyes that Joe realised it was covered in crows. When he and Sonya approached the door, the crows shuffled back. Joe expected them to erupt into cawing, but they glared down at him in silence.

'Sorry about the one who fell from the car,' Joe said, not because they'd understand, but because it felt right to say. 'I wish that hadn't happened.'

The crows gave no reply. The rat-holes at the bottom of the walls flickered with firelight from within. Standing this close to the shack, Joe could see the holes hadn't been cut into the wood. They'd been gnawed by tiny teeth.

Joe turned to Sonya. 'You don't have to come in with me.'

'I'm here, Joe. I'll come with you.'

'You can't go where he's going.' The Witch pulled the door partially open, revealing her withered face. One cheek was lit orange by firelight, the other hidden in shadow. 'You can come inside, but you won't be able to follow the path he travels.'

'You expected us.' It took physical effort for Joe to not step back from the Witch. He looked up at the crows. 'I guess you have eyes everywhere.'

'I only have two eyes.' Her voice creaked like a shack in the wind. 'But they're good for patterns and detail. I see the structure of things, and how they fit together.'

'You told me you'd help me find my future,' Joe said. 'Why?'

'Because you might save me in the end.' The Witch retreated inside. They followed her in, Sonya closing the door behind them. The air was dense with flies and other insects. Joe felt something scamper across his feet. The ground writhed with creatures. Rats, spiders, slugs and worms all swarmed over each other. The place stank of animal faeces. It was less acrid than the smell of the mountains, but still unpleasant.

Joe watched as a snake slithered through the mass, unconcerned by the rats clambering over its body. It was black and grey, with round eyes. He realised after Lily's bite he'd gradually stopped looking out for snakes on the mountains, accepting them as one of the dangers inherent to collecting.

There was a small fire in the shack's centre, contained by a ring of stones. The Witch was hunched next to it, adding broken bits of wood to the flames. Aside from lacking a window-hole, the layout was similar to other shacks, though all of the surfaces were covered in vegetation.

Moss and leaves grew up the walls and obscured the stove and sink, and grass poked up through the swarm on the floor. Vines dangled from the roof, flicking against Joe's head. He spotted an owl perched in the far corner, almost completely in shadow. Only its round eyes showed clearly, reflecting the fire's glow. It reminded Joe of the Librarian and his glasses.

'A fox!' Sonya burst out. Joe looked across and saw the fox curled up on top of the overgrown counter. The Witch cocked her head like a bird and stared at Sonya.

'I haven't seen one in so long,' Sonya said, answering the Witch's gaze.

'Yes,' the Witch murmured. She lifted a metal pot and placed it on top of the fire, dimming the light. The stones held the pot above the flames. 'The only one of his kind left here. Perhaps in the world.'

'That's so sad,' Sonya replied.

The Witch gathered ingredients from the plants growing on her walls, plucking purple flowers, yellow leaves and white buds. She threw them all into the pot together. 'There used to be many more animals that lived here. The foxes will not be the last to go.'

The Witch went to the fox and held out her arms. It climbed

into them and she cradled it like a child, its paws bent up towards her. The plants in the pot started to crisp, the smoke rising from them making Joe feel dizzy and lightheaded. He felt his balance leave him and had to sit down, placing his hands on the ground and lowering himself carefully so as not to crush anything.

Next to him, Sonya sat down in the same way. As soon as he was on the grass, his legs were submerged. Centipedes, spiders, beetles and a thousand other tiny creatures crawled over him, itching on his skin. A rat pulled itself up onto his knee, scrambled across his lap and dropped off the other side.

The Witch returned to the fire, the fox settled in the bow of one arm. She pinched the scruff of its neck and held it out, dangling above the pot. It struggled, snapping its teeth to either side. From her brown rags the Witch pulled out a knife that glittered in the firelight.

'No!' Sonya shouted. Joe wanted to protest as well, but something in the smoke muddled his mind. The Witch sliced open the fox's throat, holding the animal tightly as it spasmed and died. She directed its spilling blood into the pot, some of it splashing out over the rim. The next rat that Joe felt crawl across his lap had liquid dripping from its fur.

'Why?' Sonya asked.

'It has to be something with meaning,' the Witch said. 'For the craft to work.'

The fox's blood bubbled in the pot, the smoke rising thicker than before. The Witch placed its body down onto the ground and the rats immediately covered it. They fed, with little squelches and cracks as they tore the corpse apart.

Joe struggled to breathe, the shack becoming unbearably humid. Sonya looked like she might be sick. An age passed, Joe battling to remain conscious, then the Witch lifted the pot from the fire with her bare hands. Joe heard her palms sizzle against the metal, but she didn't react. She offered the pot to him.

'Drink this.'

'It's boiling hot,' Joe said, managing to speak despite his reeling head.

'There's always a price,' the Witch replied, and tilted the pot in his direction.

Joe leaned forward, assenting. He opened his mouth and the Witch touched the scorching metal to his lips. He would have screamed if it hadn't been for the blood pouring into his mouth. Instead he nearly choked, then forced himself to swallow the burning liquid. He knew the pain would only be over once it was done. His lips seared and his throat blistered, but he continued to drink.

Around him the walls were bleeding, burgundy seeping down from the moss and vines. Sonya and the Witch bled from their pores without showing any awareness of what was happening, beads of red dotted like sweat across their skin. Two trails ran down from the owl's eyes. The shack, the plants, the owl, the creatures on the floor, Sonya and the Witch, everything collapsed in one mighty red crash. Joe became hot liquid, hurtling down a black tunnel.

Then he was somewhere else. He stood in a dark place and heard crying. Joe saw her, crouched on the ground in her dress made of dirt, her curly black hair falling down over either side of where she sobbed into her hands. The Forest Woman.

'Why are you crying?' Joe asked.

'For the fox, of course.' She let her hands fall to reveal her tear-streaked face.

'I'm sorry that happened,' Joe said.

'And the crow as well?' she asked.

'That too.'

'Everyone's always sorry.' She stood and wiped her tears away with the back of her hand. 'But everything still dies. I'm to be your guide.'

'Where are you taking me?'

'To what you need to know.' She walked away from Joe, her hips moving with their feline turn. There didn't seem to be any option other than to follow her. As he walked behind her, he felt someone else's body around his own. His arms were inside another's arms, his legs inside another's legs.

He was no longer in the dark place. Cars rushed by in either direction on the busy road next to him. The towering buildings were resplendent in the sun, their windows reflecting vibrant blue sky. The streets were filled with people, all with places to be, things to do, purposes within the thriving network. His chest rose with joy to see it again, in all its glory.

The feeling wasn't Joe's, and it wasn't his chest rising. He had no memory of Madera, to find such pleasure in seeing it again. He marvelled behind someone else's eyes, someone who already knew the streets. The person stopped to look at their reflection in a shop window. Joe saw who he was travelling within.

It was David, wearing an ironed shirt and clean black trousers. He used the reflection to adjust his hair, displaying a pride in his appearance that Joe had never known in him. Excitement tickled in David's belly. He was on his way to meet someone he hadn't seen in a long time. Joe shared the excitement. He hoped he might meet his mother.

They entered a coffee shop, the earthy aroma sending Joe spinning inside his father's head. He'd never smelled anything as fresh and beautiful as coffee. David looked around, and Joe saw it wasn't his mother they were meeting. Instead, his father's eyes locked on a familiar face.

Demeta wore a silk dress decorated with elephant designs, rectangular jade earrings, and the same silver cross necklace that she wore in the town. A warmth rose in David's chest when he saw her. It wasn't the burning fire that Sonya lit in Joe, yet there was a quality of that same heat within it. There was no desperate yearning there, but David did carry a deep abiding care for her. Joe couldn't fully work out the feeling, the texture of it so different from his own emotions.

'It's good to see you again,' Demeta said.

There was a latté on the table ready for David. He took a sip as he sat down. It tasted smooth, followed by a bitter but pleasant aftertaste. Demeta's smartphone was on the table next to her coffee. Joe became aware of the shape of a phone in David's pocket. Knowledge floated up from David's mind that Demeta had texted him on his way to ask what drink he wanted. Joe already understood mobile phones, but the casual use of the technology amazed him. It so easily eliminated the distance between people.

'It's good to see you, too,' David said. 'I've been meaning to ask you something.'

Demeta smiled. Hers was almost the same as Sonya's. 'Of course. Go ahead.'

'Do you remember the time when we ran away from the town? When we found the abandoned shopping outlet and the restaurant with electricity?'

Demeta's eyebrows pushed in, her smile becoming bemused. 'You know I do. Why are you asking?'

'Wasn't there a computer there, in the restaurant?' His tone was more pressing now, more urgent. 'Because I was thinking, if there was, it might have had a wired connection to the internet.

All those years we were in the town, not knowing what was going on in the world, when there could've been a computer with internet in walking distance.'

'I don't know, I–' Demeta was interrupted by a rumbling from outside. The café doors slammed open, hundreds of foxes rushing in. People screamed, climbing up on chairs and tables to avoid the river of red and white. David and Demeta were calm as they stepped up onto the table, the situation frightening but nothing compared to avalanches on the mountains. Joe felt David's bewilderment as he looked down at the foxes, then his heart quickening as he noted the animals' claws and bared teeth.

Then his father split into pieces and fell away from him, and Joe was in the dark place once more. He walked behind the panther, following the padding of her paws. Joe opened his eyes in the Witch's shack, still sitting on the ground. The shack was much darker now, the fire only dying embers.

'You've seen what you needed to see,' the Witch said. Her eyes were fixed on his, echoed by the owl's eyes behind her. Sonya held on to his wrist, looking deeply concerned. Joe had the feeling that hours had passed. The pot he'd drank from was gone. All that was left of the fox was a blood-stained skeleton on the grass. Joe stood and felt rodent claws clinging to his leg. He heard a thump as the rat dropped to the ground. The Witch ducked down to gather the fox's bones, ignoring Joe and Sonya with the air that their business was concluded.

'Let's go,' he said to Sonya. His head was still light as they staggered out together. The swarm went no further than the doorway, the insects all falling or flying from Joe and Sonya's skin as they left the shack. The door pushed shut behind them. They didn't speak until they were out of sight of the crows.

CHAPTER TWENTY-FOUR

Joe walked with Sonya through the fallen forest, telling her what he'd seen in the Witch's shack. His lips and throat stung, but didn't hurt as badly as he'd thought they would. He explained his vision in detail, only omitting his father's feelings toward Demeta. Even though it might have just been fiction created in his own mind, Joe didn't see the emotion as his to discuss. He wasn't sure he understood it enough to put into words anyway.

Once Joe was finished, Sonya told him how he'd dropped forward into a trance after drinking the fox's blood. The Witch had used her bony hands to manipulate the smoke rising from the pot into abstract shapes and patterns, muttering into them before blowing them across his face. Joe had been unresponsive throughout, his mouth hanging open and his eyelids fluttering.

'Maybe it's metaphorical,' Sonya said, as they stepped

between the fallen trees, 'and you need to work out what it means. Or maybe it's real, and the outlet's an actual place. My mother or your father might know where it is.'

'If it's real, and there's a computer actually working and connected to the internet, we wouldn't just find out what's happening in the city. With somebody who knew how to use it, we could find out about the entire world. There might be places where life isn't so bad as it is here. They could send us help, like more food, or proper building materials. We could contact a doctor for Lily. They'd come to the town, or tell us what to do for her.'

Sonya stopped in front of their usual log, but didn't sit down. 'We should talk to my mother. I think she'll be still awake. She doesn't sleep very much. We can ask her and find out if they really went to the outlet. Even if they didn't, she'll help us understand what you saw. She's experienced at interpreting the Witch's visions.'

'It's late. We could ask her or my father in the morning,' Joe pointed out.

'No. We should speak to one of them now.' Sonya hesitated, then steeled herself with a deep breath. 'We both know if it turns out to be a real place, you'll try to get there. I can't wait until morning to find out if you're leaving again. I'll end up spending the rest of the night awake, and I'm already so tired. I don't know how I'd be able to work tomorrow, if we climbed the mountains and I still didn't know what was going to happen.'

'We'll speak to your mother,' Joe said, reaching out and taking Sonya's hand. 'We'll find out if the outlet's real. Maybe it was all a dream, and she'll teach us how to work out what it means.'

When they arrived outside Sonya's shack, Joe saw Demeta kneeling at the window-hole, her face lit by the moon. Her hands were pressed flat against each other, her index fingers touching her lips. Her eyes were open, but she didn't react when Joe and Sonya passed in front of her or when they went into the shack.

Joe knew to expect this when Demeta was praying. She was aware of them, and would speak to them when her prayer was completed. The walls inside the shack were covered in religious symbols. The moonlight shining through the window-hole highlighted a wooden cross, a Hanukkah menorah candle holder, and a yin-yang emblem painted in ink on a hanging parchment.

Joe didn't know how many of the townspeople had religious faith. It wasn't often talked about. Even in their shack, his father and grandfather discussed it only very rarely. David said it had as much use in the town as a TV remote, that it was an obsolete tool from another time. Grandad was less emotive, saying that he couldn't criticise faith, not when he was the closest thing to a priest the town had.

From Joe's perspective, he'd grown up with two kinds of truth. There was the truth of the world: the earth beneath his feet, the taste of oats, the waste on the mountains and the heat in the air. And there was the truth of stories, that Grandad had taught him about, found in words and thoughts. Gods, angels, devils, spirits and afterlives were the stuff of the stories, as soil and sun were the stuff of the earth. Yet, now Joe had met stories that walked on solid earth and the boundary between his two types of truth had blurred.

Sonya had always seen less of a separation between the two truths than Joe. She'd told him once, on a night together in the fallen forest, that sometimes she thought of the world and everyone in it as a big story. She'd said that if it was a story then it must have a teller, and if there was a teller then there'd be a listener, too, because a story only comes to life when it's heard. She thought that perhaps they lived in the space between teller and listener.

'It's nice to see you here, Joe. It's been a long time since you've been in this home,' Demeta said, then looked at Sonya. 'I suppose he's been dragging you into trouble again. I tried telling him not to do that.'

'Mum, he's been to see the Witch.'

'You do listen, Joe. Colour me surprised.'

Sonya described Joe's vision to her mother, focusing on the conversation in the coffee shop. Joe interjected occasionally, adding in detail.

'The shopping outlet's a real place,' Demeta told them. 'And it's possible to walk there from the town. It was David who found the way. He knew it from when he lived in the city. When he and I went, the place was empty. We slept in what was left of a restaurant, but there was no electricity that we knew of, and we didn't see any computer. It's not impossible that we missed something, though.'

Joe recalled returning from hijacking Leigh's van, and overhearing David and Demeta talking about running away from the town in the past. But they'd always been told that no one ever left the town. There was nowhere to go but burning hot desert.

'I don't understand,' Joe said. 'When was this?'

'When you two were young, toddlers still. We left you with your grandfather, and Sonya with a woman named Myleene. Myleene passed away in an avalanche, years ago now.'

'I can almost remember Myleene,' Sonya said. 'But I think it's just from you talking about her.'

'You'd have loved her,' Demeta said. 'She suggested the names Tiger and Lily for the twins. We went because David remembered the outlet, and was sure he'd be able to find it.'

Demeta drifted away from them, moving through the shack.

'We said we were going to look for supplies, but that wasn't the reason really. After living in the city, where you could always travel to somewhere else, the town and the mountains felt like a cage. We'd have taken any excuse to leave. We didn't find anything at the outlet, and considered going on and exploring more. It was you two that made us decide to come home, rather than risk heading out further. I managed to make my peace with living here. David never did. Something you've inherited from him, Joe.'

Joe felt a rush of pride. The shame his father carried on his shoulders, which Joe had so often seen as weakness, stemmed from his unwillingness to make peace with their way of life. David had never accepted the mountains of waste, where teenagers were crushed in avalanches and little girls became ill with no hope of treatment.

'He never liked all this, your father.' Demeta moved out of the moonlight and rested her hand on a statue with six arms, its features hidden in shadow. 'These artefacts I look after. He said I should trade them all to the drifters for food. But I think it does the townspeople good to have a place for sacred things to be kept. That's why they give me anything holy they find on the mountains, and even those who want to trade, prefer to do so with me than the drifters. It's the meaning people attach to these objects that gives them power, otherwise David would be right. They'd just be things.'

Demeta lifted her hand from the six-armed god, continuing her slow wander around the shack. She stopped by a pile of religious texts on top of the long-dead stove, books that had found their way to her rather than the Librarian. 'It's funny. David never saw the power that belief can give to something. But it worked on him as well. I believed in him when he guided me to that outlet, in the black of night, from one tiny place to another. It was like walking between two stars, everything else darkness. We walked during the night. During the first two daytimes, when we had to shelter from the sun, he told me he was lost, but I told him he knew the way. When the sun rose on the third day, we saw the outlet, almost next to us. If you want to find it, you'll need to have faith in him as well.'

It had taken them three nights. By Joe's reckoning, the next full moon would be the night after next. Even if Lily survived for the three nights the moon stayed full, it was still too long.

'Do you think the vision was telling me to go there?' Joe asked Demeta. She had more experience with the Witch's strange ways than anyone.

'I don't know why else you'd learn about the place. The Witch's visions have always told me things I needed to know.'

To Joe's side there was a slight nod from Sonya. He knew she'd expected this. Since hearing him describe the vision, maybe even since they decided to visit the Witch, she'd expected that he'd leave her behind again. Joe felt as if he was standing in the stream during the rain, the current pulling him towards the bottom of the hill. He was being led to the outlet.

David and Demeta didn't find anything there, he thought to himself, arguing against the pull. But it was the Forest Woman who had guided him to what he saw, and she had felt just as real as she had in the desert. She'd saved him out there in the night, appearing in the nick of time to prevent his lonely death, stranded out there in the flatlands. This could be her showing him how to do the same for Lily. He couldn't ignore the message she'd given him, even if he didn't fully understand it.

He'd head out into the desert and try to find the outlet. He had to get there as fast as he could. It was his choice, but it was a decision he was always going to make.

Joe and Sonya walked through the town, having a last moment alone together before they returned to their homes to sleep. They'd agreed that Joe would talk to his father the following morning. Then they had fallen quiet, the silence building uncomfortably between them. When they reached the edge of the dry stream, Sonya stopped. Her back stiffened before she spoke. 'I'm not coming with you to the outlet.'

'I know,' he said. 'It's okay.'

'I'm not sure I should have come the first time,' Sonya said.

He understood how being away when Buddy died had cost her. If it was his destiny to seek out help for Lily and the town, it was hers to stay and look after the people in their community. By going with him, she'd given part of herself away.

'Thank you,' Joe said. 'For everything.'

Sonya was teary-eyed as she moved in to hug him. He could smell the familiar scent of yarrow oil on her hair. Joe hoped she knew how grateful he was to her, because he wasn't sure he'd ever be able to express it fully. They held each other tightly for a while, then let go and walked their separate ways to their shacks. If Lily's situation wasn't so urgent, if the sun wasn't soon to rise, if time wasn't always passing, they'd have held on to each other for longer.

David woke up as Joe entered the shack, though Grandad stayed snoring. The first colours of sunrise were showing through the window-hole, and it wouldn't have been long till David was heading up on the mountains. Joe explained everything that had happened the night before.

'The Witch is a trickster,' David warned, speaking to Joe outside the back door to avoid waking Grandad. 'She survives on people's superstition. Most likely, the drugs she gave you just showed you the inside of your own head. You probably heard me and Demeta talk about the outlet when you were younger, and didn't know you remembered it. If she did somehow choose that vision for you, then it's because there's something she gains by you going there.'

'It's not just the Witch. It felt like the Forest Woman was really there, like she was showing me how to help Lily. Just like she helped me.'

Joe expected David to disagree, contesting the reality of the Witch's visions as he always had, but instead his father hesitated. Like when Joe had told him about what had happened after he rode the truck, there was something about the appearance of story characters that reduced David's usual cynicism. Joe suspected once again that his father had seen something similar that he'd never shared.

'I can try to show you the way,' David said, after a few moments gazing out towards the pink and amber sky behind the mountains. 'I can even try to get us there quicker than Demeta and I managed. Last time I didn't manage to get us straight there, and we had to keep walking to find it. But you have to keep in mind, there might be nothing waiting for us at the outlet. We could also get lost, and not be able to make it back to the town.'

Joe knew that David was leaving the decision up to him. 'With what I saw in the Witch's shack… it feels like I'm fated to go.'

'Fate's just what happens in the end,' David replied. 'I wouldn't go chasing after it. Do what you actually want to do, not what you think you're supposed to.'

Joe looked down at his feet. 'Lily's time is nearly up.

Whatever we think about the Witch, she's always been right when she's made predictions about people's health. If there's even the tiniest chance that this could help her, I want to try. I know you and Demeta didn't see anything like it there, but if there is somehow a working computer and an internet connection there now… that could help everyone, not just Lily. We could know what was happening in the rest of the world.'

Joe sighed, then added, 'I need to know, as well, if there's a reason I saw what I did. If there's meaning behind it. But you don't have to come with me. You can just give me directions.'

'I'm not sure that I could. There are no landmarks out there, you just have to know where you're going,' David said. He glanced back into the shack, where Grandad was sleeping. 'If you're going to do this, you'll need me with you. If there's a computer there, you'll need someone who can read, and knows how to use one.'

'I'd thought of that,' Joe admitted. 'I don't want to force you into coming. I can find someone else to–'

'I want to go with you. We'll leave when the sun sets tonight,' David said. 'I know you want to leave as soon as possible, but we can't do this walk in the sun. Get some sleep now, so you're ready for tonight. And remember that it might all lead to nothing. Sometimes that's just the way things are.'

CHAPTER TWENTY-FIVE

That evening, Joe and David stood together on the edge of the town, facing out towards where the desert rolled with cracked-dirt hills. Grandad was with them as well, to see them off.

Though the sun had set, there was enough light left to perceive the bleak landscape that swept out ahead. Two cloth sacks sat at their feet, containing supplies for their journey. At David's suggestion, they'd both slept for a couple of hours after coming down from the mountains. Now they were ready to leave.

Joe and Sonya hadn't had much time to talk on the mountains that day. Joe had climbed them late, having slept through the morning. When he found the others, Sonya was busy supporting Maya, who'd refused to stop collecting despite appearing more unwell than was usual with pregnancy alone.

Joe ended up looking after Tiger, who was slumped and sad. He'd told Joe that Lily might die. Joe could tell that Tiger was repeating someone else's words. Joe's heart wrenched as he imagined Rose and Tiger having that conversation.

Once the day's work was done, Joe and Sonya said their goodbyes at the bottom of the mountains. They said they loved each other, and she wished him luck with his journey. They spoke lightly, as if they'd see each other again the next morning. It was strange to talk that way when for all they knew this could be the last time they saw each other, but it felt better than when he'd left without telling her.

'You two be careful out there,' Grandad said to Joe and David, his wrinkled hands trembling in front of his chest. 'Make sure you come back. I like being Father and Grandfather, as well as Storyteller.'

Joe took Grandad's hands, squeezing them with just enough pressure to settle the tremble. 'We'll be safe. I've come back the last two times, haven't I? And we'll bring a story home.'

'We'll return as soon as we can,' David said. 'Hopefully the round trip won't take longer than two or three days, if I can make it a direct route this time. But we have to get going now. We need to get in as much walking as possible before sunrise.'

Then, as simply as if it was something that was regularly done, David lifted one of the cloth sacks and walked out into the desert. Joe picked up the other sack and followed behind.

When he looked back, he saw Grandad heading up towards the town alone.

For a while, Joe and David walked without speaking. David kept a steady pace, pausing occasionally to look across the seemingly identical hills and then slightly alter their course. Joe had to push himself to keep up. The sky grew darker, the distance of their vision closing in around them. Soon they could no longer see the town behind them, and even the black shapes of the mountains were hard to perceive against the night.

'When we get back,' David said, breaking the quiet as they worked their way up an incline, 'you should start practicing the guitar again properly. It's been different since you went away with Niv.'

'I know. I've been struggling to care about playing, or anything else.'

'That's a hard way to feel.'

Joe walked just behind David, speaking to the back of his head. 'I do want to learn.'

'It'd be okay if you didn't. But it seemed like you were enjoying it before.'

'Yeah, I was. I'd like it to be that way again.'

David slowed for a moment, letting Joe catch up beside him. 'Sometimes it does take effort to care. But I think you'll be able to when you next try to play. It helps that time's passed.'

Joe nodded.

'It's good to learn the skill. Even if you don't decide to play in the future, or if you end up somewhere where there aren't any guitars. It teaches you about yourself, and what you can do when you work at something.'

'I never knew how well you played,' Joe said. 'I knew you could, because of the guitar in our shack, and Demeta looking for the strings, but I never realised you had such talent.'

'Thank you. It helps that there's no one else in the town to compare me to. But I always thought I wasn't half-bad.'

They stopped at the top of a hill, and David stared out across the shadowy slopes ahead. He seemed able to read the lay of the land in some way, to look over it and know roughly where they were. After a moment, he nodded to himself, and led them down the opposite side of the hill.

'Why did you choose the guitar?' Joe asked as they descended. 'There must've been plenty of instruments you could've learned in the city.'

'Why guitar? There's a lot to explain, and I don't have your grandfather's skill with words to do it all justice.' David looked up at the stars, his expression difficult to make out in the dark. 'I first learned to play on an electric guitar. It had a beautiful sound, different from the acoustic one we play now. The nearest I can think of is the mother in the Singing Family. You know how she bends her voice? It sounded sort of like that.'

David sighed deeply, years of his life in a single breath. 'There was so much music back then. It was something called rock 'n' roll that made me pick up the guitar. Rock music was like… howling up at the moon. Howling with the pain and joy and love and sickness of being alive. That's what it was.'

'I think I'd have liked rock 'n' roll.'

'Liked it? You'd have loved it. Rock would have been perfect for you. But there was more than just that. There was the blues, which was like feeling beat up by the world put into music. The blues was sad music, but a good, rough kind of sad. There was jazz, which was all about freedom, and sounded like night-time. Then there was rap, poets throwing out a hundred verses in a minute, and hip-hop that was sort of like rock in what it meant, but not in how it was played. There was folk, which was essentially the stories your grandfather tells as songs, and there was pop, which was pure fun and dancing. There was also classical music, with all different instruments working together. If you shut your eyes and listened, classical music painted you a world.'

'You've got more of Grandad's gift for words than you think,' Joe said. He'd never heard his father speak so passionately.

David laughed. 'It was brilliant, Joe. There was so much, and it was for everyone. If you wanted music that was powerful to you, that moved your soul and sounded like what you felt inside – with all there was, you'd find what you were looking for.'

'I wish I'd been around to hear it.'

'I wish it hadn't all been lost before you were.' There was a regretful silence between them, then David added, 'But there'll be music again. That's why you're learning to play the guitar. We'll make new music, for this life and time.'

By this point, Joe had become confident in David's navigating. There was something in the instinctual way he did it, undeterred by their conversation as they walked, that assured Joe that he knew where they were going – and that he had understated his ability to lead them to the outlet when they had spoken before leaving.

As they continued on over the hills, David told Joe about the bands and musicians he'd liked in the past, punctuated by the occasional stop to regain his bearings. When he spoke about music, he described the city as if it wasn't made from bricks and walls, but from glittering sound. It struck Joe as strange that all the musicians his father talked about were either dead, or living somewhere in the wastelands that the world had become.

'Can I ask you something?' Joe said, after David had finished telling him about a band where saxophones played alongside electric guitars. Overhead, the moon was full other than a hair's breadth from its left side, lighting the desert an eerie grey.

'Of course,' David replied.

'Were you and Demeta ever together?'

He looked round at Joe, surprised. 'Demeta and I? No.

Demeta's my friend. There were other women before your mother, but she was the last. Since her, there's been no one else.'

David mulled it over as they walked. 'Maybe Demeta and I would have had something, if we'd met in a different place, or a different time. She certainly argues with me, which your mother did too, and I always enjoyed.' David laughed quietly to himself, and Joe remembered what Niv said about holding on to what made you laugh. 'I'm glad Demeta and I have been the way we are. I wouldn't change it. I've needed a friend.'

David fell quiet again. He was tense, as if he was working through a complex puzzle in his head.

'I haven't told you enough about your mother,' he said after a while. 'I'm sorry for that. I've always found it too hard to describe her. I knew her as part of the city. I remember the reckless way she drove a car, and the jokes she made about television adverts, and how she always filmed me on her phone. But what does that mean to you, who grew up in the town? I could tell you that she was kind, that she had a temper, that she was funny if you got her sense of humour, that she cared more about saying what was right than she did about getting along with people. But none of that really tells you who she was.'

'It's okay,' Joe said. 'You can't bring her back. I understand that.'

'I've been trying to make music of her, since Demeta found the guitar strings. There won't be any words. I want to play the sound of her, on the guitar. Music that sounds like how she was, if that makes any sense.'

'It makes sense,' Joe said, then hesitated, aware of the years that had passed since he'd last heard his father mention his mother. 'I know I don't understand what it was like in the city, but could you tell me what you can about her?'

David tried to describe Joe's mother and ended up telling a story about her, about when the owners of the tower block they'd lived in started kicking residents out one by one. He explained how she'd organised everyone in the building to have meetings and plan a resistance. She stayed up late at night to read through legal documentation, looking for a way to protect their homes.

When she couldn't find a legal answer to their problems, she encouraged everyone to stay in their flats even if they were evicted. She'd spit at the feet of the men who came to remove them. She could be demanding, even cruel, and spoke cuttingly to other residents who didn't understand the legal jargon around their tenancy agreements. Her intensity stemmed from her desire to help, and regardless of how frustrated she became, that deep-seated care for others was something David always admired about her. She cried for each resident who was forced out, including those who she'd clashed with.

The building was emptied in the end, but thanks to Joe's mother, some compensation was given to the evicted residents.

It at least helped them find new places to live. The story wasn't all of who his mother was, but it told Joe a little of the life she'd lived and what she'd stood for.

As David told the story, Joe felt a shadow of a woman walking alongside them, just out of sight. Maybe not his mother, but the story of her. Joe thought his father was aware of her too, but he didn't say anything aloud. He felt the second he spoke she would vanish, and the moment would be over. He wondered how often her story moved alongside David, as his father was getting up early in the morning to fill water from the well, or collecting on the mountains. Perhaps she was why David could believe Joe's tales of the magic of storytelling, and meeting the Wolf and the Forest Woman in the desert.

Eventually, the story of his mother faded from beside them. But Joe now knew a little more of his mother than he had before. David had given him something of her to hold onto to.

Joe and David walked on. They were quiet now, focusing their energy on crossing the changing gradients of the desert. They'd taken a short break to eat cold porridge that David had pre-cooked before leaving, which now sat as a stodgy weight in Joe's stomach. David stopped at the top of one of the hills, looking across the rolling landscape.

'I reckon this is about it,' David said.

'This is what?' Joe's voice creaked after a few hours of

walking in silence.

'The point of no return. If we turn around now, we should make it back before sunrise. If we continue on, then there's no going back tonight, and we'll walk far enough that we could lose the town behind us. From here on out, there's no guarantee we'll make it home.'

'Surely we'd see the mountains in the daytime?' Joe could almost feel them towering behind him. He looked back into the night, and realised he wouldn't be able to point in their direction with any certainty.

'These slopes are deceptive. Last time it took me and Demeta longer to get home than it did getting to the outlet. We'd walked for four nights before we saw the mountains again in the morning.'

'Did you stop at a place like this last time? At a point of no return?' Joe remembered Demeta's advice, that believing in his father gave him power.

'Yes.' David smiled a little. 'Maybe even the exact same place. Who knows?'

'What did Demeta say then?'

'She said that the desert looked like the sea. Because of the darkness, and the rippling earth, and the moonlight highlighting the tips of the hills. She said it reminded her of when she was young, and she swam too far from the shore. She remembered looking back, her muscles feeling weak, and not knowing if she could get to dry land.'

'But what did she say next? Did she say to go home, or continue on?'

'Continue on. She said she believed I'd find the way.'

'So do I. Let's keep walking.'

David snorted. 'You know, it worried me less when you were shouting at me.'

He set off walking again, and Joe followed behind him.

Morning approached. As the sky grew paler it revealed faint shapes in a valley between the hills ahead. The shapes were hard to differentiate from the desert, but they seemed large enough that they could be buildings. David spotted them as well, and started heading in their direction.

'Is that the outlet?' Joe asked.

'I don't know. It seems right. It's where it should be.'

They descended a slope and the shapes dropped out of view, then reappeared as they climbed the next. Under the fading stars, Joe made out that the nearest of the shapes had curved sides. Several rectangles blurred into each other behind it.

'It took you three nights with Demeta,' Joe said.

'Last time, I thought we'd be able to see the outlet on the first sunrise. But there was only desert, all around us. I had a feeling we needed to go left, that I'd got the direction wrong, not the distance. We walked that way for the next two nights, and I turned out to be correct. I took that into account this time, so maybe we've managed it in a straight line.'

'I don't understand how you know where you're going. It all looks the same.'

'It's not by landmarks. It's about staying aware of where you're coming from, and where you're going to, and trying to place yourself between them. It's keeping a feel of it all in your head.' David caught Joe's quizzical expression, even in the dark. 'I guess there's a couple of things I can teach you other than music.'

'I guess so,' Joe said. 'Though if this turns out not to be the outlet, I might skip that lesson.'

David chuckled. They headed on, but were stopped by the sunrise before they reached the shapes. An orange line traced the tops of the hills to their right, so they laid their sacks onto the ground and set up shade. They sat in the tarp's growing shadow as the sun rose, and watched the light stretching towards the shapes ahead.

When the light hit, it was as if the buildings threw off a cloak. The closest was a huge horseshoe with a white-stone plaza glinting in its middle. Behind it, there were several wide rectangular buildings with flat roofs and pastel-coloured walls, a damaged road slipping out between the hills to their side.

David jumped up, bumping his head into the tarp. 'The curved building in front, that's the shopping outlet, that's it!'

Joe leapt to his feet as well. 'One night! We did it in one night's walk!'

They embraced, bent under the tarp, then David pulled a water bottle from his cloth sack and proffered it towards Joe. 'Care for a celebratory drink?'

'Don't mind if I do,' Joe said, then took a swig. 'Tastes like the finest whisky.'

He handed it back to David, who drank and smiled. 'So it does.'

'We're so close,' Joe said, looking at the outlet and the buildings behind it. 'I can't believe we have to wait the whole day to get there.'

'Maybe not. It's not too hot yet. We could carry the shade.'

They lifted their cloth sacks and each held two of the poles that supported the tarp, pointing it towards the sun. Joe walked in front and David behind, moving like an unwieldy four-legged animal. The poles were awkward to carry, and as the morning grew hotter, Joe realised the buildings were further away than they'd initially thought.

Joe's shins were exposed to the sun and starting to burn. He felt the strain of having walked all night, but he didn't let himself slow down. The explanation for his vision was in the outlet, even if it was only that there was no real reason he saw what he did. As they got closer to the outlet and Joe spotted a copper sculpture in the centre of the white-stone plaza, he knew he didn't believe that there'd be no reason. Too much had happened to bring him and his father there. He felt something ahead, waiting for him.

CHAPTER TWENTY-SIX

Joe and David's footsteps echoed across the white-stone plaza. They still carried their shade, the tarp dipping down over their heads. The outlet curved around them, large signs along its extruding roof displaying shop names that Joe was unable to read. Each shop had wide windows and transparent doors, the glass surfaces dusted brown by the desert.

In the centre of the plaza, there was a copper statue of three people walking in a line. There were pale green streaks down their metal skin, and the detail of their faces and bodies had worn away. They had no clear gender, and two were missing limbs, but the essence of their shape remained.

David led Joe under the outlet's roof, where they packed the tarp and poles back into the cloth sacks. Joe looked through the nearest window into a room so long it seemed the ceiling should collapse. There was a sparse arrangement of bare tables and empty shelves inside, as well as a pair of stationary escalators leading up to a higher floor.

'So all of this,' Joe said, 'it was like a drifter's trade, but for the city?'

'Similar in a way,' David replied. 'Though mostly people came here because they enjoyed it, not because they needed things. Shopping was something to do.'

Joe pictured the plaza bustling with people carrying plastic bags of purchases, the shops crammed full with everything he'd found the remains of on the mountains. It was like discovering the skeleton of a grand creature in the desert, and trying to imagine it alive and breathing.

'The restaurant is on the top floor of that one,' David said, pointing towards a shop on the curve of the horseshoe. 'When Demeta and I came here, it was completely cleared out, like all the rest.'

They headed towards it, staying under the roof's shade. Joe looked through the windows, each shop long and empty. David kept his eyes down for most of the way, glancing up at just one of the shops. There was the outline of a guitar painted on its window, and Joe could tell the stands inside were designed to hold the instruments. David sighed as they walked past, but made no comment.

'It's this one,' David said, then stopped to pry his fingers into a set of once-automatic doors. He pulled them far enough apart for both of them to enter. Inside the shop, steel bars with attached clothing hangers looped out from the walls, and there were two shelving units with dirty mirrors on their ends.

On the wall behind a dismantled cash register there was a poster of a woman. She was wearing bright clothes and smiling. It was the largest picture of someone from the city Joe had ever seen. She looked like a different species.

Her lips were pure red like blood, her hair was somehow glossy, and her stomach didn't stick out like the townspeople's did. Her teeth were incredibly white. It made his own teeth – cleaned occasionally with salt, water and an almost bristleless toothbrush – feel gritty in his mouth.

'This way,' David said, standing at the bottom of a static escalator. It slanted up into an almost pitch-black opening in the ceiling. David started up the metal stairs, Joe following behind him.

'I don't know why it's so dark up there,' David said, as they ascended. 'It wasn't like that last time. There should be light coming in through the windows.'

Joe's sense of something waiting for him was stronger than ever. Whatever it was, he and his father would find it there in the darkness. They climbed into the shadows, stepping off the top of the escalator. He could see the blocked windows, sunlight bordering their edges, but could make out nothing else. The atmosphere was stuffy in here, though the heat was less intense. A smell similar to the Moonshine Brothers' whisky hung in the air. David moved ahead, tapping his hand across the wall.

'Here it is,' David said. 'Let's see about that electricity.'

There was a click, and the restaurant illuminated. Joe was awestruck by the intense flares of light trapped in the bulbs overhead, like slices from the sun captured and held. The light cast tiny stars twinkling in the wine-glasses set out across every table, their crystal as thin and clear as rain.

The silver cutlery shone as well, wrapped in napkins and laid on white tablecloths. Bronze taps glittered on the bar and were reflected in the varnished wood beneath them. Behind the bar, radiant lighting panels exhibited various bottles filled with different drinks.

One bottle separated from the rest, as the mechanical platform supporting it slid smoothly out from the wall. The platform ignited into an orange glow, tinting the bottle and highlighting the flecks of gold that moved in a slow spiral behind the label.

How can this be true? Joe thought. *How can there be electricity here?*

'I don't understand. This was a ruin the last time we were here.' David had stars in his eyes from the lightbulbs. He blinked them away, then pointed across the restaurant. 'Look. Maybe that's your computer.'

There was a tall black machine in the corner of the

restaurant, with a red light flashing below its screen. They went to it together, and David fiddled with the buttons on its side. He pressed something and the screen lit up, showing a few dots rolling in a circle. They disappeared and were replaced by text and square images, none of which made any sense to Joe.

'I'm sorry,' David said. 'It's not a computer. It's not connected to the internet.'

'What is it then?'

'It can't help anyone. But it's an amazing thing.' David tapped through options on the touchscreen. 'It's a chance for us to have something we thought we'd lost.'

'What is it?' Joe repeated.

'It's the restaurant's music system. A sort of jukebox, I think.' David pressed the screen again. The restaurant filled with a sound like brassy wind whistling through the desert hills. It was a musical instrument, one that Joe couldn't identify.

'This is what I was telling you about,' David said. 'This is rock 'n' roll.'

The brass wind faded away. A man's voice rumbled over a different instrument that played tinkling raindrops. The man sang about loneliness, and a girl's dress swaying as she danced.

'Listen, there it is,' David said, partway into the song. 'That's an electric guitar.'

The sound was brighter than the acoustic guitar, and more ethereal, as if it had been lifted away from the body of the instrument. It didn't sound like it was made from wood, copper and steel. It sounded like electricity itself, like the hot flares inside the lightbulbs transformed into music.

The electric guitar mixed with the other instruments, forming into something more complete and whole than could ever be created in the town. The song built, growing faster and louder. Joe's thoughts of the town were swept away as his heart accelerated with the music. When it ended, he was breathing hard, buzzing with adrenaline.

'What did you think?' David asked, his face flushed.

'Brilliant,' Joe said, shaking his head slowly. 'If this is it, if this is the reason we came here, then it's enough. I'm glad I got to hear the music.'

'That was just one song. There's so many on this machine. I'll find you another, one with an electric guitar solo. They sound like nothing else.'

'And imagine,' said a man's voice behind them, 'if you could listen to all that music whenever you wanted.'

CHAPTER TWENTY-SEVEN

Joe and David turned. At the top of the escalator there was a Caucasian man in an entirely black suit. His clothes were immaculate. Not a single smudge on his black shoes, black trousers, black shirt, black tie or black jacket. His hair was swished to the side, a gold watch glittered on his wrist, and his smile was as white as the tablecloths. Despite the stuffy air in the restaurant, that even made Joe and David, who were used to working on the mountains, sweat, there wasn't a drop of perspiration on his skin.

'Picture this. You drive here together in a fast car, feeling the soft purr of the engine in your legs.' The man spoke theatrically, as if addressing a rapt audience. 'You come to this restaurant first. You order a steak each, with salad on the side and a bottle of wine to share. Then for dessert, something with chocolate and ice cream, and a touch of alcohol.

'Still warm and fuzzy from the wine, you head out to do some shopping. You go to a shop that sells CDs, where the walls are plastered with the artwork of a thousand different bands, and you put on headphones to listen to sample tracks while you decide what you want. You buy the album containing the song you were playing when I came in, along with surround sound speakers that let you sit inside the music and hear all of its depth and detail.'

The man's smile grew wider, revealing more pure white teeth. His tone was friendly and confident. 'So where will you plug in those speakers? Where's home for you?'

'We're from the mountains,' Joe said.

'The landfill,' David clarified. 'And yourself?'

'From Madera, of course.' The man strode forward to shake David's hand, and then shook Joe's as well. His grip was firm. Joe noticed he was wearing gold cufflinks, that gleamed in the light.

'So, tell me'– the man swept his arms out around him – 'what do you think of my restaurant? Judge it as an example, an indicator of quality, for when we get the outlet up and running.'

'You can make the entire outlet like this?' Joe asked.

'Of course I can! We've done the same for all of Madera.'

'The whole city?' It didn't make any sense to Joe. The city had been derelict when they left. It couldn't have changed so fast.

'Young man, Madera' – the man pointed towards the black roller blinds closed over the windows, as if the city itself stood behind them – 'is the greatest city in the world. I'm not just talking about anywhere, I'm talking about any-when, the greatest city in all of history! I am in the fortunate position of being something of a business leader there. So trust me, anything you can dream, we can build.'

'If you call Madera the greatest city in the world,' David said, 'then you're a damn liar.'

Joe was startled by the anger in his father's voice. Here, finally, was somebody who could actually help the town. Whatever the truth was about the city now, someone with the ability to build this restaurant was exactly what they needed.

The man had the power of stories about him, a touch of that same feeling that Joe had encountered before, in the Wolf, and the Forest Woman, and The Boy Who Learned What Fear Was. It was there in how he looked and spoke, though he was definitely present and real. Something about that was familiar to Joe, though he wasn't sure from where. Finding him could be Joe's destiny, that everything had been leading towards. Yet, David's cheeks were pink with rage as he squared up to the man in the suit.

'We came from Madera,' David growled. 'Now we live on the landfill with everything else that city threw away. We sleep on filthy mattresses on the floors of derelict shacks. Children work every day in the burning sun, collecting rubbish to sell so they won't starve.

'Recently, a boy named Buddy died in an avalanche, crushed beneath waste thrown away from the city. He's not the first to die that way. There's a six-year-old girl in a coma, because vermin in the waste made her sick. A teenager is pregnant, and it'll be a miracle if both she and her baby survive. A great city wouldn't let people suffer like this on its outskirts.'

'You're absolutely right,' the man waved his hands as if brushing away the troubles. 'That shouldn't be happening, not with the resources we have. We'll bring you machines that provide a safe and proper way to dig through the landfill. We'll build houses, with kitchens, bedrooms and lounges.

'Every house will be stocked with food, bought from this outlet, paid for by real wages for your work. We'll build a hospital as well, with sterile white rooms and doctors and nurses, for the sick and the pregnant. There will be no suffering, not around my city!'

The man abruptly walked away from David. He stopped at the nearest table and pressed his palm down against it, rumpling the tablecloth. 'I've actually been looking for your town for a while. In Madera, I found documentation for the landfill. When I met the gardeners and the fisherpeople, they told me about the mountains, but I could never find you. Have you heard about my machines that they've been using?'

'I've heard drifters mention them,' Joe said. Leigh had said he was visiting the fisherpeople next to see their new machines, and Niv had said the same about the gardeners.

'We've not had anyone visit who's seen them working yet,' David said.

'The machines are in use, and have been hugely successful. I wouldn't want your town to be left behind.' He leaned forward, putting his weight on the table. 'Tell me, do you know a man named Charles Bradford?'

'No,' Joe said.

'We do,' David contradicted. 'But people call him the Mayor now.'

'Huh.' The man straightened up and adjusted his tie. 'A fitting title, I suppose. He owns the landfill, and the surrounding area. If we're going to make this better life for your people a reality, he'll need to transfer the rights to the area to me. Unless the landfill is lawfully mine, there's not much I can do. A man in my position has to play by the rules.'

'The Mayor would do that, wouldn't he, if it'd help the town?' Joe asked his father.

David hesitated, glancing at the suited man before replying. 'For all he likes playing at pomp and position, I think the Mayor would know this wasn't his choice to make. He'd let the townspeople decide.'

'Wonderful!' the man exclaimed. 'Who wouldn't choose a better future? A good home, safe work, and quality healthcare? My car's outside, you two can show me the way to the town. If there are lives at stake on those mountains, then we don't have a moment to lose!'

'Though perhaps,' the man added, jumping away from the table and rushing around behind the bar, 'we have time for just one quick toast. Let me see, let me see, something fitting for the occasion.'

He paused at the bottle with swirling gold flakes, then shook his head and took a dark green one from above it. He turned and presented the bottle towards Joe. 'This wine is older than you, young man, flavoured with all the time that's passed while you've been living. It's appropriate for such a momentous occasion, to drink history while we think of the future.'

The man took a corkscrew from under the bar, then plunged it into the top of the bottle like a weapon into flesh. He popped the cork out, then walked to a table and poured the maroon wine into three glasses. Joe joined him.

He had a nagging feeling of wrongness about the man's offer, and the whole situation. Something in the air of storytelling magic around him put Joe on edge. He pushed that feeling aside. This was the destiny he'd been following. He had to make sure this man helped the town. David joined them, suspicion clear in his expression.

'To a better tomorrow!' The man raised his glass. Joe lifted his, but David's remained untouched.

'Is there a computer connected to the internet here?' David asked. 'That's why we came here. It's what we were looking for.'

'I'm afraid we haven't sorted out the internet yet. But fear not! Soon there'll be internet here, and in your town. You'll be reconnected with the world as a whole.'

'I want to hear more about your plans,' David said, his voice layered with obvious suspicion. 'What are these machines for the mountains? If we were paid wages for collecting like you said, who would the employer be? Will the townspeople be able to work in the hospital you're building, or run shops in the outlet? Would we have to stay in the town, or would we be able to travel to the city and other places as well?'

Joe felt like he could not draw in the stale restaurant air. The images of a better life the man had offered, of hospitals and houses and food, were fragile and precious, as if they were painted onto glass. Too forceful a question could shatter them.

'All in good time!' the man said, and Joe breathed again. 'We'll work out the specifics in the town, where everyone can join in. This is about improving their lives, so it's only fair that they have their say. Now, to a better future!'

This time David did lift his glass, and they all drank. The wine was heady and warm. There was an amazing depth to its flavour, which Joe could only assume had developed over the years it had waited for this moment.

The man gulped down his glass in one go, and let out a satisfied sigh. 'Ah! I'll get my car set, it's just behind this building. You two finish the wine, and come down when you're ready. I'll see you shortly.'

Without waiting for reply, he strode to the escalator, then vanished down the steps. Joe was left with a lingering feeling that a story had been told, changing the reality around them. It was like when he'd told the story about the Wolf, except this time they were the subjects, and the man in the suit was the teller.

'This is why I was supposed to come here,' Joe said to David. 'He could help us have a better life in the town. He could save Lily.'

'I'm sorry, Joe,' David said flatly. 'I don't think we should show him the way to the town.'

'What?' Joe exclaimed. 'This is why we came here. It's why the Witch said I had a destiny, and why my vision mentioned this place.'

'You're smarter than this. You know what he's saying doesn't make sense.'

Joe felt like it was all slipping away. Everything had led to here. He had to make it worth something, otherwise it had all been wasted. The man seemed to have the power to make change in the world, whether that was through storytelling or money. If he had that power, surely they could convince him to use it to help Lily.

'Maybe it doesn't make sense,' Joe admitted. 'I don't see how the whole city could be so different from when we left. But we've been gone a long time. And look at this restaurant. And we know the machines that he gave the gardeners and the fisherpeople are real.'

'This place looks impressive, but I haven't seen any actual food. It could just be a well presented scam. As for the machines, we have no proof they actually work.' David looked across at Joe. He must have seen the desperation in his son's eyes, because his tone became more gentle. 'He didn't even tell us his name.'

Joe was shocked. He had been aware that he didn't know the man's name, but his mind had slipped over the fact. There was a lyricism to the suited man's words that had distracted Joe away from the details, leaving only the image of the ideal world he was selling to them. Joe thought he had been right, that the man had used storytelling power – seemingly to avoid being asked important questions. It had worked better on Joe than his father.

'I've met men like him before,' David said, taking advantage of Joe's uncertainty to press home his point. 'All promises and the clink of money in their voice. They're the most to blame, for the way the world's become. It lies at the door of men in suits and their promises. Men like him destroyed our lives in the city, and I don't know why we should believe he's been able to fix it all. We don't even know if people live there anymore at all.'

Joe was frustrated, coming up against the wall of his father. He felt that old anger, that came from being trapped in their lives scavenging from the mountains. How many times had he looked out at lights from the city and wondered if anyone lived there? And here he was, still asking the same questions with no answers.

He knew everything that David said was right, but there had to be more to it. If they weren't supposed to find the man here to help them, then Joe having a destiny was a lie. He couldn't do anything for Lily. But his vision in the Witch's shack, guided by Forest Woman, had told him to come here. It all came down to the stories.

'There's something else I need to tell you,' Joe said. He felt almost like he was pleading to his father. 'Even before I rode the truck out into the desert, I'd met characters from stories before. The Boy That Learned What Fear Was saved me from being crushed in the mountains, and the Forest Woman told me that if I looked for a way to the city, I'd find help for Lily. That brought me to the Witch, and then here. It all adds up to him. I think he might have that same power over stories, I could sense it on him. Maybe the story about the city is part of how he made this place. That power could help us.'

David crossed his arms.

'Don't tell me you don't believe in it,' Joe insisted. 'You believed me about the Wolf, and the Forest Woman. And I know you felt it, when we were walking here. When you told the story about Mum.'

David's eyes widened, but then he nodded. 'Yes. I've felt it. But just because it exists, doesn't mean that it's being used with our best interests at heart. The Witch suggested to you, somehow, to come to this outlet to find a computer with internet. That was something she knew you'd want, and it wasn't here. Instead there was this man, who's now offering more of what you want, in exchange for taking him back to the town.

'But when it wasn't true the first time, why should we think it will be the second time around? How do we know any of this is for you and for Lily? For all that's wrong in the town, people tend to tell each other the truth. I've had more experience of being lied to and manipulated than you Joe, and that's what this feels like.'

What David said about the Witch struck Joe. He'd implied that she'd used the storytelling power as well. He realised it was her the suited man reminded him of. She had that same feeling, like she was both a character from a tale and a real person all at once.

'I can't give up,' Joe said emphatically. 'If we just leave that man here, and go home, that's it for Lily. You saw the moon last night. It'll be full tonight. The Witch has always been right about illnesses.'

David let his shoulders drop, letting out a long breath. Joe knew his father had the weight of years of regrets on top of him.

'I don't know if I can show him the way back,' Joe said. 'Not without you. Please.'

'For Lily,' David replied. 'For the chance it might help her. But we can't trust him.'

'Agreed.'

They left their wine, abandoning the two almost-full glasses on the table. They searched the restaurant, including the clinically lit kitchen in the back. Like David had suggested, there was no food in the place at all, though they put some bottles of alcohol in their cloth sacks, to share with the town. There was also no computer. They looked for a generator, but could find no sign of where the electricity was actually coming from.

Maybe the power really was made by the man's story, Joe thought. Though perhaps there was a generator elsewhere, that was wired up to send electricity to the restaurant, and the rest of the outlet when needed.

David switched off the lights, and the sparkling restaurant disappeared. Joe saw his father, framed by the sunlight from the empty shop below, pause at the top of the escalator. He glanced back into the darkness, before shaking his head to himself and beginning his descent. Joe knew what David didn't want to leave behind. It had turned off, powering down with the lights.

'Dad,' Joe said, following him down the metal steps. 'One day soon we'll come back, and listen to the music for as long as we can. I want to hear it all.'

'Thank you,' David replied. 'I'd like that.'

CHAPTER TWENTY-EIGHT

The man had pulled his car round into the centre of the plaza. Joe wondered where it had been parked that they hadn't seen it as they approached. The car was red and low to the ground, shaped in smooth curves. It was much different to the cars Joe had seen drifters drive. It looked brand new and designed for speed.

The one-way glass in the windows reflected Joe and David as they approached the passenger side door, which lifted open by itself, rising up like an unfolding wing. The man grinned at them from behind the wheel and patted the free seat. Joe and David managed to squeeze themselves in, the seat just wide enough for the both of them with their cloth sacks on their knees. The spongey material sunk under their weight, pushing their legs together.

'Welcome to your chariot,' the man said, an amused note in his voice. He flicked a switch on the steering wheel and the passenger door lowered, closing out the sunlight. It was dark as night inside the car, the tinted windows shrouding the outside world in shades of purple.

The dashboard was made of black glass. When the man tapped it, a network of blue symbols and dials glowed under the surface. He manipulated the blue light with his hand, using his thumb and two fingers to turn one of the dials. A chill flowed through the material of the passenger seat, the cold sensation trickling down Joe's back and the base of his legs.

'And for my next trick.' The man moved a blue slider upwards with a swipe of his thumb. Cool wind began to blow out from a vent beneath the dashboard, fluttering Joe's T-shirt against his chest. Even in the stream during celebrations, he'd never felt such a perfect cold.

The air was bracing as he drew it in, as if it cleansed the grit and dirt from inside his lungs. It reminded Joe of the iceberg on the cover of the book he'd given to the Librarian. This is what it must have felt like to stand on the ice and breathe in.

The man pushed his foot down on the accelerator, his smile showing teeth. The car launched forwards as if weightless, flying towards the opposite side of the outlet. The shops rushed towards them, too fast for Joe or David to react.

The man twisted the wheel so that they swung under the

outlet's roof, the side of the car almost crashing into a glass window. Momentum took the car out into the desert and they sped across the dry earth.

'What's wrong with you?' David shouted. 'You could've killed us!'

'There's no need to worry, I'm an expert driver. And didn't your hearts race? I'd say the faster we're going, the more alive we are.'

'Until we hit something,' David muttered.

'There's nothing to fear! Not dying is one of my most precious skills, which I've been honing all my life. While you're inside my vehicle, you're under my protection.'

'Who's protection is that, exactly?' David asked.

Joe realised he'd stopped noticing, again, that he did not know the man's name. He focused on the fact, forcing it to stay in his awareness. Whatever power the man had, it was subtle and persuasive.

'With me, you're under the protection of the city of Madera,' the suited man said, dodging David's question.

David shook his head in annoyance. He started giving directions anyway, pointing the suited man marginally left and right as they zipped across the desert. The car swept over the top of a slope without even the slightest jolt, speeding down the remainder of the hill and then up the next.

The engine roared as they drove, much louder than the

drifters' vehicles. It took Joe a while to realise that was because the car wasn't electric, but petrol powered. Maybe what the man had said was true, and the city was functioning again. How else could he have petrol?

To Joe, nothing felt real. Not the cold, nor the unnatural speed, nor the purple world outside the window. Exhaustion from the night's walking dragged at him, and he felt like he was already dreaming. He half-expected the panther to appear and keep pace with the car.

The mountains rose into view. They grew larger, and soon the town was visible as well. After that, Joe could see the townspeople, like insects on the sides of the mountains. He wondered which of them was Sonya, or Grandad. The man drove the car over the last few hills and then guided to a stop a short distance from the stone well.

'If you'll excuse me,' the man said, then drew a mobile phone from his pocket. The screen lit up at the touch of his thumb.

Joe and David stared dumbfounded. They hadn't seen a working phone since Joe was a child. The signal had disappeared from the sky long before the last of them ran out of battery. The man tapped the screen a few times, and then put the phone to his ear. There was an electronic ringing sound, then a muffled voice answered the call.

'Send two recycling trucks to my location,' the man said. 'I've found the landfill.'

So the men in the recycling truck were from Madera too, Joe thought. *And the people living there don't know where the mountains are. I've spent my whole life gazing out at the city, and they wouldn't even know where to look to find us.*

He flopped the phone away from his ear and looked across at them. 'You two can go. Let your Mayor know I'm here. I've got a presentation to plan.'

'One of your recycling trucks left Joe for dead in the desert,' David snarled.

'Is that so?' The man didn't seem surprised. 'You have to understand that the workers get a bit irrational when they're travelling between the city and the recycling centre. There's a lot of superstition surrounding that route. They'll have thought you were something out of the shadows.'

'They knew exactly what they were doing,' Joe said.

'How troubling. I'll find out who they were for you, and have them fired.' He put the phone back to his ear. 'As I've said, you can go now. I've got work to do.'

The man flicked the switch on the steering wheel and the passenger door raised open, letting the warm air in. He started talking on his phone again, asking for something called a valuation on the landfill, no longer paying them any attention.

David shrugged at Joe and they both climbed out of the car. It was only as the door lowered behind them that Joe understood exactly what the man was discussing on the phone.

He was talking about how much the mountains were worth, as if he could place the entirety of the waste on a drifter's table.

The Mayor was speaking to Ms Winnipeg by the stone well, both of them wearing sombre expressions. Joe had a moment of déjà vu, remembering when he returned to the town with Sonya, and Buddy had died. The Mayor was stopping people to tell them bad news again.

'What's wrong?' Joe called out, as he and David walked over to the well. Ms Winnipeg's face was ashen, making her appear older and frailer than ever before. The Mayor squared his shoulders, and then stepped forward towards them.

'Lily,' Joe said. 'She's gone.'

'Lily's worsened,' the Mayor replied. 'Last night she threw up blood, and still didn't wake up. The Witch said she'll be lucky to see the sunrise tomorrow.'

Joe's heart sank. They were too late.

'What else?' David said, staring intently at the Mayor.

'When Lily threw up, the Storyteller was there. It might not be the same sickness, but he seems to have caught–'

'Has the Witch seen him?' David cut in.

'She has. We don't understand how a snake bite could have been infectious. Rose was in the shack too, and she's not ill, so–'

'What did the Witch say?' David interrupted again.

The Mayor faltered, swallowing and gathering himself.

'What did she say?' David repeated.

'She said he won't survive the night.'

Joe and David looked at each other, then without speaking both started to run towards the town, leaving the Mayor and Ms Winnipeg behind. They headed into the dry stream, up towards their home. David's face was blank as they ran, his eyes strangely wide.

'Help!' screamed a voice from above the stream. They both stopped, looking up. Maya emerged from between two shacks, staggering towards the dry stream's banks. Her hand was on her belly, and the crotch of her trousers was stained red. Blood dripped from her, splatting against the earth.

'Go to the shack,' David said, somehow calm. 'I'll take care of her. Hurry to your grandfather.'

David placed his hand on Joe's back and pushed him onwards. Joe started running again, his legs carrying him automatically towards his home. His mind seemed to have shut off, unable to process everything that was happening.

He almost tripped and fell as he rushed into the shack. Grandad lay on his mattress on the floor. His skin was pale yellow, sunken below his eyes and around his mouth. His face looked like a skull.

'Joe,' he rasped. The shack smelled like rancid sweat. Joe would have welcomed the stench of the mountains back into their home, if it could replace the humid sickness in the air.

'I'm here.' Joe crouched down next to him.

Grandad groaned, as if Joe's presence hurt. 'You shouldn't be here. I caught this from Lily. There's no need for you to catch it as well.'

'I'm not leaving.'

'Please, go.' Grandad waved one arm weakly towards him. Joe moved to the other side of the shack, sitting down on a stool by the sink.

'You're as stubborn as your father.' Grandad's voice, that could project a story over celebration rain and fire, had become little more than a broken whisper. 'Has he come back, too?'

'Yes. He's on his way.'

'You both know what the Witch said?'

'Yes.'

Grandad exhaled, the air leaking out of his mouth achingly slow. 'She's right. I can feel it in the marrow of my bones. They're crumbling away on the inside. Soon they won't be strong enough to hold me up anymore.'

'She could be wrong,' Joe said, trying to convince himself as much as Grandad. 'It could be something that passes.'

'It's not passing, Little Joe. Young people, they live or they die. But not old men. Old men always die in the end.'

Joe stared down at his hands. His eyes stung, but no tears fell. 'I don't want to lose you.'

'I'll be a story soon.' Grandad's lipless mouth formed a smile. 'And who better to tell it than you? I'm proud of the stories that will be told about me. Father, Grandfather, and Storyteller. They were good roles to be playing at the finish.'

'We'll tell a damn good story of you, Grandad,' Joe said, his chest shaking.

'Thank you.' Grandad voice was losing even more of its volume the more he spoke. 'I know everything fell apart. I know the world went to hell. But I've loved my life here in the town, with you and your father. I wasn't a storyteller in the city.

'I was just a man with a job, who liked to read old books sometimes. Living here, telling stories–' He let out a long wheeze, his chest sinking so much it almost vanished into the mattress. 'And having them listened to. I could do it for a thousand years, up and down these mountains. I loved being the Storyteller. I loved it more than anything.'

Joe's clenched hands were turning pale. His eyes burned, brimming with tears.

'I'm sorry that I don't get to find out what happens. In this tale that you've been living. With the stories that emerge from the dark and walk in the real world. With the visions that lead you places, and the crows that call out to you. With the Forest Woman who was a panther as well, who cured your injury and cried for foxes. I'm going to miss the ending, I'm afraid.'

'I can't imagine you gone. Things won't make sense anymore.'

'They'll make the sense you make of them.' That little

phrase, such a typical play on words from Grandad, freed Joe's tears. Before he could compose himself enough to reply, David burst through the shack's door.

'I found help for Maya. She's got a few people with her,' he said to Joe, then addressed Grandad. 'How are you feeling?'

'The Witch is right,' Grandad answered.

'She doesn't have to be,' David said, not leaving room for Grandad to disagree. 'There's a man here Joe and I found at the outlet. He's rich, from the city, and he wants to invest in the town and the mountains. He's spoken to the Mayor, and the Mayor's organising a meeting for sunset tonight, in the fallen forest. If people agree to it, there'll be machines to work the mountains with, and proper food to buy, and we'll have a connection with the city again. We can get you a doctor, and real medicine.'

David sounded like he was trying as hard as he could to believe what he was saying, as if he could believe it hard enough to make it real. Joe knew that deep down his father still believed the suited man was a fraud.

Grandad struggled on the mattress, turning so that he could see them both. 'What was the man from the city like?'

'He wore a suit,' Joe answered. 'It was black and shining clean, and he had gold jewellery as well. There was something about him... he was almost like a story himself. He was good with his words. When he described things, you could see them in your head.'

Something clicked into place behind Grandad's sunken eyes. 'Did you say the meeting was tonight?'

David nodded wearily, as if he didn't fully understand the question.

'Tonight's the full moon,' Grandad said. 'I'll come to the meeting.'

David started forward to protest, but Grandad pre-empted him in a pained voice. 'I'm getting tired. Can you two do something for me?'

They both agreed, anything.

'Can you play the guitar? I want to hear it again.'

For the rest of the day, they passed the guitar back and forth between them, playing for Grandad. They took turns sleeping, both of them exhausted from walking all night. As the day wore on, Grandad faded in and out of consciousness, his eyes open while his pupils gained and lost their focus. Joe and David kept playing the guitar, even when it was unclear whether Grandad could hear them. Outside, the sun moved across the sky towards the fallen forest.

CHAPTER TWENTY-NINE

When the light outside the shack was deep orange and sunset was close, Grandad sat up on his mattress with an agonizing groan. Joe stopped playing the guitar, halting the strings with his hand. David, on one of the stools, looked up from his lap. Grandad rose to his feet, lifting his suffering body through willpower alone. His legs shook. It appeared that at any moment, his knees could crunch into each other and he'd collapse.

David stood as well. 'You're not well enough to go to the meeting. You need to rest.'

'You know what the Witch said. I'll rest soon enough. If you ask for me tomorrow, you'll find me a grave man.' Grandad's voice hadn't recovered any strength, barely audible over his own wheezing breath, but his eyes held something of their old twinkle. 'I'm going to this meeting. I wouldn't miss it for the world.'

He attempted to take a step forward but his leg buckled like a snapping twig. David was ready and darted under his arm to support him.

'You shouldn't be holding me,' Grandad said. 'You'll get sick.'

David didn't move away. 'I don't know how much of what the man in the suit says is true. But if anything he's said about the city is right, we can get help for you. We might be able to call a doctor here, or even take you to a hospital. You just need to rest till then.'

'I don't want to go to a hospital. I don't want to die somewhere else.' For the first time, Grandad sounded panicked, his voice cracking.

David wrinkled his brow in frustration. 'Listen, I don't know exactly how it's going to work, but for now, we just need to do what's best for you'

'Let me come to the meeting with you,' Grandad begged, slipping out of David's grip. 'Joe's story all comes together tonight. I can feel it, in my crumbling bones. I've told stories all these years, I deserve to see this one end.'

'You're not making sense.' David was twisted under Grandad's arm, holding the old man's side to keep him upright. 'You need to lie down.'

'No, I won't.' Grandad shook his head frantically. Joe felt sure there was a risk of his neck snapping and breaking.

'We could stay here with you.' David leaned back, looking into his Grandad's eyes while still supporting him. 'We'll play the guitar for you again.'

'I'm going to the meeting. It's my choice.'

David sighed.

'Please,' Grandad said.

'Fine,' David replied. 'When we're there, we'll find out how the man can help you.'

'Get me a stick to walk with. I don't want to make you ill.'

David actually laughed. 'Have you seen the state of you? A stick's not going to help. I'm not watching you roll down the stream.'

Grandad coughed a couple of times, harsh and spitting. Joe thought he might have been trying to laugh too.

'I'll help you,' David said. 'Let me do that, at least.'

'Thank you,' Grandad said, accepting the help. They started towards the door, David leading Grandad. Joe stepped forward with his arms out as well. David subtly shook his head. Joe let his arms drop and followed behind them through the shack's door.

As they stepped outside, they saw Mr Rajarshi and the Librarian approaching the shack. The two old men cast long shadows down the hill.

'We heard the Witch's prognosis. I hope she's wrong, my friend,' the Librarian said to Grandad.

'Are you on your way to the meeting?' Mr Rajarshi asked.

With his head down, and his lips moving too weakly for Mr Rajarshi to read, Grandad replied that he was. Mr Rajarshi seemed to understand anyway, and he and the Librarian joined them on their way to the dry stream.

David had difficulty getting Grandad down the dirt bank. Mr Rajarshi went under the other arm and the two of them lowered him down. Once they were in the stream, Mr Rajarshi walked next to Grandad but let David support him. The Librarian dropped back and walked next to Joe as they headed up towards the forest.

'How are you doing, m'boy?' he asked.

'I'm… I'm just getting through.'

'It's the only way in these times,' the Librarian said. He appeared much smaller outside of his shack. His glasses glinted in the low sun's light, like the reflection of a flame. 'I've been meaning to thank you for the last book you gave me. It's wondrous to read about the weather I recall from my youth, thinking back to when the rain fell often and cold days still occurred.'

'You're welcome,' Joe said distractedly. He'd noticed there was no one else in the dry stream, nor wandering between the shacks. 'Is everyone already in the forest?'

'Yes. Mr Rajarshi and I volunteered to see if any of your family were coming. Maya's not going to be there, she's badly unwell. The Witch saw her earlier. She said the baby's still living, but there's a chance that neither of them will make it through the night. Kane's with her, looking after her as best he can. Rose is with little Lily, of course. They say the poor child's worse than ever. Apparently, she's stopped breathing more than once tonight. It's a dark time, m'boy, and sad.'

Ahead, David, Grandad, and Mr Rajarshi had stopped. Crows covered the roofs of the last two shacks on either side of the dry stream, making a black-crowned gateway to the top of the hill. The birds cocked their heads and stared at Joe.

'And the Witch,' Joe said to the Librarian. 'Is she in the forest?'

'No,' the Librarian said, eyeing the crows. 'After she visited Maya, she returned to her shack and hasn't been seen since.'

The crows flapped up from the roofs, flying above where David supported Grandad, before swooping down into the trench. They scattered around Joe and the Librarian, crying out as they did, then rushed down the dry stream like a black river. A single feather settled on the ground in front of Joe's feet.

'She wants me to go to her,' Joe said to David, who was looking back at him.

'Go,' David replied. 'Maybe you can get some answers.'

'I don't want to leave,' Joe said.

'We'll look after Grandad,' David said. 'You find the Witch. You tell her we went to the outlet like she wanted, and now we're done playing her games. Demand an explanation from her, of everything she's said to you.'

Joe recognised David's anger. It was rage against a world that wasn't how it should be. A world where Grandad was dying, and they'd been away when he'd fallen ill. Joe knew too well how that sort of anger could hurt inside. He'd felt it so many times looking up at the mountains. He couldn't help Grandad, but he could at least try to ease his father's pain.

'I love you, Grandad,' Joe said. 'I'll see you at the meeting.'

'Yes,' Grandad answered, his voice already ghostlike, whispering from the other side. 'I hope it's a good story, Little Joe.'

Joe wanted to hug him, to wrap his arms around the old man and hold him close, but he knew Grandad would fear passing on his sickness. Instead, Joe strode down the stream, following a trail of fallen crows' feathers.

Anger grew inside him, mirroring his father's. He was like one of the crows, following the Witch's commands. She'd tamed him for her own use. He took a deep breath, and let the feeling pass. It wouldn't help him to confront the Witch, nor decipher her riddles. All he wanted was to find out what he could, then get back to Grandad.

Joe reached the end of the dry stream. He saw the suited

man's car still parked next to the stone well, now with two recycling trucks behind it. The crows were flying in tight circles above the Witch's shack. He walked to the door and pushed it open. Lit by the evening sun, the inside of the shack lost its mystical quality. The grass on the floor was bent and yellowed, and the moss on the walls was grey. The rats and insects ran from the light, into the shack's corners.

The Witch leaned on her stick, standing next to the ashen stones where she built her fires. The right half of her face gave nothing away, as usual. The left half, in a line that cut down through her nose, was crumpled with sadness. From her left eye only, she was crying.

'Why are you crying?' Joe asked.

'For Lily.' Her voice sounded younger, weeping along with the left-hand side of her face. 'And for your grandfather, and for Maya and her child.'

Tears ran down her left cheek as she sobbed louder. Joe recognised the sound of her crying. He'd heard it before.

'And for the fox I killed,' she moaned. 'And for the crow that died in the desert. For Buddy, for your mother, for everyone who's died in this town.'

'You're the Forest Woman.'

One cold eye and one crying eye looked into his. While the left half of her face continued to cry, she spoke in the impassive tone of the elderly Witch. 'Yes. I am, or was.'

The Witch was the Forest Woman. She'd told him he had a destiny as the Witch, then appeared alongside Leigh's van to tell him to try to get to the city to help Lily. She'd been motivating him to travel out from the town, first towards the city then to the outlet.

Then Joe had a thought that triggered an anxious sickness in his stomach.

'You can control the animals,' he said, his voice shaking. 'The snake that bit Lily. Was that you?'

'Like the fox, there has to be sacrifice for the magic to work. But I always hoped that you would save her, and myself, tonight.'

Joe felt as if the mountains themselves were falling, the waste crashing all around him. She'd done this to Lily. It was her all along.

'You made Grandad ill as well,' Joe accused.

'I didn't mean for that to happen,' she replied, her voice still old. 'I didn't expect the sickness I gave her to spread.'

Joe expected rage to rise up inside himself, but instead all he felt was disbelief and disgust. She had lived among them. She drank whisky with them at rain celebrations. How could she have done this?

'Does Maya have the sickness too?'

'Not the one I put in the snake,' the Witch said. 'Maya's illness was not my doing. This town is no place for new life to come into the world.'

'You have to make Grandad and Lily better. Maya too, if you can.'

The youth and sobs returned to her voice. 'I can't, Joe. I can't make any of them better now. Only you can, with your power that you've learned. The one you used to defeat the Wolf.'

'The storytelling?'

She nodded, weeping. 'I'm sorry. I used you for my own ends.'

'I don't know how to use the storytelling to help,' Joe insisted. 'The Wolf was a character from a story, so I was able to change things by adapting its tale. But I don't know how to do that here. I don't know what the story is that I'm supposed to change.'

'By the end of the night, you'll understand,' she replied, in the impersonal tone of the ancient Witch. 'You may even be able to influence the way the narrative concludes.'

No answers, again. Joe considered demanding an explanation as David had told him to, but he knew it wouldn't work. If she'd been going to tell him what was going on, she'd have done so a long time ago. He'd find out nothing else. He turned away from the Witch, meaning to head back up the dry stream to Grandad.

'Joe.' It was the younger voice again. He looked at the damp left side of her face. A few of the hairs on that side were no longer grey, but curly and black. 'I wanted to tell you that I'm glad I could help you in the desert. Not because you might do the same for me tonight. Because it's good that you're alive, and it'd pain me to see you die.'

Joe nodded. There was nothing to say. She had threatened Lily and Grandad's lives, and set in motion the events that had put his own at risk. Yet still, she'd saved him in the desert, when the truck left him for dead.

'It's your time to go to the forest,' she said, as the old crone once more. 'I'll follow when it's mine.'

She grasped the shack's door with her bony fingers and waited for him to leave. Her face was no longer split into two personalities. She was entirely the elderly Witch once more, though her left cheek was still wet. Joe walked away and she pushed the door shut behind him.

He heard the flapping of wings overhead. The crows that had been circling above the roof flew away from the Witch's shack, passing low near the parked car and trucks, then up and over the mountains and out of sight behind them. Next came the rats, pouring out of the holes in the walls of the shack, followed by the spiders, snakes and insects, all of them heading to the mountains to vanish amongst the waste.

Finally, the owl flew upwards from an unseen hole in the roof of the shack, utterly silent in the air. With its white wings wide, it glided away, following the crows' path towards the mountains.

Joe walked in the opposite direction, up to the stream and towards the fallen forest.

CHAPTER THIRTY

The fallen forest was busy with chatter. Nearly the whole population of the town was sitting across the logs and talking to one another. The suited man stood at the far end of the collapsed trees, lit by the sunset behind him. He was engaging with several townspeople at the front, switching back and forth between different conversations.

Four heavy-set men formed a guard around him, wearing the same bottle-green jumpsuits as the men who'd attacked Joe in the desert. They weren't wearing the gas masks, displaying their uniform faces with buzzcut hair and alert eyes. Like the man in the suit, these guards must have been from Madera as well. Their hands were clasped in front of their waistbands, not far from pistols holstered on their hips. Joe's limbs tensed as he remembered being thrown from the truck, the night he'd met the Wolf.

The Witch suggested that the same storytelling magic he had experienced that night would come into play tonight, and Joe could somehow use it to help Lily and Grandad. His grandfather clearly had similar suspicions. It was why he was so insistent on coming to the meeting.

But how would the suited man's offer, or scam, become a story? Why would that put the Witch under a threat that she'd hoped Joe might save her from? It was like he was trying to find his way through a labyrinth, in pitch darkness.

Joe scanned his eyes across the crowd, looking away from the suited man and his guards. Grandad, Mr Rajarshi, and the Librarian sat on the log furthest removed from the rest of the forest. David sat with Demeta, repeatedly looking over his shoulder at Grandad. The Mayor and the Artist Sisters were at the front, part of the crowd competing for the suited man's attention.

Alice was further back, speaking to Bill and his daughter, Hope. Matthias and Scott, the Moonshine Brothers, sat behind them. The Singing Family were gathered across two logs, entertaining the surrounding townspeople with brief snatches of song. Ms Winnipeg and Mrs Polward were talking with another pair of old ladies, their conversation punctuated with glances across at the suited man and his guards.

In the middle of it all, on their log, Sonya sat with Tiger. She saw Joe and leapt to her feet, running through the fallen trees towards him.

'Oh Joe! I'm so sorry that I haven't come to see you. I didn't know you were back until I came to the forest. I've been in Rose's shack all day, Lily's worse than ever, I think she's dying, and your grandfather… I'm so sorry–'

'It's okay,' Joe said, taking her hands. Her usual calm was cracked and broken, her expression frantic.

'Marco and Harvey are with Rose,' she said, speaking fast, 'which is good, because most people have been afraid to go there since your grandfather became ill. Rose shouldn't be alone, not when Lily might not make it through the night. I've just found out about Maya's bleeding. She's only got Kane with her. Maya's like a daughter to him, and he's barely been holding it together as it is. I don't know if they'll be okay with just the two of them.'

'Sonya. Go to Maya and Kane, and look after them. There's no one else who'll make them feel as safe as you will. It's who you are. Don't worry about me. I'm managing alright.'

'I'll still worry about you,' Sonya said, then slipped into Joe's arms and hugged him. 'Are you sure you'll be okay?'

'Yes, I am. You can go to Maya. She needs you.'

Sonya took a few long breaths, steadying herself and regaining her natural composure. She said goodbye, and then strode off towards the stream. Joe edged through the townspeople. He sat down next to Tiger and patted his shoulder. Tiger barely reacted, the bags beneath his eyes far too large for his young face.

'Oh, Joseph, you're here!' The Mayor shouted across from next to the suited man. 'I didn't see you arrive. That's everyone we were waiting for, isn't it?'

There were mumbles of assent from the townspeople on the logs.

'Well then,' the Mayor declared. 'We're ready to begin. As I'm sure you all know by now, this man has come to make us an offer of investment in the town, in exchange for my ownership of this land. As this is too momentous a decision for me to make alone, first we'll listen to what he has to say, then we'll have a discussion of it. When all of the terms are decided, we'll end on a vote of whether or not to accept his offer. Now, good sir, I concede the floor to you.'

The Mayor sat down. Joe noted that he'd given no name for the suited man. It seemed that only David was immune to being distracted from that detail. Joe thought it might be his father's cynicism that let him refuse to be influenced by the story the man wanted to tell.

The suited man stepped forward, his manner confident and warm. 'A pleasure to meet you all. I'd like to tell you a story. Who in this town knows stories well?'

All heads turned towards Grandad, out on the edge of the

forest. The Librarian and Mr Rajarshi each supported him with an arm behind his back, propping him upright. Grandad's eyes were attentive, but he gently shook his head rather than trying to raise his voice to reply.

'He's the Storyteller, and I'm the Librarian,' the Librarian said. 'I keep my library in my shack, and he keeps his in his mind. He tells stories better than any other.'

People nodded in agreement, and the man grinned. 'Excellent. It's good to know that stories are valued here. I'm going to tell the story of how your lives will improve, if you let me reconnect your town with my city, Madera.'

The man began, and Joe knew without doubt that this was storytelling, with the touch of magic within it. He told a tale of the townspeople waking up in the morning, and if it was too dark, flicking a switch to illuminate the room, and if it was too hot, turning a dial to cool the house. He told them about the smell of meat and eggs frying on the hob, and about drinking cold orange juice from the fridge.

He described how some of them would take jobs driving machines up onto the landfill, collecting in short shifts and returning home before half a day had passed. The machines would be equipped with technology that gave prior warning of avalanches. With appropriate safety procedures, no one would ever be caught in one again.

He told them how other people would run restaurants, shops,

bars, theatres and galleries, making the town a happier place to live. Everyone would have a car, and the roads would be rebuilt so they could drive to the shopping outlet, the recycling centre, or the city – even to the gardeners or the fisherpeople, whom he'd already struck similar deals with. They'd work out an agreement for buying the hunters' meat as well, once he'd located their roving band in the desert.

He spoke about reconnecting the town to the internet, so that they could find any film or song they remembered from their past, and be part of a whole world communicating in the present. Everything would be new, sparkling clean and made especially for them. The stream would no longer be dry, but always running with fresh water.

It was a wonderful story. As Joe listened, he felt joy rise inside himself. He knew he had been swept up by the same magic that had made him not worry about the man's name. He knew, but didn't care. If the man's story could make the world he described, it could save Grandad and Lily too. This was the destiny Joe had set out to achieve. A peace had settled over the townspeople, and they knew all would be well.

The sun had set behind the suited man by the time he stopped to ask if anyone had any questions, the early stars visible in the evening sky. Matthias of the Moonshine Brothers raised his hand, asking how it would be decided who did what work in the new town.

Everyone had already accepted the suited man's ability to bring all these changes about, and all that was left was detail. The man answered by saying it was a good question but before he could expand further, he was interrupted by the sound of rattling wheels.

A black van appeared over the hill, skidding to a stop before the first of the fallen trees. It was Leigh's van. The drifter climbed out, his hat on his head and his rifle in hand. He stood tall and fixed his stare on the suited man on the opposite side of the forest. The guards moved their hands to their holsters.

'This man is a liar,' Leigh announced. 'The gardens are dying. The earth is ripped apart, the plants shredded by his machines. He's done the same to the fisherpeople, their waters poisoned and empty. They're all starving, because of him.'

The suited man stepped forward, ready to argue. The townspeople's spellbound calm was interrupted, confusion crossing their dreamlike expressions. Joe felt his own head clear, his absolute faith in the suited man rapidly fading. He looked around and saw the Witch approaching the fallen forest, walking with her stick. The suited man stopped dead as he saw the Witch too.

'Yes, you're right. That was the plan,' the man said.

His manner had completely changed, all pretence of enthusiasm and vigour dropped, replaced with a menacing tone. More of the townspeople sat up properly, coming out of their stupors. Their eyes widened as they looked at Leigh's rifle, or the guards' fingers primed by their holsters.

'I was planning to remove the resources from your hovels and let you all die out,' the suited man said. He was looking beyond Leigh, watching the Witch. 'Madera has to be perfect. There can't be poverty surrounding the greatest city in the world, and the simplest solution to that is just to get rid of you all. But right now, I don't care.'

The townspeople kept still on the fallen trees. They were fully alert now, the silence across them fraught, as if any sound or sudden movement could start gunfire.

The suited man imitated the shape of a gun with his hand, and wagged it at Leigh. 'When I discovered this place, I was quite eager to clean it off the map, along with its disgusting residents. Yet just now, in this moment, I couldn't care less about any of that. Do you know why?'

The Witch stopped beside Leigh, leaning on her stick. She was entirely her ancient self.

'Because she's here!' the suited man went on. 'After all this time, after all these years, I've finally found her!'

What's he talking about? Joe thought. He couldn't make sense of any of it.

The man spread his arms and laughed wildly, revelling in some private triumph. Leigh squared the rifle against his shoulder and took aim down the barrel.

'You know what to do, boys!' the man shouted, arms still wide. 'The two old men!'

A pair of guards swivelled and drew their weapons, aiming towards where Grandad sat with Mr Rajarshi and the Librarian. For an awful moment, Joe knew *what* was about to happen, without understanding *why*.

Gunshots exploded out and the elderly men fell from the downed tree. There was chaos as everyone dived for cover behind their logs. Joe seized Tiger and pulled him down onto the ground. He held onto the cowering young boy, like when they were under the weight of the mountains together. He felt the same panic as he had then, as if he was trapped under the bin bags all over again.

The sound of Leigh's rifle cracked in the air and the suited man fell. It cracked again and one of the guards dropped, too. Another guard fired and the drifter's knee shattered into blood. He collapsed, dropping the rifle. Ms Winnipeg ran past Joe, shielding Leigh with her body. Suddenly there were no more gunshots, only a ringing in Joe's ears.

The three remaining guards advanced towards Ms Winnipeg, pointing their pistols at her. Joe gazed across the dirt towards where Grandad had been sitting. Mr Rajarshi was crawling away, splattered with somebody's blood.

The Librarian was crumpled on the wood. His lifeless eyes stared at Joe, his glasses snapped under his cheek. Grandad had fallen forward so that his face was hidden, but Joe knew that he was dead as well. His back had been destroyed by a bullet, and Joe could see bone.

Joe felt his heart break. Seeing Grandad and the Librarian laid side by side, all he could think of was Grandad's tale that had moved the Librarian the most. It was the story of the Library of Alexandria burning to the ground. Looking at his grandfather's body now was like seeing that great library burning, the books within reduced to ash and flame.

All that knowledge, all those stories, blown away as smoke on the wind. At least the Librarian's shack and his books would survive him. So many of Grandad's stories left the world in the same moment he did. It was waste, greater than anything thrown away on the mountains. The world was made less by Grandad being gone.

Grandad never got to see the end of the tale. That fact made Joe's eyes blur with tears. He'd come to the forest because he'd loved storytelling, and he thought he'd get to see the end of Joe's story. Instead all there had been was chaos, and death, and Joe was left with the same question he was always left with.

Why? Why had Joe been led to this point, and told there was some way that he was meant to help? Why had the suited man asked who knew about stories, and then killed both of the people who did?

The suited man climbed to his feet and dusted off his

shoulders, unhurt even though Joe was sure he'd been hit. Ms Winnipeg cowered in front of the three guards, Leigh collapsed in a puddle of blood behind her with his rifle to his side. The Witch stood in the same place, her weight on her stick.

The man raised his arm, his hand clutched as if holding something. With his other hand he gestured at the horizon. In that moment, Joe saw how truly within the man's power they were. At his command the moon began to rise, its grey light stretching out across the fallen forest. The moonlight touched the base of the man's trousers and the black material glittered with stars.

As the moon lifted into the sky, more stars emerged from the fabric, the suit no longer black but blurring between deep blue and purple, with swirls of galaxies and mists of nebulas moving across it. In his clenched hand was a dress woven from the same night sky.

'It's time now,' the Prince in his night-sky suit said. 'It's time you wore this. Time for you to be my queen.'

The Witch let her stick fall as the moonlight reached her, becoming the young Forest Woman. Her brown rags solidified into a dress made of dirt, encrusting over her skin and then flowing down around her legs.

'Never,' the Forest Woman said.

David jumped to his feet, letting out an angry roar. He charged forward, Demeta grabbing at him too late.

'You bastard!' David shouted, and swung his fist at the Prince, who turned his chin as he took the blow, showing no pain from the impact. He caught David's arm and twisted it around into a lock, still holding the night-sky dress in his free hand.

One of the guards kicked Ms Winnipeg, who'd tried to lift the rifle in the diversion, and she fell back over Leigh. Another guard placed his pistol against David's temple, the Prince keeping him bent forward by his trapped arm.

'What will you do?' the Prince asked the Forest Woman. 'Will you let the people of this town die, one by one, or will you wear this dress and be my queen?'

She glared back at him, her eyes pricked with angry tears. Joe watched in horror. His grandfather was dead, his father about to die. Then he remembered the Wolf. He knew why the Prince had asked who knew stories well, and killed those who did.

'*You will hurt no one else tonight*,' Joe said, standing. There was a new depth and resonance to his voice. One of the guards aimed a pistol at him, and Joe's legs threatened to give way. The Forest Woman looked at Joe with grim determination, as if willing him on.

'That's rather a big statement to make, not to mention most likely untrue. So why exactly would you think that?' The Prince's casual manner had become forced, a facade of his earlier self-assurance.

'Because,' Joe said, then hesitated. The guard pointing the

gun at David was red in the face, his finger trembling against the trigger. He was trying to fire, but couldn't. Joe's voice deepened again. '*Because of where we are. There's a reason these fallen trees remain, though all else around is gone.*'

'Explain that reason to me, then,' the Prince said, releasing David's arm and stepping towards Joe. The guard kept the gun aimed towards David's head, still attempting to pull the trigger.

'*Because this is where you made love.*' Joe knew the story he had to tell. '*Where the trees opened above you and you could see the stars together. It was you who caused these trees to fall, long ago. By now, they should have disintegrated into the earth, but like you and her they've lasted through the passage of time.*

'*All else was destroyed for your city, left as barren desert, but not this fallen forest. Your power, that's kept you alive since the time of sultans and horses and djinns, has preserved this place as well. These trees are sacred to you. Now that you know where you stand, you can do no more harm here. Your men, under your power, are bound by your laws as well.*'

Joe recognised the way his voice had changed. When he was injured in the desert, and the Forest Woman had turned into a panther and carried him on her back, he'd heard this deep version of his own voice. It had narrated his healing and return to the town. The voice sounded the same internally, with himself as the speaker, as it had when he'd heard it outside of his own body. Back then, it had reminded him of Grandad.

He understood now his voice's depth and power. It was

something Grandad had once explained to him. When Joe told the Prince's story, a thousand different voices spoke along with his tongue, and a thousand meanings from a thousand listeners sounded in his ears.

His words had to ring with truth, as balanced and clear as a correctly-played guitar chord, or the tellers and listeners would abandon him. His voice would lose its magic, and the guns would fire once more.

'Your story doesn't work,' the Prince growled. Sweat ran down the side of his brow, disagreeing with the tale costing him great effort. He lifted the night-sky dress, displaying it as evidence. 'I know the place where we looked up at the stars together. Why would it take me so long to find her?'

'She was always too good at disappearing from you, at stepping out of sight between the trees. She hid this place, in such a way that you'd never discover it. That's why you couldn't find the town and the mountains when you searched for them.

'You never did track her down. By making a young girl ill, she set events in motion to bring you here. She sent me towards your city, and then the outlet, as bait for you. This was her plan.'

The Prince grasped the pistol that was aimed at David, and pulled it from the guard's hand. Resisting the story, struggling against it, the Prince raised the weapon and pointed it at David's head himself. David didn't take his eyes off Joe, and made no attempt to escape.

'Why? Why would she bring me here?' the Prince asked through gritted teeth. He was trying to break the story. 'Why would she bring me here, if she was hiding from me?'

'*Because you've been wiping out the world, one bit at a time, for your city. Because she knows, despite the love you once had, what you've become.*'

It wasn't enough. The story needed something more, something strong. Joe closed his eyes, listening to the thousand voices speaking inside his mind, trying to hear all the tales that had come before. It was impossible to make out what individuals were saying while everyone talked at once. But he heard one story being spoken over the rest, and it was Grandad telling it. It was one that he could use.

'*Because every man has his own death. The many deaths you've avoided, with all your power, were never yours. Your death has been waiting for you all this time, and who or what else could it be but her.*'

'No,' the Prince said. 'No, the end is that I find her, then she wears the night-sky dress and marries me. She has to marry me. That's the ending.'

'*You made your own death. Once, she would weep for the passing of a fox or a crow. But you filled her with death, so she could slit a fox's throat without flinching, or poison a young girl to achieve her plans. You cut down her forest, so her home was dead. You reshaped her people, from forest people to city people, and killed her way of life. You tore wounds in her night sky and tried to clothe her in that butchered skin.*

'*She, who once walked naked and free, instead wrapped herself in the dirt from the ground, which was the last remains of her murdered home. She hid from you, trying to stop the killing.'*

In the corner of Joe's eye, the Forest Woman grew large and dark.

'You took everything from her. Her home, her people, and even herself. All that you left in their place was death. You've dodged all of the other deaths that have come for you, but not this one of your own creation. You made death out of the woman you loved.'

The Forest Woman had become a giant black panther, her haunches higher than Joe's head. She prowled past where Ms Winnipeg and Leigh lay together in a puddle of the drifter's blood, swinging her neck to look at Joe, then at David, and finally at the Prince.

The two guards still holding guns aimed up at her. The Prince waved them away and placed his own pistol on the ground. He draped the night-sky dress across his palms and offered it up towards her.

'My love,' the Prince said, and then spoke as a poet:

'Where the trees opened
we made a world from the stars,
drawing lines between them
to form shapes and stories.

When I felled the trees

I made a home for you,
a city built not from dead wood and stone
but faith and desire.

When I took the stars from the sky
I did not steal but borrow,
we'll return them to their rightful place
when we climb to the heavens together.

The city is our spiral staircase
skyscraper towers reaching high into the night,
King and Queen ascend dressed in galaxies
to step together from the peak.

We'll walk between planets and gods
on the pathways we drew in the sky,
we'll wander through the stories we told
living together in the love we made.'

The Forest Woman's head transformed back into her own, the rest of her body still panther. 'That was where our love was, up in the stars with our stories. I did love you once. If we could live within our stories in the night sky, then maybe I could love you again. But as beautiful as your words are, I know you to be a liar. I won't let you trap me, nor let you kill more stars for me.

You'd even kill our stories, in the end. Your words are pretty, but his?'

She looked at Joe and her head became the panther's. She swayed her amber eyes back to the Prince. 'His are true. I am your death.'

She struck out with her paw. When it made contact with the Prince, for a single moment there seemed to be two of him, an Arabian noble with desperate love-filled eyes next to the cynical Caucasian businessman.

Then both men were gone, leaving the dress and the suit behind, drifting towards the earth. Before the clothes hit the ground, they evaporated into two blue-black clouds sparkling with stars, which rose up until they filled a pair of empty slashes in the night sky. The guards were gone too, having disappeared in the same moment as the Prince.

The townspeople clambered to their feet, dazed and confused. The giant panther, in the centre of it all, bowed her head. Joe saw Bill and Hope helping Alice back into her office chair, and the Artist Sisters embracing each other. He looked at David, alive and with no gun to his head, and a wave of relief washed through him.

Joe nearly laughed with the joy of survival, but then he heard Leigh moan in pain. It brought it all back. Grandad and the Librarian were dead. Lily was dying, and possibly Maya too. Joe's work wasn't done yet.

'The forest woman was grateful to the town that had hidden her and helped her to defeat the prince.'

The Forest Woman shrunk from the panther back into her young self. The dress made of earth crumbled and fell from her, back into the ground. She stood naked and free, and smiled up at the stars returned to the sky.

'In gratitude, she took all the death from the town. She took the death out from the drifter lying on the ground, removing the bullet from his flesh and healing his injury.'

Leigh sat up, his hands going to the missing wound in his knee. Ms Winnipeg threw her arms around him and wept.

'She took the death from Maya and her child, so that they would reach the time of birth unhindered, and both would live through it. She took back the death and sickness that she placed inside little Lily through the snake, removing that illness from the town altogether so no one else could become infected.'

'She took the death from the boy's grandfather,' Joe said, then stopped. His voice had lost its power. He'd felt a block, on the side of his mind, just before he'd spoken. He knew why. It wasn't true to the world he lived in or to the story he'd told. Once someone's death had come, it was too late to save them.

'I'm sorry,' the Forest Woman said to Joe, her eyes brimming with tears. 'I didn't mean for him to get hurt.'

Joe felt the story inside him, unfinished. There was more death yet. 'I don't think I can save you either. I would, if I could.'

Her smile returned. 'You let the stars my lover had stolen rise back into the sky. You let the dirt I wore from my forest fall back into the ground. The earth and stars are part of who I am, and they will go on. You saved more of me than I'd dared to hope for. It's time to finish the story, Joe. Make it as good as you can.'

'*The forest woman was full of death, the death that her lover had left in her and she'd carried all those years, the death that she'd taken from the town in gratitude, and the death of her lover himself. But just as there was so much death in her, there was also so much life to be given back to the world.*

'*Her soul floated up and joined the stars in the sky, and her body fell down and joined the earth in the ground. Her heart, that had felt the greatest love and the greatest sadness, became in the earth an acorn that would grow into the first living tree seen in that forest for a very long time.*

'*Her acorn heart gave the last of its magic to the memory of those who'd passed away: trees growing in the fallen forest for the boy's grandfather, his mother, the Librarian, Buddy, and all the others who'd died in the town. Trees grew for the fox and crow, and when the owl and the other animals died they'd have their own trees, too. This final gift was even shared with the prince and his guards, five trees growing together for them.*

'*It became a promise for the people of the town, that when they died their tree would grow in the fallen forest, so one day the forest would stand again. This is the end of the story of the forest woman and her foolish prince.*'

The Forest Woman was gone, the tiny sprout of an oak tree

in her place. Throughout the fallen forest, saplings poked out from the ground. Joe walked to where Grandad's body had been, the townspeople parting to let him past.

A stalk poked out of the earth with two delicate leaves open at its peak. Joe dropped to his knees in front of it. Another sapling grew nearby, the Librarian's body gone from the log. The two old men had vanished like the Forest Woman and the Prince, existing only as stories now.

David knelt beside Joe and put his arm around Joe's shoulders. The other townspeople began to move around the forest and speak to each other. They seemed disorientated by the storytelling magic, uncertain what had just occurred and the part they played in it. Joe heard Hope asking her father Bill about the panther, and the Moonshine Brothers Scott and Matthias perplexedly discussing the baby trees. Everyone seemed to understand enough to recognise they should give Joe and David space.

Joe looked at his father, who met his gaze. In that moment, Joe knew that his father's mind was as clear as his own. They both remembered the storytelling and the deaths, and always would. Joe leaned into his father. They stayed there kneeling together for a long time, staring down at Grandad's sapling tree.

CHAPTER THIRTY-ONE

The next morning, Joe was woken by David propping Grandad's mattress up against the wooden-panelled wall. Without it, the floor felt too large. They sat on the stools and ate porridge that David had made. They recounted the night before, putting the events in order. None of it felt real by the morning light, but there were still only two of them left in the shack, not three.

Partway through their breakfast there was a knock at the door. It was Sonya and Demeta, letting them know that the Mayor had called another meeting. They walked down the dry stream together, Joe and Sonya lagging behind Demeta and David. Joe told Sonya everything from the journey to the outlet and the amazing music, to the suited man and the night in the fallen forest that she'd missed while looking after Maya and

Kane. She'd already heard some of it from Demeta, but it was obvious her mother's retelling had been confusing and missing key details.

Sonya didn't seem to have any issue believing in the magic, despite it being even more bizarre than when the panther had returned Joe to the town. She told him about a dream-like memory of seeing stars rising back up into the sky from the window-hole, and then moments later the colour returning to Maya's skin and her groans of pain stopping.

They followed David and Demeta out from the base of the dry stream and towards where the townspeople had gathered under a circle of shade around the stone well. The Prince's car and the two recycling trucks were still parked nearby, like monuments of the night before. They joined the rest of the townspeople under the shade, a discussion already under way.

Joe saw Rose on the other side as he stepped into the circle. Tiger was holding her left hand. Lily, pale but awake, was holding her right. The twins appeared shy of each other, as if after so long apart they didn't know what to do now that they were together again. Rose smiled at Joe, then spoke to someone behind her. Maya stepped into view, one of her hands on her belly. She mouthed 'thank you' to Joe.

The discussion the townspeople were having was about the events of the night before.

'What panther?' Mrs Polward asked, in response to

something said by Lacey the Artist Sister.

'I think I saw the panther too,' interjected Alice. 'Looking at me with orange eyes.'

'I don't remember any of that,' Matthias said gruffly. 'But there was a businessman from the city, and he brought thugs with guns.'

Joe had been right that the storytelling magic had muddled the townspeople's perception. They couldn't recall the night in full, and disagreed on the bits they did remember. It was the same as the hazy effect of the Prince's storytelling, that made important details slip out of focus. Looking across the group and seeing certain faces remaining stony and silent, like Mr Rajarshi and Ms Winnipeg, Joe wondered if those who were saying less were actually those who remembered more.

Eventually, though, the townspeople came to a consensus of sorts. They remembered a man in a suit, who brought men with guns and threatened the town. He was responsible for the shootings, of Grandad and the Librarian. The Witch was mixed up in at all somehow, and Joe told a tale that saved them, and now there were new trees growing in the fallen forest.

The whole night became a story, the tale I told just one part, Joe thought. *There were stories within stories, and Grandad didn't even get to see it.*

It was the Mayor who brought some order to the meeting. He said that the news Leigh had shared regarding the harm done to the gardeners' and the fisherpeople's ability to provide food must be discussed, but that first they'd organise funerals for the Storyteller, the Librarian, and the Forest Woman who was the Witch.

There was some muttering over giving the Witch a funeral, while another conflict arose around whether the funerals should take place together or over separate days. Demeta suggested having each of the dead's stories told on the same day might give them all the chance to process what had happened, and get some closure on it all. There was widespread agreement with her, and a decision was reached to hold the three funerals together the next evening.

They discussed practicalities, agreeing that even without bodies to burn they should still build a pyre for each of the dead. It was decided to move the funerals from their usual place beyond the end of the fallen forest, as several people expressed worry about the effects of the smoke, if the wind took it towards the sapling trees.

With a regretful look at Joe and David, the Mayor reminded everyone that as they no longer had the Storyteller, they'd need individuals to take up the role for each of the dead. Joe recalled Grandad saying he was proud of the stories that would be told about him.

'I'll tell my grandfather's story,' Joe volunteered. There were approving reactions from the townspeople. Joe knew they'd wanted him to offer. Mr Rajarshi said he'd tell the Librarian's story, and David whispered to Joe, 'Don't feel you have to. It's up to you.'

'It's okay,' Joe replied. 'I want to do this.'

David nodded. 'As long as you want to.'

The Mayor asked who would tell the Witch's story, and no one volunteered.

Demeta turned to Joe. 'It might be good for everyone to hear the tale you told last night again. It could help us to make sense of it all.'

David's expression told him once more that he didn't have to. Joe acknowledged his father with a brief smile, then spoke up. 'I can tell the story of the Witch.'

Once they'd finished organising the funerals, Leigh stepped forward, tipping his hat to Joe before speaking. He explained that the gardeners had managed to break the machines before all their crops were destroyed, but now they had few tools left to tend the plants that remained.

They'd been conned by the suited man, also known as the Prince, into handing over their old equipment, after he'd convinced them that they'd no longer need it. The fisherpeople had abandoned their old homes and taken their boats down the coast, travelling away from the poisoned waters to find new places to fish.

Leigh asked the townspeople to search the mountains for

tools for the gardeners, and for materials to build new homes for the fisherpeople. Several of the drifters were assisting the hunters in finding more meat, which, alongside any food the gardeners of fisherpeople were able to spare, they'd distribute out equally regardless of trade. With food scarce while the gardeners and fisherpeople rebuilt, they wanted to make sure everyone had enough to survive.

It's all changing, Joe thought. *Things aren't going to go back to the same after this.*

Leigh also said there was a risk that after the Prince's death, the recycling trucks would stop running. It was only after the Prince's recent appearance that they'd learned that at least some of the trucks were no longer automated, and were driven by his men. If the trucks were halted, there was a possibility that the recycling centre's system wouldn't function and the machines would no longer top up their vehicle charging cards.

Many drifters still had credit left, enough to get them back and forth till a new system was in place. If needed, the drifters would work in teams to undertake the several day walk between the different areas, protecting themselves from the sun in the daytime like Joe and David had in the desert. Even if the recycling centre continued to allow them to charge their vehicles with waste from the mountains, Leigh said the drifters would still plan out this system. They needed to be prepared for when the chargers stopped working.

That day, when the townspeople climbed the mountains, they looked for anything that could help the gardeners and the fisherpeople, as well as keeping an eye out for ruined wood for the funerals. At the meeting it was decided that Maya, Rose and the twins, and Bill and his daughter Hope, wouldn't climb the mountains. As they were no longer collecting trade to buy food and had agreed to divide out equally whatever they received through the drifters, those few could be kept safe.

When Joe and David returned home in the evening, Joe's collecting sack was mostly full of wood, including some broken pieces of furniture for funeral pyres, as well as wide panels that could be used for building shacks for the fisherpeople.

Word had spread on the mountains to take screws and nails from any materials they found them in, so at the bottom of his sack there was a scattering of those as well. Joe hadn't collected much for the gardeners, but David had brought back a shovel, and Sonya and Demeta had carried a wheelbarrow down the mountains between them.

Throughout the evening, it was Joe's task to listen to everyone's stories about Grandad, David waiting at the door and letting people in as he had for Buddy's funeral. Maya was one of the early arrivals.

She told Joe that a few days ago she'd been afraid of what it would be like to bring up a baby in the town. She'd talked to

Grandad about it, and he'd told her miraculous tales of babies floating down streams in thatch baskets, of children raised by jungle beasts, of lost boys and girls becoming kings and queens. The stories didn't all have happy endings, Maya said, but after hearing them she felt like her child had a chance in the world.

Alice visited next and told Joe about a time when she'd been exhausted by her 'Office Chair' title and being the townspeople's symbol of cheerful perseverance. Because of it, she'd felt unable to complain, even on days when collecting was going badly. She said Grandad had told her a story about a land where names were magic.

In the story, people had a public name that others called them by, as well as a hidden name that truly defined them, only revealing the latter to those they trusted most. The story wasn't meant to comfort, Alice said, or to justify how things were. All it did was give her another way of thinking about names, and that at least had helped.

Neither Maya nor Alice wanted Joe to speak at the funeral about their personal situations, but they both asked for the tales they'd discussed to be mentioned. The townspeople visiting the shack all asked for the same, for one of Grandad's stories that had touched their lives to be referred to during the funeral.

How did he do it? Joe asked himself, after being told yet another story of Grandad's. *How did he carry all these stories up and down the mountains with him each day, and remember them all?*

Joe knew he'd find it difficult to remember even just the titles of the different tales that people wanted him to mention, let alone remembering the complete stories like Grandad had. Of everyone that visited, only Sonya and Mr Rajarshi didn't talk about Grandad's stories.

Mr Rajarshi, who came between receiving his own visits for the Librarian's funeral, spoke about Grandad not as the Storyteller, but as his friend. Grandad was patient if Mr Rajarshi or the Librarian slowed or struggled while they were collecting, and the three of them had grand discussions about art and philosophy as they filled their bags. Mr Rajarshi said it sometimes felt like they were keeping the ancient ideas alive, out there on the mountainside.

Then, before leaving, the last of those three old men sat and watched Joe's lips as Joe told him about going to the Librarian's shack and giving him the book with the iceberg on the cover.

When Sonya visited, she just wanted to know if Joe and David were alright. It felt strange for Joe to tell her that they both were. Their day had been busy, with the meeting in the morning, the unusual collecting on the mountains, and receiving the townspeople in the evening.

It wasn't that they weren't sad. He and David had both cried a few times on the mountains that day, but there'd been work to do. Each time they'd let the tears flow, then dried their eyes and continued on.

Eventually, long after the sun had set, no more visitors arrived at the door. Joe and David looked at each other in what felt like the first silence they'd had all day.

'Is there anything you want me to say tomorrow?' Joe asked, realising that his father hadn't shared any memories for the funeral.

'He wouldn't want much said about his life in the city. It's who he became here that mattered to him most. But tell them that he used to read me bedtime stories when I was a child. I think he'd have liked people to know that.'

Later on, when Joe was lying on his mattress and trying to get to sleep, he thought about telling the Witch's story as well. He didn't know how much of her manipulation to include, and was uncertain whether to describe her as a clever old crone who lived in their town or as a magical forest woman from a story.

Only a few of the people who visited had spoken about her, those who'd been to her for visions, or those who'd used her herbs and remedies to deal with illnesses. Demeta talked about her a little, saying that she'd always believed the Witch cared deeply for the townspeople. But even Demeta had more to say about Grandad than the Witch.

He didn't know how she and the Prince had stepped out of their story and into the real world, but then again Grandad, the Librarian and Buddy had lived in the real world, and they were stories now.

The following night, a line of three fires burned near the stone well. The townspeople sat on the ground and watched the flames. The funerals began with introductions for each of the dead. David stood and introduced Grandad, then the Artist Sisters spoke together for the Librarian, and finally Demeta for the Witch.

Following that, it was time for Joe to tell Grandad's story. As he walked to the front, he saw Tiger and Lily sitting with Rose, the twins preoccupied with a counting game played on each other's fingers. Rose wrapped her arms around their shoulders and guided their attention to Joe. He smiled at them before he began.

Joe spoke briefly about Grandad's personality, talking about his kindness and his wisdom, then moved on to the stories he'd told. Simply describing the stories didn't feel adequate, and Joe ended up telling shortened versions of several of Grandad's tales. This was well received, with murmurs of recognition during the beginnings and applause at the endings.

Joe didn't manage to tell all the stories they'd asked for the day before. In those he did tell there were times when his memory slipped and he improvised the narrative, but his audience just seemed pleased to hear any version of the tales. Joe finished by asking for a moment of silence for Grandad, bowing his head as it was observed. After that he joined the crowd again, sitting next to David.

Mr Rajarshi went to the front, and told the Librarian's story. He described townspeople visiting the Librarian's shack in the evenings to read with him by candlelight. It let them escape the town and the mountains for a while, going instead to the worlds inside the pages. He spoke about the Librarian's belief in a future where young people would be taught to read once more, and how that made the preservation of his books even more significant to him.

Mr Rajarshi said that the Librarian would want the books to stay within his shack, and that the library he'd built there was special and should be looked after. The library was a symbol, Mr Rajarshi said, of faith in the future and of commitment to providing a better life for children not yet born.

Many of the townspeople had thought the Librarian was an old fool for keeping books that had good worth for trade. Yet when Joe saw the firelight reflected in the crowd's glistening eyes, he knew that Mr Rajarshi's speech had made the shack into a sacred place. Even without the Librarian, people would take books there to be stored.

The shelves will fill faster now, Joe realised, *than they did when the Librarian was alive.*

Mr Rajarshi held a silence for the Librarian and then Joe stood again, to tell the story of the Witch. He adapted Grandad's tale of How The City Came To Be, telling it with the Forest Woman as the protagonist rather than the Prince. He began with her living in peace with her people, meeting travellers from distant lands when they visited her forest.

The Prince arrived, and she fell in love with his words but hated his actions, as he cut down her forest to make his city and ripped wounds in her night sky. When he tried to convince her to wear the dress made of night, she created her own dress from earth and hid from him, even after he stamped the ground and the last of her trees fell.

The Forest Woman stayed hidden in the fallen forest until mountains of waste from the Prince's city rose up above the dead trees. A town formed at the base of the mountains, and she left the fallen forest to join the people living there, taking on the identity of the Witch.

Having blended Grandad's tale into the reality of their lives in the town, Joe then spoke about her existence among them, including her animals, her healing herbs, and the visions she gave. Finally, he described how in order to stop the Prince and his destruction, she'd made a young girl ill and used a boy with stories in his blood as bait. He hesitated over including those details, but it seemed fairest to tell every bit of her story that he knew.

Joe said that she was desperate by then, otherwise she would never have put his and Lily's lives at risk. This was a kind way of perceiving her, and he hoped it was true. Whether it was or not, it was how the townspeople would remember her now. He finished on how she sacrificed herself in the end, encouraging Joe to tell the story that resulted in the death of her and her once beloved Prince.

They held a silence for the Witch, then Joe sat down. He suspected that many of the townspeople couldn't quite believe any of it as literal fact – but even so they seemed to respect the story as a way of understanding who the Witch was, and what had happened to them that night. It gave them a way of moving on.

The mother of the Singing Family stood. She said that though they didn't know the details, the guards that had come with the Prince had their own lives and stories. She announced a moment of silence for them, and for the Prince as well.

As with the Witch, there'd been disagreement at the meeting the day before over whether the Prince and his guards deserved a silence, with some townspeople arguing vocally against it. Those who'd argued that all deaths should be given their due had eventually won out, on the argument that those who did want a silence should be allowed one. Despite unimpressed expressions on a few faces, the silence was not interrupted.

Good, Joe thought. *Grandad would have wanted them all to have a silence.*

The funerals were finished, three fires burning on under the night sky. The Moonshine Brothers brought out a whisky, which they'd named Three of Stories, and the townspeople shared a drink. The night became like a gentle celebration. The Artist Sisters etched designs into the earth, the Singing Family performed slow songs, and David played soft music on the guitar.

Sonya sat by Joe's side, drinking whisky with him. They spoke about the stars from the dress and the suit returning to the sky, and at the same time both tried to point out where the stars had returned to. They laughed as they realised they were pointing opposite ways. Demeta wandered over, and told them she thought she remembered the rising stars as well, only adding to the confusion when she pointed in another new direction. The three of them had a happy argument over which stars were new and which had always been there.

Joe fell silent after a while. He listened to Sonya and her mother laughing and debating the stars, and to the music made by his father and the Singing Family. His chest filled with love for it all: the earth and the stars, the town and its people, even the black mountains that loomed behind the fires.

Demeta drifted away from where Joe and Sonya sat, going over to look at the huge and curling pattern that the Artist Sisters were carving into the ground. Sonya wrapped her arm around Joe's waist, and rested her head on his shoulder.

Joe's mourning had mostly been for Grandad, but now he took time for the other two stacks of burning wood. He'd never again see the Witch make a celebration bonfire blaze and dance in different colours, nor hear the Librarian's voice rise in excitement at the prospect of a new book.

An uncanny sensation tickled across Joe's skin, a feeling that it took him a few moments to recognise. He knew it from inside the Prince's car, and from ducking under the stream when the rain fell. Sonya stirred against him, having felt it too. There was a chill in the night air.

Later, when the fires had diminished to glowing orange mounds, Joe sat in the same place with half a glass of whisky next to him. Sonya was almost asleep on his shoulder. Most of the townspeople were still around, drinking and talking, though the music had stopped, and the Artist Sisters had given up on their patterns in the earth.

Leigh, who'd been staying in Ms Winnipeg's shack, approached Joe. 'Can I talk to you, kid?'

Sonya squeezed Joe's hand and said she'd check how Maya was doing. She got up and moved away through the townspeople.

Leigh sat down next to Joe, his face lit by the firelight. 'I don't quite know what happened that night, but I know I wouldn't have made it if it wasn't for you. I figure I owe you something.'

Joe shook his head. 'I didn't do it because I wanted anything from you.'

'Listen to what I'm offering first. I'll be staying here a while. A man doesn't nearly die without having to stop and do some thinking. Reckon this town's the nearest place I've got to a home. I don't know if you know this, but the woman I stay with here's my mother.'

'I'd guessed you were related, but I didn't know how.'

Leigh snorted. 'That doesn't surprise me. Ma's not one for talking much about herself, but she'll know every bit of gossip in the town. What I'm telling you is that my van's free, and almost fully charged. You want to drive to the city, it's yours. Only obligation is that if you're able, you bring it back.'

'You'd be stuck here?'

'I'm going to try to start up the Prince's car, though that'll only last as long as there's fuel in it. Even if I don't manage, other drifters will be coming through. I can get a lift with them, if I want to.'

Leigh pushed his thumb against two of his fingers, as if rolling an invisible coin between them. 'I might not be the only person travelling that way. When I left the fisherpeople, some of them were talking about coming by the town, and I've been told a few of the gardeners are saying the same.'

Joe drew in a surprised breath. 'I've never heard of someone from another place coming here. That doesn't happen.'

'That's because of us drifters. We refused to take anyone with us for so long that people stopped asking. Thing is, owning electric vehicles gave us a decent life out here. Unlike everyone else, we could always be pretty certain of getting fed. Once you've had the thought that somebody might try to take your vehicle and your decent life from you, it's awful hard to trust a passenger in that big empty desert.

'But now a lot of the drifters are changing their tune. They're saying we've been keeping things as they are by forcing everyone to stay separate. That if we'd carried people with us all this time, rather than just stuff to sell, then everyone together might have worked out a better way of living. It's high time the drifters took some responsibility.'

He looked Joe in the eye. Joe remembered that he'd once met that steely gaze when they'd been pointing guns at each other. 'This new plan we got, of walking from place to place if the recycling centre doesn't let us charge up anymore, I think that can work. There ain't going to be anyone walking the distance to the city, though, especially with the strangeness out that way.

'If the vehicles do stop charging, this might be our last chance to find out if there's anything better for us there. If I were a braver man, I'd go myself. From what I can tell, you've at least got something of a handle on how to deal with the shadows you'd meet on the way. So what do you reckon?'

'Yes,' Joe said, noting the decision as he made it. He wouldn't just be going for the sake of the town anymore, but for all of the people who were trying to work out a way to survive together.

He'd be going for himself as well, to finally fulfil his yearning to see the city.

Leigh stretched out his back with a yawn. He climbed to his feet, then drew the van's key from his pocket, his plastic charging card attached to it by a key ring. 'I appreciate what you did for me, even if I don't understand it. Find me tomorrow, and I'll teach you how to drive the van.'

He threw his key to Joe, who caught it, clenching plastic and metal together in his hand. Leigh walked away, leaving Joe sitting with it in his hand. Joe looked out across the flatlands, where on the horizon a single light twinkled like a fallen star.

CHAPTER THIRTY-TWO

The next morning, Joe and David ate porridge together. They had smaller portions than usual, aware of the shortages that were sure to come. It was cool inside the shack, the chill still in the air from the night before. Through the window-hole, the sky was grey with clouds. Joe started to explain Leigh's offer, but David interrupted him. 'He wants you to take the van. I know. He asked me first, if I was okay with it.'

'What did he say?'

David sighed, laying his spoon down into his bowl. 'He said that he didn't want to take a son away from someone who's just lost a father, but I don't want that to stop you from going.'

'You could come with me.'

David took a long drink from his water before answering. 'No. I don't think so. Life here's worn away at me. I'm old and tired now, worse than I should be for my age. I'd only slow you down.'

Joe watched David eat another spoonful of porridge. His face was covered in nicks and scratches from collecting on the mountains. Joe had once thought his father was weak.

'No,' Joe said.

'What?'

'You wouldn't slow me down. It was your sense of direction that got us to the outlet. I think you'd remember your way around the city, too. Plus, you used to drive. It's your choice either way, but you'd be able to help if you came.'

'I don't know if it will be the city I remember. The Madera that we lived in wasn't really built by a Prince. That was just one of Grandad's stories. I don't know if we'd find our past there, or more fiction. He had a lot more tales about the city.' David hesitated with his empty spoon above his bowl. 'I don't think it would take me long to get the hang of driving again. I'll come with you.'

'Are you sure?'

'Yeah. I never much liked this place anyway.' David turned and looked at the guitar leaning in the corner of the shack. The strings glinted in the overcast morning light. 'We should take that with us. You've still got lots to learn.'

An exciting idea struck Joe. 'After all this is done, we should go back to the outlet. See if the restaurant is still the same, even with the Prince gone. If it is, we could stop for a little while, and listen to more songs on the jukebox.'

David smiled. 'Yeah. We could definitely do that.'

Joe sat on the earth and watched Leigh's van disappear around the edge of the mountains, his father driving and the drifter in the passenger seat. He didn't need shade, the sun obscured behind the clouds. He guessed there'd be rainfall soon, but this was different from usual celebration weather. The air was even colder than it had been the night before. He found himself shivering a little as he waited for David and Leigh.

David was better at driving than Joe had been, controlling the van without jerky accelerating or braking. The van reappeared around the other side of the mountains, passing near the three black marks on the ground from the funeral fires, before stopping next to Joe.

David disembarked, followed by Leigh holding several sheets of paper torn from a notebook. Leigh laid them out over the van's bonnet, pencil-drawn maps of the routes he commonly drove, as well as handwritten notes that were maintenance instructions for the van. After wishing them luck for their journey, the drifter headed away towards Ms Winnipeg's shack. As he left, he turned around and lifted his hat to them both in a gesture of farewell.

Joe and David had decided to depart that day, due to the

limited food that would be arriving in the town. Delaying would likely leave them with fewer supplies for their journey. They had already packed the van with everything they needed, including the guitar wrapped in clothes to keep it safe.

David drove them down to the stone well, where they filled water bottles and packed them into the rear of the van. All that was left to do was to say goodbye to Sonya and Demeta when they came down from the mountains.

After receiving the key from Leigh the night before, Joe had told Sonya what had happened. She'd seemed unsurprised, both that Leigh had made the offer and that Joe had accepted it. He and his father waited by the well until the townspeople started descending the waste, a few of them commenting on the cold weather as they passed by.

Marco stopped by to draw water, chatting with Joe and David as he did. When David explained their plans, Marco said he thought it was a good idea to try to get to Madera. He said they needed to know what was happening there, now more than ever. He said he'd miss their music at the celebration that was surely coming with the clouds overhead, and asked Joe to tell him a tale of how the city was when he returned.

Not long after, Sonya and Demeta walked towards the well carrying collecting bags. David smiled at Demeta, indicating with his hand for her to follow him and talk elsewhere.

'We're going to leave today,' Joe said as Sonya placed her

collecting bag onto the ground, though he could see in her eyes that she'd already guessed.

'I didn't realise it'd be so soon,' Sonya said.

'My father's coming with me. He's going to drive the van. We thought if we waited we'd have less food to take with us.'

'I'm glad you're not going alone,' Sonya said. 'And you're right. It's better to leave sooner.'

They spoke pragmatically to each other, as if there was no emotion between them. Yet Joe remembered sitting on the back of a recycling truck, weeping and cursing himself for leaving Sonya behind, and he remembered finding Sonya in the fallen forest with the red tracks of tears down her cheeks.

Joe knew that this could be the last time he saw her, that the journey he was taking was dangerous, and that the mountains couldn't be trusted to be kind. Knowing that he might not see her again didn't hurt any less that it had previously. They'd just become better at saying goodbye.

'It might be that I'm gone for a long time, and you won't know if I'm coming back,' Joe said. 'There'll be people visiting the town, from the other places. If there's ever someone else–'

'Shush.' Sonya shook her head. She pushed her hands into his, interlocking their fingers. 'You don't need to say that.'

'You're good at loving people,' Joe said instead.

'When you're gone,' Sonya replied, 'I'll tell myself stories of you. Tales of the boy who went away, and his adventures.'

Joe gripped her hands, holding back tears. 'When I'm away, I'll tell myself tales about the girl who stayed. The girl who was made from the town and the mountains, from the celebration fires and the flowing stream, and from night-time in the fallen forest. I love you so much, Sonya.'

'I love you too, Joe.'

They kissed, eyes closed and gentle. Joe felt cold flecks tingle against his cheeks, and Sonya's fingers slipped out from his. He opened his eyes. Sonya was looking at the sky.

'Snow,' she said.

It fluttered down like white feathers, touching against their skin and then vanishing. It didn't disappear when it landed on the waste. It stuck to the bin bags and the rest of the rubbish, gradually colouring the mountains white.

Sonya smiled sadly at Joe, her braids crystalline and twinkling. Then she led him over to the van, where his father and Demeta were waiting. David saw them coming, and gave Demeta a last hug before getting into the driver's seat.

'Take care of him, Joe,' Demeta said. Joe nodded, then climbed into the passenger's seat and closed the door, looking out at Sonya in the falling snow. David looked over as if he was about to speak, then changed his mind and turned on the van.

They pulled away, leaving Sonya and Demeta waving behind them. Joe watched in the wing mirror as Sonya let her hand drop and said something to her mother, who squeezed Sonya's shoulders and kissed her on the forehead. Then they were out of sight, David guiding the van around the edge of the white mountains.

Joe saw Rose sitting on the side of one of the landfill slopes, with Tiger and Lily below her. The twins ran back and forth, scooping the snow from the bin bags and hurling it at each other. David started to smile and Joe couldn't help but do the same. He'd hold on to that memory, of the twins playing in the snow, for times to come. For now, they drove away from their home, away from the town and the mountains, heading towards where stories dwelled in the shadows and the city lay waiting.

The End.

ACKNOWLEDGEMENTS

Firstly, thank you to you, for reading. Stories come alive when they are read, or heard.

Thank you to my parents, Janet and Jim Ferguson, for supporting my writing from the beginning, when it was about murderous bus drivers and men trapped in sci-fi boxes (I still think that one was pretty good!).

A big thank you to everyone who gave feedback on the book along the way, especially Sean Ferguson, Malcolm Foster, and Dr Pam Wells. Landfill Mountains is a better book for your efforts!

Similarly, thank you to my editors with Onwe, Stephanie Stahl, Donna Hillyer and Kim Halstead, who all helped to improve the way this story was told. And what's this all about, if not storytelling?

Also with Onwe, huge thanks to Kosi Amayo and Alice King, for fighting to make this book the best it could be in every single way, and to get it out into the world!

Thanks to Cath Heinemeyer, and the York Theatre Royal, for introducing me to performed storytelling. Thanks to the Cumbrian youth theatre, including the Theatre By The Lake in Keswick, for starting me down this path.

A debt is owed to all those who tell stories aloud, and have passed stories down through generations. Another debt is owed to those who have written some of those stories down.

Thanks to everyone who was part of my York St John Creative Writing and Literature course, both staff and students. I learned something from all of you. Special thanks to James Parker, for the help and the friendship.

Cheers to Joshua Burnell and Fe Sladen, for the music and the art. Your creativity inspires me to push onwards and keep writing.

Lastly, my deepest and most heartfelt thanks to Ashton Bauer for being alongside me every step of the way, and for putting up with me constantly asking how different sentences sounded. Thanks to Hazel, for giving me a future to write for. And of course, thank you to Hugo, for being a cat and not being fussed about any of this.

RAB'S LIST OF ENVIROMENTAL CHARITIES

Fridays For Future

fridaysforfuture.org

#FridaysForFuture is a youth-led and organised movement that began in August 2018, after 15-year-old Greta Thunberg and other young activists sat in front of the Swedish parliament every school day for three weeks, to protest against the lack of action on the climate crisis.

Earth Guardians

earthguardians.org

They inspire and train diverse youth to be effective leaders in the environmental, climate and social justice movements.

One Tree Planted

onetreeplanted.org

One Tree Planted is a environmental non-profit tree planting charity that plants trees in countries around the world.

Practical Action

practicalaction.org

They help people find solutions to some of the world's toughest problems – made worse by catastrophic climate change and persistent gender inequality.

Global Giving - Climate Action Fund

globalgiving.org/climate-action-fund/

By providing ongoing support for local leaders who understand the challenges facing their communities, the Climate Action Fund is redefining business-as-usual.

Climate Emergency Fund

climateemergencyfund.org

They are turbo-charging the climate movement by supporting its most brave and adamant activists.

Client Earth

clientearth.org

They are an environmental charity with a unique approach.

They use the power of law to change the system for a brighter, healthier future.

World Wide Fund for Nature

wwf.org.uk

WWF is the world's leading independent conservation organisation. Their mission is to create a world where people and wildlife can thrive together.

UK Youth Climate Coalition

ukycc.com

UKYCC mobilises and empowers young people to take positive action for global climate justice.

UK Student Climate Network

ukscn.org

UKSCN is a group of mostly under 18s taking to the streets to protest the government's lack of action on the Climate Crisis.

Climate Coalition

theclimatecoalition.org

The UK's largest group of people dedicated to action against climate change.

Green Alliance

green-alliance.org.uk

Green Alliance is an independent think tank and charity focused on ambitious leadership for the environment.

Friends of the Earth

friendsoftheearth.uk

Friends of the Earth England, Wales and Northern Ireland is a grassroots environmental campaigning community. They push for change on the causes that matter with the help of their campaigners, lawyers, local groups and supporters.

Woodland Trust

woodlandtrust.org.uk

They plant woods and trees to combat climate change, build a greener future for the UK and create havens for wildlife.

Wildlife Trust

wildlifetrusts.org

They are a grassroots movement that believes we need nature and it needs us.